THE FIRELANDS

KAREN HARPER

CHARTER BOOKS, NEW YORK

THE FIRELANDS

A Charter Book/published by arrangement with
the author

PRINTING HISTORY
Charter edition/July 1990

ISBN: 1-55773-342-2

Charter Books are published by The Berkley Publishing Group,
200 Madison Avenue, New York, New York 10016.
The name "CHARTER" and the "C" logo
are trademarks belonging to Charter Communications, Inc.

PRINTED IN THE UNITED STATES OF AMERICA

10 9 8 7 6 5 4 3 2 1

The Firelands is dedicated to the memory of two dear and dynamic women who were born in the late nineteenth century in the Firelands. Although different in backgrounds and personalities, they were firm friends for nearly ninety years, bound together by their childhood memories and love of their hometown, Milan, Ohio. Their lives are not this fictional story, but their tales of times past inspired me to write a novel of love and friendship which survives the "firelands" of all our lives:

Mabel Loher Mudge, my maternal grandmother

Virginia Smith Collister, my "Auntie Midge"

Author's Note

IN THE SPRING of 1777, the American Rebellion for Independence was yet young. The apparently overwhelming British forces commanded the Atlantic, held New York City, and threatened the capital of the colonies, Philadelphia. But American hope was on the upswing for the dubious reason that Commander-in-Chief Washington and his ragged, infant Continental army had shown great talent for clever retreats that had, so far, kept them intact to fight again.

At this early stage in the war, American Brig. Gen. Benedict Arnold was greatly admired, especially in Connecticut, where he was the local hero. Born only fourteen miles from New London, Connecticut, where this story begins, Arnold had built a brilliant reputation. He had led an inspiring winter march on Canada; he had fought the British navy at Lake Champlain with a ragtag flotilla of small vessels; and he had harassed a British force burning Ridgefield and Danbury, Connecticut. For these bold deeds, the colonies, especially Connecticut, were hysterically grateful.

As a result, anyone related to Arnold was riding high in public favor. As we know today with the hindsight of history, such popularity by association with Arnold was tenuous and dangerous. And therein lay the smoldering embers that ignited the fires of one war—and of two women's hearts.

Chapter One

"Simples are herbs to heal a deep-rooted specific pain or illness. Benefits are herbs used before suffering strikes to prevent it. Would that the Lord God in His wisdom had given us simples and benefits of the heart and soul as well as for these corporeal frames. My dear daughter Althea, I hope you will take to heart your mother's advice on the art of the apothecary and the art of living."

May 22, 1777

POUNDING ON THE door below pulled her from ragged dreams. Althea Arnold's bare feet hit the rag rug on her bedchamber floor as they had a hundred times before in the middle of the night to answer some summons for aid. One could not hope to prosper one of New London, Connecticut's two apothecary shops without occasional, desperate interruptions in the dark of night. As she pulled her homespun shawl around her cotton night rail, Althea only hoped it was a call for some herbal simple or benefit she had already made and stored in the shop below.

The rapping resounded as she shoved her feet into sturdy leather pumps, hurried into the narrow upstairs hall, and then down the creaking back stairs. "Coming!" she called. Althea had no fear the knocks nor her voice would wake the Widow Middleton, her housekeeper and companion who slept in the next bedchamber. The elderly woman had been nearly deaf for years.

But this knocking which rattled the front door again might have wakened even the dead, Althea thought. She had no notion of the hour, but daylight had not yet grayed the sky outside. She scratched flint on steel to light the betty lamp she kept on the counter for such emergencies. In her orderly shop, the woman the town knew as Thea Arnold could move in the dark to locate the drawers of dried leaves and roots, the elixirs, and precious tonics she had sold to make her livelihood these last two years. But without a light in the orderly shop, her visitors might suffer a broken bone to add to their other ailments.

The lamp flared and smoked; she turned down the wick and opened the bolted front door. To her surprise, her dear friend Varina Lockwood, called Rina, stood there on the top step with her maid Cassie behind her. On the street, a familiar Lockwood carriage and matched pair of bays awaited with the driver Silas perched on his seat. Both guests hurried in past Althea before she could speak.

"Rina, whatever is it? Not your father taken ill in the dead of ni—"

"He's fine as ever, considering I roused him after two of the morning clock," Rina admitted with a shake of her blond head, which sported curl papers, it was revealed, when she threw back the hood of her ruffled blue pelisse. "You can imagine how his mettle's up that I told him I simply had to come for help now and not in the morning!" Cassie hovered near, but her eyes wandered to survey shadowy corners and then drifted back. "Thea," Rina rushed on and thrust out her wrist in the wavering light, "look! It's that vile, scratchy, blistering rash from ivy at the edge of the woods. It burns like fire! I just know I got it traipsing about with you near your precious herb beds on our picnic today! I'm going crack-brained itching in the worst places so I can't sleep. And with the parade honoring your cousin Benedict next week, I'll be a strawberry-blotched sight at the reception Father's giving at the house!"

"Drat, but you always were vulnerable to that ivy!" Thea commiserated with a hand on Rina's shoulder. "Can't you just learn to watch for the three telltale leaves and avoid it? I've told you 'Leaves of three, let it be!' "

Rina sighed and shook her hand off gently. "Don't scold, Thea! It's partly your blame for picking the place. Besides, nothing dire ever happens to you outside!"

"I get sunburned," Thea offered patiently.

"Oh, you know what I mean. I told you I would rather have gone somewhere different for once since we were out on our own! And," she addressed Cassie now, "I don't want to hear another word from you either about this being some curse the Irish fairies put on me! Irish fairies don't live in American forests!"

"But me ma and I come here from Ireland, din't we, so they could have come, too!" Cassie insisted. Trailing her fingertips down the counter, she moved away toward the display table where Thea kept the licorice and rock candy for the children.

After all these years, as used as both women were to Cassie's living in her own inner world, they both stared momentarily after her as if waiting for some reasonable response. But she only hummed another of her strange tunes with no melody at all. The one song anyone ever recognized that the sixteen-year-old, freckle-faced maid hummed in her haunting voice was "Danny Boy," her dead mother's only heritage to the girl besides her rampant superstitions about the Irish fairies called the *Sidhe* and pronounced "Shee."

The three young women had been constant companions before Thea left the Lockwood mansion two years before to restore her deceased parents' apothecary here. Yet familiarity hardly bred similarity among them, as they seemed quite the mismatched trio. Cassie McCrea's wandering mind and wandering ways made some of the superstitious townfolk almost believe the milk-skinned, reed-thin girl could live on forest moonbeams as she sometimes claimed. The orphaned colleen was still dubbed everything from town sprite to town idiot behind Rina and Thea's backs. Protecting Cassie from the amused, amazed, or abusive stares and comments of New Londoners over the years had helped to make the other two fast friends. But even Cassie's strangeness was not what drew most glances the trio's way. Rather, it was how different Althea and Varina looked from each other.

Thea, at six feet tall in shoes, towered over Rina—as she did over many New Londoners, including, unfortunately, most of the men. Thea's thick, flame-hued, flyaway tresses escaped proper bonnets and lace caps. Her hair curled naturally into waves and ringlets while Rina struggled to crimp hers nightly with papers and hot irons. Thea's heavy copper lashes framed green eyes that sparkled like great, glittering gems. All this made Rina's cameo beauty look pale and ethereal by comparison. Yet, with the graceful, slender ideal of colonial beauty, Rina was gilded perfection, while Thea's shapely bosom, which corsets and stays could hardly contain, seemed quite blatantly improper.

Though everyone's gaze jumped first to Thea's blazing coloring and curvaceous form, it was her friend, honey-haired, blue-eyed, and petite, who was considered the beauty, for her Lockwood breeding as well as her looks. The British might be the enemy in this War for Independence, but the dominant English heritage was yet admired. Amidst New London's marriageable women, Rina Lockwood was a canary among the sparrows. Thea Arnold, only a tradesman's daughter, though lately well enough connected through the meteoric rise of her cousin Benedict Arnold, was a vibrant parrot like one a New London privateer brought back from a raid but could not train or cage.

Well, at least, town talk declared, it was just fortunate with Althea Arnold's strange looks (Could it be the taint of West Indies or Iroquois blood, or maybe even infidel Catholic way back there in her ancestry somewhere?) that the rich and respectable Moses Lockwood still formally served as her guardian. And, after all, anyone connected with Brigadier General Arnold was quite acceptable, however she looked or however independent she acted. Arnold himself had been an apothecary once in a Connecticut town. Then, too, Thea's good-heartedness to townfolk, whether they could pay her or not, was earning her the reputation of Angel of Mercy even if she did literally look down on almost everyone and appear so colorful like that.

"I'm not scolding you for catching the ivy scratch, Rina," Thea told her as she led her into the small combined kitchen and dining room behind the shop. "I'm just saying, since you are so tender to it, you've got to beware those poison leaves. And if it's really that far up the backs of your legs, you must have almost had your skirts hiked up to sit in it!"

" 'Twas since she drank so much of the dandelion wine we sneaked out there," Cassie put in with a roll of golden eyes. She lowered her voice. "She had to make water twice in the woods, she did. She got that rash from squatting. The forest folk don't like their floors stained by mere mortals, and—"

"Cassie, enough!" Rina declared as she discarded her pelisse and lifted her pistachio green sprigged gown to display her blotched legs. "And if you chatter that nonsense to anyone in town but Thea, I shall trounce you!"

"I can't believe it," Thea said and shook her head as she studied Rina's legs.

"It's that bad then?"

"I mean, even with Cassie and the carriage, you got out of the house without the proper silk stockings and petticoat in the dark of night under Father Lockwood's nose!"

Despite the hour and the predicament, the two women shared a little laugh. Sometimes, they need say but a key word or exchange a certain look to send them both into gales of giggles or a common, unspoken reminiscence. Since Thea's parents had caught the typhus trying to cure Rina's mother of that dread disease when both girls were seven, they had been reared by Rina's father Moses Lockwood almost as sisters.

At times, especially before Cassie came, they'd had only each other in the Lockwood mansion with Rina's elderly, stern father. Yet the differences of inherent temperament and family status had perhaps caused whatever few barriers there had been on the common path to womanhood. Despite the fact Rina coveted Thea's independence and Thea yearned for Rina's elegance, they had shared so much—especially these days, with both on the threshold of spinsterhood in a town temporarily devoid of eligible men when most were off fighting for freedom.

"I've just the prescription to soothe that rash and help you sleep tonight," Thea promised as she bustled behind her long, oak work counter. Even away from the lamp, her capable hands went by touch to a particular unguent pot among the neat shelves of delft jars, spouted syrup bottles, and wicker-sheathed demijohns.

She ignored Rina's continued sputterings about not being able to act as hostess for the private Benedict Arnold reception after the town parade next week if she didn't lose this rash. After all, Thea fretted, Cousin Benedict was going to address the entire town from the front steps of this very shop, right under her newly painted sign depicting the traditional apothecary golden phoenix with outstretched wings above the weights and scales and the bold words ARNOLD'S APOTHECARY. But as pretty and popular as Rina had always been— a petted, sleek house cat when Thea herself felt the floppy-footed outdoors Irish setter at times—Thea could certainly understand Rina's concern that all should go well at the reception. Besides, Cousin Benedict was bringing Lt. Col. Cullen Varner among his aides-de-camp. Rina's father had long been promoting him to Rina as a beau, so no wonder she wanted to look and feel her best.

"You're so blessed to live here on your own," Rina was saying with another long-suffering sigh. "You know, to come and go as you want, even at night. I had to beg and fuss to get Father to let me come now instead of in the morning, as if I were some bond servant instead of cherished daughter—or one of them," she added quickly.

"But you managed, didn't you? You always manage your heart's desire somehow, Rina," Thea said as she hurried back with the unguent jar. With her three middle fingers, she dipped out some of the pale greenish salve and smoothed it gently on the backs of Rina's legs. Cassie came forward to hold the lamp and watch.

"Mm, it feels cooling. Something you got out of your mother's pharm—that book she left you?"

Thea glanced at the thick vellum, Moroccan-bound volume resting on its special place on the shelves. It was the fourth edition of the *London Pharmacopoeia*. With the long ban on British goods that had forced her to make so many more of her own simples and benefits, pills and tonics, plasters and elixirs than she used to, the guide was irreplaceable. But it was even more precious for her mother's delicate handwriting in the margins with additional comments about healing and life. It was truly the closest thing she had to her mother's long-lost, loving voice.

"Yes, from the pharmacopoeia," she told Rina as she

soothed the rashes and blisters behind her knees. "This is a mixture of dock roots for skin rashes and loosestrife leaves and aloe juice. Hold still!"

"Oh, I didn't mean for you to have to put it on with your bare hand, Thea, really. Won't you catch it, too?"

"Not with this balm between my skin and yours. Besides, a cloth would have scratched you more. But if you actually squatted in those leaves I showed you time and again, you may put it on your own petite bum when you get home!"

She gave Rina all she had of the ointment along with a sleeping mix of powdered red clover heads, lettuce, and hops to be taken with wine at home. Her patriotically homespun shawl tight around her in the cool May night air, Thea walked Rina outside to the waiting Lockwood carriage just as the portly town crier, Amos Jameson, ambled by. He doffed his bicorn and lifted his lantern as he called out, "Clear skies and all well at half past three of the morning clock!" Cassie dawdled in the doorway behind them, swinging the netted bags of violets Thea had hung there overnight to dry.

"My dear Thea to the rescue again!" Rina whispered and gave her friend a quick, upreaching hug with her rashless arm. "I feel a bit better already. And I still miss you at the house, Thea. Come more often, won't you? You know how Father is about my 'just wandering out and about without parental permission,'" she added, imitating his low, sonorous tone.

"I come when I can, my Rina," Thea said, her long, wild hair bouncing along her back as she nodded.

Cassie's singsong voice came from behind to make them both turn to her. Etched by pale lamplight in the doorway, she recited: "Rina and Thea, two peas in a pod, have been best friends every step they have trod."

It was a silly, old childhood rhyme, one of Thea's many creative whimsies. But it made both women shiver in unison, even standing close together.

"It's true isn't it?" Rina asked, her light blue eyes glazed with sudden tears as she stared up at Thea. "And we always will be friends like this!"

Rina's little-girl pout to have her own way thrust Thea back fifteen years. But in those early days, hadn't Rina resented her intrusion into her home and her father's care as passionately as she demanded eternal friendship now? Quickly, Thea shoved that dark thought back into a crevice of her mind.

"Of course," Thea said, her eyes smiling with her mouth. "Forever! Now, I'll be to see you first thing in the afternoon after my daily visit to Charity Payne. And don't fret. I predict you'll look as beguiling and unscathed as ever when Cousin Benedict and a certain handsome officer come calling at Lockwood House next week."

"Well, that certain handsome officer is only father's idea and not mine—so far!" Rina teased. She stood on tiptoe to dash a quick kiss on Thea's cheek. "I'll send Cassie over to help you and Widow Middleton clean shop in the morning." Holding the driver's hand, she stepped up into the carriage and perched gingerly on the edge of the leather seat to keep her skirts away from her itchy spots. "Come on, Cassie! No more night rambles, even if that's when your fairies are about!"

Quick as the breeze, Cassie leaped unaided into the coach. But Thea heard the girl protest, "Afraid the forest folk will snatch me up? But the English soldiers are out there somewhere in the dark, too, worse than the *Sidhe,* I tell you, mistress!"

The old driver Silas closed the carriage door, bid Thea good night, and clambered back up on his seat. He clucked the horses away down cobbled Water Street toward the Lockwood mansion across town. Such wisdom from the mouths of babes—and Cassie—Thea thought with a night-breeze tremble as she wrapped her shawl closer and hurried back inside.

Just over a week later, parade day dawned bright and warm. The town turned out to cheer Benedict Arnold, newly promoted to general, who had been born but fourteen miles away. He had done glorious deeds. Surely, he and the Connecticut regiment he had brought today would protect New

London from the British, who had burned other Connecticut towns, including Danbury and Ridgefield just last month.

Thea shivered with excitement as she stood on the steps of her apothecary shop, waiting for the parade to come to her. It would march down Main Street, then cut down Hill Street and along Water Street to her flower-bedecked shop where Cousin Benedict would make a speech and take a brief respite while the parade halted. Then he and his splendid retinue would continue down Bank Street to Lockwood House for a reception, which Thea would also attend. Some state officials waited there, including their admired Gov. Jonathan Trumbull.

Thea could hear crowd noise and the rattle of drums now. Fifes shrilled the state song, "Yankee Doodle." Her heart thudded in her throat. Resplendent in her best, if three-year-old, salmon silk gown that highlighted her vibrant eyes and hair, she tugged again at her netted wrist-length mitts. Her hands were ever scratched and dirtied by plant and soil stains, however much she scrubbed them. She tried to ignore broken fingernails outlined with half moons of brown. Drat, how she wished, at least just for today, she could flutter a fan with the grace of Rina's pristine, soft, delicate hands!

Her nerves jangled as the parade swung around the bend toward her, past the wooden warehouses and wharves. With its fine wood and granite houses, its grassy knolls and stone fences and narrow streets, the town of New London lay in a sweeping curve above the Water Street docks and the ferry slip to Groton. But despite its apparent placid riverside and hillside charms, the town had always been a hotbed of independence and rebellion.

Even before the revolution, the Sons of Liberty inspired its people to independent thinking and rabble-rousing. Perched on the Thames River which led to Long Island Sound, New London was now the premier privateering town that harassed British shipping. Big-bellied sails brought back local brigs, sloops, and schooners, laden with captured British riches to support the rebel cause and enrich New London citizens who financed or sailed such risky ventures. Though the town's location made it vulnerable to British chastisement from nearby New York, everyone remained brazenly defiant. That fiery bravado singed the air today as Thea caught sight of Cousin Benedict himself upon a smart black stallion.

She cheered and bounced and clapped now, too. Rina would have told her it was most unladylike, but she didn't care. A bright new American red, white, and blue banner flapped stars and stripes she had heard a widowed upholsterer from Philadelphia had recently sewn for George Washington's generals at his behest. Today, the glory of the cause had come to New London and to her! Today, she basked in the reflected light this great man shed on her departed parents' memory, her shop, and her town!

She waved wildly and her cousin deigned a nod when he caught sight of her. At age thirty-six, the widowed Benedict Arnold still cut a fine figure, riding at the head of the Connecticut regiment brought in for the day. Its ranks were smartly attired when rumors said so many Continental army boys were still in tattered hunting shirts and homespun. How grand the general looked leading the columns of men in brown coats with yellow facings. He glittered in bright blue and red with gold, bouncing epaulets and a pink satin ribbon of his new rank across his waistcoat. His sword and his horse's sleek flanks glistened in the noontide sun.

Thea regretted for just one flash of moment that this regiment was not that of her friend Evertt Edwards, the journeyman cooper from across town who had come to court her last year before enlisting. He was, after all, about the only bachelor in town who was tall enough to look her in the eye and who thought she was pretty, too! But despite Rina's romantic promptings, Thea had not let Evertt turn her head. His persistence had both frustrated her and endeared him to her, but she knew she could never love him, nor accept his hand in wedlock. Rina had urged her to give him more time, but now the war had separated them and just as well. Thea knew Evertt did not evoke the depth of feelings and commitment she would surely feel when "the one" came along, if he ever did. So Rina said she understood and insisted that Aide-de-Camp Cullen Varner was probably not "the one" for her, either. She'd pick her own husband, just like Thea, she'd declared much too vehemently. Yet it rankled Thea just a bit that Rina would have her soldier paying her court today when she herself had no escort anywhere in sight.

The crowd had swelled before her shop, though, blessedly, few stared up at her. Standing on tiptoe, Thea skimmed the rest of the parade. She picked out the stiff-backed, aristocratic-looking Lt. Col. Varner in the press of officers behind the regiment. Somehow Cullen always reminded her of that marble bust of Julius Caesar in Charity Payne's fine house. Cullen was educated at Yale and had enjoyed the Grand Tour of Europe. He often quoted Latin phrases, so he had that in common with the stone-hewn Caesar, too! Five other officers rode with Cullen, and all wore matching brown bicorns, some sporting bright cockades and feathers. But their coats were blue and buff, not as bright as Cousin Benedict's. Thea had seen one other military parade and wondered why he didn't have his officers surrounding him.

Behind the six mounted officers came the regimental band, and then a wooden longboat with an unfurled sail, mounted on a sailor-drawn wagon bed to symbolize the privateering pride of New London. And there, in the boat draped with blue and white silk bunting to look like cresting waves at its prow, bold as you please, as if he had risked his life and not just his invalid wife's fortune, sat the town's wealthiest man, Thea's nemesis, Avery Payne. He looked as smug and sleek as ever in his powdered wig and silver silk breeches and coat, as if a real captain setting sail would ever wear such finery!

She looked away, thrusting Avery from her thoughts as she had Evertt, but not for the same reason. Evertt was ever polite and kind to her, though she did not encourage him to court her. But she did all in her power to discourage the tenacious Avery! The way he looked at her, she knew he did not really value her advice about his ailing wife. He was married to her dear friend, Charity Payne, whom Thea had nursed these past two years. Thea was convinced Avery's oily politeness and kindness to his wife's apothecary were mere sham, and all he really valued was getting her alone someday. So she beat frequent hasty retreats from the Payne mansion if he came home. She tried to call on Charity when he would not be in. When he cornered her somewhere or visited the shop, his eyes always examined Thea in places they should not and made her feel prickly discomfort and bottled-up anger to tell him exactly what she thought. But, for Charity, whose fortune he was squandering here again today for his own glory, Thea had held her tongue so far.

When the parade halted before her shop, a hush hovered in the air. Then the little fife and drum band struck up a fanfare, and Cousin Benedict dismounted with a flourish. Thea had not seen him for nearly five years since, usually when he returned to Connecticut, he only visited his sister Hannah and his three sons in New Haven. He was nicknamed "The Dark Eagle" for good reason, Thea thought. His complexion was swarthy, and he emanated quickness and swooping power. His eyes were sharp and dark; his beaklike nose dominated pronounced jowls and a pointed chin. As Thea went down the two steps of the shop to greet him and looked awkwardly down at the top of his black head, she recalled something else: Benedict Arnold had always been quite short. The parade paused; the shuffle and rattle and music stopped.

"Well, well, you've grown more since I've seen you, dear Althea," he said up at her with a taut smile that fought becoming a grimace. He bounced up the two steps she had just descended to stare a bit down at her before he bent under her straw bonnet brim to peck at her cheek. The crowd roared; Thea felt herself blush hot. Benedict Arnold doffed his hat to his audience. His officers dismounted, their saddles creaking and swords clanking. When the cheers subsided, Gen. Benedict Arnold spoke in a resonant voice to the crowd.

"This is a great and memorable day for New London and the Arnolds of Connecticut!" he announced. "To be honored in the area where I had my humble beginnings as an apothecary just like my father's brother's daughter, Althea here, moves me deeply. But this is a day to be engraved in our memories for another reason. Here again, in this place, we boldly cast the gauntlet in the face of the raving English lion and declare, 'This shop is independently owned and shall not be taxed by distant nations!'" He pointed grandly at the newly painted sign that made Thea so proud over her front door. "This street," he went on in a ringing voice, "is free for us to walk in our own individual ways! This town shall be governed by a Congress elected by its citizens! This collection of colonies—this new nation—is ours together and not the possession of some overweening, foreign power! We shall fight for our right to be free, and I am proud to be in the vanguard of this battle to the very end!"

The crowd exploded with wild huzzahs. Shop boys—Thea saw her own delivery boy Jemmy in the crowd—merchants, mothers with infants in arms, pig-tailed privateering sailors on leave, everyone whooped and hollered. Thea wondered if Cousin Benedict would say more, perhaps introduce his officers, though they seemed to keep their distance as if they knew this was his day and his town. Thea nodded her greeting to Cullen Varner, whom she had met several times before when his merchant family from Danbury had come calling on Father Lockwood and Rina. With the Lockwood fortune tied up in lumber mills, and furniture- and ship-building, the Varners had enjoyed business as well as social ties with the Lockwoods for several generations. Cullen nodded back at her with a stiff smile and a squinty stare.

Cousin Benedict seemed to wring cheers from the frenzied crowd with each thrust of his bicorn, then his sword in the air. And then, Thea saw another man beyond Cousin Benedict and behind Cullen.

Her body jerked as if a steeple bell had clanged. Everything blurring by so fast seemed to slow, then stop. Though Cousin Benedict had made her want to slump and hang her head to decrease her height, she jolted upright to see this other man better. He stood at the back of the cluster of the general's aides; he must be one of them. She was sure he stared at her, too. She felt as if he reached across the heads of men to touch her shoulder or take her hand. Or was it even more? Her knees suddenly shook, and her stomach cartwheeled.

Yes, he looked at her *over* Cullen's dark brown head. He was as tall as she, maybe taller. His hair was a golden brown that glinted reddish in the sun. A roughhewn face, not really handsome. His square jaw and broad nose offset a thin, determined mouth. Thick, straight eyebrows shadowed deep-set eyes so she could not discern their color. Even through his sun-struck coloring, he had a slightly wearied, peaked look she had seen on far too many feverish faces lately. Perhaps he was actually ailing and forced to ride and stand there in the sun! She had the urge to dash away from her long-awaited cousin and help the man at once. Then, when the officers replaced their hats, he swept his bicorn back on with the jaunty green feather that did indeed mark him as one of the general's aides-de-camp!

"Thea," Cousin Benedict's strident voice repeated until she jumped as if surprised to see him. "I said, I'll step inside a moment now before going on to Lockwoods'."

"Oh, yes, of course. Please," she said. She tore her gaze away from the stranger and hurried up the steps toward her cousin.

Benedict Arnold moved in the door before she could get there. "You won't mind if a few of my men and my friend Avery Payne come in for a moment, too," he told her in a voice far more used to giving orders than entertaining suggestions.

"Of course not," she said with a darted glance back at the door to see if that included the aide she had seen behind Cullen on the street. Town faces, mostly children she knew, pressed noses to the thick window glass to peer around the pear-shaped apothecary jars as the officers filed in. Unfortunately, Avery Payne made himself immediately at home with a glass of porter from the Widow Middleton's proffered tray as he swaggered in to join General Arnold. But worse, she did not see the tall man now.

"I had no notion you knew my cousin personally," Thea told Avery Payne with a rapier edge to her voice.

"We hold business interests in common as well as appreciation for the glorious cause, et cetera, my dearest Mistress Arnold," Avery retorted with a quick, ingratiating smile. The thirty-two-year-old Avery was sleekly handsome and he knew it. Despite embargoes both economic and moral, he yet garbed himself with English flair and elegance—some of it looted from recently captured British packet ships. His keen, darted look swept her now in that too familiar way, head to toes, then back up again. He dared wink at her, then strode over to clink his pewter mug with the general's glass, just before Benedict Arnold sank gratefully in the chair Thea offered him as guest of honor. She turned her back to Avery to cut him off from her cousin. She noted then that the general and several of his officers sported small tin pins on their lapels painted brightly to look like the new American banner. But before she could remark on them, Cousin Benedict spoke.

"Ah, memories, memories of the old days before the war," he announced to all as if to change the subject of whatever common interests Avery Payne alluded to. The brooding, almost bitter look that flitted over her cousin's face, even when he commanded center stage like this, surprised Thea. "The pungent aromas of paint, varnish, and linseed oil of an apothecary shop," he went on with a grand sweep of glass and arm, as if he toasted the shop itself. "The scent of sawdust on the floor, though I see this one's well swept, the copper still in the corner bubbling away with something or other—"

"Water of mint," she put in.

"Ah, yes. And that heady, sweet smell from the back drying room, too."

"I grow honeysuckle and roses just out the back door, Cousin, though my herb gardens are on the edge of town near some Lockwood forest land. And I'm so used to it all, I almost don't smell those flowers anymore," she added.

"Yes, well," he said and in one gulp tossed back his porter from the only glass goblet she owned. "Enjoy it while you have it, I always say, for who knows what the morrow brings. I shall see you shortly at Lockwoods' then, dear Althea."

Her face fell and her heart, too. All the expectation and planning for this, only to have it end so fast? On to Lockwoods' where Rina would be hostess and Cousin Benedict would belong to them all again. It had been so strange to have him here today, as he did resemble the father she barely recalled—but for father's height. And that tall man outside she so longed to meet was still nowhere in the press of these officers. She could hardly just blurt out a description of him, nor was she adept at approaching strangers at a proper gathering. She sighed deeply as General Arnold vaulted to his feet from her hoop-backed Windsor chair and strode for the door.

"Damnation!" he cracked out and turned back. "I nearly forgot. Thea, I have an aide who's feeling a bit feverish and weak-kneed. I told him to just go 'round in back so my crowd out there won't crush him. Can't do without him long. Get him a bit of ague tonic or something to buck him up, what say, then bring him along to Lockwoods', that's the girl."

As stunned as Thea was by that request from the blue— as though heaven had heard her silent plea—she noted Cullen Varner's tightening frown. Did he not trust the ailing aide here with her? The feverish man just had to be the one she'd seen on the street! But to have him here when everyone else went away and to be expected to nurse him shook her more than Cousin Benedict's visit had!

Despite the rush out the door in the general's broad wake, only Widow Middleton went along to wave Benedict Arnold on his way. Hesitantly, Thea peered into her small back room that served as kitchen, dining hall, and work room. It was deserted but for the marmalade-colored cat that sometimes wandered in to sleep on the cool hearthstones.

The cheers and marching music on the street swelled, then muted in her ears. That crowd wouldn't miss her, anyway, she thought. From where she stood, she gazed out her back door, which overlooked the old West Indies import sugar, coffee, and rum warehouses, now bulging with privateered British goods. She tiptoed closer until she could view the jut of Shaw's Wharf and the pewter-hued River Thames beyond. She heard the neighing of a nearby horse before she saw the man seated on her stoop as if he'd wilted there among the roses. His back against the stone wall, he held his cockaded hat on his knees with his strong profile sketched by the sun. He only turned to face her when he heard her skirts rustle. His deep-set eyes opened under that thatch of eyebrows.

Gold, she thought. His eyes looked the hue of tansy blooms in the slant of sun, although they must truly be dark as garden loam. A tiny white scar threaded his brown brow. He wore his own hair pulled straight back in a plain leather queue. His hands on his bent knees were big—much bigger than hers, for once.

"Oh, there you are!" she said.

He snapped straight up to his feet, as if he had been called to attention. He topped her by a good two inches, even hatless. It was a strange, exhilarating sensation for her. The oddest fluttering swept her, like tiny, gilded hummingbirds trapped inside her belly.

"Aide-de-camp to General Arnold at your service, Mistress Arnold!"

"I'm sorry to hear you're ailing," she managed, clasping her hands so hard around her closed fan she felt its ivory ribs bend.

"I, too, Mistress Arnold. I'm usually as healthy as my horse Charger here."

"Oh, yes," she said, uncertain if he had made a joke. "Cousin Benedict says I'm to give you something for your condition and escort you down to Lockwoods'. He has need of you, it seems."

She studied him while he tied Charger's reins to a rambling rosebush. He followed her inside. Despite his verve, he spoke and walked a bit shakily. It touched her heart to note that he had to stoop slightly to get through her door when its lintel only brushed her bonnet crown.

"Greatly obliged," he told her, his voice deep and slightly drawling. "Hate to admit how poorly I feel. I get hot, then cold, then hot again."

"Please sit here," she said stiffly, and motioned toward the chair where the general had sat. She wanted to help this man badly, but it was so different from having just any ill person in her shop.

"As I said, I don't get sick much. And when I do I just go to bed. Don't trust many fancy cures."

"I assure you, the medicinal cures I practice are a far cry beyond the old superstitions, sir. I'm hardly going to slice a chicken in two and put its split body parts around your feet."

She could have bitten off her tongue at her tart reply, but when she saw a hint of a grin crook his mouth, she relaxed a bit. She realized if she weren't so nervous with this compelling man, she would not have been so defensive. A loud silence stretched between them. He appeared to be trying to see what her hair really looked like under her bonnet. Boldly, she removed it and lay it on the counter amid the empty mugs as she turned away to fetch the powder she'd have him take with parsley wine. She almost yanked her netted mitts off before she remembered her hands. Yet it encouraged her that his had looked rough, too, calloused and even scarred.

"I'm sure I have a thing or two to help cure your fever, even if it gets as far as the shakes," she said to make amends.

She could feel his eyes on her as she got up on her wooden step stool to reach up and open the ceiling drawers. But she had no idea of the impact she had on him.

Despite his bodily discomfort and dismay at not accompanying his general, this stunning woman's presence forked jolts of feeling through him. He had never beheld anyone quite like her, a larger-than-life goddess who emanated both power and peace. So this was the young female apothecary cousin of the general's whom Cullen Varner had told him of. Still, he supposed her Arnold ties alone might make her off-limits to a backwoods-bred officer, however dedicated to the general.

But Cullen had told him she was gangly and awkward. And here was this clever, ravishing, unique woman. He hadn't been alone with—even near—any woman for so long with all the months he put in to help the cause and General Arnold.

"I have what you need," she interrupted his frenzied thoughts. "This goldenrod pulp mixed with marigold leaves will soothe most fevers." She turned to face him across the counter and their eyes held again. "You don't know the specific cause, do you?"

"I might now," he teased with a wan smile that flaunted strong, straight teeth. He immediately regretted his heavy-handed humor when he saw her cheeks flame as hot as his skin felt. "No, not really," he said quickly, "though we've hardly had a moment's rest since we chased the lobsterbacks out of Danbury last month, unfortunately after they'd burned half the danged town to get to the big military depot there."

"I heard," she said as her skilled hands mixed a paper packet of the powder in a bit of greenish liquid she'd fetched from a huge, pear-shaped carboy in the front window. "My dear friend Varina Lockwood's friend—your friend, Cullen Varner—" She seemed to be struggling to find her words as she walked over to extend a leather flagon to him with the drink. "I mean, the British burned Cullen Varner's family home and their warehouses there. No doubt, he wants justice and recompense for that."

"Not quite sure what Cullen Varner wants beyond everything to be perfect," he said, but he downed the drink. He thought it tasted grassy, outdoorsy. It jabbed him with the homesick memory of the Pennsylvania farmstead and the family he hadn't seen for nearly two years. He pictured the Lehigh Hills again at wheat-cutting time with the tall grass waving. He saw and smelled twisting Tahicox Creek, rampant with wild honeysuckle in the grassy summer as it edged God's green fields. Something here with this woman whose first name he could not recall, made him think of those lost golden days before the war—or was it just the scent of that rambling rose and honeysuckle out back? This woman was not like his mother or his sisters. Their hair was not that ravishing red, though they had inherited theirs from some copper-haired Glenn or Buchanan ancestor from Scotland's braes and glens.

And this woman was dead wrong about Cullen Varner being his friend, though, on his part, he admired the Danbury gentleman for the lofty standards he demanded of himself and his men. Cullen's whole life seemed consecrated to winning. The farmer couldn't help admire how the gentleman had stoically accepted the ruination of his heritage—and much of his rich inheritance—in the burning of Danbury. But he wished Cullen would accept him as an officer of the same rank, the way Benedict Arnold did.

Why, the general had even accepted the towering height that made others so leery of him. Maybe, it was because the general knew his Pennsylvania aide-de-camp was loyal to the end, no matter how others like General "Granny" Gates, or even congress, refused to recognize or reward Arnold's greatness. Sure, he was danged proud General Arnold had promoted a Pennsylvania farmer and trapper right along with the highborns, but he regretted there was yet a wall to breech with a man like Cullen Varner.

"Would you like to sit for a while before you ride to Lockwoods'?" Mistress Arnold interrupted his drifting thoughts again. Hang it all, he cursed himself. Was he actually getting delirious with this damned touch of ague so he'd just been sitting here woolgathering?

"I'm fine," he told her and rose from the chair. She saw he, too, wore on his lapel one of those tin, painted American banners Cousin Benedict sported. He moved slowly toward the back door. He nodded to the old woman now clearing up the mugs from the counter as if this were a tavern and not an apothecary shop.

Thea noted he walked with a casual, lanky grace that neither his height nor his military training could stiffen. His broad epauletted shoulders and strong chest narrowed to hard hips and thighs that plunged into knee-high boots polished to such a sheen she could see her elongated reflection in them as she bid farewell to Widow Middleton and followed him out.

"I'm right sorry," he apologized on the stoop out back as he fished in his waistcoat pocket for a coin. "I'm so addle-brained, I forgot to pay you."

"No," she said and shook her head to cascade a curly crimson tendril loose just before she replaced and retied her bonnet. "Please, it's gratis—for the cause and for one of my cousin's dear men."

He noted she colored slightly at her own choice of words. Despite his age of twenty-seven and his experience in battle beginning with the siege of Boston that had catapulted him into Arnold's favor, he suddenly felt as awkward as a schoolboy gawking at her like this. But either she or the fever had fuzzed his brain. He felt soft and woolly inside. He'd like to curl up here somewhere near her and go to sleep—if a man

could really sleep near a woman like this without touching
her first. Surely, she had a suitor she was promised to. He
should ask her, because it was one of his iron-clad rules that
if a woman was spoken for, that was that.

"You know, I feel so silly," she said. He watched her lips
move. Shapely and soft, her lower lip looked like a tiny red
pillow. "Cousin Benedict didn't mention your name."

"Beg pardon. And I don't recall your given name," he ad-
mitted. "I'm Morgan. Lieutenant Colonel Morgan Glenn of
Pennsylvania, and right proud to be aide-de-camp to General
Benedict Arnold, a great man—him, not me, at your service,
Mistress Arnold."

"And I'm Althea, but please call me Thea," she said and
shyly, charmingly, he thought, extended her hand.

He took it. It fit his beautifully, not lost in his big paw at
all. He had the foolish hankering to pull off her lace-netted
mitt to touch her skin, but he'd tarried too long already. He
turned away, or he was sure he'd fall right into her pond-
green eyes.

"You have a horse?" he asked as he untied Charger.

"I'll walk along to get you there."

"Nonsense. I'll put you sideways in the saddle and ride
behind. You've ridden pillion?" he said and lifted her up with
no more ado.

She gasped at the way he made the decision for her and
the quick, sure touch of his hands on her waist. She marveled
at how easily he lifted her when she was certain his strength
was drained. Why, she must be as heavy as she was tall. But
with this man, Morgan Glenn, she almost forgot about that
and her hands and her wild hair and—drat, she was being
silly. A man like this was perhaps even married, and he
would be gone tomorrow.

At that thought, her silly heart fell to her feet, even as he
mounted behind her. But it still beat with unheard drums
when his strong arms came around her to hold the reins and
keep her in the saddle. Her body tingled all over at his touch,
as if fiery fife music still raced up and down her spine.

Chapter Two

*"The mixing of elixirs is a most delicate charge of the apothe-
cary, and care must be taken as in the mingling of certain
volatile temperaments of persons. Therefore, seal strong and
diverse elements away from each other with wood and wax
stoppers in glazed pottery or glass demijohns protected by bur-
lap and sawdust between. Dangerous brews co-mingled may
turn desired good to harm."*

VARINA LOCKWOOD SURVEYED the crowded drawing
room of her family home and smiled behind a flutter of
painted paper fan. She tried to listen to the mayor's wife, but
she felt so excited she hardly heard one word. Wishing she
had hired a violoncellist despite what Father had said about
overdoing ostentation, Rina tapped her foot impatiently to
her own dissonant, internal music. Even today, her memories
clashed and darkened, though she reveled in one of the few
times Father let her hostess the sort of social gathering the
house had once gaily resounded with years ago. But she also
recalled that nightmare time that ended it all when Mother
died and Thea came to stay.

Rina kept the set smile on her face and breathed in her
own essence of roses to calm herself. From ringlets of wheat-
hued hair swept up under a butterfly lace cap to pink, silk-
slippered toes, Rina Lockwood exuded the scent of the sweet
sachet Cassie had made from Thea's discarded petals at the
shop. Even Rina's pink-and-beige striped satin skirts and embroidered buff stomacher smelled like the pale pink rosebud
peeking out from her bosom bottle.

For once she had willingly worn a lace modesty piece to
cover the bare skin above the low, square-cut necklines Father said were sinful. There, where she had scratched in her
sleep, and on her ankles remained her only traces of ivy rash.
Thanks to this frothy lace and Thea's ministrations, even a

poison rash could be hidden so as not to spoil this day. Why, if it had not been for Benedict Arnold's triumphal return, even this soiree would have been forbidden, and Rina had no intention of missing one moment of it!

Especially during the war, Father was adamant they not take on the appearance of "revelry and cavortings." But Rina felt a good mixing of people just served to buck one up for whatever came tomorrow. Perhaps while General Arnold and Governor Trumbull were here, she could get their agreement on that to use as a wedge to budge Father later. She excused herself from the little cluster of avid-eyed guests embroiled in their own chatter. In a rustle of satin over wire panniers and tight elbow sleeves dripping lace, she traversed the thick, imported flowered carpet to rejoin the group of dignitaries seated around her father.

The sixty-seven-year-old, white-wigged Moses Lockwood sat ramrod straight in the wheelchair to which painful gout had consigned him five years ago. "Why are you here with us old folk, dear girl?" he asked in a scolding tone, which no one else seemed to heed. General Arnold still perched on the edge of his petit-point chair as if ready to explode to his feet to lead a charge into battle, while the somberly attired, unimposing Governor Trumbull nodded eagerly, and Avery Payne hung on their every word. Despite all that, Moses told her in a too-loud whisper, "Arnold's officers will be here today and gone tomorrow, my girl. You'd best be about amusing Cullen!"

Father's insistence mixed with the fact Thea had not put in an appearance yet because she was nursing some laggard aide of the general's prickled Rina, despite her soaring mood. For far too long Father had decided everything for Rina, while Thea had too often either backed him up or been off having such a fine time she wasn't around to defend her. Father had told his daughter—his real daughter, Rina fumed silently, the one he never really trusted to think for herself— whom to bring in to visit, when it was proper for her to go out, and how to act on all occasions. And now, deep inside like a yanked embroidery knot, Rina felt the tightening panic

that he would also simply decree when she must wed Cullen
Varner and in what gown!

Not that there was anything truly wrong with Cullen, she
admitted to herself as she fanned her flushed face. Despite
the recent catastrophe where Cullen's family had lost their
Danbury home and warehouses to British torches, she was
yet impressed with Cullen's heritage, his demeanor, and appearance. But it riled her that Father—Cullen, too, just like
Thea, no doubt—expected she would fall in line just like
some green soldier boy taking orders! And, all the while,
there was Thea, whom Moses Lockwood had reared as if she
were bone of his bone, too. The moment Thea had asked to
return to her parents' shop to live her own life her way, he'd
allowed it! Well, it just wasn't fair, and Rina Lockwood was
going to wage her own war for independence the moment
she saw a way!

"Father," she began, choosing her words carefully, "Cullen is just fine without me for a moment. We do have other
guests, you know. If he wishes to stand like some silent sentinel by the window, staring over here and brooding, that is
his choice and not mine."

Her protest went unheard by everyone else as the heated
conversation in the group plunged on. Father just grunted
and scowled but turned away to listen, too. From what Rina
could gather, the governor and town mayor were quite distraught at something General Arnold had just revealed.

"You're being sent to New York State under General
Gates!" Governor Trumbull, their houseguest for a few days,
protested. "Heaven preserve us! With Connecticut towns
being burned and us perhaps next on the blasted British list,
we need you to remain here!"

"You do understand for the good of all Americans we
must stop the enemy from sweeping down the Mohawk and
Hudson valleys, sir?" Arnold demanded and jumped to his
feet. Rina had noticed he only chose to stand when others
were seated. "They would cut off the northern states for
troops from Canada to gobble up, and I'll not sit by and allow
that!"

"But, damnation, General," Avery Payne put in, his high

brow crumpled with concern. "We New London privateers have risked everything to bring British shipping down. And to leave us here, naked and undefended but for a few old, understaffed fortifications and rusty cannon from the Indian Wars—"

Arnold held up his hands for silence and got it. "I realize that. Don't forget I know this area like the back of my hand. I don't favor reporting to old 'Granny' Gates with his sluggish, spineless ways, either, I tell you. All I can advise is that you send the strongest worded protest to congress or even Washington himself if you want me here to guard our beloved shores from more British flame-tossing and pillaging! Perhaps that unruly congress will see fit to give me my proper due then. But I'm hardly to be personally berated, friend Avery, for your bold—and lucrative—escapades here. Now, with all your wealth, I'd say you could hire someone to patrol the shores of the River Thames and Long Island Sound, or work out some personal protection. You know what I mean," Arnold's voice trailed off as if there was much yet to say on that.

Rina listened to the growing alarm. The tenor of the times agitated her own inner seething. Just let Father with his merchant interests and men like Avery Payne and his rich fellow privateers know how it felt to be beset by rules and regulations one did not like. To be told whom to mingle with and whom not. Even to have one's own house and private lives perhaps invaded!

"Rina, my dear, don't just glower and gawk!" her father said up at her in the continued rumble of men's discussions. "Go tend to Cullen, I said!"

She flounced away without another word, but took her time weaving through the other groups of guests and clusters of Chippendale- and Hepplewhite-inspired furniture Father's craftsmen had made before the labor drain of the war. Strident conversations mingled to a droning buzz in the tall-ceilinged, foursquare granite mansion. Standing behind the linen-covered serving table laden with pewter platters and silver chafing dishes, Cassie beamed at her as if nothing were amiss. Rina paused to tell her how pretty she looked in a canary ruffled gown and stiff-starched apron. No need to take things out on Cassie, as she was also innocent in all this, Rina thought.

She moved on, sensing that Cullen watched her meandering progress across the crowded room; she could feel his exacting, dark blue eyes on her. She took a fresh glass of punch to him for an excuse to seek him out.

"More punch?" she asked as she joined him by the front damask-draped window. "I have no doubt it is hard for you to be here with the loss of your own dear home last month," she added, with a sudden stab of sympathy for him.

"I am grateful, Varina," he said and took the cup, "for the drink and the understanding." His fingers lightly brushed hers. She savored the little tingle that coursed through her from his look and touch and compliment, then glanced out the window. "I dare say," he plunged on in the lull from her usual talkativeness, "all of us will be facing hard times until we win this dreadful war *pro patria.*"

She looked back at his serious face. No sign of emotion there for his own losses or the future dangers he faced. Only a flicker of curiosity when he looked at her like that. Yet she saw his chiseled nostrils flare at the sweet scent she exuded, and his eyes studied her. But, devil take him if he thought he had some unspoken eternal hold over her the way her father did!

"You are always so calm, Cullen. But not in battle, I presume."

"In battle I do what I must to win, at any cost to myself or my men!"

"How noble," she began, then caught herself. "I mean— I don't know how I'd react in the heat of battle."

"Pray God, if I and men like me are willing to spend everything to protect you, you shall never have to know." He put his cup down on the gateleg table and took her hands in his. He lifted her right hand to his lips briefly in a gesture that was surprising for Cullen. He had always been entirely proper and formal with her before. But perhaps the war pressing in on them changed even Cullen Varner, she thought with a delicious little shiver. Perhaps losing what he had once

thought was his future in Danbury made him think of other
things, of what really mattered in life. If he would just court
her and ask her opinions and share her feelings sometimes,
and let her make up her own mind—

"It's important for me to know you will be here waiting
when this is all over, Varina," he interrupted her thoughts.

"Father will certainly be waiting to hear how things have
gone for you," she parried, but she felt breathless, waiting
for what he would say next.

"Your father and I are of one mind on this *ad perpetuam,*
Varina, though it's you I am speaking to now," he pursued.
"I'm afraid certain things are already being changed by the
war, traditions ignored. For example, not that I blame General Arnold for wanting bold men around him, but, right up
with commissioned gentlemen, he's promoting homespun
volunteers like that Morgan Glenn Thea's stayed behind to
nurse. I don't blame Glenn, for he's a brave, moral man."
He lowered his voice even more, but not for the intimate
whispers she longed for in her ear. "*Inter nos,* Varina, I can't
help but think a former tradesman like Benedict Arnold is
just trying to surround himself with men of his own status
in promoting Morgan Glenn. Just as he can't abide most men
taller, he can't abide most men higher in birth. I'm ever loyal
to the general because duty decrees such, but standards must
be maintained, even in war. We're fighting for freedom from
foreign tyranny, but not for the blurring of social distinctions
and standards here at home!"

"But aren't the homespun volunteers, even green privates,
putting their lives just as much on the line as you gentlemen
officers?" she retorted. Cullen sounded so much like her father she wanted to scream. She hadn't met or seen this Morgan Glenn, but she almost wished he were here so she could
give him *two* glasses of punch and the best chair and her
fawning attentions so that both Father and Cullen would see
what she thought of their standards. Especially when they
included telling a young woman who she must love and
honor and wait for and be bound to when that man himself
just prated high-flung ideals as coldly as his precious Latin
phrases!

"If you'll excuse me, Cullen, I—"

"Wait, Varina," he insisted and seized her right hand again in both of his. "You do understand that there will be a necessary rebuilding of things after the war, don't you? Standards must be sustained to lay the foundation for that day in our new nation. The old trading routes by which our families once prospered will be restored. New houses and families must be built, and when that time comes, I only hope that you will be willing to—"

Rina tugged her hands away to halt his words. If this was something special coming, she wanted it in private, away from Father's eagle eyes and half the city's stares! She wanted to be wooed and written to, not included in a list of complaints. She longed to be given little gifts and poems—even if lighthearted ones like Thea made up on the spur of the moment. She yearned to have her beau passionately distressed that some other man might catch her eye and sue for her hand while he was away at war. She desired emotion, not iron control. She wanted freedom to choose, not to be told. She wanted—

"Varina, listen to me now—"

"Oh, Cullen, look!" she cried and darted back. "Here's Thea with the general's favorite aide you were telling me of." She fled toward the nervous-looking Thea and the tall man standing with his bicorn in his hands just behind her in the foyer. The conversational buzz in the room muted; heads turned their way.

"Thea, finally!" Rina greeted her with a quick peck on her very flushed cheek. "And this must be our belated guest, Lieutenant Colonel Glenn," she said and smiled up fetchingly at the tall man as Thea presented him and he bowed over Rina's delicate hand. Rina ignored Cullen's approach as she inquired about Morgan's health. "Well," she declared, so Cullen could hear, "since Thea says it takes awhile for that ague tonic to work, I'll just take you upstairs right now and show you to a room to rest no matter how General Arnold fusses. Until you're much better, you just leave that to me!"

"Indeed, he could use a bit of rest," Thea admitted, though she could have pinched Rina right through her widepanniered skirts for pulling her special patient away like that and stranding her down here under everyone's curious gaze.

But Rina, as hostess, was in control and she knew it. To apparently everyone's dismay, including the tall lieutenant colonel's, Cullen's, and even, strangely, Thea's, Rina locked her arm in the tall man's and marched him right up the stairs. Let Father fume and Cullen fuss, Rina thought defiantly. She was making this decision, and, after all, she had the rules of hospitality on her side!

She darted a glance back down the curving staircase at Thea, standing with the wide-eyed Cassie now at her elbow. Cullen glared up, too. Fine, just let him, Rina thought triumphantly. And she would gladly enough face down her father when she had this handsome hostage safely ensconced in the bed just down the hall from her own!

"I can't thank you enough for knowing exactly what I needed," the deep, drawling voice of this big man interrupted her private victory parade. "Just an hour's sleep or so, then I'll be off and away with General Arnold. But, please tell Thea again how grateful I am."

Rina loosed his arm and opened the guest room door. "Thea. Yes, of course, I will. She's been the dearest friend of mine for years."

"Like a sister, she said." His voice sounded weary as he headed straight for the bed. "Say, forgive the personal question, Mistress Lockwood, but Thea isn't—betrothed or promised or such, is she?"

Rina studied the imposing man as he sank wearily on the side of the bed. Her thoughts seethed like bubbling liquids too long bottled up. Feelings toward Thea, Cullen, her father, this man who emanated power and pride however ailing he was—churned through her. The words came to her in a swirling rush.

"But didn't Thea tell you? You must not have asked, then, as she's so proud of it. She was courted all last year by Evertt Edwards, the town's journeyman cooper. He's taller than her and her match in every way. But they aren't wed legally yet—not quite, if you catch my drift."

She trembled at the look she saw on his face. The hurt in

his eyes went far deeper than the weariness of the fever. "But, well, you know how that is," she plunged on, suddenly panicked at what she dared. "People have said for years I was meant for Cullen Varner and it's not true and I'm not promised to nor in love with anyone like Thea is, all out there on her own and free as a bird by her own choice. Just rest now, and I'll explain things to General Arnold downstairs," she added, suddenly desperate to change the subject. "And I'll send you my father's valet to help."

"No need, Mistress Lockwood," he said with a shake of his big head. "You've helped enough." He did not meet her eyes, and she turned quickly away. But not before she saw an endearing, errant lock of hair dart down to cover the thin white scar on his broad brown forehead.

She closed the door quietly and leaned against it in the hall. She took a deep breath. Whatever had possessed her to say all that? She could hear her own heart thudding at her bending the truth about Thea. And what if he said something of it to her? Well, she'd just have to be sure Thea and he had no more heart-to-heart talks. Besides, he'd be leaving soon and that would be that.

She stood away from the door. Her knees felt as weak as Morgan Glenn's had looked. She stiffened and started away just as Thea and Cassie appeared at the top of the stairs.

"Should I fetch more tonic for him?" Thea whispered down the dim corridor lined with gilt-framed portraits of Lockwood ancestors. "The ride over here must have been too much for him right now."

"I think he'll be just fine," Rina said and hurried toward them. She refused to meet Thea's penetrating gaze as she bustled past to go back downstairs. "Don't worry about a thing, Thea. He'll be just fine."

Though she mingled with the guests as a social equal, Thea did not feel a part of them. Yes, she had helped the mayor's wife through painful shingles this last winter, and nursed others in the room. That garnered nods and waves, but not heartfelt invitations to the tradesman's daughter to enter into conversation. Unlike Rina, she had never been comfortable just joining in large groups. When he saw her across the room, Cousin Benedict boomed out a story of his and her father's boyhood days, but then he became engrossed in the men's discussions again, unfortunately, with Avery Payne. Father Lockwood pulled her into his group, but he spoke so earnestly with others, she went on again. And Cullen Varner looked too forbidding to approach, especially when Rina spoke with other guests right in front of him. Rina as hostess was too busy to spare anyone more than a moment's chat.

Though Thea had been reared in this house, somehow, it had never been quite hers, she realized as she momentarily watched the room from Cassie's side near the long food tables. Perhaps if she had been younger when her parents and Mrs. Lockwood had died, the place would have seemed more naturally hers, too. Father Lockwood always said it was her home every bit as much as it was Rina's. If only each time he insisted the three of them were a little family, she had not recalled so vividly the apothecary shop just as it had once been! In the years when Father Lockwood had stored its goods in a warehouse and leased it out to be a wiggery before she got it back, she still stubbornly had thought of it as home. If she wouldn't disappoint Rina and Father Lockwood and Cousin Benedict, she'd like to head back there right now or take Cassie and walk out to the woods to find some fresh sassafras root to brew Morgan Glenn some good, hearty tonic when he awoke upstairs.

She jumped when Avery Payne loomed before her as if to pin her to the wall. "I've had a bit of unsettling news, and I wonder if you would help." He seemed genuinely distressed when nothing about the man usually seemed genuine. Yet, even now, his probing gaze unsettled her. She mistrusted the sort of help he really sought from her. "It's Charity, having a bad spell," he rushed on. "My stableboy just ran over to tell me. With essential business being decided here for the good of all New Londoners, I just can't rush away, so—"

"So I can," she cut him off. "Yes, I'll go to help her, as you can't afford the time," she said before she could halt her words.

"Now, see here, Thea, I didn't mean—"

"I'll just slip out to see how she is," Thea added before he could make a scene. While Avery stalked back to huddle with Cousin Benedict, Thea hurried toward Rina to explain where she was going. Rina frowned when she saw Thea bearing straight for her, but nodded quickly when she heard she had to leave.

"Avery Payne would never depart for one of that poor, besotted woman's spells," Rina whispered, "even if he was just having his boots shined!"

"Poor, besotted woman," the words rang in Thea's brain as she hurried four doors up Bank Street to the Paynes' large, imposing granite home. The house had been part of Charity's vast dowery as the spinster heiress of the Mumford fortune when she'd married her dashing, younger husband ten years ago. Then, the thirty-year-old, plain and sickly woman had been swept off her feet by newcomer Avery Payne's attentions, which everyone else in town saw for what they were. For a while after the marriage, Charity's health had seemed to improve. But these last eight or so years, she had slipped more and more. Now, after risking his wife's capital in many unprofitable ventures, Avery was the town's most brazen and rich financier of privateering vessels. And Charity was the town's most reclusive invalid. Over these last two years that Thea had nursed her, she sometimes wondered if the dear woman's asthma spells weren't worsened at times by Avery's blatant interests in all else but her.

Thea dashed up the stone steps under the Georgian pillared portico and pulled the bell rope. "Poor, besotted woman," Rina's words taunted Thea again. She had no desire to be like Charity. Perhaps it was best that Morgan Glenn was leaving town today with her cousin's retinue and she would not see him again. How easily she could be swept off her feet by him. Though neither of them had broached the subject, he must have a wife or beloved waiting somewhere.

Charity Payne's lady's maid Susan was out of breath by the time she pulled open the big wooden door. "Oh, Mistress Thea, thank ye for coming. I would ha' sent for ye direct, but I knew it was your big day down there, so I sent the boy for the master."

"How is your mistress?" Thea asked as they hurried up the wide, curving staircase together.

"Breathing real hard, beet red, then bluish, like before. A-coughin' and a-gaspin' for breath."

Thea heard Charity at the end of the long upstairs hall. Even the thick carpets and rich paper wallhangings, the damask draperies and canopied bed could not mute the heart-wrenching sounds. "Charity, I'm here!" Thea called as she rushed to her bedside. The frail woman clasped her arm with amazing strength as Thea plumped her pillows up behind her. "Get a coal from that bath stove," Thea ordered Susan, "and fetch that piece of acacia gum I brought last week to burn."

At age forty, Charity Mumford Payne looked years older. Her chestnut hair was etched with gray; her once sparkling deep blue eyes now seemed faded; her roses and cream complexion had gone papery pale. Lines webbed her thin face, and her voice trembled even when she was not wracked by "a spell." Her body, now more gaunt than slender, was yet delicately graceful the few times she rose from her bed or left her room.

But, especially lately, when she realized it pleased Avery quite well enough to merely visit her here briefly once or twice a day on his way out to the vast world he coveted, she had kept to her room and bed. Now, even when he brought that world to the house with boisterous visitors downstairs, little dinner parties 'til all hours, or that noisy, exotic parrot he usually kept in his big, sunny bedchamber down the hall, Charity seldom made the effort to get up. But it twisted Thea's heart to see how the dear face would light at the merest sound of Avery's voice outside or downstairs. Poor, besotted Charity loved Avery blindly and completely, and that made Thea protect him, yet detest him all the more.

Charity and Thea were friends, closer than anyone, including Avery, knew. The Mumford heiress and the tradesman's daughter called each other by their given names in private and talked of much more than Thea's cures and Charity's labored breathing. For Thea was the only one who had been honest with Charity about how she looked and what her prospects were for future health. She was honest with Charity about all but what she knew of Avery's attentions to other women, for that would have destroyed Charity's will to live. If Charity knew Avery eyed Thea the way he did, that, too, might have ended everything the friends had built together over these last two years.

"Breathe slowly, shallow at first, dear," Thea crooned as she wafted the aromatic smoke of the suffusement Charity's way. When Charity stopped gasping and coughing, Thea dosed her with syrup to soothe the spasms of her asthma, then sat on the big bed to hold her hand until her pulse quieted, too.

"You would . . . think . . . I could do all that . . . myself now," Charity whispered raggedly and held tight to Thea's hand. "Didn't mean for you to come . . . from your special gathering . . . your special day."

It pained Thea to know who she did mean to come, but they both let that pass unspoken. So Charity would rest her voice, Thea regaled her with stories of the parade, of Cousin Benedict's grand speech from the steps of the apothecary shop, the gathering at Lockwoods', and even Morgan Glenn.

"Ah, he sounds a fine figure of a man for you," Charity murmured, and the corners of her mouth twisted up in a hint of an encouraging smile.

"No. He's leaving."

"Maybe . . . he'll be back sometime. But tell me then, how did my Avery look standing . . . in the prow as captain of his ship?" Charity inquired between careful breaths. Her eyes glistened at the merest thought of that sight, Thea fumed silently. And to think, the faraway, awed look on the flushed face seemed to say, whatever Avery Payne does, he is mine and I shall love him until the day I die!

Thea looked away and cleared her throat. "He looked just right for a privateer who never goes to sea," Thea told her, "but very much in his element on dry land. And I do hope that fine silk bunting he bought for waves will be sold for soldiers' shoes or food."

"He's always giving goods for the cause, Thea," Charity

summoned a bit of spunk from her sunken frame to punctuate her words.

"Of course. He's well-known for that, and you, too!" Yet, Thea thought, he only donated publicly with much acclaim to polish his own name with the town hierarchy and now Cousin Benedict. But today, he seemed to have realized at last that such brazenness might make him a special British target, she mused, ashamed at her own smugness over that when this dear woman's health rose and fell by the smattering of affections he occasionally flung her way.

"You go on back, my friend—and tell me all about everything else next time," Charity insisted over Thea's protests. But she knew she had to go. She oversaw Susan's sprinkling alcohol over the small pillow stuffed with hops to induce sleep. She bid the frail woman farewell and left her resting under Susan's care with the promise they would fetch her right away if the asthma became agitated again. Thea went down the silent stairs by herself, past the bulge-eyed white marble bust of Caesar on the landing under the oval window overlooking the fine back gardens. She paused in the large foyer hung with painted paper of pastoral meadow scenes she loved. Then she heard the screech nearby, and she jumped.

She peered in the open door of the south drawing room from which the sound had come. Bottle green damask chairs, twin settees, and matched brass wall sconces perfectly balanced the large, marble-tiled hearth and flowered rug. The chartreuse and yellow parrot Avery had flaunted about town when it was first captured from a British ship sat in an ornate cage by the front window. While she watched, the feathered fellow preened his wings and picked at first one lifted talon and then the other with his green beak. He seemed very cramped and closed in there, flustered and annoyed. She had a sweeping urge to free him. There was a perch for him in the corner he no doubt would have much preferred.

"If you want him, he's yours," the male voice said close behind her. "He's a stubborn little bastard, but I'll break him. He'll say and do what Avery Payne wants, or he'll be sorry!"

Thea was jolted by his words as much as by the surprise. She stepped farther into the room to put a space between her and Avery. His satin waistcoat and breeches shown pearly gray in the muted light. "I didn't hear you come in. Nor think you would."

To her dismay, he followed her into the drawing room and closed the door behind him. A frown stretched his high brow. "Damnation, I do not need your pious judgments, Thea. No, that's not what I need at all from you," he dared and shot her a blinding smile that echoed the hue of his elaborately curled wig.

"Let me pass, sir. I must return to Lockwoods'."

"In a minute. How bad is she?" he asked with a nod upward.

"Your wife is better. Forgive my openness, sir, but do you not realize her spells worsen when she wants to be out with you?"

"Nonsense. She knows my abiding affections!"

Thea said no more. No good to blurt that it would be the death of Charity if she truly knew of the "affections" he kept in a little house out by Shaw's Cove. But at least whoever the current woman was, she was never there for long and, so gossip said, was soon enough replaced. Thea tried to skirt around him for the door, but he put out a stocky arm to block her way. They stood, neither moving for a moment, sizing each other up as adversaries.

"Thea, I see no good reason for your sharpness with me. And you do look lovely today in that salmon hue to set off your stunning hair. But sincere compliments aside, why alienate one of the town's leading citizens when you are trying to build your trade? You have a competitor shop in town, you know, and my dear wife would miss your ministrations greatly, as would I, if we began to buy our medicinal cures and other sundries there."

For Charity alone, and not that heavy-handed threat, Thea again held her tongue. She was no dunce. Though yet a virgin, she knew what such looks and innuendos from a man meant. But he never quite crossed the line of forcing her to cut him off. And he knew, all too well, she would never tell Charity if he did overstep. Thea jumped again when the parrot squawked.

"So nervous today, Thea," he murmured. "So unlike you."

"That bird can't abide your keeping him caged here, nor do I, Mr. Payne," she managed, but cursed her shaky voice.

"Just a word of business, then. You didn't think I wanted aught but a word of business, did you? I've rats on my ships that need to be dispensed with. And now that I'm going to be taking your illustrious cousin on as a partner—"

"Cousin Benedict is throwing in with your privateering?"

"He at least knows whom to trust," he countered. "Now, down in that precious little shop of yours, do you have something we could put in cast-off food to be rid of the vermin rats, or shall I go to Greenwoods' Apothecary for something?"

"Poison snakeweed might do, or that East Indies poison nut, though I've little left of the latter," she admitted.

"Whatever will do a quick, clean job, et cetera, fine. I'll be to see you about it, but don't tell a soul as I don't need my sailors, investors, or anyone else thinking I'm stooping to such petty concerns in these tumultuous times. Agreed?"

She never thought she'd agree with Avery Payne on much of anything except the need to sever British shipping lines. She didn't want him to have any new excuse to call on her, but she could help with ridding the ships of rats, and she certainly could use the money with swelling inflation when half the town owed her for goods. She had no intention of asking Father Lockwood for funds to help her keep the shop afloat through these hard times. She had told him she valued her independence, and she meant to.

"Agreed," she said.

He smiled and opened the door behind him a crack while he extended his hand to her. That last gesture reminded her of Morgan just this afternoon. But Morgan's hand was big and calloused, while Avery's looked smaller, smooth and soft. Yet Avery's gall had kept him from ever seeming one bit disturbed by the fact she topped him by several inches. Perhaps this harmless—to all but rats—bargain, fairly offered and accepted would be a bridge on which they could build a business relationship. For Charity's sake at least, she had to try. She took his hand, but withdrew it quickly when he clasped it between both of his and his eyes heated again.

"A deal for the poison only," she told him, and stepped quickly past into the foyer and out the front door. "Poor, besotted woman," the words came to her again as she headed back to Lockwoods'. But she still didn't trust Avery Payne at all—nor her own foolish heart when it came to Morgan Glenn.

Chapter Three

"Never heed superstitions or pure emotion with no root in rational thought. I have never seen good luck charms, chants, or magic potions truly cure one ailing soul."

CASSIE MCCREA SPOTTED another four-leaf clover and put down her hemp sack of newly dug sassafras roots to pounce on it. "See, Thea," she called and held the clover out, stiff-armed. "One for your hatband, too!"

"I've never yet seen one of your forest folk with or without one of your magic clovers, Cassie," Thea said and went on down the path toward town, lugging her bag.

They had spent all morning digging roots and tending the straight lines of herbs out on the edge of Father Lockwood's rolling land to the northwest of town before the Cedar Swamps began. There had been thick forests here once, but it had mostly gone for logging to help make the Lockwood fortune years ago. Here Thea had built a crude, bark cabin to store her hoe and rake, and to shelter tender blooms or herself if a quick storm came up.

Usually Cassie was a better worker, but today she had been especially distracted and needed prompting to help dig and pull. Sometimes, Thea was sure the girl was a mirror of moods for both her and Rina, as if she were somehow mystically tied to them both. It was as if Cassie had sensed her dismay at not seeing Morgan Glenn again, but she refused to interrogate the girl about what was going on at the Lockwoods'. She believed and trusted her friend Rina, and that was that!

More than once out here today, Thea had been tempted

to just agree with Cassie's occasionally voiced belief that Thea had met a *Sidhe* out here in the woods once. *That* might make the girl work harder. But once she assented to go along with Cassie's falsehoods, Thea scolded herself as she trudged along, it would breed all sorts of other lies. And surely, Cassie would blurt something to Rina when the two friends had vowed long ago there would be no secrets or lies between them!

Thea turned back and sighed. Cassie was plucking the white-balled blooms of clover and weaving a crown of them with her deft fingers. "Here, Thea," she cried as she scooped up her sack and came to join her. "A clover crown for you! Fairies sometimes give the gift of healing, and you have that, you do, so the crown is yours!"

"I got my gift of healing from my parents' talents and lots of hard work, not some fairy's whim, I told you." But Thea bent down to let Cassie settle the wreath over her straw bonnet brim. "At least I prefer that tale to your fear that the *Sidhe* take lost forest maidens for concubines," she teased as they went on together.

" 'Tis true enough!" Cassie protested as she loped along to match Thea's strides. Out here, Thea noted, Cassie looked like she'd been put together with strings like a doll and not earthly bones and sinews. She listened halfheartedly as the girl went on with her story. "Disappeared for seven years, a woman did once in County Cork. When she came home, she'd danced with the *Sidhe* so long, her toes were all worn away!" she declared, awed.

"Indeed, mine will be worn away if we don't get back soon. Just sing a bit then while we walk along," Thea urged to calm her.

But if she expected a tuneless, wordless ditty she could just ignore with her own thoughts, Thea was mistaken. Cassie sang "Danny Boy," that Scottish-Irish one she loved. Cassie's words even included Morgan's last name, Thea noted as she bit her lower lip and headed south for Lockwoods' at a good clip, as if the haunting song chased her.

Oh, Danny boy, the pipes, the pipes are calling
From glen to glen and down the mountainside . . .
But come ye back when summer's in the meadow
Or when the valley's hushed and white with snow . . .
Oh, Danny boy, oh, Danny boy, I love you so!

Thea walked faster despite her load of roots, tears glistening in her eyes. Angry tears, not just hurt ones, she told herself. Whyever had she become so emotional over a man she had only been with for less than an hour? Yet it cut her to the quick to know that he had remained at Lockwoods' these four days and told Rina he didn't want to see anyone, not even, evidently, the woman who had nursed him gratis and still sent, through Rina, tonic for him to take to regain his strength before he rejoined General Arnold in New Haven this week. And here she had been so foolish to instantly trust Morgan Glenn, every bit as much as she always had Rina. It made her wonder if her judgment were askew. Perhaps she was wrong even to distrust someone like Avery Payne. If she hadn't judged Morgan Glenn right, who knew?

As they crossed where Tilley and Blinman Streets met on the corner by the Lockwood mansion, Thea wiped her eyes before she went up to the house. Perhaps, she lectured herself again, it was only the deflation of spirit after Cousin Benedict's departure when she'd been looking forward to his visit for so long. She had to drop this fresh root off to Anna, the Lockwood cook, quickly, then be on her way home. Business was brisk in the glow of Benedict Arnold's address to the town from her front steps, and the Widow Middleton sometimes confused orders, even when customers shouted right into her ear trumpet. Cassie followed her to the back entrance of the house, still singing.

To Thea's surprise, as soon as she gave several roots to Anna with directions for their shaving and brewing, Rina joined them. It wasn't often she came into the big-hearthed kitchen, as overseeing the cooks was the least favorite of her household tasks.

"Out scrounging for more cures for Morgan Glenn, Thea?" Rina asked and gave her a quick hug. "But he is much better now, really."

"Is he coming downstairs then, or leaving soon?" Thea asked in a stab at nonchalance. Cassie passed by with a dish of strawberries, and both women took several before she drifted off, still humming her song.

"I really don't interfere in his rest or recuperation," Rina said, without meeting Thea's steady gaze. She popped the crimson berry in her mouth instead of inserting her foot there again. She panicked every time Thea appeared lately. Although she had learned these last few days that Morgan Glenn was a man of bedrock honor who would not seek Thea out since he believed she was promised to another, she was still terrified he would talk with Thea and she would learn that Rina had lied. She hadn't meant to! She regretted it already, along with the web of other lies it had bred. She regretted if she had hurt Thea, but something had made her just blurt it out! All she wanted now was for Morgan to leave before he saw Thea again and they both discovered her guilt. Devil take it, every time she saw Thea these last four days, her stomach felt like she'd eaten a bowl of green apples, not just strawberries!

But more than she wanted Morgan Glenn to leave because of Thea, Rina thought, she wanted him to stay forever! She adored him, maybe loved him, yes, she was certain of it. It was her decision, her choice, for once. Whatever anyone said when and if they found out, she loved him! He was so different from anyone she had ever known. So blessedly different from Cullen; Morgan was open and straightforward, warm and endearing, though a bit rough around the edges. He knew how to tease and smile. She could tell he was in awe of her, too, as if she were some precious porcelain doll placed in the dressmaker's window to display the newest imported fashions before the war! But she wanted more than his interest or his awe! The deceit she'd used to have him all to herself these past days made her hate herself sometimes— and yet she felt compelled to take it all out on Father and Thea.

"I'll be running now," Thea's welcome words punctured Rina's guilt as she took a few more strawberries. "Come on, Cassie, and then I'll send you back."

"But you could just take a horse to carry those sacks," Rina offered.

"And have Cassie riding about town on her way back when she's worse than ever obsessed with the forest today?" Thea whispered. "She would probably just ride off into the woods. We'll walk."

"Do it your own way, then," Rina called and forced herself to give a gay little wave. *You always do anyway, and now, I am too,* she thought to herself and hurried back upstairs before the back door even banged.

Morgan Glenn sat on the wide window ledge of his room on the second floor of the Lockwood mansion and listened. He no longer heard the Scottish song sung by a heavenly-voiced woman going by. Like too much lately, it made him think of home and family in Pennsylvania. Now, if only that voice had been his angelic Rina's, he would for sure think he'd died and gone to heaven.

He sighed and crooked one long leg up on the ledge. It had been quite a week. He had enjoyed several hours speaking with Moses Lockwood, a clever merchant and pillar of this community for years. He and Gov. Jonathan Trumbull had shared a fascinating discussion before he had returned to his War Office in Lebanon. Morgan's strength, which that danged fever had leeched from him, was slowly returning. The sassafras tonics Thea had sent through Rina had bucked him up. He thought a great deal of General Arnold's young female cousin, especially for not coming up here bedside with him since she was betrothed. He let his thoughts wander over possibilities for one moment, then shoved them all away. It had been a godsend that he got ill here in New London, but not because he'd met a skilled healer. Wonder of wonders, it was his growing attraction to pretty, petite Rina Lockwood that was flourishing like a wild weed under Rina's careful tending.

But, in all decency, he could hardly expect a well-bred

woman like Varina Lockwood to considering a permanent commitment, however much she hinted at it. He could never ask her to wait for him while he was away with General Arnold for who knew how many years. Their lives were so different. The women he had known were a far cry from Rina. Strong, sturdy, willing farm girls in the Tahicox Valley. Supple, brown Iroquois gals who reveled in the custom of tending to a visitor's needs at night—all night, especially a young trapper who gave fair trade for furs and spoke, though haltingly, in their tongue. But now that he worked with Arnold and mingled with his officers, he had put that world behind him for a while. Could he ever go back to it with a woman like Rina Lockwood at his side?

He shook his head and shrugged. The thought was ludicrous and very unfair to Rina. He had been woolgathering as sure as her strange Irish maid always did. He stood and stretched. The Indians thought that crazy folk had been touched by the gods and always spoke the truth. But that was so much superstition, too. Still, they'd have a real shock meeting someone like Rina's Cassie.

At Rina's familiar knock on his door, his heart leaped. He straightened his waistcoat and wished she hadn't taken the coat of his uniform out to have it laundered. He brushed back his hair with both hands. "Come in!"

She bore a small engraved silver tray with a pewter mug of steaming tonic and a plate of fresh-sliced walnut bread. Their eyes met and held as she sat it on the gateleg table near his bed. "Your daily dose," she said, "fresh from the forest."

"Thea dropped it by?"

Rina's smile faded. Perhaps he had seen Thea out the window, she thought. "She's busy and gone on back to her shop. She only dropped it by as a favor to me," she told him stiffly.

"Your mouth looks crimson."

Her hand shook as she extended the pewter mug to him. Just because he inquired about Thea didn't mean the warm, intent look on his face that heated her blood wasn't for her, she assured herself. He cared greatly for her; she was sure of it. But she had given him every opening to touch her, to kiss her and he was proving to be as stiffly honorable as Cullen!

"My mouth," she ventured as their fingers touched over the steaming cup, "is crimson from eating strawberries, though I wish it were from something else."

"Such as?"

She shrugged prettily, not budging a step. He had the wildest urge to pull her into his arms, to sweetly bruise those pert lips with his own. But, dang it, he was her father's guest, and in his bedchamber, no less! She was intentionally tempting him. She had been all along. Was it all fated to happen to him this fast? She had vowed that Cullen was nothing to her and that she cared for him, the edge-of-the-frontier-bred Morgan Glenn.

"You know, Rina, I feel a good bit stronger today," he told her, his voice raspy. He pressed his hands over hers on the mug. "Maybe the tonic I need is a little walk in the gardens with you. And if there are more strawberries, we could eat some out back together, the same one at the same time."

She laughed delightedly. "And tomorrow, if it doesn't rain, we can take a ride out to get you some fresh air and a constitutional walk," she told him. "I know the best parts of the forest and what to avoid."

"Then let's," he agreed and lifted a big hand to stroke those other strawerries that always bloomed on her cheeks. Fine, pale down covered her silky skin against the gentle rasp of springy hair on the backs of his bent fingers. His hand looked so big next to her petite face. Yet she filled such a big hollow spot inside him with her warmth that he had no doubt her slightest rejection could crush him. But would someone like Varina Lockwood ever wait for him until this war was over?

"The strawberries were quite sweet," she said, to interrupt his agonized musings. "See?"

She pulled him down by his buttoned brown waistcoat to dart a quick kiss on his mouth. He lost his head then. He got rid of the cup and pulled her up to him and slanted his mouth over hers hungrily. She felt so delicate, yet strangely sturdy, too. "Rina, Rina—" he rasped, as his hot breath brushed her temple and swayed a loose golden tendril there.

Her insides went hot and shaky. The forbidden allure of the man, the way he had not been able to resist her, the obvious passion in his voice and on his face swamped her senses so she swayed against him, barely on her toes. "Please, again," she breathed the words.

"Best walk outside," he managed and carefully set her back as if she would break.

"Just in the private Lockwood gardens," she whispered. "Today you're mine, all mine, forever and ever."

He almost said "amen," but he just nodded, stunned. Not even being promoted to General Arnold's aide over several others obviously favored by his staff had hit him with such a heady feeling of victory. With a dream like Rina to love, he could fight any war, win any battle! His motto never seemed more solid: Just do right and trust those you care for and you will be rewarded. He didn't even need that sassafras brew they left cooling on the table. He escorted her out to the private gardens in back and kissed her again and again until they both clung together, trembling and breathless in the leafy shade.

Rina hurried downstairs on Morgan's last day in New London. She fixed a set, little smile on her lips when she saw him waiting for her in the parquet front foyer, hat in hands. But she was still so furious with her father that her hands shook when she held the buff lapels of Morgan's blue uniform to pull him down for a quick kiss.

Earlier this week, Moses Lockwood had been either busy with the New London Citizens' Committee for Public Safety or incapacitated in his bed by another gout attack. Fortunately, he had paid her and Morgan little heed then. He had hardly noted their growing attraction—or else, he was just so certain she was to be Cullen's bride someday, he thought she dare not dally with their houseguest and Cullen's fellow military aide.

But today, it was as if Father had tried to ruin everything! She had arranged for Morgan and her to take a private jaunt out of town to say a proper—which meant, to her, a passionate—farewell. She was certain she could encourage him to propose marriage. But now Father had not only said they must take Cassie along for a chaperon, but he had asked Rina in front of Morgan at breakfast to stop by Thea's shop to fetch him some gout powder and pills for his painful joints! Morgan, dutiful gentleman that he was, had readily agreed to both!

When Cassie joined them with the loaded basket, Morgan took it from her, and the three of them strolled down the front flagstone walk to where the horse and cabriolet awaited their outing. Morgan lifted them both up, then climbed up and unwrapped the reins. His broad smile bathed them both in more sunshine than the clear blue sky. It was lovely outside, but Rina could not still the storm inside.

"Ready, Cassie?" Morgan asked the girl, squeezed in on the other side of Rina with their hamper of food wedged under her feet. Cassie grinned and nodded until her straw bonnet brim bounced. "Then, I'll take another rendering of that 'Danny Boy' you sing so well!" he added as he clucked the horse and snapped the reins to move them on.

Rina silently cursed Morgan's high spirits as Cassie began to sing the mournful song over the clip-clop of the single horse's hoofs. How could he be so happy to be leaving her tomorrow and going back to war and battle? she fumed silently. And why had he asked for that dour song when the two of them should just be chatting about happy things?

But Rina admitted to herself she could not hide her plans or her desperate feelings for Morgan any longer. She knew he wanted to speak formally with her father about his intentions to court her. So far, she had deflected that. She had convinced Morgan their relationship must be their own affair, at least until she had time to beard her father in his den about it all. Nor could she have this trustful, honorable man blurting out their plans in front of Cullen or General Arnold until she had laid the groundwork for their future together. Devil take Morgan Glenn! Why did she have to attract such overly dutiful, truthful, honorable men? And now, in such a short time, how had she gotten herself so deeply snared by such little lies to those she loved? Morgan, her father—worse, Thea. Rina could not help but groan in trepidation as Morgan pulled the horse up in front of Arnold's Apothecary shop, singing in his deep bass with Cassie as if to announce to the whole blasted world they were here!

He jumped down to tie the horse's reins to the hitching post, then reached up to lift Rina down. Thea, obviously hearing them, had come to the door, wiping her hand repeatedly on her work apron. Rina merely glanced at her at first, then back at Cassie, who giggled as Morgan swung her down. Rina clenched her hands tight around the string of her equipage bag until her fingernails dug half moons in her soft palms.

How hard, Rina thought, she had tried these last intoxicating days to pretend that Thea had not discovered and, perhaps, cared for Morgan Glenn first. How fast she had tried to rush through it all to pretend she hadn't lied both to and about her friend. But, however much guilt gnawed at her insides, she had no choice now but to play it out. After all, Thea had always prided herself in being independent, and she was not Thea's keeper! Still, she couldn't look in Thea's wide green eyes even as she spoke to her.

"Thea, dear, we really can't stay. Just popped by for more gout curative for Father."

"He's poorly then? Good to see you again, Lieutenant Colonel Glenn," Thea said, but just wrapped her hands in her wrinkled, stained apron when Morgan extended his hand. Rina stared up at them both through slitted eyes, but breathed a sigh of relief when Thea added, "Sorry, but my hands are a mess. I've been making pills, you see." She indicated her equipment as she led them both inside while Cassie dawdled in the doorway.

"Oh, you roll them out in a little brass tube form," Morgan said, much too interested, Rina thought. He followed Thea over to her long wooden work counter while she fetched what they came for from a narrow drawer.

Rina also hurried closer as Thea turned away to rattle through some paper packets for Father's germander gout powder. "Yes," Thea was telling Morgan over her shoulder in a voice Rina recognized as forced nonchalance, "I mix the paste for the pills, mold them in that tube, then just—" she turned back to face them with the gout powder, "cut them off and store them away until someone needs them."

Rina bit her lip while Thea's stare held with Morgan's. At last, he looked away. "Father will bless you for these, Thea," Rina put in quickly. "He always did. Well, we really must be off now." She wanted to tug Morgan away by his arm, but she didn't want Thea to think she owned the man—not yet at least. She'd have to find a way to tell everyone after Morgan left.

"I know you were kind enough not to take money the other day, Mistress Arnold," Morgan said, not budging one bit, even when Rina took the packet of pills and made for the door. "But I wish you would accept this as a token of my thanks and esteem, especially since you're kin to my general."

Rina thought at first he was fumbling with the buttons of his uniform. She hurried back over to the counter across which Thea stood facing the man, almost eye to eye. Suddenly, the air in the little shop seethed with unspoken thoughts and feelings, louder than the noise of Thea's little copper still which steamed and bubbled in the corner as it mingled elixirs.

"Please accept this little tin flag," Morgan said. "There's a tinsmith in General Arnold's honor regiment, a friend of mine from home. He made these for the general's officers. The general wears one, too," he said and held the small metal piece out in his big hand.

"Yes, I noticed it," was all Thea managed, staring down at the proffered gift. At that moment, though she was grateful no one knew it, she literally ached. She ached to touch Morgan's hand, to hold him here somehow. She ached to let him know how deeply she felt—and how much his obvious rejection had hurt. But after all, she scolded herself, what had he rejected? There had been nothing understood or promised between them. But she yearned so to reach out to him, as

loosed emotions she had never known existed screamed and
crashed inside her.

When she did not reach for the pin from his hand, Morgan
put it on the counter next to her marble slab with the roll
of pills. "Someone like you ought to have it—someone as
close to the general in her own way as I am," he said. "And
I'm real glad Rina has a fine friend like you, especially during
the hard war days to come," he added as he turned away to
shoo Cassie through the door and wait for Rina there.

"See you soon!" Rina called to Thea with a flutter of her
hand as she hurried out. Morgan steadied Rina's elbow while
she climbed back up into the cabriolet. It could have been
worse, Rina thought. They had escaped unscathed and
undiscovered from Thea's clever gaze and brain. Or had
they? Well, Thea would forget him soon enough, and
anyway, there had not been time for anything to really
develop between them. And when Rina finally told her, Thea
would come around to being happy for both of them. But
if Morgan was going to leave smiles and gifts behind him for
Cassie and Thea, Rina was now more than ever determined
she would have the man's heart itself—and not just some tin
pin he had fastened over it!

As he drove the carriage out of town, Morgan Glenn felt
he'd just sobered up from a week's binge on Pennsylvania
lightning. He'd been intoxicated by his nearness to the lovely,
strong-willed Rina all week, sequestered as they were from
reality in the Lockwood mansion. She had gone right to his
head, and then his heart. But seeing Thea again had somehow
brought him back to earth, albeit momentarily. That original
sparkle he had seen in Thea's eyes had dulled. That expectant
look on her stunning face he recalled even through the eyes
of feverish misery had gone wary and cold. Had she resented
that he had not pushed more to pay her for her services that
first day? At home, when someone offered a gift, it was
always heartfelt and simply understood that, when the time
came, favors would be repaid. Did his presence with Rina
make her miss her own love, Evertt Edwards? Or, if Thea

Arnold had an inkling of his and Rina's mutual attraction, did she not think he was good enough for her friend Rina?

"Turn right here, and we'll take the little road up along Jordan Creek," Rina interrupted his thoughts. She shifted on the seat next to him to rattle his agonizings. Her soft thigh lay pressed to his hard one, with only his breeches and her yellow flower-sprigged gown and maybe just one petticoat between. It was his turn now to shift on his seat. Too long living just with men at war, he scolded himself, and he fought to keep his physical feelings for Rina bridled.

"Isn't it lovely here?" she asked, her hand on his arm. "That's the gristmill in that rocky cove down there and just across the creek is Bolles Wood, an ancient hemlock forest. We'll stop just up there where there's a little bridge to cross."

The mention of the ancient forest sent Cassie into one of her warnings about appeasing the forest fairies. Morgan annoyed Rina by asking the girl all about them. "The forest folk where I come from are called Indians," he told Cassie after her breathy recital, his face and voice absolutely serious. "Sometimes they go naked and grow their hair long and have bows and arrows, just like you say these *Sidhe* do."

"Morgan, don't encourage her!" Rina scolded with a jangling laugh as they alighted from the carriage. *Don't encourage her or Thea, either,* she wanted to demand. She felt all pent up inside, almost panicked. This man was so open, so easy to love and desire, when she felt so tight and closed inside. Before the day was out, she must have his word they could wed someday, when she decided. She felt driven by her need for him, the need to choose him and then let everyone know she had decided her fate on her own. She would keep him no matter what any of those others who thought they laid claim to her would say! "Oh, look," she cried and took Morgan's free hand that did not hold the hamper to pull him on. "The perfect spot for a picnic! We can sit beside the little bridge before we take a walk!"

They downed chicken, bread with apple butter and preserves, ale, and strawberries. Cassie wove enough dandelion and clover chains to stretch from here to town. The girl seemed strangely disturbed by this unfamiliar place, but Rina had been adamant they not picnic near Thea's herb gardens in the Lockwood forest on the other side of town. Perhaps Cassie's nervous state would work out for the best. Rina intended to get Morgan off alone to settle things between them, and Cassie would no doubt balk at crossing the little footbridge as she refused to ever take the ferry to Groton over water.

That fear was some remnant, Rina was convinced, of Cassie's superstitious mother's imprint on her mind as a young child. Well, even that at least was something she recalled of her mother. Thea had her mother's notes to her in that herbal recipe book in the apothecary shop. Cassie had the heritage of her mother's songs and stories. So why couldn't she, who lost her mother at the same age as the other two, recall one blessed thing of her mother but the lovely parties she used to have at the house and the way she used to laugh? Why could she remember nothing of what her mother had given or said to her?

"Cassie, Morgan and I are going to take a little walk across that water there," Rina said, getting hold of herself. "Want to come along or stay here with the things?"

" 'Tis best I wait here. I'll not be falling in the water without a four-leafed clover. All these be in leaves of only three!" she bemoaned and held out the clover chain for Rina to see.

They left Cassie humming over her flower chains and traversed the narrow, little wooden bridge, which swayed under their weight. Once they were across, Rina felt as if a great burden of worry and doubt had lifted from her. Annoyance at Father's attempt to send Cassie along as a chaperon and nagging guilt over letting Thea down fell from her with the warm June sun and sprightly breeze. When they were out of Cassie's sight, Morgan took her hand and they kissed repeatedly. Groves of stately, gray-barked elms towered over them here, rustling their newborn leaves laced by birdsongs as if they, too, were beautifully bewitched. They paused at the edge of the ancient hemlock forest on a mossy-lipped ledge overlooking a ravine half full of tumbled boulders. She took off her hat and let it dangle down her back by its blue ribbons, which matched her gown.

"Rina, everything's happening so fast between us," he began.

"But time is of the essence these days! Besides, Father told me he fell in love with my mother the first moment he saw her."

"You know, my father wooed and won my mother in a week in Philadelphia before setting out to farmstead in the Lehigh Valley, so maybe it's in our blood."

She nodded fervently, but silently rejected the thought of ever living away from real civilization. The notion of homesteading in some far-off place with Indians running loose scared her, but they could settle all that later. *"Something* is in my blood on a day like this," she teased to banish the bothersome thought.

"You mean the sun's enough to warm our blood," Morgan jested back, but his eyes returned to her flushed face in a caress warmer than the sun.

"Anywhere we are together can be just like this," she told him. "Private, special, ours to share together away from the world outside, no matter what happens!"

He sighed deeply as he wove his big fingers through her slender ones. "There's much to do yet in that world outside to protect all this from the British foreigners," he said, his voice suddenly bitter.

"But let's not think about anything dire today!" she pleaded. A slanting stroke of sunlight made her mouth pucker in a frown. At that moment he sounded entirely too much like Cullen Varner when she needed real promises and commitment. Then he jolted her as he almost repeated Cullen's exact words to her.

"I'd like to ask you to wait for me, Rina, and I want that more than anything, but—"

"But of course I am going to wait for you, for our marriage and life together we've spoken of!" she cried and clung to him on tiptoe to place the top of her head under his chin. He was so much taller and bigger, she couldn't reach or touch quite enough of him. "Here, please, let's just sit," she implored. "We have to talk this all out now, before everyone bothers us again."

"Bothers? But surely Cassie, Thea, and your father—"

"Over here where the grass starts, just sit down and listen, please, my darling!" She tugged him down, but not before he removed his coat and spread it, lining down, for her to sit on its sturdy blue and buff. She cuddled to him as they sat until he pulled her into his lap and held her to him. She spoke in a rush of words to challenge the breeze rattling the leaves overhead.

"Before you go tomorrow, Morgan, I have to know that you and I are really promised."

"Promised, yes, though I must ask your father for permission—"

"But I told you he can't readily accept the idea of my pledging myself to anyone just now, not with his painful physical condition. And since Mother died, I'm the only family he has left, real family, so he just can't let me go the way he has . . . others," she added as thoughts of Thea intruded again before she thrust them back. "Please, Morgan, I'm asking you to let me tell him in my own time, my way, after you've gone. I'm asking you to let this be our sacred secret from everyone just for a while."

He cradled her head between his large hands to tip her face up to him. She was astounded that tears gilded his eyes, too. He held her very, very still, gazing at her, his calloused thumb brushing her pouted lips back and forth. She could feel a trembling in his big body. She was suddenly very afraid of what he might say. "You know," he whispered as if regretfully, "I can't deny you anything."

That vow was what she needed to hear. She shifted closer in his lap, her hips yearning and demanding against his hard thighs, against the thrust of his desire, which he could not hide. Though he held her head still, her thoughts spun inside. If only she could belong to him completely, here and now, he would never forsake her! Ideas whirled through her brain so fast she could only grab at her own feelings.

"I love you, my darling, want you desperately," she heard herself say. "Please, show me you do, too!"

"You know what you are asking!" he demanded, his voice both awed and harsh.

She ignored that protest; she threw herself beyond reason. She clung only to the terrifying need to have and keep this man at any cost. She heard the woman's voice again like one bewitched: "We're promised now, Morgan. Please just show me how much you love and want me!"

Amazingly, he shook more than she did as he began to love her. It was she who pulled her lawn modesty piece away to bare her throat and bosoms to his lips and hands. She helped his big fingers unhook her stomacher to bare her to the waist. She pressed his big head to her as he fondled her shell-hard nipples with calloused fingers, and then with his insistent tongue. She welcomed his hot hand as it crept up over her cotton stockings to her bare, opened thighs above. She felt beyond her body, yet mentally in control. She wanted this, she chose this! It was everything she and Thea had thought they would find when . . .

Thea! Her face intruded momentarily with a stab of guilt. Guilt not for this act of surrender and conquest, no, but for the lies to Thea . . .

"I love you, only you!" she cried to spur him on when his hands stilled and his big body tensed. "Morgan, please, I'm fine!"

"You *are* fine, Rina, the finest thing that's happened to me. And that's why we can't do this, not now. I refuse to leave you compromised or with child if—if I should never come back."

Her hands clasped the nape of his neck. "Not come back! But you will! You have to come back to me—only me!"

He pressed her down flat on his coat and leaned over her. His hand remained on her thigh, but unmoving now. He tugged up her bodice to cover her breasts. Slowly, she came back from the whirlwind brink where they had almost gone together. She stared dazedly up at his taut face framed by tousled hair and blowing branches and shattering blue sky arching over him. Her skirts and petticoat still ruffled up between them.

This overwhelming man tried so hard to keep his weight

from pressing her down. The heat of his hand left her thigh. He leaned now on both elbows over her, close, looking as if he meant to memorize her lying there. The inner iron control she thought she had breeched had asserted itself again. She clung to him, but knew now she would have to wait to fully possess him. She felt mingled relief and disappointment. And yet, man of honor that Morgan Glenn was, this passionate time here would surely bind him to her and keep him from telling Father as he had wanted to. Strange how, especially when he drew away, longing forked like summer lightning through the black sky of her inner being.

All too soon, Cassie grew tired of tossing clover boats in the creek and wandered back up to the remains of the picnic. She wiped the plates with leaves and put them away in the woven hamper. She took another swig of tepid ale. Then she remembered how much the forest folk liked a little offering of food or whiskey. 'Tis true, ale was a far hue and cry from whiskey, but perhaps just a bit of it would be better than nothing.

Venturing one step out on the bridge before it spanned the water, Cassie dumped the contents of her mug. She watched it swallowed by the rushing stream. Holding tightly to the rough handrail, she felt very brave and bold. Some wavy memory of her mother's story of falling from the ship in New York harbor jumped at her and then was gone, like the ale. She tossed the mug back on the bank, then glanced over at the other grassy side of the stream. A circle of big white clover heads!

" 'Tis a fairy ring!" she cried. No one must ever stand in one, but they often led the way. Perhaps this forest was blessed and not cursed since it had not been cut down by Mr. Lockwood for his big mills and warehouses that chewed up and ate the forest. It was her lucky day, despite how Rina had been glaring at her all the way out! Before she remembered to be afraid of crossing the water, Cassie darted across the bridge to gaze closer at the nearly perfect circle of clover.

She edged around it carefully, then peered into the forest

fringe beyond where Rina and Morgan had disappeared. Just like Thea, Morgan liked her singing, he did, Cassie thought proudly. She would like to sing now, but the hair prickled on the back of her neck, and her stomach shook. What if the *Sidhe* lived in this ancient wood, after all? What if they shared their power with Rina and Morgan within so they could have anything their hearts desired? Or what if they were annoyed at mortals trespassing here and put curses on them all?

She gasped when she saw a second circle, this time of toadstools, just a ways farther in. She bent over to examine it, then walked way around. A little path lined with toadstools beyond that! But then she heard the sounds and clasped her hands to her breasts. Just the wind? Moaning? Crying? A chant to cast a spell? Had she found the fairies at last as she'd promised Mother so long ago and her not here to see?

She peered between rustling branches, half-expecting to see a fourth circle, this time of dancing, naked forest folk. She bit her lower lip hard before her mouth dropped open. It was another sort of dance! Morgan's mouth was on Rina's bared breasts! His hand was up her skirt. Rina's legs were moving. Cassie felt dizzy, as if she herself danced and spun. Then Morgan leaned over Rina and her skirts seemed ruffled up between them like a yellow and white flower seeking the sun! Rina and Morgan pressed together on the grass, staring and whispering! They must have—must have . . . Saucer-eyed, Cassie clapped her hands to her open mouth and bumped back into a tree trunk. Those two were bewitched, indeed!

Cassie turned and fled all the way back to the creek. She hesitated there, trembling, afraid to go back over the bridge. But if she did not, Rina would find her standing there. Rina would ask where she had been, and she could not lie to Rina or Thea either if they asked. Desperate, scrabbling on hands and knees, Cassie searched the clover-peppered grass until she found one that was four-leafed. Holding it in her sweating, trembling hand, she edged back across the little bridge and grabbed up all the picnic things.

*   *   *

When Rina and Morgan emerged from the screen of trees a half hour later, they found Cassie sitting bolt upright in the carriage, staring straight ahead. Her hair looked like a windblown haystack under her askew straw hat. Her arms, like iron bands, clamped the empty picnic hamper as if to hide her grass-stained skirts.

"Cassie, are you all right?" Rina demanded.

"Fine. Good as you!" the girl retorted without a look their way.

Rina and Morgan exchanged quick, guilty glances. "Did you see someone pass by?" Morgan ventured.

"No. Found a lucky clover, I did."

Morgan lifted Rina back up into the carriage and she settled in carefully by Cassie before Morgan joined them on the single seat to wedge them tightly in. Rina linked her hands around his upper arm and leaned her head on his shoulder as he clucked to the horse to move them on.

Let Cassie sulk that they'd gone off and left her, Rina thought. Even if she told Father the two of them had wandered off together, it didn't really matter now. She and Morgan were committed to wedlock in the future. He had proposed marriage as they lay there together! She hid her smile against his uniform just under the golden epaulet, which tickled her nose. She didn't regret or fear a thing right now—neither Father, nor Cullen, nor Thea, nor the dark forest places in her own soul that Cassie sometimes made her dread. Defiantly, Rina pressed her leg closer to Morgan's as they bounced along on the road toward town.

Chapter Four

"For nightmares that make the heart pound, two trustworthy mixtures are camomile tea and, as ever, the old lean-to, treacle water. If one's stomach rebels it may be illness or worry, both internal caused. If basil cannot quell it, look to the very heart and soul."

THE SUMMER COUSIN Benedict and his soldiers came to call, Thea's shop was ever full of customers. Each New Londoner had his or her own story of seeing Connecticut's fabled hero during the parade. They stood on her steps where he had addressed the crowd; they asked to sit in the chair where he had sat. Thea finally put both the goblet he drank from and the little tin flag like the one he had worn on display in the window for folks to stare at. She, after all, had stared too much at that pin Morgan had given her, when she had it all to herself in her bedroom.

The town gazette had erroneously reported that "the glorious general had given the brooch of a patriotic banner he was seen to wear on his lapel to his dear cousin, Mistress Althea Arnold, as a sign of his pride in the country and his love for New London in particular." Even folks who had never set foot in her shop before, those who patronized Greenwood's Apothecary on the other side of town, came to look and chat and buy.

Her coffers swelled. She even began to make payments, as she had long yearned to do, to Father Lockwood for the two-acre piece of land where her herb gardens grew. At least this boom in trade kept her so busy that it somewhat helped her to forget she still thought and dreamed of Morgan Glenn much too often.

As busy as she was—she had even hired a second shop boy

now to mix substances with mortar and pestle—she still recalled Morgan's face or voice at the oddest times. Unlike most of New London's citizens, she thought not of Cousin Benedict's hallowing her shop by his presence. When she saw her Windsor chair or put the little tin flag in the window each day, she recalled Morgan Glenn. More than once, she dreamed that he came back amidst the chatter and bustle of the shop and just stood tall and strong in the front doorway and beckoned to her. Fighting her way through the people, pushing past Avery Payne and Evertt Edwards, she struggled toward Morgan. But if the dream got her as far as the door, it soon turned to a nightmare that made her pulse pound. For when she reached him and held out her hand, he just turned and went off with Rina in a Lockwood carriage. Once, Thea had even dosed herself with treacle water, which she detested, to make the dream stop. At last, but for sporadic returns, it had subsided.

"Mistress Arnold, did General Arnold tell you when he'd be back to New London?" Old Mrs. Truman Gwin, who seldom cared for aught but her churchgoing and the status of her own parlor, was peering beady-eyed over the counter at her. Thea snapped back to the present. This cool morning of August 27, 1777 was no exception from all the other summer days, but for its hint of coming autumn and another new customer. "Us being so close to New York City where those British vultures are nesting, I mean, we need some protection here! When is he coming back?" the woman demanded.

"I really have no notion of that, Mrs. Gwin, as he's gone to fight off the British approach from the north, you know," Thea answered as she wiped her hands on her apron.

"But I heard tell the latest news comes into this shop before anywhere else! Well then," she said huffily, "I'll just take me home some of that fever mix I heard tell of. You know, what the gazette said you gave the general's aide-de-camp. Never can tell when a body's going to get a fever, and anything for General Arnold's men is good enough for me!"

Thea filled the order. She had given up telling people that the marigold and goldenrod powder needed to be fresh, so it could not be purchased far ahead of use. She was also weary of telling folks what brand of porter she had served the general in his brief respite here and every word he had said. The weekly gazette had printed everything, anyway. Something new appeared about Cousin Benedict's two-month-old visit just as often as they printed the extensive lists of privateering booty. She handed Mrs. Gwin the packet of what most folks were just calling "Arnold Powders" and took her coin in return. And then, just when another customer asked another question, Avery Payne's voice made her jump as he hurried through the door.

"Great news, everyone, and I knew this would be the best place to announce it!" he crowed and beamed across the room at Thea.

The fourteen customers in the shop murmured and crowded around Avery. After all, the man had somehow established himself as one of the pillars of the community since he had wed the last of the respected Mumfords. In these war times, power and money talked louder than a fine heritage of past dedication and service. Thea would very much have liked to order him out, but she held her tongue and even managed a tight smile. Avery was one of her best customers for rat poison in years. Despite how he had told her once he wanted no one to know he was buying the poison, he had praised her publicly as a patriot for helping him rid his ships of vermin—and therefore the seas of British vermin. But once again, she mused, that had gotten *his* name in the weekly gazette, right along with Cousin Benedict's. It galled her that Avery carried on as if he himself dared his life on raids, when he never sailed farther than the river in the seven privateers he owned and provisioned. For Avery, though, he had been quite kind and controlled of late.

Yet he still took the advice of the song "Yankee Doodle" a bit too literally, especially the line "with the girls be handy," she thought. Thea still mourned poor Charity's passionate adoration of the man. For Charity's sake—and for the fact Cousin Benedict was a silent business partner to Avery now and that, too, gave Thea a new measure of protection with him—she had decided to get along with Avery Payne if it was the last thing she did.

"News of a military victory from Cousin Benedict, I hope," Thea called over the hubbub to him when he stared pointedly her way.

"Better than a military victory!" Avery told them as dramatically as if he were making a speech for governor. "Benedict Arnold has beat the British under St. Leger, all right, but he's managed to make fools of them and their brutal Indian allies, too! And he used their own superstitions to do it!"

Everyone listened raptly as he recounted the news one of his ships had discovered when they'd captured a British packet. In glowing terms and with grandiose gestures, Avery explained how Arnold, with a small force of Americans, had volunteered to relieve the British attack on Fort Stanwix at a key point on the Mohawk River. Knowing he was outnumbered by the enemy and the swelling numbers of their fierce Iroquois allies, he hit upon a brilliant scheme. His troops had recently captured a Tory named Hon-Yost Schuyler, who was soon to be executed as a spy. But Hon-Yost suffered from some sort of feeblemindedness and acted quite the raving lunatic. Realizing the Indians feared and revered such folk, Arnold told the man he could have his life in exchange for a favor.

So Arnold sent Hon-Yost running to the British camp with the wild message that there were swarms upon swarms of armed Americans approaching under the command of the general the Indians called The "Dark Eagle." To the British officers' dismay, vast numbers of their Indian allies believed the madman's words and went home. St. Leger's officers also got cold feet and talked him into lifting the siege on the American-held fort and even retreating without a shot being fired!

"And now," Avery concluded his tale, "all we have to do is wait for word of Arnold's next victory, this time over the entire northern army under General Burgoyne! I just knew Thea Arnold's cousin would bring us all good luck!"

The little crowd huzzahed her, much to Thea's embarrassment. Blushing, she shot Avery a look as if to say, "I wish you'd not rouse them all like this!" Others began to wander in from the street. The little crowd in the shop grew. Even Widow Middleton heard the noise without her ear trumpet and tottered downstairs from her afternoon nap to see what was the stir. Avery sidled over to Thea in the growing celebration.

"Can't say I'm not helping your precious business interests lately," he whispered warmly in her ear before she managed a step away from him. "I told you we'd make excellent partners, dear Thea."

"Believe me, Mr. Payne, privateering has no place in the apothecary business," she told him. "And why not just announce publicly that you are business partners with my cousin, since you seem to revel in his adulation much more than I do?"

He seized her wrist hard before she yanked it free. "I said, Thea, both he and I want that to be a secret for now. I'm very good at keeping secrets," he murmured with a leer, getting entirely too close to her again. She took another step away from him behind the counter. It was the first time since the day of the parade he had let his friendly facade slip.

"Please, just leave," she said. "Your stirring up this crowd is just too much, and—"

He frowned. "You've got to learn to play along," he said, his voice suddenly threatening. "If you really want the crowd quieted, there is more. I thought I would spare you, but, perhaps not." He looked at her strangely; she could almost see behind that high forehead, under that immaculately curled, pristine white wig at something dark he was thinking. Then he held up his hands for silence in the increasingly noisy shop and announced, "There is more. I had thought to spare you this, but I realize now I must not."

Slowly, the room quieted. People shushed others coming in off the street. Thea stood behind the counter, her hands pressing her apron flat to her belly. A nightmare of fears assailed her. Would he say that despite this victory, one or more of General Arnold's aides had somehow been wounded or killed? Not Morgan! Not Cullen!

"There's been a brutal murder and scalping, maybe ravishment, too, of an innocent young woman in a New York forest. The villains are two Indian allies of the British whom their General Burgoyne has made no move to punish so the British don't lose more Indians. This heinous deed was done to a Tory woman named Jane McCrea, whom the Indians were supposedly guiding safely to her Tory fiancé at Burgoyne's camp. This McCrea is evidently not related to our own town half-wit, Varina Lockwood's Irish maid, Cassie McCrea. But just think, if the British and their Indians ever dare to storm New London, maybe we can send our own little madwoman out to tell them that the whole Continental army, et cetera, awaits them here before they swoop in to grab any of our own young women?"

Thea gasped at his poking fun at Cassie and making light of this horrid tale and Cousin Benedict's clever deed. "Mr. Payne, I hardly think you need to embellish such a tragedy with—"

"Just let it be a warning!" Avery's strident voice cut her off. "If even Tory women aren't safe from the Brits and their Indians, who knows what can happen here with rebels!" He glared right at Thea. His jaw clenched as if he fought to keep from blurting more blatant threats. The veins in his neck stood out and throbbed. Then he shoved his way through the crowd and out the door.

The tension in the air uncoiled. Folks murmured, shook their heads, and clucked their tongues at the fate of some poor woman named Jane McCrea. Some left whispering; some went back to their tasks of talking or buying. Thea felt drained: she knew the press of people this whole summer had sapped her inner peace. She had been trapped here so much in the store, she hardly had the time she needed to tend her herb beds and just be outside. And now she had to head for Lockwoods', not only to take Rina some fresh chamomile for the undiagnosed stomach pains that had plagued her for weeks, but to try to explain this latest war news to Cassie before she heard it somewhere else. Who knew what word of a young woman named McCrea being murdered in a forest would do to Cassie's strangely inventive mind. How dare that wretched, self-aggrandizing Avery Payne just march in here to rile everyone and leer at her like that! And just when she thought perhaps she could at least tolerate him!

In the next half hour, Thea managed to clear the shop of customers and send Widow Middleton back upstairs to bed. She propped a "Shop Closed For Now" sign in the window. She knew she did not have time to go way out to her peaceful herb gardens, but she would take some flowers to her parents' graves on the way to Lockwoods'. She cut some leggy, late-August rose blooms out back and put them in water in a glazed jar. With the chamomile for Rina in her netted equipage bag and the jar cradled in her hands, she went out the back door and up the hill on Shapely Street.

As much as she loved her shop and chosen trade, she breathed easier now, just to be away for a while. She stopped on the slant of street and gazed back at the buildings crowding the stretch of bustling river wharves. Peeking over the rooftops of warehouses and shops, the masts of the privateering fleet poked the sky like church steeples. But then she thought of Avery Payne again and turned away.

She hoped Rina was doing better today, especially since Cullen Varner was visiting the Lockwoods for the night on his way through on business for Cousin Benedict. Selfishly but truthfully, Thea admitted to herself, she was glad Cullen's visit proved there was nothing but friendship between Morgan Glenn and Rina. Rina had told her so and she believed her. Only, one annoying thought nagged her. If it were only friendship, why could not all four of them have shared that, instead of just the two of them and Cassie? Cassie hardly sang a thing these days but "Danny Boy," because it was "what my friend Morgan likes. And he said the Indian forest folk where he comes from sometimes go nearly naked and have long hair, too, just like the *Sidhe* I been looking for, I have."

On the crest of hill near the Town Meeting House, Thea slowed her steps and turned into what New Londoners had long called Ye Olde Ancientest Burying Grounds. It was green and quiet here. She strolled straight toward her parents' graves and wedged the jar of roses between their rectagonal stones, carved with beautiful praying hands which

Father Lockwood had erected when they'd died. His own wife, the beautiful Samantha, who had died at twenty-eight, was buried just down the way, but Thea wouldn't visit that today without Rina. That's all Rina would need today to sink her spirits even more, Thea thought. Rina was unstrung for days after visiting her mother's grave, bemoaning that she could hardly recall a thing about her. If it weren't for the stunning portrait of Samantha over the hearth in Father Lockwood's bedroom, Rina said, she might not have any memory of what her mother even looked like. So strange, Thea thought. But perhaps the shock of Rina's losing her mother had done all that, though she herself and even Cassie recalled their departed mothers quite well.

Thea heaved a sigh for Rina as much as for herself. She brushed a few dried leaves away from the base of the four clearly marked Arnold stones—her father's parents lay here, too—and turned to go. But, as if the mossy turf and stone-carved words could hear, she whispered back, "Thank you for the apothecary book and shop and all the love, both of you. I'm carrying on as best I know how—for all of us Arnolds." She lifted her hand in a brief wave and walked away, feeling somehow much calmer inside for being here to touch the past.

Despite her twisting stomach pains, Rina sat stock still while Cassie coiffed her hair. After having dinner with the Lockwoods last night and speaking with her father 'til all hours, Cullen was waiting downstairs to bid her farewell before he rode off this afternoon. General Arnold had kept Cullen quite busy on some sort of personal business that entailed delivery of sealed letters and private meetings with New London's town leaders, including Avery Payne. Fortunately, Rina thought, all that meant Cullen had not been around Morgan Glenn much, as Morgan remained at Arnold's side. So, even if Morgan let something slip to his comrades about Rina, Cullen was not usually there to hear it. Nor had Rina breathed a word of her betrothal to Father or Thea yet, as she had once intended.

"Ohhh," Rina moaned as Cassie put the final touches on her upswept hair.

" 'Tis the stomach knots again, mistress? Thought maybe Mr. Varner's visit would help, I did, him being a friend of Morgan's and all."

Rina's narrowed pale blue eyes met Cassie's golden ones briefly in the mirror before Rina looked away. She refused the straw shepherdess bonnet Cassie proffered and pulled her lace mitts on. Ever since that day of the picnic when Rina and Morgan had found Cassie sitting like a statue in the wagon, the girl had said the strangest things at times. Oh, well, Rina assured herself, that was just Cassie, and she'd never change. But Rina knew she herself was changing in her feelings toward Morgan and Cullen, and it scared her.

She was certain it was not just that old adage, "out of sight, out of mind," for Morgan Glenn was on her mind a great deal. It was just that sometimes she had these overwhelming rushes of remorse for what she'd done. She'd lied to Thea and Morgan and treated poor Cullen dreadfully. In a moment of possessive passion, she'd wanted Morgan to tumble her, and it was he who had kept a cool head to stop. And, that other saying, "Absence makes the heart grow fonder," seemed to be true for Thea and Morgan, though Thea tried to hide it. Devil take Morgan Glenn for ever coming here and confusing both of them so! These stomach pains had only started after everything happened in June as if they were punishment for what she'd done. Especially with Cullen here and so attentive, her stomach was no better.

Worse than all that, the nightmares about her mother had begun again, the ones she was certain she had outgrown two years ago. She dreamed she was searching for her mother in the mist, in the fog off the river. Everything was gray, but she heard her silvery laughter. Then mother began screaming, screaming Rina's name, a cry that shot Rina bolt upright in her bed, her heart pounding from her breast. She'd wake up in a cold sweat to sleep no more that night.

Rina stared at herself now in the mirror with eyes big as saucers. She supposed she looked a bit like Mother in the portrait. But Mother had glowed with life, hadn't she, and her own face looked pale as whey right now. She pinched pink into her cheeks and stood so quickly she tipped her dressing table stool back into Cassie's knees.

"Sorry, dear," Rina said and hugged her friend. "Just in a rush to bid farewell to Cullen."

He was waiting for her, his hands rotating his cockaded bicorn around and around. Rina, graceful hand trailing along the curve of banister, swept down the stairs in a rustle of pale blue skirts. His face lit to see her.

"I've bid your father farewell already," he said. "And have his permission to take you for a walk out back."

She acquiesced, despite the queasy feeling in her belly again. She and Morgan had walked those gardens, but they had not asked Father for permission. Yet that tiny rebellion had shrunk in importance to her now. Cullen looked very solemn and handsome today. She cursed herself for not just having the pluck to blurt out to him and Father, too, that she and Morgan were promised to each other, but something held her back.

"I realize I made a royal fool of myself the last time we were together here," he began as they strolled the gravel path amidst the clipped boxwood and beds of August flowers. "I was speaking in such elevated terms to you that night, so philosophically. But Rina, dearest, I was working up the backbone to ask you to look favorably upon my suit, to consider waiting for me. And to tell you how very much I admire and want you at my side *ad perpetuam!*"

"Want me at your side? But what exactly does that mean to you, Cullen? You're always so reserved and formal, so—"

He swept her into his strong embrace so fast her senses reeled. He kissed her cheek, her nose. He tilted her chin up and kissed her mouth, stiffly at first, and then with a beseeching softness that melted her bones. No! a voice shouted inside her. But she did not pull away.

"Look, my dearest," he apologized and bent over her hands to speckle them with kisses between his rush of words, "I didn't mean to hold all that back. I have always meant to have you as my wife, but after my home and the family business burned I realized nothing can be taken for granted.

And perhaps, I thought, I have not enough to offer you now. All sorts of matters I didn't see coming have changed things lately. The war—the big battle no doubt I will face with General Arnold. How he's sent me hither and yon as some sort of messenger boy while his other aides are kept at his side—"

"But it means so much to New London, Father says, that he takes such an interest in us yet and sent you to see to that, even when he's up on the Hudson. And it did mean you had time to come to tell me this!"

"Yes! And will you consider my plea, think about it, my dearest?"

She almost wavered on her feet. It was exactly what she had longed for from Cullen. Passion, yearning words. He wanted *her* to decide, to think and feel that perhaps she might be his. For one moment, Morgan Glenn's countenance almost faded in the mist of threatening dreams, like Mother's face.

"I—yes. I will think about it, Cullen, but I can promise nothing yet."

"Then that's enough. We won't say a word to others, except your father—Thea, too, if you want, of course—until we are fully committed. As much as I want to be back with the army, I'm cursing having to leave you so soon!"

He kissed her again so that, blessedly, her head spun and she could hardly think. Of course this was all impossible. She was promised to Morgan, already committed. She had to tell Cullen and everyone else so. But he would soon be facing perhaps the biggest battle of the war to stop the British. He looked so happy, so fervent! She had cracked the stiff, brittle veneer of Cullen Varner to prove that he shone brighter than ever under the cool facade!

She let him kiss her hands again in the front yard and hug her briefly to him. She waved up at him as he mounted. And then they they both saw Thea coming up the flagstone walk from the street.

"Thea! My best to you!" Cullen called out with a broad smile that made Thea halt in her tracks and shade her eyes with her hand to see him better as he rode by to the street.

"I'm off to rejoin your cousin and the army. Any message for him or Lieutenant Colonel Glenn?"

Rina gasped as Thea startled. "Just tell them God bless them and their next American victory," Thea said up at the mounted man, but her shaky voice hardly matched her bold words.

"Yes, tell them that from me, too!" Rina called and waved even harder as Cullen spurred his mount to a gallop.

"I'm so pleased to see you and Cullen part very good friends this time," Thea said as Cullen disappeared up Bank Street. She fished the packed of fresh chamomile for Rina's stomach from her equipage. "A bit more chamomile and Cullen and maybe your stomach pains will just float away."

"You're not a doctor, Thea," Rina retorted more harshly than she intended. Devil take it! Her stomach cramps were worse again, and she knew that Thea knew, too.

"Then shall we send for the doctor again?" Thea asked as she put her arm around Rina's shoulder to help her up the steps to the house.

"No, no. I don't intend to be bled again! These dried old herbs will do just fine for me. I was much better when Cullen was here, really."

"And didn't have the slightest twinge at all until after Morgan left here months ago," Thea said. At that, Rina felt wracked by pain she wasn't sure just stayed in her stomach or went right into her mind and heart. She had never wanted to hurt Morgan or Cullen, and certainly not Thea. How had she spun this web of deceit? And despite her good intentions, she continued to spin new disasters. Thea sat her in a brocade chair just inside the front door. Rina grasped her hand as she started away for help.

"I'm sorry if I was short with you, Thea. And, really, I can tell I'm feeling much better already."

Thea's eyebrows only lifted at that, but she knelt by Rina's chair to better hold her hand.

Two days later, the hot, humid weather returned to coastal Connecticut. Thea did not bother to light a lamp at dusk as she bustled about the shop to weigh some pleurisy roots in her hanging scales and put things away. Despite the oppressive heat, her spirits were lighter than they had been all summer. Father Lockwood had told her privately today he considered Rina and Cullen as good as betrothed and, after all, she had seen Rina in Cullen's arms before he rode away to battle. If Cullen made it through this war, at least Rina would be wed and happy. That also proved that Rina had spoken the truth about her week with Morgan Glenn. Thea's decision to believe Rina that there was nothing but friendship between her and Morgan Glenn had been sound. She had just imagined deeper feelings between them, the same way Cassie imagined her *Sidhe* peeking from the forest fringe.

Though she could have gotten herself into a real fret wondering why Morgan's warmth to her that first day had seemed to cool during his week of recovery, she tried to put all that aside. Other than her continued prayers that he, too, would survive the war, Morgan Glenn was out of her future for good. Her life was here in her dear New London with her shop, blessed from afar by her guardian angel Benedict Arnold. She was thankful for the luxury of heading to bed early tonight and to her herb beds in the morning!

She sighed and went to answer the insistent rapping on her back door. Her heart fell when she saw who stood there. Avery Payne, looking flushed, with his fine velvet hat in hand. How dare he come after dark, and after his crudeness here the other day! She knew well enough when Charity had a spell at home, he sent the servants to fetch her, and never came himself.

"I'm closed now, Mr. Payne. I really think—"

"It's Charity. She wanted so badly to see that new privateer I've been outfitting, the *Speedwell*. I knew I shouldn't agree, but the poor dear never gets out anymore, so—"

"She came clear down to that schooner?" The whole town had been buzzing about Avery Payne's newest three-masted vessel lying at anchor to be refitted just a few blocks from here by Shaw's Wharf. Thea could see the forest of spars from right out back. "Does Charity have her medicine?" she demanded as she darted back inside to seize some.

Before he even answered no, Thea had rifled through her

drawer in the dark for more precious acacia gum to burn and grabbed the whole big, dark brown bottle of comfrey syrup. "We can go out the way you came!" she ordered Avery. Quickly, he followed her. She did not protest when his hand steadied her elbow as they cut down the uneven cobbled lane toward the wharf. Time was of the essence when Charity had a spell, Thea thought, and they both knew it.

. The docks seemed quite deserted. Their feet sounded hollow on the gangplank as he hustled her aboard. They slowed their pace to walk around obstacles still littering the deck, including cannon not yet mounted and two swivel guns. Privateers, built as they were for chase and capture, sported sleek, narrow hulls and decks. The *Speedwell's* new rigging and shrouds lay in huge rolls and piles along the bulwarks, ready to fill the sky with the sails that meant speed. Thea's nose, often dulled by the continual aromas of her shop, flared at the pungent, different smells here: fresh barn-red oxide paint; turpentine; the pine of the spars; tar, which the so-called "jack-tars" used to waterproof their hats and trousers.

"In the captain's cabin below," he told her. "I thought she'd be more comfortable there."

He led her down the companionway steps by the quarterdeck. A lantern hung below. The ship, like the docks, seemed deserted. "Didn't you bring her maid along at least?" Thea asked, breathless at the pace he set.

"Watch your head," he said as he opened a cabin door with a single lantern lit inside. "Low beams, as we never sign on jack-tars as tall as you."

Thea's eyes swept the small, oak paneled captain's cabin, fully expecting to hear and see Charity gasping for desperate breaths. In the four chairs at the narrow table, even in the recessed bunk—no one. But the table was set for two, with a wine decanter and two goblets, which shone in the lantern light. The blanket was turned down on the built-in bunk to reveal white linen sheets. Thea jolted to a halt and shook off his hand as Avery snapped the door shut behind him and bolted it.

She spun to face him and backed away. "She's not here is she? You lied!"

"I thought we needed a private little chat at last. I grew weary of waiting. I regret to say, I'm not a very patient man."

"You mean you grew weary of pretending to be polite— a gentleman. You know, despite your cowardice, you *are* a privateer at heart! You love to feed off others! To chase and attack them—even New London's war effort, not to mention Charity, me, your string of women down at Shaw's Cove—"

He shouted a sharp laugh to cut her off, but it did not reach his narrowed eyes. He leaned against the bolted door with his arms crossed over his stocky chest. His teeth flashed as white as his fine cravat in the light of the hanging lantern. "Jealous, Thea? And oh, so passionate. How I adore that quality and would like to see more of it! And I vow to you, Thea Arnold, there will be no need for my 'string of women' after I show you all there can be between us this night!"

"You are demented! Let me out of here or I shall scream this precious new ship apart! I'll have it all over town and tell Charity as well as my cousin what a deceitful wretch you are!"

He lunged for her. She swung the bottle of syrup at him. It thudded off his shoulder and broke on the floor. She was two inches taller than him, but he was far stronger than she had expected. She had no practice wrestling with men. He bent her wrists back behind her hips and grasped them with one hard hand. She tried to kick, but he pinned her down against the table, sending wine goblets flying to shatter on the floor.

"Now you listen to me, spitfire! *I* am the money and the power in this town! *I* give the orders here, not you! Shall we just make it my word against yours if someone hears you scream? You are here, evidently of your own accord, alone with me in the captain's cabin of my ship. Let me tell you, your precious Cousin Benedict would side with me! As for Charity, I'd have to tell her you were lying, that you had made me an offer of this lush body in exchange for my buying medicinal supplies for my fleet, let's say, or even all that rat poison, eh?"

Pressed back along the hard table, her head half off the edge, she gazed up aghast at him. This was a nightmare! His face was livid, distorted by rage and passion. His eyes gleamed demonically. His words, his threats didn't even sink in, but only stunned her as he speckled her face and throat with saliva.

"Now, the truth is," he was saying, "I've been lusting after you for more than one reason. That voluptuous, untamed body, yes, but your fierce independence, too. I have to have you, just as I covet this ship, and the power I've nurtured in this town. Charity won't mind, my dear. She and I no longer share the passion that you and I are going to share tonight, this first night of many that will be our solemn secret. And I'll make you rich, Thea Arnold, rich in many ways! No one's on this ship tonight. Relax now and enjoy this while I make you completely mine!"

Slowly, holding her frozen gaze like a snake might before it strikes, he wedged a knee between hers and lifted it to spread her legs. Her skirts rode up. He chuckled in anticipation of what he had desired for years, the flame-haired temptress, perhaps the only unwed tradeswoman in town he could not possess if he put his mind to it. No one—*no one!*—challenged or threatened Avery Payne's new vision of his greatness, the personal portrait of himself he had been painting ever since he'd arrived here ten years ago. He had never wanted a woman more than this, no, not even Charity Mumford with all her thousands of pounds just waiting for him to spend. Charity had been so easy, no contest at all. And with her wealth, everything else had fallen into the hands of the handsome, runaway carpenter's son from New York who built only big dreams.

The wealthy Dutch widow who had taken him in in Albany had taught him manners and rich tastes while he learned other delights in her bed. And when he finally got off a ship in New London, looking for perhaps a younger, richer widow, there had been the lonely spinster Charity, sitting in her front yard to take the air. Damnation, it had taken him only two months to have her with his cock-and-bull story of being the impecunious son of the Paynes of Wyebrooke. And everything had been so easy up to his encounter with this stubborn little bitch with the full breasts he was going to ravage tonight until she moaned with pleasure. But now, he thought, as he lowered his head to kiss her breasts right through her gown stretched so taut under him—

He gasped hard for breath as pain sliced through him. She had kneed him—in the groin. Agony wrenched him in two. He crumbled off her to the floor when she shoved up at him with all her might. He sucked in a desperate breath again—just as Charity did to stay alive. He doubled over on the floor in the broken shards of glass goblets and sticky liquid from that bottle she brought. Damnation, the glass pieces ground in his palms! Then he vomited his dinner, while he still shuddered with pain.

He heard her rattling the door bolt, but he couldn't even rise to chase her. He had wanted to bed her, to show her all that could be between them—and instead she had done this to him. Defied him, unmanned him, hurt him. Didn't she know, if he couldn't have her, he would destroy her? But now, he lay there momentarily helpless, gasping in his vomit and blood. He heard her thudding up the galley steps, running across the deck.

He knew that Thea cared for Charity too much to reveal this episode to her. If she told Benedict Arnold, she'd be in for a surprise to learn he was invested up to his neck with Payne privateering, hoping to compensate for past expenditures congress would not reimburse him for!

Moaning at the pain in his belly and his hands, Avery Payne got awkwardly to his knees, then stumbled to his feet. "No one, but no one," he croaked out, "defies me!" However long it took, he vowed furiously, as he bent under the lantern to shakily examine the slivers of glass dribbling blood from his palms and wrists, he'd get Thea Arnold for this! He'd have her crawling to him through slime and broken glass and begging to spread her legs for him! He'd break that defiant, independent bitch one way or the other, if it was the last thing he did!

Thea had a stitch in her side by the time she fled headlong up the cobbled hill to her shop. She let herself in the back door and fumbled with the lock she seldom used. She leaned against the door, trembling, teeth chattering, reliving it all in her mind again. Such deceit! Such brazen defiance of all that was good and safe and right! And she had no idea that just trying to kick him away would do all that to him. She wanted to feel triumphant that she had accidentally found the way to get him off her, but she only felt sordid and sick.

She hurried into the darkened shop and felt her way along the counter. By touch and a nose newly cleansed by river air, she located the bin of fresh spearmint leaves. She made certain the front door was latched, too, then took a huge handful of the mint upstairs to her room. Though she knew it was foolish, she wedged the back of her rush-seated chair against that door.

She moved quickly, deliberately, though she still shook. Using her flint kit, she lit a single, thick candle by the bed. She bruised and crushed the mint leaves between her palms and dropped them in her white porcelain washbowl. No time to fetch heated water from the kitchen hearth now. She poured all that was in the pitcher over the leaves and swished them around to release their cleansing essence in the water. Then, although Avery Payne had not touched her bare skin, she stripped off her clothes and scrubbed every inch of her flesh, face to feet.

Only then, as she patted herself dry with a square of flannel, did her brain really begin to work again. Only then did she see clearly that, even if he never cornered her alone again, she was as trapped by Avery as that poor parrot he had caged at the house. If she told Rina, she would tell her father and the burden of all this would fall on that old, suffering man, who had been such a kind foster father to her. Who knew what that desperate wretch Payne would do if someone like old Moses stepped into the fray? Old Widow Middleton who slept the sleep of the deaf, if not the dead, in the next room, offered no real protection. Benedict Arnold, her nearest male relative, was miles away and obviously had far more important things to concern him. Besides, more than once, Avery had hinted that her cousin would side with him in any disagreement. Was that all bluff, or did Avery indeed have some hold, financial or otherwise, over Connecticut's hero, "The Dark Eagle"?

If she tried to publicly denounce Avery, it would be her word against his. The fine reputation she had built here for herself and her shop would suffer. Avery Payne, the rich and powerful privateer and Committee of Safety member, against Thea Arnold, the tall, gawky, flame-haired tradeswoman spinster who had never quite belonged before all this Arnold glory. And then, there was poor Charity. Friends though Thea and Charity were, the woman was slavishly in love with her husband. Could Thea bear to ruin that friendship and that love, and perhaps Charity's fragile life, too? And yet, despite the good he was indirectly doing for the rebel cause as he built his own power and wealth, Avery Payne had to be stopped. Thea, for one, had never believed that any ends justified any means.

She left the candle burning; the darkness would hardly soothe her tonight. Despite the fact she'd been without her parents for fifteen years, she yearned for them now as she pulled on her night rail and got into bed. They would tuck her in. Mother would sit here until she fell asleep. She would hold her hand. But now, they were gone, and she had no one here to comfort her tonight.

She rolled back and forth until she had churned her sheets to a wavy sea. Then, she got up, opened a drawer in her low-boy, and took out the tin pin Morgan had given her. She pinned it right on her night rail. For some reason she could not explain, that helped. She even blew the candle out. Though thoughts paraded back and forth through her mind like marching men, she no longer trembled. And at dawn's first light, she slept.

Chapter Five

"For certain herbal leaves and blossoms to do most good, they must oft be torn or bruised. Only then can we realize how potent they may be and, eventually, what curative powers they possess."

IN SEPTEMBER 1777, the British captured the colonial capital of Philadelphia after defeating Washington at the Battle of Brandywine. This main American army settled in at nearby Valley Forge to remain a threat to the British. That same month, the northern American army under Generals Gates and Arnold prepared to stop a British invasion along the Hudson River under General Burgoyne. If Burgoyne could march to Albany and link up with General Clinton's British forces which held New York City, the new United States of America would be sliced in two.

So, before the British arrived, General Gates, first in charge, ordered fortifications dug along the wind-washed river valley on a hill called Bemis Heights, eight miles from Saratoga, New York. Despite limited supplies and reinforcements, Burgoyne's well-trained army attacked. The land was hilly and woody all around but for a fairly open twenty-acre farm between the two camps where the soldiers fought.

At that first Battle for Freeman's Farm, September 19, the second in command of the Americans, Benedict Arnold led a furious assault to turn back the British. But Gates, being overly cautious, kept the vast majority of his forces behind entrenchments and refused General Arnold the reinforcements that could have insured total victory. After all, "Granny" Gates had as good as told "The Dark Eagle" to remain behind the lines and just let the British under "Gentleman Johnny" Burgoyne try to take their lofty, dug-in position!

Gates's conservative approach clashed as mightily with Arnold's fiery heroism as the two armies did. The British won the first encounter, but at a staggering cost of redcoat and Hessian lives. Both armies hunkered down for nearly three weeks, trying to heal and prepare for the next decisive encounter. The British dug and mounded up a pair of well-defended barriers called redoubts, which the Americans would have to take to win the day or make the British retreat.

But, in the American camp, the officers were taking sides and feuding as fiercely as were their generals. In protest of Gates's bumbling, Arnold had resigned from Gates's service, though he still held his rank. But masses of officers begged the dynamic Arnold to remain, so he stayed behind, technically without a command. In retaliation for Arnold's popularity and insubordination, in his report to Congress, Gates intentionally failed to mention Arnold's bold attack on the enemy. After nearly three weeks of bickering, the entire American camp tensed with the threat of a new assault on October 7. And in the mess tent for Arnold's aides-de-camp, the long-simmering unease between Cullen Varner and Morgan Glenn exploded at last.

"I tell you, Glenn," Cullen Varner insisted, leaning over the plank table toward the tall Pennsylvanian, "General Arnold badly overstepped to challenge Gates. Gates is as much a Virginia gentleman as Washington and deserves to be obeyed!"

Morgan banged his tin mug down. "You mean to say, you agree we should just wait here like sitting ducks for another fierce attack that's evidently coming today? You know General Arnold was right to lead our regiments and sharpshooters into the redcoat ranks like that! And we'd have breeched them, if General Gates had sent him the reinforcements he asked for! No, I'll take a tradesman general with a bold heart any day over a gentleman general with a nice set of manners!"

"I for one admire the standards Gates lives by! There's no pride in General Arnold's rushing hither-thither with hit-and-run savage tactics where he might get picked off! Gates

recognizes the danger of reckless officers, even if you do not!"
He rose from his camp stool to poke a finger at Morgan's
lapel, punctuating his accusations.

Cullen's voice was almost condescending now, and Morgan had had his belly full of that since Cullen had been back
in camp. Dang, the man had even stayed at Lockwoods'
while he'd been gone and obviously spent some private time
with Rina. Morgan had written to her to ask about that. Why
he had ever vowed to her he'd keep their love a secret was
beyond him, but he sure wasn't gonna keep quiet on this mess
going on here in this army!

"Look here, Varner," he said, his voice as taut as his face,
"we don't have time to play Gates's namby-pamby, war-of-
attrition games. I don't care how many volunteers are joining
us every day. It's a good, hard, decisive, offensive attack we
need!"

"Now you listen to me, Glenn," Cullen's voice went maddeningly on. "Fighting a few Indians in the wildwood is your
background, so perhaps you just don't understand. General
Arnold's passion to do things his way sent the wrong message
to our rank and file!"

"It sent the message that's holding this whole ramshackle
army of half-trained individuals together!" Morgan exploded
and jumped to his feet. "Each man's gotta stand up for what's
right and what will win this war. And you might as well get
off your Connecticut-bred high horse on this one, because it
was only Arnold's charge that saved us from a rout at Freeman's Farm. What this army needs is *more* inspirational heroes like Arnold! He says 'follow me, boys,' not 'go on out
and get shot up, boys, while I'm back here in these nice, safe
entrenchments!' "

Cullen lowered his voice, despite the fury that had finally
ripped free. Too long he'd acted the gentleman with the backwoodsman aide that General Arnold so favored while he
played messenger boy to prideful windbags like Avery Payne
over Arnold's personal investments. And he'd never gotten
over the way Rina had snubbed him to rush to Glenn's aid
that day of General Arnold's parade. Now, the two men
leaned on fists across the narrow table, nose to nose.

"Arnold's a reckless hothead," Cullen clipped out, "and I'm with Gates when the call to arms comes today!"

"Arnold's a bold leader, worthy of loyalty, and I'll be at his side if he rides out today, come hell or—or high and mighty critics on his own side *and* the British against him, too!" Morgan countered.

They did not speak after that, but filed out to join other officers waiting for assignments on the hill between Arnold's and Gates's tents. To calm himself, Morgan strode to the riverside edge of the Heights and gazed down through fir trees to the tumble of red sugar maples and gilded oaks along the twist of river. That red-gold reminded him of Thea Arnold's hair in the sun, he thought, then chided himself for thinking of her instead of Rina. He breathed in deeply of tangy autumn air and fingered in his waistcoat pocket the last well-read letter he had gotten from Rina. It was nearly a month old, received while Cullen was away. There had been a lag in her letters lately, and that worried him. But since he'd found out from Cullen she was safe, danged if he was going to ask him anything else about her!

Then he heard the first crackle of distant guns and ran to General Arnold's tent. The general, sword in hand and bicorn on head, tore outside at that first retort. He looked as if he breathed fire. Quickly a handful of whinnying stallions were brought up from the corral for him and his officers. "Lieutenant Colonel Glenn, any new orders for me?" he demanded.

"No, sir! General Gates's decree that you're to stay back of the lines is still in effect," Morgan told him as, over the general's epauletted shoulder, he saw Cullen Varner storm into General Gates's tent as if to report that Benedict Arnold was chomping at the bit to charge again. Then everything happened.

"The hell with Granny Gates! He'll lead this fine army and this fine nation to defeat with his damned dithering!" Arnold shouted. "No one will keep me in my tent this day! Are you with me, man?" he cried to Morgan as he sprinted toward his waiting bay stallion.

"All the way to victory!" Morgan cried as he gave his general a boost up on the big brown horse, then ran for his black stallion Charger.

Morgan Glenn ripped the wind as he followed his leader into battle. Neither of them could know that, behind them, General Horatio Gates emerged from his tent with Cullen Varner at his elbow to curse them soundly. And he sent Cullen and another officer flying toward their horses to order Arnold back behind the lines.

As Arnold and Morgan Glenn spurred their horses down the hill toward Freeman's Farm, they could already see the line of crimson coats and glint of bayonets ahead. They rode down, then up the first ravine and plowed through an uncut wheat field under a hail of bullets. How fine it looked, Morgan thought, this farm about to be chewed up again by horses hoofs and cannon balls and bloody swords.

Now they could glimpse the British Balcarres and Breyman redoubts on hilltops ahead with their log breastworks and blazing guns. One or both of those would have to fall for the Americans to win the day. Morgan caught up with General Arnold's fierce charge just as Arnold came alongside the first American regiments General Gates had sent to battle without their bold commander of the left wing.

"Victory or death!" the impassioned devil of a man beside him shouted. "Victory or death!"

Morgan heard the astounded word passed from man to man in the running ranks. "Arnold! Hellfire Arnold's come to lead us on again!"

"What regiment is this!" Arnold thundered to the men with muskets raised and canteens and bullet pouches bouncing as they ran into the heat of the battle.

"Colonel Lattimer's troops from Norwich and New London, sir!"

"God bless you all! My cousin lives in New London, you know! Let's take the field for her and all the brave ladies left behind, boys!"

Those words sobered the passion pulsing through Morgan's veins. Thea's own fiancé, her beloved journeyman cooper, Evertt Edwards, might be here, charging the enemy. But he had no more time to think. They were caught in enemy crossfire at the very vanguard of the charge. Already, men around them began to drop like stones.

Clouds of smoke choked them; bullets fell like hail. A great surge of emotion and energy poured through Morgan. He assisted and protected Arnold as the general seized command of any regiment in sight and hurled them at the British toward the Hessian-held lines, marked by the green German coats. Like a whirlwind, Benedict Arnold rode up and down, exhorting, cursing, swinging his broadsword to make himself an obvious target.

It was then Morgan saw Cullen Varner chasing Arnold back and forth in the fray and realized he had been sent to recall him. Morgan smiled grimly, but that moment's respite let the fear crash in. As if that very human emotion uncovered Morgan, a bullet slammed into his left arm. At first he felt just a slice of cold, but then the pain began to chatter at him. He held his horse's reins with one hand now, ducking, shouting, ordering men on with Arnold. When dusk began to fall, they had fought their bloody way to the north sally port of Breyman's Redoubt, which General Gates had said they would never reach. Grenadiers, Hessians, and Mohawks retreated before their fierce offensive, the first victorious American one of the war so far.

It was the gates of hell here. Din and confusion in the gathering dark. A cacophony of wounded horses and men with smoke-blackened faces. Shouts, shrieks. The stench of powder and flesh. But above it all, even in the face of heavy Hessian fire, rode Benedict Arnold, shouting, "Death or victory!"

In that strange moment, Morgan thought his entire life flashed before him. The early days on the farm along the rippling creek, the Indians who came to trade. How as a boy he had loved those big red and blue Conestoga wagons on the road and vowed to have one someday. The faces of his mother, his brother, his cherry-cheeked sisters. Father, bent over the plow. And then that week in New London where Thea had cured his fever and Rina had stoked it so high again—

But if he thought in the haze of pain and exhaustion and thirst and battle-stupor he must surely die, he was wrong. It was his general whose horse went down with a bullet. It was his invincible general on the ground under the big beast before some soldiers dismounted to roll the dead horse off.

"Damn, damn! Leg crushed, I think!" Arnold said up at Morgan as he knelt over him. "You're shot, too. Tell them to get those damned Germans off those guns back there!"

"They are, sir," Morgan assured him, amazed at the general's steely command when his left leg looked flat and twisted. "The enemy's retreating. And they're going to execute the man who shot your horse."

"No! Spare him! They all shot at me and only one soldier did his duty to get me. Now, listen, Morgan Glenn," Arnold said and grabbed his good arm in a fierce grip. "I am commending you for coming along for the ride. A man after my own heart, I knew it. But," a grimace contorted his face before he went on, "I am commanding you not to let the damned surgeons cut off this leg, no matter what. I'll die first, you understand? And if Granny Gates tells them to, I order you to desert and take me with you. Take me home to Connecticut, even if you have to bury me there, but in one blasted piece!" he gritted out before he slumped silent at Morgan's knees.

It was then Cullen Varner appeared amidst the churning smoke and hubbub of American cheering over the British retreat. "He's not dead?"

"Unconscious. His leg's a mess, but the victory is his. See that your General Gates remembers to tell Congress so this time."

Morgan stood and bellowed for a stretcher for the general. He wavered on his feet from blood loss and exhaustion. When Cullen reached out to steady him, Morgan saw he, too, had been shot, though not severely wounded. A bullet had cleanly taken off his right earlobe. They looked dazedly at each other one moment.

"I thank you for your help," Morgan said most sincerely at Cullen's supporting him. "Despite our differences, I've always wanted us to be friends."

Cullen frowned, gazing first out over the smoky, bloody enemy redoubts the Americans had stormed, then back at Morgan. All Cullen could think of was that years from now when anyone—his and Rina's children—asked him how he lost his earlobe, he would have to tell them that he was playing messenger boy again, even on the battlefield in the war for freedom!

"Friends? Never!" Cullen clipped out before he could stop himself. When Morgan's knees went weak, Cullen sat him on the ground next to the prone Arnold, mounted, and rode back to report to General Gates.

It was ten days later when Morgan was well enough to visit General Arnold in one of many field hospital tents at Albany on the very day General Burgoyne surrendered to General Gates back at Saratoga. Arnold sat propped up in a narrow camp bed, his leg encased in the big wooden fracture box. "Come in, come in!" Arnold ordered when he saw who it was. He returned Morgan's sharp salute. "At last, someone I trust! Sit there!"

Morgan folded his big frame onto a three-legged camp stool that put him far lower than the general. "How long for that apparatus, sir?" Morgan asked.

"Until my tormentors decide to take it off," he groused. "Three, four months. I'll get home to New Haven to recuperate when I can. But at least I'm in one piece, still a whole man to attract the ladies who like to dance, eh?"

Morgan saw he was not smiling despite the jest. "I don't know about the ladies, sir, but General Washington will have need of you!"

Arnold shrugged, a strangely bitter look on his hawklike face. "Too late."

"Too late for what?" Morgan blurted, but Arnold changed the subject.

"I heard you had a blood fever from that infected arm after they dug out the bullet. Bet the healers weren't half so pretty as my cousin that time in New London," he feigned another tease, though his voice was still grim and heavy.

"Yes, sir. I mean they surely weren't. General, I was thinking perhaps you should write to Mistress Arnold to tell her that her fiancé died, loyally following you into battle in the New London regiment. It would surely mean a lot to her and—"

He stopped at the general's puzzled expression. "Her fiancé?" Arnold demanded. "Who the hell is that?"

"*Was,* sir. Evertt Edwards, a journeyman cooper from New London who got killed in our final charge on Breyman's Redoubt."

"Thea was never betrothed to anyone as far as I know, but then that day in New London was so hurried, she probably just forgot to tell me. So, tall, flame-haired, independent Thea found a man to take her on and then lost him. Yes, I'll write her, though probably from New Haven later. You know," he plunged off on another tack as though that was enough of Thea, "Granny Gates jumped at Burgoyne's surrender terms when it should have been the other way around. And he'll have all the glory."

"Not when everyone hears what you did, sir. The men know. *I* know!"

"Not enough. Not anymore," Benedict Arnold declared and dismissed Morgan with best wishes and a terse farewell. Morgan stood in the warming sun outside on this surrender day, not feeling very victorious. Until General Arnold went back to active duty, Morgan was being reassigned to his old job as attaché on Washington's staff at a little place called Valley Forge in Pennsylvania, but he had received permission before he reported there to visit his parents just north of Valley Forge. Still, he'd almost rather be riding to New London to see Rina, maybe to pay a condolence call on Thea, too. Funny how Thea hadn't told her cousin about her betrothal when Rina knew all about it. But, then, that's what real friends were for. Despite everything, he wished he hadn't failed so miserably to be such to Cullen Varner.

It was nearly nine months later that Morgan was finally reassigned to Benedict Arnold. Cullen served now with General Gates, who'd been promoted to president of the Board of War for "his glorious victory at Saratoga." And it took that long for Thea to begin to visit Charity Payne more frequently again.

For a long time after Avery's attack, even when she knew Avery was down by the docks or in a town meeting, she had gone only sporadically to his house. She had suggested that Charity use a doctor's services and sent herbs over at his request. But she had missed conversations with her friend and been ashamed of her fear of facing her, almost as she feared facing Avery. It was not that she really believed he would dare such a scene again, since he had been pointedly avoiding her. Rather, she worried Charity would discover something in her voice or on her face to give away what had happened. But this summer evening, Thea knew Avery had gone out for a sail on one of his vessels, so she came calling unannounced and was warmly received. Tears misted her eyes at how pleased Charity was to see her.

"It's just that your business has boomed in direct proportion to your cousin's reputation—that's why you haven't been by much," Charity told her graciously as Thea prepared to leave after a chatty visit. Charity's delicate, birdlike hands clung to Thea's much larger one. "I can't tell you how much good your visit has done me. I think I shall swear off all your herbal cures and tell Doctor Nelson never to come back. I shall simply mend myself on good feelings—and, of course, my love for Avery."

Thea tugged her hand away, then regretted the quick move and leaned over the bed to kiss Charity's powdered cheek. "I think it would be wonderful if you could join him downstairs once in a while for dinner," Thea said as she plumped up the pillows behind her. "At least, don't breathe in the hops and alcohol from that sleeping pillow until after you've bid him a good night's sleep."

In a lighthearted and uncharacteristic move, Charity lifted and hugged the lattice-embroidered hop pillow across her meager breasts. "And give him a good-night hug like this, you mean, friend Thea?" she asked with a wan smile. "I tell you, those first two years of my marriage there were nights I treasure. Nothing was more wonderful than to be in

Avery's arms, before—before I became too weak and ill with my spells."

Thea's heart wrenched even more now at Charity's love for such a man. Whatever sort of blackguard Avery Payne was, at least he had given his wife some happy days and nights to recall. But who was to say part of Charity's asthma could not be alleviated if he would just pay her heed these days when he had her fortune firmly in hand? Embarrassed to be privy to such longing for a man Thea detested, she hurried to the door. But something made her look back. Charity in that moment looked almost pretty. She was as Thea recalled her from years ago. Charity's pale face glowed as if transported, no longer waxy in the lamplight. Her chestnut hair seemed not etched with gray but gilded; her blue eyes shone, staring off in some vibrant memory. But they shifted back to Thea and she waved her out the door.

Charity sighed and wished she could walk in and out the door like that. But perhaps when Avery came in tonight from his little cruise, she would go down to meet him. She would not even summon Susan. She would brush her own hair loose to her shoulders the way he used to like it and just go down for a simple good-night kiss. Ah, she used to live and breathe for Avery's kisses and his quick, fierce possessions of her in the nights as dark and warm as this one!

Later, when she heard his carriage arrive and the front door open and close, Charity did exactly as she'd planned. Her heart beat very fast, but she moved slowly, stopping every few steps to take a careful breath. One hand heavily on the banister, she went slowly, quietly down the carpeted stairs of the silent house, which had once rung with the voices of her parents and their friends, her own friends, too, before everyone had wed and had children, while she had borne none. But then her handsome, dashing Avery had come along to save her life.

Trembling in wild anticipation, holding her red satin fringed shawl close about her slender frame, she sat on the bottom step to rest just a moment before going into his study at the foot of the staircase to surprise him. But then she realized he wasn't alone. Avery's voice, yes, but another man's, too, one she had not heard before. Her spirits plummeted. Now, she would have to go back up and wait with her door open to catch him before he went to bed, however late it was. For now, even the closeness to his voice soothed her and gave her strength.

"Your accent's really not so pronounced, and that Yankee garb suits you," Avery was saying. "I can see why General Clinton sends you on little errands, et cetera, like this."

General Clinton? Charity thought. But General Clinton was the British Commander in British-held New York City! She clutched her shawl tighter as if the hot summer air had chilled her.

"Stow the compliments, Mr. Payne," his guest was saying. "Clinton is most interested in your offer, and that's all you have to know. Now, if and when we come calling in New London, you've clearly marked what's to be spared from torching on the map. Your directions are most clear. Clinton does wish, though, you'd lay off taking our packets and transports, or he might not be so inclined to delay our arrival or hold the torch on this house or your warehouses."

"I realize we have more negotiating yet to do," Avery put in hastily. "I hope I'll be dealing with you for that."

"Perhaps. Perhaps not. Now, what the general is really avid for is more information about this Benedict Arnold partner of yours. Arnold's quite disgruntled by congress and this General Gates, you say. If anything at all can be worked out there, it will be worth more to you than a few buildings spared when we turn this rebel, privateering port into another firelands."

Charity gasped in shock when she realized what they were discussing, and she feared she would start a spell and cough to give herself away. Did she know her husband—her patriotic Avery—at all? She half crawled, half scrambled up the stairs and sat, propped against the banisters that hurt her thin back, while Avery and that traitor—no, Avery was the traitor—finished their business. She heard Avery, bold as brass, let the man out the front door! No one—no one would ever believe this! She had to confront Avery to stop him, but first . . .

She crawled into her room and pulled herself up by a chair near her bed as the desperate wheezing started. She fumbled with the writing paper, quill, and ink from her bedside table drawer. Her hands shook. She spattered ink, but managed to scrawl, "Thea—help. Avery & Brits. B. Arnold. They are going to burn—" before her gasping for breath weakened her too much to go on and she shoved the pen and ink back in the drawer. She jammed the note inside the hops in the sleeping pillow either Susan or Thea usually dotted with alcohol to make her sleep. She reached toward the bell rope for Susan, but it was so far away. Then Avery suddenly loomed in the door.

"How could you? How could—you?" she gasped out as she sucked in air. "I trust—love you—"

He lifted her in his arms and lay her on her bed. How strong and good his arms still felt around her. She realized then she mustn't let him know who she had heard. "Susan! Call Susan—and Thea!" she cried, her voice so feeble now.

And then she saw, draped over his arm, her red shawl she must have dropped on the stairs. "You were downstairs listening, weren't you, wife? Damnation, what an unpleasant surprise! You actually came down to see me but picked such a wretched time!"

"Can't breathe. Call—help," she croaked out and reached for the bell rope, but he pulled her to the far side of the bed and went quickly over to close the door.

"Poor Charity, having a spell and hallucinating," he said, looming over her again. "You know, I was willing to let things just drift between us because you weren't really in my way, but now, I'm afraid you are."

"Aver—y, please—"

"Don't worry, my dear. It will be better this way for both of us. You do see you've pushed me to this?" he murmured as he reached for the lattice-embroidered sleeping pillow and gazed narrow-eyed down at her. She began to gasp so loudly then, he was afraid it might summon Susan or the other servants, so he pulled her flopping arms down and held them with one hand over her stomach. Then he lifted the pillow and pressed it over her face.

"Sleep. Sleep forever," he muttered as she kicked, struggled, then went still. He loosed her thin arms and took a larger pillow and pressed that down with both hands over the smaller one. He lifted both pillows and listened for her heart. She lay bluish, just as she got in a particularly bad spell sometimes, but she was definitely dead. Then he rang the bell rope and bellowed out with all his might, "Susan! Everyone! Help me! Fetch the doctor and Thea Arnold! The mistress has had a spell and fainted!"

Tears glazing her face, Thea stood beside the body of her friend Charity Payne as Doctor Nelson pronounced her dead. Charity's faithful maid Susan sniffled loudly just behind. "I heard her gasping for air when I came upstairs after I'd been home a while," Avery was saying in a shaky voice. "By the time I'd called the others, she was gone, my poor, ill wife."

"I just saw her earlier tonight," Thea put in, her voice a monotone.

"How much earlier?" Avery demanded. "If you hadn't been too busy to see her lately, maybe you could have told us this was coming!"

Thea just gaped at the man's audacity, but Doctor Nelson cut Avery off. "We're all distraught here, Mr. Payne. I actually thought your wife was a bit better in these warmer months. Now, I'd best cover the deceased so her maid and your servants can prepare her laying out."

Thea leaned down to kiss the waxy, quiet face, just as she had earlier tonight when Charity looked so hopeful. This close, in the slanted lantern light, she could see a faint crisscross impression on her right cheek and chin, as if she had tried to go to sleep against a pillow. Yes, that was it, the lattice pattern on the sleeping pillow filled with crushed and bruised hops. Thea touched her lips to the cold cheek and recalled bidding farewell to her parents this same way when the typhus that took Samantha Lockwood took them, too. As a memento, she lifted the sleeping pillow she'd given Charity. She would not be needing it anymore. Thea stayed only until Doctor Nelson covered the body with a sheet and asked the new widower, "Should Thea send you some sleeping potion 'round, Mr. Payne?"

"Yes, something from Thea might be helpful," Avery dared and levelled a look at her that chilled her to the bone. Gripping the pillow to her, she hurried from the room and down to Lockwoods' to tell them what had happened.

"I detest funerals and funeral feasts!" Rina whispered to Thea behind her fan as they sat on the royal blue brocade settee in Payne's parlor. Townsfolk circulated from the table laden with food in the dining room through the hall and drawing rooms and even the parlor where Charity had been laid out before they'd buried her two hours ago in the burial ground up on the hill. "And I vow, I'll never wear this ring," Rina added as she glared down at the expensive onyx mourning ring, which all the guests had been given as a remembrance of Charity Mumford Payne. "I feel like that parrot over there in the cage, trapped here."

"I know," Thea whispered back. "But I just tell myself I'm doing it for Charity."

Rina rolled her eyes and flicked her fan in the July heat. "She's finally past her pain, that's the way I look at it. We're the ones left behind to suffer, though I don't know about the so-called widower."

Thea forced a quick glance at Avery across the room. He looked somber enough right now in his mourning black, speaking to the mayor, but he hadn't taken one day off work—and he eyed her every chance he got. Now, more than ever, Avery Payne made her skin crawl. And she kept wondering why Charity had the imprint of the sleeping pillow pressed so hard against half of her face. Or had it actually been pressed down over both sides of her face? Perhaps on that night of shock and sorrow, Thea had only noted the half the lamplight fell on. Drat, no used agonizing. Some thoughts she'd entertained were absolutely impossible, weren't they? Charity was gone now, and Thea regretted her dwindling visits to the ailing woman. She had stayed away because of Charity's vile husband. Suddenly, Thea couldn't stomach being here—if for different reasons—any more than Rina could. Besides, she wanted to show Rina the strange letter she'd received from Cousin Benedict in Philadelphia, where he was now military commander since the British had vacated the colonial capital.

"Let's just slip down to the house and see your father," Thea suggested and stood to shake out the skirts of her only black gown. "But I'm afraid we'll have to bid farewell to Avery first. You go ahead and do the talking, or I'm likely to say something I'll regret in front of everyone," she said and thrust Rina slightly ahead of her.

Rina made the proper comforting remarks, fortunately, Thea thought, without the usual, "please let us know if we can do anything to help."

"I'll be seeing you, Thea," Avery said as they moved away.

Rina spun back, putting her petite body between Avery and Thea again. "I don't think you have the need of any apothecary services anymore," Rina replied, to both Avery and Thea's surprise. She lowered her voice to a near growl. "You, unlike the rest of us poor mortals, seem healthy as a horse, Avery Payne. So just keep clear of my friend Thea."

Outside Thea hugged Rina with a quick arm around her shoulders. "What would I do without you?" she told Rina.

"Don't think I haven't seen how that pompous ass looks at you," Rina told her pertly. "If he ever dares anything, you just let Father and me know! After all, what are friends for?"

But her own words haunted Rina as she went up to visit her father, now bedbound with the gout. Friends were to confide the truth in, to really trust, that's what friends were for, Rina berated herself silently. These last months she had been tormented by what she had done to Thea, who still talked about Morgan Glenn.

Rina also regretted the rash rebellion that had driven her to tamper with Morgan Glenn's affections. She had been so sure she loved Morgan then! He had swept her away with his dynamic warmth and openness, qualities she admired so, but could not emulate. Yet, she was still stringing Morgan along when she knew in her heart and mind Cullen Varner would be a more suitable husband for her. Cullen had even written he would settle in New London after the war, now that his Danbury home was burned. She just could not picture Morgan, the brash frontier Pennsylvanian, doing such! She had thought once how much she wanted out of the childhood home that she and Thea entered now, but it seemed suddenly so dear. She had to clear everything up! She had to tell Cullen she would be proud to be his wife, but she must let Morgan down first. Though she had not seen him for months, his faithfulness and dedication had not wavered in the winds of time as hers had, and he deserved better. As Thea did. As Cullen did.

"I said, Rina, let's let him sleep and not disturb him," Thea whispered at her side to snap her from her agonizings. They stood in the doorway of the sleeping Moses Lockwood's big, sunny bedroom where the shaft of late afternoon sun gilded the golden frame of Samantha Lockwood's portrait over the marble mantel. Thea saw Rina's eyes move to her mother's painted face, so she pulled her away out into the hall and down to Rina's room.

"I don't know what will happen when I lose him, too," Rina confided as they both perched on Rina's big canopied bed as they had over the years to share secrets.

"You will go on and take control of your own life, my Rina," Thea told her with a decisive nod to encourage her. "Just as I have. You can do it."

Rina nodded, too, feeling so much better. Her stomach didn't hurt so much, and her heart didn't ache when Thea was here to buck her up like this. Just like Thea, she was going to take control of her life and do the right thing!

"What's that?" Rina asked when Thea produced a piece of parchment and smoothed it open on the bed between them.

"A very odd letter from Cousin Benedict I want to share with you. It seems he is living the good life in Philadelphia as Washington's military commander there, and he's even found a young lady to court, a Mistress Margaret Shippen, nicknamed Peggy."

"Really?" Rina marveled. "Won't the New London gossips have a day with that news? I—I heard Morgan Glenn's still with him."

"Yes, Morgan's there—probably enjoying the young ladies

of Philadelphia, too," Thea joked, but frowned and bit her lip. "But here's the strange part. He writes, 'Dearest Cousin Thea, I regret I have as yet been remiss in not offering my condolences in the loss of your New London betrothed, Evertt Edwards. His conduct in the Second Battle for Freeman's Farm showed he was a loyal, brave lad. He followed me and Lieutenant Colonel Glenn right up to the British-Hessian lines and did his duty to the end. He was interred in a mass grave near the farm. Please know that he was indeed a fine American patriot, which is yet greatly admired by those of us who have borne the brunt of so much unpatriotic handling throughout these days.'

"Now," Thea asked, "wherever do you imagine he got some cockeyed notion I was affianced to Evertt Edwards? I never said a thing to make him believe such!"

Rina shrugged her shoulders and stood abruptly to look out the window toward the street. "Who knows?" she blurted, then cursed her cowardice that she had not confessed and asked Thea's forgiveness. But how could she when they were such good friends again? "Maybe Evertt talked of you, and it came to Arnold's ears all bent out of shape. You know how gossip goes."

But silently again, Rina vowed to end all this deceit so Thea would never have to know. That decision calmed her racing pulse and aching belly. She would write Morgan a letter in Philadelphia, telling him how wrong she had been about their love and asking him to forgive her for no longer planning their future together. And she would write Cullen she would marry him. At least he and Morgan no longer served together. Morgan would probably never show up in New London again. And she would be the best friend to Thea from now on, no matter what befell in this war or ever after!

Chapter Six

*"As an apothecary, one must learn to write things down:
herbal recipes (R_x), supplies, receipts, memoranda of what is
discovered. And so, my dear and only child Althea, in case
you ever take up the honored trade, I have written additional
notes to you in the margins of this precious book."*

BY HIS SECOND day back in Philadelphia, Morgan Glenn
had memorized Rina's letter rejecting him and dashing all
his hopes. "And above all, Morgan, I pray you will forgive
and understand," she had dared to conclude. Right now, he
wasn't certain he could do either. He was still reeling from
his father's sudden death. He had been called away from
General Arnold's staff here in Philadelphia for the funeral.
He had obtained permission to stay home for several weeks
to help his brother get the winter wheat crop in. At least,
next to the grief he'd seen in his mother's eyes and the
wrenching agony of the widows and orphans who had escaped their men's massacre, this letter from Rina was nothing, he tried to convince himself.

While he had been home for his father's funeral, the British
and their Indian allies had committed a terrible massacre on
a frontier colony settled by Connecticut folk. Nearly three
hundred men had been slaughtered on the banks of the Sus-
quehanna River before the horrified eyes of their women and
children. Survivors fled in a death march over the mountains,
and many arrived at the Lehigh settlements. The Glenn farm
had taken in nearly twenty of these wretched people until
they could find a way back to Connecticut or dare to return
to their frontier homes. It made Morgan more determined
than ever that settlers who came in peace should be able to
farm the westward lands.

How desperately he longed for a force of men to lead against the British in retaliation for the massacre, just the way he had swept into battle with General Arnold. Yet he had returned to Arnold's staff here in Philadelphia and re-dedicated himself to victory for America. He had vowed he would always keep his Connecticut fiancée Rina safe, even if he brought her back to the edge of the frontier someday. But then, Rina's months-old letter had massacred that hope for their future together. Since then, he'd run the gamut of emotions: denial, anger, resentment, hurt, worry. If he was ever to feel the understanding or forgiveness Rina had requested, it was down the road a ways.

But he had other things to agonize over also. General Arnold had settled too completely into the life of commander here in Philadelphia now that the British army had vacated the capital. The general was still bitter toward congress and even toward his friend Washington. Financially, he was living far beyond his means, just as luxuriously as the British commander had with a large home and coach-and-four to take him to the city's soirees and dances. He was obviously slighting his administrative duties and had many citizens angered with him. That same rash, mercurial nature that had inspired men to follow him in battle made them want to desert him here. Worse, he was obviously smitten with a woman nearly twenty years younger who, dang her pretty hide, was a dyed-in-the-wool Tory, and General Arnold knew it! One glance at them at a dance like this showed she was leading the "Dark Eagle" around on a very taut chain.

Morgan glared past the couples dancing the minuet at this elegant party at rural Chew House. There at the very center of attention, stood the belle of the ball, laughing Peggy Shippen and her starry-eyed suitor, General Arnold. War austerity or not, the revelers had turned out in satins and silver buckles to partake of laughter, music, and tables of food. Morgan could stomach no more of this high life, not while widows went hungry and mourned their dead, and the war was far from won!

Seething, he glared once more at his commander and jolted to a halt on his way out the door. For one moment, it was as if, in his mind's eye, he saw himself and Rina. Pretty, petite, and blond Peggy had stolen General Arnold's heart away in a brief whirlwind romance, just as Rina had his. And there sat Arnold, bad leg propped up on a chair, unable to dance or barely walk well, yet while Peggy almost perched in public on his lap! How achingly familiar! That woman could no doubt talk the wily soldier into any whim: stolen kisses in the garden, a betrothal kept secret from her father, a tryst in the woods, and passionate commitment for the future all so lightly taken.

"Be ye not unequally yoked," his mother had often quoted the Bible about looking for a mate for life. So how in blazes had Morgan Glenn, the backwoodsman from Tahicox Creek, ever thought he could wed a woman with Varina Lockwood's heritage? He would have been better off not to have ridden into New London at all, or at least to have stayed all feverish and sick in Thea Arnold's apothecary shop that day!

At the door, he took his cloak from the soldier who held it for him, but did not put it on. He banged outside onto the snow-swept lawns of the estate to walk his grief out in the cold.

During the next year, for their own private reasons, both Rina and Thea tried not to think about Morgan Glenn. Rina publicly announced her betrothal to Cullen Varner, who arrived for the engagement party on leave from General Gates. All the war talk that day was on the new British raids against Connecticut towns: the torching of much of New Haven, Fairfield, Norwalk, and the saltworks at Greenwich.

Miraculously, New London, that defiant hotbed of privateering, went yet untouched as if the town were specially protected by Providence. New Londoners clamored for aid from Governor Trumbull, who had no militia to spare. Town troops sporadically drilled at the ancient forts on both sides of the river when some soldiers came home at planting time. A single cannon was hauled to the Common on Manwaring's Hill, and the old guns on the parade were cleaned and pointed toward the river by the sparse local militia. Privateering vessels briefly in port kept armed men aboard. When Cullen returned to General Gates, he vowed to request aid, but he told them what they already knew: General Benedict Arnold, native son, was the one who might heed such a petition. But no one sent protection, and somehow life went on.

It seemed to Thea that women, boys, and old men—and Avery Payne—ran New London. At least Avery was steering clear of her, thanks perhaps to Rina Lockwood's words to him at his wife's funeral. Rina now donated hours to charity work. She organized knitting committees to make socks for soldiers. She spearheaded clothing drives. She held parties where women tore and wound bandages from old clothes and curtains. She urged donations of jewelry and proudly offered up pieces that had belonged to her mother.

"If I can't recall that she gave me this jewelry before she died, what does it matter?" she retorted bitterly to Thea. "Now, that herbal recipe book your mother wrote little notes in, or those stories and songs of Cassie's—those things mean something. But Father only insists I keep a few specific pins, earbobs, and necklaces. Anything I can do to help Cullen and the cause from afar, I will!"

Thea donated medicines and money. Because of her Benedict Arnold connection, she assumed, business was still booming despite rampant inflation where it took a wagonload of Continental dollars just to buy a wagon. She had purchased the acreage near the forest for her herb gardens, and Father Lockwood had even insisted on doubling the land she had asked for. "An early wedding gift to you, in case I'm not here then," he'd told her. Indeed, he might never see that day, Thea thought, but not because he was about to die. Gout wracked his joints in his seventieth year, but his heart was strong. Yet he could live to be ninety, she mused sadly, and never see her marry like his own elegant, lovely daughter Rina.

Thea stopped by Lockwood House on her way home from helping birth a premature child in September of 1780. Here she had gone to see Mercy Bigler with betony tea just to calm her nerves and ended up assisting the midwife in the delivery! Rina would want to know, as Mercy's husband Simon served with Cullen in General Gates's forces. Simon had been taken prisoner by the British during General Gates's ignominious defeat in the south by Lord Cornwallis. Though Cullen had escaped to fight again, Rina had been as good a friend to Mercy lately as she had always been to Thea.

What a changed person Rina had been lately, Thea mused as she banged the familiar brass knocker on the front door of Lockwoods'. Rina had taken in Charity Payne's maid Susan when she'd fled lecherous Avery Payne's attentions, and without a fuss as she had as a child when Father Lockwood had taken in both Thea and Cassie. But, Thea wondered, did Rina remember those early screaming protests any more than she recalled her mother's death?

"Oh, Mistress Thea," the old, peruke-wigged butler greeted her and swept the door open. "Mistress Rina's out for a meeting at the Episcopal Church, but the master's awake and would be glad to see you."

"Thank you, Joshua. I'll just go on up for a visit then."

"Thea, my dear!" Moses Lockwood greeted her and clasped her hand as she bent over to peck a kiss on his cheek. Though many, including his own daughter, thought Moses to be crotchety and stubborn, Thea had never been afraid of him. And she was eternally grateful for all he had done for her, more than his own daughter would ever be.

"Just thinking of you, really I was, Thea. You've been as busy as Rina during this blasted war. You haven't been to the meeting of church-knitting ladies and Rina's back, too?"

"No, but I just helped bring a new child into the world at Mercy Bigler's. It was a terribly hard birth, but the babe should live. Luckily," she told him to soothe his frown, "the new lad's a bit too young yet to serve in the ranks with Cousin Benedict at his new assignment at West Point Citadel."

Moses's thin shoulders shuddered as if he would laugh but could not afford the pain of movement. "If West Point's safe with Arnold, then the whole Hudson Valley and the north is safe!" he told her. "Yet it seems our favorite Connecticut general finds time to marry and have a son of his own these days, and poor Cullen can't even get free again to come wed

Rina. I'm going to be here for that day, I tell you—and be around for the country's independence, too!"

"I hope you'll be here long after that, Father Lockwood," Thea said and put her hand over his on the sheet. "I don't know what New London or Rina or I would do without you."

"Humph! Rina will have Cullen then, and you—"

"Will still have my shop."

"And a good man someday, I warrant. There's someone smart enough out there to snap up a fine woman like you. Maybe I should have the Committee of Safety or Governor Trumbull fetch that tall Morgan Glenn fellow back here to protect us, eh, on special assignment from your cousin! Governor Trumbull liked Morgan Glenn, and I just wonder if you didn't, too."

Thea felt her cheeks heat even at the teasing mention of that faded name and face. Still, the impact and the aura of Morgan Glenn encompassed her after three years apart. Perhaps if Cousin Benedict came to Rina's wedding, her thoughts wandered, he would bring his favorite aide-de-camp with him.

"Thea, since Rina isn't here right now, there is something I would tell you, and ask you."

Thea's eyes focused on the dear old face again, wigless but encased in a fringed bed cap. "Of course. Her stomach complaints have not begun again, have they?"

"Not at all. Close the door for just a moment, will you?" She did and sat again, hands pressed in her lap. "It's something I've wanted to entrust to you for a long while, something that might be a bit of a burden to you, but I see no other way."

She leaned forward in her chair. "Your health. If I can help—"

"No, you already have in that. It is this," he said and sighed as he rolled his eyes to stare over Thea's head at the portrait of his lovely Samantha on the wall. "You know Rina claims she can't recall much about her mother."

"Yes—just a few little things like her laugh and the parties."

"Now, listen, dear Thea. Rina may be back at any moment, and there's no time like the present."

Thea sat enraptured, then stunned as he explained his marriage to Rina's mother. Samantha had been barely sixteen when he wed her, Moses said, and he had fallen in love with her at first glance the year before. "She was so delicate, so beautiful, just like that, Thea," he said, and grunted in pain at his own efforts to turn his head to look at the portrait again. "I daresay, she was a child in her delight with life and I, a rich man, greatly her senior, indulged her whims terribly."

All that jewelry Rina's donated, Thea thought. All those parties Rina recalls when Father Lockwood was obviously never one for parties. But why was he unburdening his soul to her like this? And then he told her.

"We had eight lovely years of marriage with no child. My age—I blamed myself. It was almost as if my laughing, charming Samantha was not only my wife but my cosseted child, so I never longed overmuch for an heir. But when she conceived Rina, it was awful for her. Your mentioning Mercy Bigler reminded me. Pain, bleeding—your mother dosed her with wild raspberry tea, I recall, so she would not lose the babe early. The thing is," he said and pinched his eyes tightly closed, "she might have welcomed that."

"No! No woman who loves her husband would ever—"

"It wasn't that. It's just she hated losing her petite form, her independence to do what she wished, her joy of life. And after she suffered through a protracted labor, she—she did not want a thing to do with the child or me again."

Clanging bells sounded in Thea's head. "Never wanting anything to do with Rina? Even when little Rina grew a bit and turned so fetching?" she asked. "Not when Rina turned quite the image of herself?"

"Especially not then. I hired a wet-nurse, then a nursemaid. I tried, Lord knows how I tried, but she would scream, 'Get her away from me!' She was never herself after that, not really. And when she caught the typhus fever that swept the town and the little girl went into her room to see her—" he floundered, tears in his eyes, "she was out of her mind with fever then. She screamed at Rina that she hated her, that she should have died before she was born, that she never wanted her. It was the last thing poor Rina ever heard her mother say, and she was shattered. But then Samantha died and I was shattered, too. Rina said nothing of what her mother had said. I thought she would forget, I prayed she would."

"I think that—she has, maybe intentionally," Thea managed and swiped tears from her own cheeks. "But, if you haven't told Rina this, why did you share it with me? You can't expect me to tell her."

"No, no! Perhaps she should never know, now that she's doing better. But her rebellious behavior in the past, and her moods, not to mention that strange stomach complaint and the way she frets for not recalling her mother—I just thought someday someone dear to her would need to know this when I'm not here."

Thea nodded, but she wasn't certain she agreed. Did Rina recall those horrid scenes with her mother or not? Should she be told? Thea knew nightmares of Rina's mother had haunted her years ago. "I should not be the one to tell her," Thea said, her hand over Moses's crooked fingers again, "but perhaps you should. Perhaps before she weds Cullen and has children of her own to deal with, perhaps just knowing would help her."

"No! I think it would destroy her now when she's doing better. I only told you in case sometime in the future there *is* some reason she should know. I told you it would be a burden to bear."

"You realize," Thea said and stood to gaze fully at Samantha Lockwood's portrait with new eyes, "Rina might not believe me if I ever told her. She resented me when I first came to this house. *I* recall things she perhaps never will, you see."

"I know that, Thea."

"So perhaps you should at least write it down somewhere. My mother always said you should write important things down."

"I shall do that and leave it with my will."

"No, not there. Then, when she learns of it, it would be

like losing both of you at the same time. You know, although it helps me to understand her better, Father Lockwood, I am sorry you told me. I feel the traitor to be harboring something like that and not tell her. Rina and I vowed long ago to always share the truth with each other."

He kissed her cheek as she bent over to bid him a subdued farewell. He wasn't sorry, he told himself, as he went back to staring at Samantha after Thea left. Having told Thea, he would not have to write all that sorrow down where someone he didn't trust might come upon it someday. Thea was the one to entrust that horrid secret to. Thea had the gift of healing. If anything happened to him, she would have the truth and the love to keep Rina strong. Thea was worth so much more than he had ever given her in terms of money or trust or time or love. For one moment, he wished someone like Thea had been the daughter of his body—or even his wife.

He shook his head, even though that hurt, too. He closed his eyes to shut out the picture of his wonderful and terrible Samantha.

Thea could not sleep that night, haunted by what Father Lockwood had shared with her. How could a woman not want her own child, a beautiful child? Perhaps Rina's earliest objections to Thea, and later Cassie being taken in by Father Lockwood, had been not only her reluctance to share her father, but also some sort of reaction to her mother's cruelties. Perhaps someone who had never experienced a mother's love could not love others easily without years of practice. And had Thea's parents known the truth about Samantha in those days they nursed her and caught the typhus from her? If only Mother had written something down in the pharmacopoeia to help her know how to deal with this!

Thea tossed and turned and thrashed. Finally, she got up and searched through her pine storage chest until she found the sleeping pillow she had taken from Charity Payne's deathbed. She went downstairs to fetch a handful of fresh hops and a small bottle of alcohol to flick on the pillow. She seldom used soporifics, but she was exhausted. She padded back upstairs to light the candle by her bed and dumped out the dried contents of the pillow into a basket. And then she saw the crumpled, ink-speckled piece of paper.

"What?" she said and bent to unwrinkle it in the light. She flipped it over and read in her dead friend Charity's shaky but unmistakable handwriting: "Thea—help. Avery & Brits. B. Arnold. They are going to burn—"

"What?" she said again. When had Charity written this desperate, disjointed message? And who was going to burn what? The British? But Charity had been dead for two years! Since then, some Connecticut towns had been burned, of course, but how could Charity have known that? "Avery and the British. Benedict Arnold? Tell Avery or tell Benedict Arnold that the British are going to burn something?" Thea puzzled aloud.

And then, as she stared down at the empty pillowcase in her lap, she thought of the imprint marks on Charity's face again. What if Avery and his silent business partner, Benedict Arnold, had thought they could keep the British away from here with their privateering ships? Perhaps Charity had found that out and been terrified Avery and the general would be hurt. But why the haste with this note, and why was it stuffed, hurriedly half-written, in this pillowcase that had marked her face the night she died?

And then another possibility staggered Thea. What if Avery Payne were actually working both sides? What if he told Charity he needed more of her fortune—or all of it—that last night after Thea left her? And when Charity refused or protested, or had a spell in her agitated state, what if Avery took this pillow and . . .

She began to shake as if a chill wind blew right through her. No, Avery's ships were attacking the British, not helping them. But she kept fingering the raised lattice-pattern embroidery on the pillowcase. Even someone just snuggling close to breathe in the soothing fumes would not have marks embedded in the skin. Charity would surely have called her maid Susan for the alcohol to release the fumes, but she had not. But Avery . . .

"Damn him for a seducer and a liar! But a murderer? Then he might as well be a traitor to his country, too!" she snapped.

She dressed and paced downstairs in the shop until dawn yellowed the sky. She would have to tell someone her suspicions, take someone with her to confront Avery. How she dreaded that; she recalled his threats the night he'd trapped her on his ship as if it had been just last night. She could never risk facing him alone. But she dared not endanger Rina or involve poor, suffering Father Lockwood. And, if Avery were guilty of playing both sides, did it mean his partner Benedict Arnold was involved in this, too? Surely not! And yet, whatever it meant to herself and her business, she had to go to the Committee of Safety with this information. Then, they could face down Avery. If she further hurt her cousin's reputation, stained lately with a public reprimand from General Washington for his misuse of Philadelphia funds which Cousin Benedict claimed congress owed him, anyway, so be it.

She sat on her tall stool behind the counter. She forced herself to drink a cup of catnip tea to calm her nerves. Funny how something that could stir a cat so calmed a human, or was it just that—

She jumped straight off the stool when a rock shattered her front window. "Traitor! Arnold traitor and liar! Arnold traitor! Arnold traitor!" a rough chant rose outside to stun her as another rock splintered another window to shards. Trembling as if her own heart had screamed those things she feared about her cousin, she held the stool before her as a partial shield and shuffled to the window.

A growing crowd had gathered outside, mostly people she knew. And they were hoisting each other up on shoulders to take her painted apothecary sign down! Anger made her bold; she yanked open the door.

"Stop it! What are you doing and saying!"

"Arnold traitor, Arnold traitor!" the crowd chanted. Two women shoved her back when she tried to stop the boys from stomping on her sign. Someone hacked at it with an axe, and someone else speckled it with tar, which they also splattered on her windows. It mottled her skirts like black ink. Widow Middleton stuck her head out a window above and yelled, but everyone ignored her.

"The Arnold name's cow dung from now on!" a voice in

the crowd shouted, and she realized they were throwing that, too.

"Stop it!" Thea screamed. "Stop it! Have you gone mad? What is it?"

"What is it, she asks real innocent like! News just come that your cousin turned tail and gone to the British, that's what!"

"No, that's impossible!" Charity's note inside! Then was Avery Payne involved, too? "No, no!" Thea cried, but the rattle of a carriage racing up the streets drowned out her words. Rina! Rina leaned from the carriage window before it even stopped.

"Thea, get in! It's true! Word came from Morgan Glenn to Father! Get in before you are hurt!"

"No! I'm not leaving my shop! I cannot believe it—and even if it's true, I haven't done—"

"Been living off his glory!" an old man who was one of her best customers for Blistering Plaster bellowed. "Prob'ly privy to all his plans! Sold a few New London secrets to the Brits, hain't you?"

The crowd backed her to the door of the shop. Then, as Rina scrambled out of the carriage, Avery Payne thundered up on a large white stallion. "Get back, back, all of you!" he ordered the crowd. When he edged his horse in closer, Thea gaped up at him. "I'm here to protect you, Thea. Give me a hand up now, and I'll just tell the Committee of Safety—"

"Get away from me, you deceitful bastard!" she shrieked. How could this nightmare be so real? She was the one who had to see the Committee of Safety! She had to take the pillow and the note and tell the committee that Avery—

"All right, you stubborn, little Arnold bitch," Avery leaned down to hiss at her, "we'll do things your way then until you learn your lesson that's been so long coming! I'll have you crawling to me for protection! You don't think I've forgotten, do you?" He sat erect on his horse and shouted to the crowd while he gazed intently down at Thea and Rina clinging together. "I hear there's a gathering of rather unruly citizens defacing Arnold graves up in the Olde Burying

Ground. I just thought perhaps you'd like me to stop them, Mistress Arnold, but if you're not going to cooperate any more than your traitor of a cousin—"

It was all he got out before Thea shrieked and clawed her way through the crowd. Rina grabbed for her, but she was gone on a dead run up the hill. Pictures of her shop windows being broken, her painted sign ruined were nothing compared to her fear of a crowd attacking the stones and graves of her parents, just because of the cursed Arnold name.

She ran without looking back until she was gasping. She heard Rina's carriage rumble up beside her. Nearly hysterical, she got in with Rina at the corner of Main and Hill, and the driver whipped the horses on. "Rina, Rina, I've got to tell you," she began, but could not go on. Anyway, Avery could now just claim that Thea had forged Charity's note to get sympathy for herself or to throw blame on others. Trapped! Too late!

"What—what happened? Why has the town gone mad?" Thea asked, though she was too panicked to digest much of Rina's answer.

"General Arnold was going to hand over West Point and a lot of American troops to the British. He's been in contact with them for a long time. Morgan Glenn sent a message that Arnold's British contact was captured with the evidence. Arnold fled to New York to the British."

"Damn him! Damn him!" Thea got out as the carriage turned in the wide open gate of the burial ground. Rina scooted out behind Thea, who was already running again.

Thea screamed at the crowd and charged them. Some of the rabble ran away when they saw her. Some dared to shake their fists first. But they all melted away toward exits as she saw what they had done. All four gravestones were shattered to shards. Ragged effigies of a man and woman hung by their necks from a nearby maple tree. For one moment she had actually thought they had dug into the graves and . . . and . . .

She collapsed to hands and knees among the shattered stones. Suddenly Rina was there, kneeling down, her arms hard around her. Sobbing, Thea clung to her, but no sounds came. And the hanging effigies with crudely printed signs about their necks reading "Benedict Arnold" and "Thea Arnold" just twisted and twirled in the gentle morning breeze.

Two days later, Lt. Col. Morgan Glenn waited under house arrest within the West Point Citadel. Washington was personally fortifying the site in case the British attack still came. Morgan awaited a military inquiry and another interview with Washington, who, ironically, had arrived the day Arnold heard his plans had gone amiss and fled to the British. Now, Morgan paced the tiny room they'd put him in; he leaned his head against the walls and banged his fists on them.

Why hadn't he seen this dreadful possibility of Arnold's actual defection—of treason—coming? With the general's young wife's wheedling and her Tory ties? With Arnold's ever-present need for money? With his dark hints even years ago of "too little, too late" from Washington and congress? At his thwarted need for glory, which men like Gates had robbed him of? Morgan Glenn had been unswervingly loyal to the man—even as he had been to Rina—and been burned again.

Morgan's entire career and his relationship to many people now hung in the balance. Family, friends, fellow officers. Thea Arnold. He had dispatched a note quickly, with Washington's permission, to save Thea, but had it been in time? And would Washington's panel of inquiry believe the tale he'd told of his stupid innocence and blind dedication? Yet, he took comfort in the thought that Washington had also trusted Benedict Arnold until the last, and had come to have a friendly breakfast with him the very morning he fled.

Morgan spun as a sharp knock resounded in the little room. He turned to face the stern Lieutenant Fitzwalter, one of Washington's aides. "Orders for you, Lieutenant Colonel Glenn," he told him after a crisp salute and handed him a folded page.

Morgan's hands shook as he opened it. Orders to a court-martial, to prison, or worse? Arnold's captured British contact, Maj. John Andre, was to be hanged, and Washington had vowed to get Arnold at any cost. He skimmed the writing to the bottom. Governor Jonathan Trumbull! He was being assigned to the governor of Connecticut?

"General Washington says to convey to you his regards to a man of honor. The panel has ruled you were not privy to General Arnold's dealings. And General Washington thought this assignment, for which a request came through last week, would be appropriate to show Connecticut that General Washington trusts you and feels Benedict Arnold acted alone. He knows you will do as fine a job for Governor Trumbull as you've done for him off and on over the years, sir."

Clutching the precious paper, a veritable pardon, Morgan Glenn saluted. "Tell the commander in chief I will not let him nor the traitor's abandoned Connecticut down, Lieutenant."

Fitzwalter nodded and was gone. Morgan Glenn crumpled back against the wall and read the paper over and over again.

Americans, Connecticuters especially, went wild repudiating the man they had long enshrined as a hero. Benedict Arnold was hanged in effigy in New Haven, Boston, Philadelphia, and many small towns and villages. He was drawn on tavern walls standing beside the devil, smiling, though some wag declared it wasn't fair to the devil. Effigies and pictures of him were burned in public bonfires. Many people with the first or last names Benedict or Arnold changed them.

Governor Jefferson of Virginia offered five thousand guineas for Arnold's head to add to the usually tight-fisted congress's one hundred thousand dollars. When it was learned Arnold had taken thousands of pounds from the enemy as prepayment for his defection, people denounced him as "the Judas of the Revolution." And when it was discovered that his Tory wife had maintained a long correspondence and friendship with Arnold's British contact, Maj. John Andre, she was branded everything from Delilah to Jezebel.

When Arnold got his first assignment as a British general to ravage the Commonwealth of Virginia, Washington sent his French friend and protégé the Marquis de Lafayette after him with troops and orders to bring him back dead or alive. But Arnold's raids there were even too brutal for the British to stomach, and they recalled him to New York before Lafayette could catch him.

Caught up in this hateful frenzy, anyone who had been close to or related to Benedict Arnold, especially in Connecticut, was suspect and abused. In his first weeks in Lebanon, the wartime capital of the state, Morgan Glenn was continually cursed and spat at on the streets. In early summer, when Governor Trumbull sent him to New London with extra ammunition supplies, he dreaded his reception there. Meanwhile, Thea Arnold's little apothecary shop's booming trade slammed to a halt, and she was shunned. Thereafter, anytime folks turned deceivers or traitors, even in life's little daily deceptions, they were branded by that most hated of names, "you Benedict Arnold!"

Chapter Seven

*"Some say that medicines, like the rod on a willful child,
must taste bad to do their good. But I say a bit of mint water
or licorice mixed in to soften the blow is not amiss, and that is
the way your father and I are trying to rear you, my Althea."*

"ONE GOOD THING has come from Benedict Arnold's defection anyway, Cassie," Thea told her friend as they dug
white-flowering blood root along the forest fringe. She didn't
expect Cassie to answer. The girl only dug and pulled up the
herbs sporadically while she hummed. She spent most of her
time squinting over her shoulder into the woody depths laced
by dogwood and pink mountain laurel while warblers lilted
from tree to tree overhead. Thea was used to talking to herself lately, since a deaf old lady and the Lockwood family
consisted of her only acquaintances in months. "At least with
the shop so empty, thanks to Benedict," Thea went on, "I've
had lots of time to be out here on my land to tend the herbs.
The nation's going to need my medicines and, if they won't
buy them from an Arnold, Father Lockwood will see the
army takes them *gratis.*"

Thea's thoughts spun off to four years ago this month, almost to the day, when she had given herbs *gratis* to Benedict
Arnold's aide-de-camp Lt. Col. Morgan Glenn. The weekly
gazette had spilled a lot of ink over the fact Morgan was now
working for Governor Trumbull as liaison to Washington.
She had read just last week that "the governor has praised
Morgan Glenn's fine record of service. However, the gazette
must note, Glenn was rather too close in proximity to that
Judas to our cause to be so lauded." Drat, Thea thought, as
she wiped the orange stain from broken blood root stems off

her hands in the grass, I can understand and feel for Morgan Glenn now!

"Come on, then, Cassie. We've got to leave some so it will spread next year. Besides, we're a mess."

Cassie stood and stared at her orange hands. "I don't care!" she replied defiantly as a child might. "I think it's pretty! Nothing better than a day's ramble in the woods, me ma used to say. I'd just like to see the British come through these forests, I would, to try to take us by surprise like everyone's afraid of! The forest folk don't allow no iron or steel passing through, and they'd capture every last one of them British, they would!"

"And save us all a great deal of time and worry!" Thea played along as she hoisted the basket of fresh herbs over her arm and they started away. Cassie walked backwards to be certain they were not surprised from behind by either British soldiers or forest fairies. There had been numerous false alarms lately about British ships in Long Island Sound. Avery Payne and others who owned the large and successful New Londoner privateering fleet were always spreading word that attack was imminent. And so, like the town which had heard the boy cry "Wolf!" too often, folks were starting to ignore such dangers. And therein lay a danger of its own.

As they headed back to town, they laughed and joked about their sticky, "bloody" hands. "I'm going to be an Indian!" Cassie declared and broke a fresh stem to draw warpaint on her freckled cheeks and brow while Thea laughed at her antics.

It felt so good out here in God's green land to laugh and loll about a bit, Thea thought. Months of bearing the burden of what Benedict Arnold had done—she could not bear to think of him as cousin now—had really worn her down. If it weren't for Rina and Father Lockwood and Cassie, especially now that Avery had begun to bother her again, she did not know what would have become of her and her empty shop. She smiled as Cassie held another stem up toward Thea.

"What must I paint on you for all the town to see?" Cassie demanded, her face bright with mischief.

Thea put her basket down and stood there still and somber. "Can you spell Arnold, A–R–N–O–L–D, Cassie? I'm still branded that by them all, so I might as well have it on my face as on my shop."

"Can't spell that," Cassie insisted. "Can't spell but X for my name."

"You know Rina and I taught you more than that! All right, then, just put war paint on me, too," Thea volunteered. The wet tip of the blood root stem tickled, and she laughed again despite it all. If she didn't keep busy, if she didn't laugh, what would there be for her but to cry or give up? It wasn't fair the way the town treated her, for she had done nothing but go along with their adulation of Benedict Arnold. Perhaps after the war ended, perhaps when they won, things would be better again.

They strolled back into town, swinging the basket between them. On Hempstead, then Coit Street, too, people gawked at them and whispered, and Mrs. Renquist tugged her youngsters over to the other side of the street. Defiantly, Thea tried to harden her heart, but all that hurt. Even more now, she sensed the cruelties Cassie had long endured as the town's "half wit." Thea realized how brave Rina was being to publicly stick by her when she, too, became tarnished by her association with "the traitor's cousin."

"Do you want to help me rip and wrap some of those soldiers' bandages for Rina this afternoon?" Thea asked. She kept herself very busy doing things for others, whether they appreciated it or not. They probably wouldn't even take Rina's bandages if they knew who had torn and wound most of them.

They had to raise their voices to be heard on Bank Street as two noisy wagons approached them from behind and rumbled by. Soldiers! Four soldiers with piles of cannon balls and barrels marked "grapeshot." Two big draft horses pulled each of the wagons, and a big black horse walked behind the first wagon, tied by the reins. The instant the tall officer in charge turned back in his seat, Cassie and Thea recognized him. From the first wagon, he squinted back toward them in the noontide sun.

Thea stopped swinging the basket and it bumped Cassie. Thea gasped, stood, and stared while the tall officer told the driver to halt the wagon. Dusty, a bit bedraggled, but wonderful-looking to Thea, he climbed down. He took off his cockaded bicorn and stood on the edge of the street. His golden-brown hair, pulled straight back in a queue, glinted reddish in the sun. It was Cassie who moved. She left Thea holding the wicker handle of the basket and sprinted up the street, shouting, "Morgan! Morgan Glenn, do you want to hear me sing 'Danny Boy'?"

Thea walked slowly closer while he greeted the paint-faced girl. And then Thea remembered. Her face was smeared orange, too, her gown was brown with forest soil, her hands . . .

"Mistress Arnold," Morgan said with a solemn nod as he approached her. It was the first time in months someone on the street had greeted her or said that name with kindness. She felt her bones dissolve; her heart pounded so hard her hands shook the basket. She blushed under his scrutiny at the thought of how she must look.

He wondered if she knew all about him and Rina, or if, now that Rina was publicly betrothed to Cullen Varner, she still kept the secret, even from Thea. At the powder magazine at Shaw's Cove where he'd just delivered some of this ammunition, he'd heard about Rina's betrothal and how this town was treating Thea Arnold. The sparse local militia had been glad enough for the delivery, but shocked at who had brought it to them. So the taint of traitor was yet on all of them who had trusted and been doubly betrayed by Benedict Arnold.

"Lieutenant Colonel Glenn," she managed. "It has been a while. So much has happened."

"Yes. You see, we're taking these wagonloads over on the Groton Ferry to Fort Griswold," Morgan told her. "General Washington doesn't call Connecticut 'The Provision State' for nothing. Why don't you and Cassie just climb in and I'll drop you by your shop? Here, let me take that," he added, and grasped the handle of her basket.

But she clung to it. They held it between them in a little war of wills. It frightened her how glad she was to see him and how much she wanted to go with him. "No need," she insisted, "really."

"No bother," he insisted. With a stronger tug than she could muster, he brought her ᴜᴏ his side, along with the herb basket. "I'd love to see their faces when we two ex-Arnold-followers get together and then give them the danged shot and powder they've been begging for. Besides, the men at Shaw's Cove tell me some folks here believe New London might have been spared so far because Arnold especially favors the town and might be pleading in New York on its behalf."

"Is he our hero again, then?" Cassie cut in as Morgan hoisted her up on the long plank wagon seat before Thea even acquiesced to the ride.

"No, Cassie," Thea remonstrated. "Never again, and no more parades for him!" Her heart soared as Morgan lifted her up as if she were as small as Rina.

They made their own parade down Bank to Water Street. People stared, stopped right in their tracks. Drat them, Thea cursed silently. But it couldn't be much worse than it had been for her this past winter, that is unless Morgan planned to stay at Lockwoods' again as he had that first time.

"Have you seen Rina yet?" she asked him warily.

"No. I suppose I should pay a call to wish her the best for her coming marriage with Cullen Varner, though. I hear she's announced that betrothal," he said, then went on quickly. "Funny, how it seemed Cullen would come out smelling like one of your roses when he picked General Gates and escaped the shame of being with Arnold." He shook his big head at the memories. "But Gates's defeat by Cornwallis in South Carolina and his cowardly flight and demotion didn't put much polish on the Varner name, either."

"No. But Rina's still loyal and loves him, anyway!" Thea blurted, though she wasn't sure why she saw a frown crunch Morgan's brow. Before her shuttered shop windows, he jumped down and reached up to assist her. She took his hand. It was so strong and warm. His mere touch shot shivers of soaring strength mixed with a strange, trembling weakness through her all at once. His driver handed Cassie and the basket down. There was a moment of silence then, as if something were being mutually mourned.

In his dusty blue and buff uniform Morgan Glenn stood staring at the bedraggled front of her shop, which had looked so grand before. Her ornate painted sign with the phoenix rising and the weighing scales was gone. Her shiny windows with their glittering glimpse of glass carboys and huge flasks inside were boarded up. But she had boldly painted across the rough wooden planks, THEA ARNOLD'S APOTHECARY SHOP. It had obviously been reprinted and defaced more than once in some defiant contest she waged with this danged town, Morgan fumed.

"I'm real sorry," he said and turned to gaze deep into her grass-green eyes.

"Thank you. I'm sorry for you, too. I—I know you admired him. At least, you were loyal to your superior when he was not. And I'm glad the governor sent you—that he's showing everyone you are innocent," she declared with a decisive nod of her head that sprang two coils of crimson hair loose from under her lopsided bonnet.

His eyes studied her face, and a wry grin lifted the left corner of his firm mouth. "Even with that orange stuff all over your skin, you're still a sight for sore eyes. It kinda' goes with your hair. Look, I'm here for the summer. I'll be working with the men in charge of Fort Trumbull and Fort Griswold, so I hope we can talk more later. The ferry to Groton's right down on Market Wharf, isn't it?"

"Yes. Yes, that's where it is!" Thea said so loudly she almost shamed herself, but her mind was on the fact he wasn't leaving right away! Here was someone—Morgan Glenn, *Morgan Glenn!*—who really understood what she was going through. Her mind treasured his earlier words, "we two ex-Arnold-followers." That little phrase seemed to say and promise so much! He had wanted to publicly show the town they were together today. He had brought New London aid for its defense! And he hadn't even laughed, at least at first, at how awful she must look. If some shiny-armored knight had thundered down Water Street on a white steed to take her to his castle, she could not have been more touched and thrilled.

"I think we all better wash up," he said as he climbed back in the wagon and hit his hat on the knee of his breeches. Dust flew. He laughed just once, a deep, rich sound. His driver chuckled and elbowed him. Thea smiled, tears stinging her eyes. And Cassie sang "Danny Boy" at the top of her lungs while she jumped up and down and waved good-bye.

Morgan's calling on Thea caused more gossip, more snide comments in the gazette, and Rina's fussing about "what the town will say about both of you together!" But despite all that and the fact Morgan was only here for a few months, Thea Arnold was the happiest she'd ever been. She regained the weight she had lost, so that her gowns no longer hung oddly on her; she sewed herself a new frock from old curtains; she hummed while she worked. There were no more customers than usual, but through Rina she distributed medicinal supplies for the cause. Taxes and inflation ate away at what she had saved in the boom times, but she smiled again, even when she was in town. If it hadn't seemed that she saw Rina so much less and Rina was so much more on edge, that summer of 1781 would have been entirely golden for Thea.

Morgan was very busy. Though the local authorities mistrusted him enough to stubbornly go their own ways, he met with Col. William Ledyard, the military commander of the district, who oversaw Fort Trumbull, which guarded New London, and Fort Griswold, guarding Groton across the river. With Capt. Adam Shapely, Morgan supervised the strengthening of Fort Griswold's ten-foot stone walls and deep ditches. He met with the Committee of Safety in public, and with Moses Lockwood, member emeritus, in private. They decided on a two-shot alarm from Fort Trumbull if the British were ever spotted at the river's mouth. That made the townsfolk rest easier—too easy, Morgan told Thea. He met with privateering investors and captains, unfortunately, Avery Payne included. Only last week Thea had told Avery to stay away when he came to offer a large purchase of her cures—*if* she would just bring them down to his office on the wharf in the evening.

But Morgan still found time to call on Thea. They walked out to her piece of land for a picnic with Cassie in tow, though he had seemed reluctant at first to do that. Despite the glares and whispers, they attended the Fourth of July celebration at the public square called the parade. "I always said the best defense is a strong offense," Morgan told her that night while a big bonfire gilded the buildings facing the parade. "I believe it's best we be seen together publicly, not to defy the gossipmongers, but to show them we're hiding nothing, ashamed of nothing. I've made the mistake before of doing things in secret, and it didn't turn out to be anything but bad."

Certain there was more he meant to confide, she had waited for him to explain. Did he imply that General Arnold had hinted to him he might turn traitor? But Morgan just tucked her hand under his arm. They walked back to the shop while the Independence Day revelers bayed at their bonfire, as if to challenge the British in New York right from the town square.

Thea was so aware of herself as a woman each time she was with Morgan Glenn. Somehow, he made her feel pretty, even petite—at least not gaudy and gawky. Her new square-necked gown with its graceful box pleats across the back and its quilted petticoat and embroidered pale blue satin apron, instead of the stained muslin dress she always wore in the shop, made her feel so feminine. The robin-egg-blue skirts that had once been draperies only had paper stiffening over the panniers, no horsehair or buckram. But they swished elegantly when she walked. The whalebone stays in the bodice enhanced the full breasts that used to make her so shy standing next to slender Rina. She knew Morgan Glenn gazed appreciatively at her, and that made her feel so very special and alive.

"The sky's beautiful tonight—sword points of stars," he told her as they strolled around the back of the shop to sit on the wooden bench he'd made for them. He had placed it near the stoop where they had first met. They overlooked the busy wharf and harbor from her little patch of grass.

"It is beautiful in New London," she said and adjusted her skirts as they sat. His big thigh pressed against her paper, and it crinkled. "Despite everything, it's always been home. I'm hoping after the war ends, people will forgive and forget."

"Sometimes, I think, it's even easier to forgive than forget," he told her while people's voices drifted to them from the distant celebration. He thought of Rina then, but he wasn't ready to share that with Thea yet. He had avoided Rina at first, but had literally run into her when he went to report to her father at Lockwood House yesterday. She had been on her way inside when she'd bounced in then out of his arms as he headed out the open front door. She'd asked how he was doing, but then chattered to him about Cullen before he could answer.

Then she had asked about his family. He had told her of his father's death and about the massacre survivors he'd helped. Thea knew all of that already; it had helped to share it with her, but he was sorry he'd told Rina. He wasn't bitter, he told himself, even now. It was just that her desertion of all the precious things they had planned still hurt deep inside. It was the first time he had felt betrayed and deserted—a harbinger of the devastation coming with Benedict Arnold. And he just wasn't sure he was ready to trust anyone again, including the stunning Thea, who sat here with moonlight dancing copper on her hair and promise in her eyes.

"Thea, our growing friendship has meant a lot to me this summer so far," he began awkwardly.

"So far? You haven't been recalled?" she asked. The alarm in her voice made him smile in the dark.

"No, not that. Just giving you a progress report like the one I send to Governor Trumbull, I guess. I think we have something good to build on."

"Oh, yes, I do, too!"

"Friends, maybe more. I always felt more about you, even from the first before things got so—confused."

"I, too!"

He took her hand from her knee, then decided to hold it on her knee. His hand settled down. Her shapely knees emanated warmth right through her skirt and fancy apron. When she shifted slightly, her skirts rustled and she smelled wonderful, as intoxicating as her roses. He leaned forward, breathing in her sweet scent. He hesitated.

Thea leaned forward, too. She felt suspended in a dream. Morgan's head tipped so he missed her nose. His lips touched hers, tentatively tasting, then with strong determination. She felt her lips soften against his. He slanted his head more to deepen the kiss. His free hand lifted to her elbow, to her shoulder, to her bare throat to caress her, light as the breeze.

And then, despite her wobbly knees, despite his desire to take this slowly, he stood and pulled her to her feet. Pressed together perfectly, they embraced. He kissed her even harder. It was wild; she felt so free. She sailed like ships on the sea. Her knees braced against his strong legs, which crinkled her gown flat between them. The big brass buttons of his waistcoat pressed against her belly and her breasts. Her arms wrapped around his strong neck; their breathing and their heartbeats and their tongues entwined. He tasted of the spearmint they had been chewing; he smelled like leather and outdoors and something tangy and undefinably precious up so close. They melded closer, closer, like the elixirs that swirled and seethed in her copper still inside. His big hands measured her waist. His warm, luring lips pulled just slightly back to whisper, "You don't need these stays and stomachers and padded things. You're beautiful just the way you are."

A breathy, little moan escaped her lips as he took them again. She wanted to thank him for everything. For the desire and power that seeped into her, staggering her with new heights of awareness. For his admiration, his companionship, his protection. But she only held to him to stop the hillside from spinning. To keep it from tilting them together into the river where they would surely drown in more of this until there was no coming back to sanity, ever!

"Thea, sweet—" he began, then clipped off the word. He sighed so heavily it slumped his big body for a moment. Regretfully, she could tell, he clasped her wrists and lowered their hands to make a little barrier between them. Her head still spun. She gloried in his closeness, his kiss, his caress. Yet she already bemoaned that he stepped back with only one brief peck on her nose. She sat her down on the bench by herself.

"Didn't mean to lose my head with one little kiss," he tried to apologize as he forced himself to gaze out at the winking, bobbing lanterns that marked the ships at berth below.

"Maybe it was more than one little kiss," she protested.

He turned back. "Yes, but I'm just not ready for it again, not with the war."

"Maybe it will go on forever," she replied petulantly. "Maybe we'll all be as old as Father Lockwood when it finally ends! And what do you mean by 'ready for it *again*'?"

"Nothing worth repeating right now. Listen, I'll stop by after I watch them drill the local militia across the river tomorrow, all right?"

"Of course."

She went to her back door as he started away. He knew he had ended things badly tonight, but that first kiss had rocked him to his bootsoles. And now that he was certain Rina had never told Thea about their betrothal, he should really tread carefully here. Besides, in September he'd be leaving again, for who knew how long. He was not going to leave a woman behind to wait for him again and possibly send him a note someday saying that she had upped and changed her mind. Nor was he prepared to take a wife!

A wife! The thought hit him hard as he strode down Water Street toward the room he rented beyond the lumberyard at Winthrop Cove. Old Moses Lockwood had invited him to stay at their house, but he'd made that mistake before. Thea Arnold—a wife. But he'd have to tell her about Rina, and things would never be so pure, so pristine, and smooth then. Hell, he'd been burned before, so he'd be careful now. Those you thought you could trust most, you sometimes couldn't trust at all. He had to try to keep his hands and mouth and thoughts off Thea Arnold, as he had to worry about more dangerous assaults than that.

He glanced down at the newest, big British prize that New

Londoner Captain Saltonstall had hauled back into port last week. It was the *Hannah,* a rich three-master merchant ship once bound from London to New York, now stripped of its goods, just waiting at the wharf to be outfitted for a privateer herself. The city had celebrated, but he—and Avery Payne, who of all the privateers seemed to have the coldest feet of late—had worried. Yes, he had a lot more to worry about than keeping his hands off Thea Arnold. The governor had sent him here to tell the local militia to be sure the British kept their hands off this danged entire area!

During the next two months, Morgan Glenn still called on Thea, but he seemed more busy and distracted than ever. Thea realized they both walked on eggshells with each other: there was tenseness between them like a string pulling them tighter together, and yet, Morgan seemed to fight it. At times she longed to push him over the edge of his restraint, to have more from him than the quick kisses he bestowed stingily to bid her farewell each time he left her. She longed for him desperately. From the way she caught him watching her, she was more than certain he wanted her, too. And yet he remained achingly polite and restrained until sometimes she thought she would scream. But, as deeply honest as she was, she resisted the desire to flirt or tempt him if he wasn't ready to trust her.

Still, she had decided to do one other thing she had been pondering all summer. She had worked herself up to showing him Charity Payne's desperate deathbed note. When Benedict Arnold had defected, she had told no one about the note. After the fact, no one would believe her, and it might tip Avery off about her theory he had murdered his poor wife.

But now, Morgan seemed to be trusting Avery too much. Morgan considered Avery prideful and pompous, but he did not realize how tricky he could be. Granted, it had been Avery who had twice sounded the two-gun alarm from Fort Trumbull when his vessels had spotted British ships near the mouth of the river. And it was Avery, Morgan had said, who was trying to hold down the number of British prizes lately to not further goad the British. But if Morgan deemed that proof of Avery's patriotism and good sense, she felt it her duty to inform Morgan of Avery's other side by sharing the note.

The day she decided to tell him the details, Thea and Morgan borrowed a rowboat from his landlord down by Winthrop Cove and rowed up the Thames in the lovely afternoon. Weeping willows trailed graceful fingers in the water where they stopped to eat. They waged a miniature war of fleets in which her ships were waxy, white-flowered herbs called Indian pipe, and his gaudy cardinal flowers. They shared biscuits with honey and even sweeter, hotter kisses that made her so dizzy she could hardly breathe.

Yes, she vowed, as they headed back, she would show him Charity's note at the shop. His time in New London was dwindling. With Washington and the French marching south to meet Cornwallis, Governor Trumbull believed the British in New York dared not venture north again to attack Connecticut's coasts. Too soon, Morgan would be recalled. Treasuring in her heart each moment they were together, Thea Arnold trailed her hand in New London's river and smiled shakily into Morgan's eyes as he rowed.

"But was Charity Payne on any sort of laudanum or opium for pain?" Morgan asked her later when he'd listened to her and read the note.

"She had no pain—well, only Avery," she murmured, half astounded at her feeble pun, but it was true!

He shook his head and frowned. "So he has no idea you have this nor entertain this theory he might have killed his wife."

"No. You do believe me, don't you?"

"Sh!" he comforted and sat beside her at the table to put a quick arm around her shoulders. "With the marks on her face from the pillow, it sounds very suspicious, but it isn't solid proof. You'd need to get him to confess. If he's a liar in that, perhaps his rabid concern about a British attack is somewhat suspect, too. But we can't put you in danger with him one way or the other."

She almost blurted out the rest to him then, about Avery's

attack on her, his attempts to bribe and coerce her since. But that would somehow ruin things between them. Would Morgan believe that she hadn't led Avery on? He'd seen she was eager every time Morgan had showed her the slightest affection. Besides, sometimes she had the strangest feeling there was someone from his past in Pennsylvania he wasn't telling her about, either.

"Thea, I'm glad you shared this. Without revealing what I know, I'm going to test Avery Payne somehow tomorrow. I'd best sleep on it tonight. And I can see why you didn't come forward with this when General Arnold defected."

She walked him to the back door that stood ajar to catch the crisp September air off the river. She was sorry their beautiful day had ended like this. She had to say something before he left her just standing here again.

"I will always treasure today, Morgan."

He took her hands in his. "I, too. The best ever."

"Really? Ever? Then there was no one to row boats with up your dear Tahicox Creek in Pennsylvania?"

"No one this special," he whispered. "No one like Evertt Edwards was to you."

"Evertt Edwards? Did General Arnold tell you that?"

His big hands tightened over hers. "No, I told him and suggested that he should write his condolences to you."

"But I was never betrothed to Evertt Edwards! He was a dear man who cared for me much more than I did him. Wherever did that idea come from?"

Rina! Morgan thought. Little pieces of a puzzle clicked into place in his mind. Rina had actually lied about Thea being taken by another man. And after she'd won his heart, she'd insisted on secrecy—though her later engagement to Cullen Varner was front-page New London gazette news! Rina Lockwood had taken him and used him and then tossed him away. Damn her! Now he had her to talk to, as well as Avery Payne tomorrow.

"Thea, I've got to go," he told her and dropped a quick kiss on her sweet slant of cheek. He felt a cur to leave her like this after the day they'd shared, but he could not explain his feelings right now. She had a winsome, honest way of wiling things from him he wasn't ready to share. And he kept fighting himself to not show her how much he desired her. He did not want to use her the way Rina had apparently used him. "I'll see you tomorrow, sometime early," he said. The words were true, but he had no idea how early.

Realizing that the day had glowed but the evening had been tarnished by Morgan's sudden departure, Thea labored over the brews in her copper still until she felt sleepy. She paraded today's scenes and words and kisses back and forth in her mind. Until Morgan returned again, Thea would cherish this day. Perhaps she should write down little things about it, as her mother always had, and press them in the pages of a book as well as in her mind.

When the sharp knock rattled the back door, her heart leaped. He had come back! It certainly was no customer for nighttime help from Thea Arnold! She dried her hands, hurried to the back door, and opened it.

She gasped and tried to slam the door! As if her worst worries had conjured him up, there stood Avery Payne. "What is it?" she demanded. "I told you I want no part of your offers for my so-called services."

He looked ruddy, his face aglow with excitement as he shoved the door to force it open. She retreated as far as the hearth and hoisted the heavy iron lid of a cook pot. "Put that down, damn you, Thea! I've only come to tell you that tonight's the night you crawl to me and beg me to do all I've been waiting for."

"Get out of here, Avery, or I'll scream."

He hooted a laugh. "Now, really, not that dire threat again. Who would come to rescue Benedict Arnold's little cousin?"

"You were partners with him, and I'd just tell—"

"And you think they'd believe you? Besides, it's all too late now. I just want you to know I've never forgotten how you tried to defy me, et cetera—put that damned lid down, Thea. I'm not going to touch you again, far from it. You're going to crawl to me and beg, I said. You're going to beg me to touch you anywhere and any way I want before I—"

"Get out of here, you vile bastard! Don't think I won't tell Morgan Glenn at least, and he'll believe me!"

"Morgan Glenn. Yes, I don't doubt you've spread your legs for him, but perhaps you won't be so stiff and virginal for me then, eh?"

She heaved the heavy lid at him but he sidestepped, and it thudded hard to the wood plank floor.

"I've a lot to do tonight before I have time for you, my little Arnold whore," his horrid voice went on. "And you don't really think a man like Morgan Glenn whose already ragged reputation is going to be in tatters by tomorrow really cares a fig for you, do you? I imagine he just saw someone he pitied, someone he knew would be very willing to turn tail for him because she was so lonely. Lonely and quite the outcast—to all but that spoiled little twit Rina Lockwood, and me. See you tomorrow and thereafter, my dear," he said and, with another demonically triumphant laugh, went out and slammed the back door. She rushed over to shoot the bolt and leaned against it, shaking, gasping as hard for air as his poor wife had once done.

Avery Payne joined the two men waiting for him down by the wharf. Jedediah Clapper was a lackey who seemed to value only money, which Avery supplied him with in abundance for his unquestioning loyalty. Levi Dobson, whom he had dead to rights on embezzlement if he ever stepped out of line, was another man he could use, though he had a hair-trigger temper.

"It's after eleven. Let's head out to meet them," Avery told Jed and Levi. They mounted horses and rode south out of town through Brown's Hill Gate toward the lighthouse, being careful to skirt the few defenders at Fort Trumbull in the dark.

"You both have your maps?" Avery asked as they approached the lighthouse that marked the entrance to the river. The men nodded and grunted. "Good." He had picked and molded these two from many possibilities in his privateering crews. He trusted them to obey him implicitly, simply because he had a firm hold over both. "Levi, you'll be rowed across to the Groton side to whatever British officer is leading the attack on Groton and Fort Griswold. Jed, you'll stick tight to General Arnold himself and make sure he orders only the buildings I have marked to be burned."

"Sure, sure. But, you know, it blisters even me to have to work with that one."

"Just shut your trap and there will be handsome rewards, et cetera, for you when everyone else is burned out and we only seem to be. The one warehouse of mine they'll burn and that derelict ship are as good as empty. And I'll be conveniently away from my mansion and they'll only torch my carriage house. You be sure that's exactly what happens, Jed!"

"And Mistress Arnold's shop?" Jed asked and hunched his shoulders farther forward as if he would spring over his horse's neck. "I can't read this damned list in the dark. What's the final say-so on her place?"

"It's to go up in flames. Arnold's agreed, he thinks so she won't be singled out as having made a deal with him. But, as far as I'm concerned, it's so she'll be destitute. And with her protector Moses Lockwood's warehouses and mansion turned to ashes, I'll have her at last," he muttered, more to himself than them.

Years of work were culminating in this night that would turn this whole area to a firelands, Avery Payne thought, and he would be there to help rebuild it. At least he had been farsighted enough to get on the Brits' good side while he played his trump cards here in town. So, whichever way the war went, the best of everything—and Thea Arnold humbled at last—would be at his feet. He just hoped things got off to a good start when Fort Trumbull finally spotted danger and shot off two warning cannon. He'd told the Brits to answer with the third shot, which signaled a celebration. That would cause confusion, and delay that wretched neighborhood militia from falling out.

He laughed aloud at the whispered notion that Arnold's favoritism of New Londoners had made the enemy spare their town while others burned. Damnation, he and Benedict Arnold had not been silent partners only for Arnold's profit in the privateering trade! The British owed him as much as they did Arnold's Tory wife for talking the man into defecting! He congratulated himself smugly and spurred his horse to a gallop to meet the incoming British fleet and their commander. The Judas of the Revolution, Benedict Arnold, was coming home to take care of his favorite town of New London, all right!

Chapter Eight

"Never get too near the flame of the copper still or the heating crucible. Dry suspended herbs away from fire, or what was meant to heal your suffering customers will make you suffer, too!"

MORGAN GLENN SLEPT fitfully, and the lovely dream began again. He was taking Thea home to the farm as his bride in their big red and blue Conestoga wagon, with its proud sweep of canvas shading them like a full set of sails. His family, Father, too, waved to welcome them. They rolled on through golden fields of ripening, swaying grain along the creek. But then, from all sides came the charge of Gen. Benedict Arnold's men, back and forth, daring the British to fire. Cullen Varner was there, chasing General Arnold, shouting that Rina was his. Morgan stood in the tall driver's seat of the painted wagon. Thea tried to grab his arm to hold him back. But Morgan had to take one of the new horses from his team; he had to ride back to war and leave her here in the churning, dangerous sea of men and guns and . . .

Morgan sat bolt upright, wet with sweat. What had awakened him? Just the dream? A distant cannon? Yes, a second shot. The warning attack from Fort Trumbull as if his dream had been prophetic!

He was into his stockings, breeches, and boots when the third, more distant gun boomed. Three shots? What in blazes was going on? The town would panic, he thought, as he jammed his shirt in, grabbed the rest of his uniform and weapons, and dashed out the door.

He cursed the time it took him to saddle and bridle his horse, but he was thundering down Water Street in ten min-

utes. It was pitch black, one or two of the morning, he esti-
mated. In the confusion of those guns, he wondered if this
were the long-dreaded attack—or only a dream.

Around him, all was chaos. Crowds in nightclothes,
mostly women and children, thronged the streets. They
carted what precious possessions they could carry in pillow-
cases or stockings. Infants wailed. Panicked dogs barked and
skittered away from his horse's flying feet. An occasional cart
with household goods rumbled by; one woman rode along
perched on her feather mattress atop a horse. He had to pick
his way slower now. And then he saw Thea.

She was hastily gowned and her glorious hair flowed wild
and free in the flare of occasional torchlight. "Thea!" he
yelled and rode to her. "Thea!"

"Everyone's going to the hills!" she shouted up at him, her
hand grasping his boot toe as if for comfort. "Someone from
Fort Trumbull just rode through to say there's a fleet of ships
off the river!"

"The wind's to the north, thank God! Big ships won't get
up the river. They'll have to march—"

A brash boom-ba-boom began, making his horse rear and
the crowd stop and turn to listen. Thea darted back until he
quieted his mount. It sounded like a heavy, deep, distant bar-
rage from at least five warships, he judged, so there must be
a couple thousand soldiers coming ashore. "They're here en
masse, that's for certain." He leaned down to tell Thea. "I'm
going to try to assemble some militia to stop them if they get
past the fort. Clear out with the others, and take what you
can!" he shouted before he spurred his horse on again.

Farther up the street, he stopped a lanky boy who seemed
to be alone. He leaned down to shout at him, "Go back along
the wharf and yell at the captains or any sailors aboard to
loose their vessels and flee up the river! If the lobsterbacks
get in town, they'll burn the anchored ships, too."

"Too, sir? You mean they really gonna burn this town!"
the boy gawked up at him, but then he ran in the direction
Morgan pointed.

Morgan rode on through swarming, shouting crowds. If
he could somehow discover who the attacking commander

was—General Clinton or Royal Governor Tryon—it might tell him something about their strategy here. So many things he'd like to do: take Thea out to one of the surrounding hills where she'd be safe; help these wandering children and women along; make sure old, crippled Moses Lockwood was safe. Despite the fact the local militia had told him they would handle any crisis in their own way, he would fight alongside the stubborn New Londoners to the death to protect their town.

When he reached the vicinity of Fort Trumbull, he was appalled to hear from fleeing citizens that it had already fallen. "Yep." An old man running with two muskets in his arms stopped momentarily to speak to him. "Captain Shapely fired one good volley at them British bastards and retreated real quick to Fort Griswold 'cross the river to fight from there. Redcoats thick as hornets on the other side a' the river, too."

"Damn! We need help to delay them here until more of the neighborhood militia gets in! Any word who commands the Brits?" he asked, but the man jogged on toward town.

Morgan spurred his mount north around Shaw's Cove, past the magazine where he had delivered powder and shot that first day. Some of it had been distributed; some was still stored there. Every time he spotted men or big boys as he galloped along, he shouted, "We're going to make a stand to delay them! We're going to make a stand on Manwaring's Hill!" Soon some men, a few of good fighting age, joined him there. They primed and loaded the single cannon on the hill. Morgan positioned men with muskets behind trees and stone fences along the route the incoming horde would have to take. It was the same desperate way the Americans had been forced to fight British might since those first days at Lexington and Concord.

He rode from house to house along the streets between the hill and the enemy, shouting to people to get out or take cover. Dawn tinged the sky as they heard the tread of troops. And then, for the first time in months, Lt. Col. Morgan Glenn saw the crimson-colored coats and pristine white and gleaming metal of the matched ranks of hundreds of British soldiers. And just behind came their green-coated German mercenaries, marching in noisy precision.

"Damn them all to hell," he gritted out through clenched teeth. "A huge force, and the Hessians, too! We're doomed, but it doesn't mean they're not gonna pay for it first!"

The big old gun on the hill boomed out its smoky welcome to the enemy, blowing the front line apart. Rebel guns crackled to pick off others. The British and German ranks bent, filled, and came on again.

Morgan ducked from fence to house to tree with his hastily assembled force as the British took the cannon on the hill and set Manwaring's house afire. "Retreat, reload, shoot!" he encouraged the rebels time after time. Already, somewhere along the Colchester Road outside of town, smoke smeared the sky. Here, the British swarmed up Blackhall Street, evidently heading for the higher hills overlooking the town. From there they could wreak devastation with their own cannon or several they had captured. A clever plan, a perfect way to oversee both the shooting and the burning, Morgan admitted grudgingly, as he cut one street over to parallel the enemy's march. But then, of course, they might have captured some locals or even have Tory informers from the area to advise them.

As Morgan reloaded his musket and both pistols and peered at the enemy from behind a lilac thicket on a private lawn on Hempstead Street, he saw the cluster of British officers. And there, holding a spy glass and pointing to the burying ground hill they evidently intended to occupy just beyond the meeting house, rode the unmistakably short but imposing figure of Benedict Arnold!

Morgan gaped, then swore. Tears stung his eyes at the perfidy, the ultimate, final betrayal by the man he had once admired. He would betray and burn his own town, the place that had honored him—only yesterday, it seemed—with a fine parade of American soldiers!

"I'll have your head or die trying, bastard—sir!" Morgan ground out. He untied his horse and, on foot, led him by the reins to find a spot from which to shoot.

*   *   *

When Morgan Glenn thundered off toward Fort Trumbull, Thea found a spot for Widow Middleton in an evacuating neighbor's wagon. At least their distrust and dislike of the Arnold name did not extend to the old woman, Thea thought gratefully. She ran back inside her shop and carted out a few things to hide in the root cellar dug there. If the British dared to burn the entire town, they would not get everything she owned. Besides, she had been threatened by several townfolk that she deserved to be burned out when General Arnold was burning tobacco fields in Virginia, so who knew what a few vindictive elements in the town would do when given the chance.

In the dark she dumped things on top of her roots and slammed the cellar door. A few mementos of her parents, the precious pharmacopoeia her mother had written in, her scales, mortar and pestle, the little tin flag Morgan had given her so long ago would now be safe. The expensive copper still was too heavy for her to lift. Drat this war and General Arnold who had made things so bad for her and New London! Years ago he'd tried to save Danbury from such an attack, but he could just go to the devil now! He evidently hadn't been able to talk the British out of a raid here on what was as good as his hometown!

She wished she had a musket and knew how to shoot. She took some food, a bottle of drinking water, and a ball of bandages she'd been rolling for Rina's donations. First, she was going down to Bank Street to make sure Rina and Father Lockwood were safe. But as she hurried out, she saw two lagging, lost children she did not recognize. She decided she must take them up to safety in the hills. At least these little New Londoners held to her gladly. In their terror, they did not know or care that her name was Arnold.

Thea arrived out of breath to hide the children in the bushes on the hill just below the graveyard. A woman there with a brood of wailing youngsters spat at her, "Happy at what your Arnold kin done this time?"

Exhausted and bereft, Thea spun on her. "I am not my cousin's keeper! Leave me alone and just pray they'll spare the city if they've come to burn the privateering ships and warehouses!"

"Pray! With Satan hisself here?" the woman hissed and pointed up at the cluster of distant red uniforms on the edge of the burying ground hill.

"Satan himself? Here?" Thea echoed as she put down the small clinging girl she'd been carrying. She straightened and shaded her eyes. "Dear God in Heaven," she prayed aloud as her sharp eyes took in the short, stocky man among the others, the one pointing with a spy glass across the river at Fort Griswold and the fleeing privateering ships in the river. A cannon the British had positioned on the hill boomed, belching black smoke, but that did not obscure her view of the man she knew all too well. "No, no!" Thea tried to deny the awful truth. But there, in broad morning sunlight, gloating over the city he had come to burn, was Cousin Benedict.

"Damn!" British General Benedict Arnold clipped out. "You might know the wind would shift now to let those vessels get upriver when we couldn't sail in earlier! And Fort Griswold's been much built up since I've seen it."

"Mr. Payne told you, sir," Jed Clapper put in at his elbow, "how much trouble that Glenn fellow's been, rousing folks to action 'round here."

Arnold pressed his lips together and nodded grimly. "Perhaps I trained him all too well," he said. He beat down a sharp stab of regret for all that was now lost to him: Morgan, Thea, New London. But, damn them, congress and Gates and Washington had driven him to it! He gazed once more around the pretty hillside cemetery and at the town below still cloaked in the summer greenery of early September.

"Send a message to Captain Eyre across the river not to bother taking Fort Griswold unless the rebels capitulate," he ordered. "But have them burn Groton to its foundations. And now, men, lift your firebrands here to do your duty against this rebel town! I'll indicate which buildings go as we ride. We'll meet the other half of our forces coming along Bank Street and have this privateering nest in ashes by sunset! On then! Follow me!"

*   *   *

Morgan Glenn heard the cheer rip from British throats as the men crowded around his former commander and they moved off down the hill. Dang! He had crawled on his belly up along the stone fence around the cemetery and, just when he had a bead on their commander, they'd surrounded Arnold and rode off! Exhausted and filthy, he lay with his face to the mossy turf a moment, cursing Arnold, cursing the war. And he soundly cursed himself for being just a minute too slow no matter what they would have done to him.

Arnold had once spared the life of a man who had shot the horse beneath him in the battle at Freeman's Farm. But there would be no reprieve for Morgan Glenn from the British, especially after he executed their prime political prize, Benedict Arnold. Thinking of his own death at the hands of the British, Morgan pictured Thea's face, smiling at him yesterday when they had rowed together up the river, now jammed with fleeing ships. When they had strolled through the peaceful town out to her herb gardens. That first time she had greeted him behind her shop, the day General Arnold came here as a welcomed, instead of cursed, conqueror. Slowly, Morgan rose to a crouch and skidded down through the thick underbrush to where he'd tied his horse. He mounted and circled far around until he could get a clean shot at the enemy commander.

When the marauders came along Bank Street burning houses, Rina Lockwood went out on the front portico to face them down. She was afraid, but even more determined to save her home and her father upstairs. He had cursed and swung his arms at her and Cassie when they'd tried to put him in his wheelchair to get him downstairs in case the worst occurred. So they'd reluctantly left him where he was for now. The carriage driver Silas was ready to help them carry the master down in his chair, but the old butler Joshua had taken a musket and foolishly tried to halt the British down the street—and never returned. Rina had sent the Lockwood maids and cooks up to the hills with many others.

She gripped her hands tightly together until she felt her

fingers go numb. House after house down the way began to glow orange with flames, then black with belching smoke. It looked to her as if they went in to burn Avery Payne's—surely they would target the privateers' homes—but when they emerged, she saw smoke only from the carriage house out back. Perhaps if they spared a privateer's home, they might also spare her father's house.

She walked down the flagstone path to the street to block their way in. Four men held torches, and their faces were sootsmudged. "Please, sir," she asked the soldier who seemed to be in charge, "I've an old, sick father inside who ought to have the right to die in his own bed. He's been ill for years and confined to a wheelchair with the gout. And I assure you I've done naught but knit a few socks and wind a few bandages. I am asking yōu to spare our house."

To her relief, the officer doffed his bicorn, and his eyes went over her. She breathed a little easier. She'd seen that look of appreciation from men often before.

"This is the house, sir," an aide behind the officer told him. "You remember, where there was that reception the commander told us about."

"Then, mistress, I am to inform you, your house will be spared if you will but offer General Arnold another reception on his way out of town. The choice, he says, is yours, so—"

"General Arnold!" her voice rose. "He's—he's here with you? That traitor Arnold?"

"Arnold!" was repeated from the upstairs window. Rina gasped and spun around just as the British men bearing torches gazed up. Somehow, Moses Lockwood had managed to get out of bed and drag himself to the window. He hung halfway out, shaking a thin fist, though the gesture wracked his body. And he was shouting things Rina wanted to gag him for!

"If that foul, deceitful, son of a bitch Arnold has dared return at the head of this ruinous, hell-bent, whoreson rabble, burn the place, you bastards! I'll have it burned before I'd ever offer him a mouthful of river water! Tell the turncoat he isn't worthy of this city, his cousin, his nation! Deserted us all, so let him go roast in hell with the rest of you fiends, and—"

"Father!" Rina shrieked upward, then turned back to the astounded officer. "Please, he's out of his head, that's all!" she shouted to drown out the tirade from above. The officers yelled up at the frenzied old man as if they, too, would shout him down, but then the other voice boomed out above all.

"Two of you go up and drag the rebel Moses Lockwood down," Benedict Arnold bellowed from his horse. "He can watch this place burn from the street with his daughter."

Everyone swung around to stare at General Arnold. Rina spit at him, but only got his boots and breeches as a soldier dragged her back and two others ran into the house. She screamed, begged, she wasn't sure for what, but Arnold kept his face impassive. He was recalling that other day he'd come in welcome triumph here. The thought of what he'd come to do today twisted in his gut. But he had his beautiful young wife and two infant sons and a new British reputation to protect now. And the more devastating this raid on New London, the more his praise would surely resound in British ears and in old London, where he would eventually go to live.

He glanced down the street at the burning houses. He had intended to overrule Avery Payne and leave the Lockwood house standing, so Avery's wouldn't be the only one left along here. But the old man had defied and insulted him. He had to take a strong stand before these British. He was fed up with being publicly reprimanded by Gates, by Washington, and now this old Lockwood codger who could have had his house for just one little gesture, one little glass of port or Madeira. But now Avery Payne's spirit of revenge on this house would be satisfied as they burned it, and they would leave one or two other homes standing down the street instead.

"Your father will be right down, Mistress Lockwood. I hear you are to wed my old aide Cullen Varner. He deserted me for General Gates, you know, so you might ask him a thing or two about betrayals. Torch the place," he ordered gruffly. His voice caught in his throat when she shrieked. "Now!"

He turned and rode off to check the burning of the central city. Behind him at Lockwood House, his soldiers ran inside with firebrands. Soon Rina saw the draperies at the windows flare. Even the upstairs rooms glowed crimson. "Father!" she screamed. "Father!"

"They no doubt carried him out in back," the officer said and finally ordered her released. The soldiers moved away as she tore around behind the seething, glowing house.

But there was no one in the backyard. She ran in front again. The two soldiers sent to bring him out were there, coughing, bent over. She grabbed the first man's arm to spin him around. "Where is he? Where is he?"

"Wouldn't come. Had a gun and said he'd shoot us. Said he'd die there with that woman's painting—"

Rina screamed and tried to run into the house. The downstairs belched blasts of yellow-orange heat, driving her back. The inferno roared and crackled at her. "Father! Father! They said they'd bring you out! Father!"

She tore around to the back again, but a neighbor woman halted her and embraced her. "Too late, Mistress Rina! You can't go in there now!"

"They can't! They can't. Father!" she pulled away and shrieked so loud the woman tried to cover her ears. Others ran around into the back gardens of the burning house, where they could only stand helpless and stare.

Shaking with rage and indignation, Thea left the shelter of the hill where women and children huddled. On foot, she stalked Benedict Arnold and his mounted, firebrand-toting cohorts. Arnold and his officers rode toward town through Richards Street, then went off at a quicker clip toward the south end. She felt furious he had eluded her. She wondered if he might have gone down Bank Street and decided she should head over to see if the Lockwoods were all right. But on her way, she heard General Arnold had ridden back toward the central part of town, and she started off to locate him again.

When she spotted his vanguard, she hurried along in a daze, keeping his distant cluster of officers in sight. She ran through back lots of houses, out of breath, a stitch slicing her side. She had to try to stop him. Plead, beg, lecture him, entreat him—something. If not, she would find a gun. She must get closer to those fiends in case she could get her hands on a loaded gun!

She ran faster when she realized Arnold's men were setting fires on both sides of town. They were not just going to burn the warehouses and privateers' homes. The town mill, the print office, houses out on Winthrop's Neck spewed telltale black smoke. Her stomach churned when she realized Arnold's obscene calling card also stained the sky near where Rina lived.

When she saw Arnold and his men enter Main Street itself, she ran beside the ranks of redcoated soldiers, her eyes always up ahead on the mounted officers. They wreaked fiery havoc on the fine old family homes here as they passed through. She gasped at flames chewing up the beautiful Saltonstall house, and prayed Lockwood House was safe. If they were burning homes of community leaders, she had to go help Rina. She did not trust Benedict Arnold to spare Lockwood House just because its owners had once played host to him! But she had to stop Gen. Arnold here first, before he went a step farther!

At the corner of Shapely and Main, screaming his name, Thea ran into the ranks to reach the general. Soldiers shoved her back. As the British torched the Customs House, one of Arnold's officers rode over to her through the milling troops. The words scraped her throat raw, but she said them: "General Arnold is my cousin. I need to talk to him!"

The officer dismounted and escorted her to the general's side before the devastating troops rode on. Trembling with fury that overcame her fear, she glared up at Gen. Arnold. Her fists clenched; her face, streaked with soot, sweat, and tears, tilted up to gaze at him. The afternoon sun made a ragged aureole around his head. He swept his cockaded British bicorn off and gazed down solemnly at her, wondering what she would dare after that tirade he had just suffered from her little Lockwood friend on the other side of town.

"Thea! Get up in the hills with the other women!"

"They hate me because of what you've done! And why should I flee while you burn this town? Some Arnold has got to stand up for it since you don't anymore!"

He sidestepped his big black horse closer to her. He leaned down, an elbow to his thigh, and lowered his voice. "You don't understand how things were, how I wasn't hearkened to or admired."

"So you defected! Everyone hearkens to and admires traitors, of course!" She could not stem her tirade of bitter sarcasm. "You little, little man! No wonder you always have to sit if others stand, to mount the steps above them even. Your morals are as tiny as your stature, you vile, wretched betrayer, and you little, little man!"

She saw with mingled elation and agony how her words pierced him. The flaccid jaw set hard; the narrowed eyes snapped fire. "I was going to burn your shop out," he told her quietly, "so the townfolk would realize you were not in collusion with me—to protect you. But now, I believe we'll spare the Arnold shop," he hissed, "to let them wonder what you pranced out here to tell me in our little reunion." Then he bellowed so that everyone would hear, "Get my dear cousin out of harm's way and, for all she's helped me, don't let one spark touch her shop!"

"No, no, you vile, foul—" she screamed as hard hands hauled her off. Now New Londoners would think she had only pleaded for her shop to be saved! Now perhaps they would believe she had actually supplied him with information for this raid! Now everything would be so much worse.

"Do your duty along the entire waterfront, men!" her cousin shouted as her two soldier-captors dragged her back up Shapely Street and shoved her in the direction of the hills. Stunned, she fell to her knees amidst the acrid smell of smoke and the roar of spreading flames. She put her face in her hands and sobbed until her tears smeared to gray in her filthy palms. Rina, she thought dazedly. She had meant to get to Rina since this morning. She had to go to Rina.

And then she heard the galloping horse and looked up to see if the soldiers were returning. But it was Morgan! Morgan!

She stood as he reined in. "I talked to him. I tried—"

"I saw," he clipped out. "And just as I got a good drop on him from an upstairs window. But then, he bent down amidst his mounted men to talk to you, and I couldn't shoot him with you there, even when he sat up again. The British might have thought you set it up—decoyed him to stop—and I couldn't risk that. Then he rode off and it was too late—for all of us," the broken thoughts tumbled from him.

She explained how Benedict Arnold had made it look as if she had begged him to spare her shop, and maybe fed him information, too. Morgan nodded grimly as he listened. His uniform and skin were black with dirt and smoke. Sweat ran tracks down his gray skin. But he had come to her! No one had ever looked more wonderful to her! "Too late for so much," she concluded as he reached down to haul her up behind him on his horse. "If he'd captured you, Morgan, no telling what he would have done," she tried to comfort him. "You tried. We both tried, and it wasn't enough. Now, I've got to get to Lockwoods'. Where are you going?"

"There's no stopping the burning here in the central town. I'll take you there and hope it's not too bad—" he got out before a huge series of earth-shaking blasts slapped the sky. "The powder magazine at Shaw's Cove!" he told her as he quieted his shaken mount and spurred it to a gallop with Thea hanging on behind. "That means they're already burning both ways along the waterfront. They may have reached Rina's already. Hold on!"

As they rode toward the south end of town to Lockwoods', they could see flames creeping across the waterfront from both directions. Warehouses, piles of lumber, rigging, and vessels became black clouds in the sky.

"Look," she said and held tighter around his waist, "they're even burning all the public buildings around the parade—the church, too!"

When they rode past the warehouses beyond the parade, the stench and sights panicked the horse; it balked and nearly threw them. The British had smashed hogsheads of molasses, sugar, coffee, and Madeira, and had lit the piles to bubbling, smelly puddles in the cobbled street. Melted butter ran in the gutters. Beyond, two anchored ships that had not gotten away flamed heavenward, like torches floating off to watery river graves. As they emerged from the stinking inferno to ride up Bank Street, shops, spars, and shipyards behind them soared to incandescent sky-bound hues amidst choking smoke.

They gasped when they saw the destruction awaiting them here. Morgan spurred the horse faster. "No. No!" Thea cried when she saw the seething skeletal facade of Lockwood House, all blackened wood and ashes and tumbled granite. "Father Lockwood! Rina!"

Only three houses stood along the street of mansions, and one was Avery Payne's. Morgan helped her down, and she darted up the path, screaming Rina's name with him right behind her. "Here, back here," a neighbor woman called and gestured from behind the house.

Thea ran into the backyard, past the first row of clipped hedges, singed by the heat still pulsing from the glowing shell of the house. Rina, with four other women, including Cassie and Susan, sat on two benches they had pulled together, slumped over, heads down, as if in prayer. Cassie jumped up. "Thea! They came and burned the house with Mr. Lockwood in it!"

Rina's tragic gaze locked with Thea's shocked stare. "You weren't here," Rina accused. She looked blanched, stricken. Her eyes didn't really focus; it was as if she looked through Thea. "Benedict Arnold came here and told them to burn it. You could have stopped him."

"I tried uptown. I couldn't even—"

"Did he burn your shop?"

"No, but he only did it so—"

"They killed him, Thea!" Rina cried and embraced Thea so hard she couldn't breathe. "Father cursed them and wouldn't leave his room. Wouldn't leave Mother! If you had been here, you could have saved him, but your parents couldn't save Mother, either!"

Thea gazed wide-eyed at Morgan over Rina's head. Rina's arms held her tight, but her words were loaded with blame.

"It's like some men when they get battle frights, Thea,"

Morgan told her and stepped closer to embrace both women. "They don't know what they're saying. They strike out at everyone!" Though it had only been this morning, it seemed ages ago that he had decided to find Avery Payne and Rina because he had bones to pick with both of them. But then this wanton, massive destruction had overshadowed both those things. He pitied Rina, pitied Thea—pitied all of them, himself included. Next to Rina's possible lies and Avery Payne's trickeries, this devastation and the war still awaiting him loomed so large. Morgan Glenn vowed to himself then, that somehow, he would find a way to compensate these firelands sufferers for what that ultimate betrayer and traitor Benedict Arnold had done to them.

Morgan left the women in the garden and rode out to help harass the British when they finally retreated. But it was then he heard news more dreadful than anything he'd encountered. At first the Americans holding Fort Griswold across the river had put up a heroic fight and refused to surrender to the overwhelming British might. Though some claimed Commander Arnold had sent an order across the river to the British not to take the fort, they had somehow done it, anyway. Enraged by the defiant rebel stand and the punishment their ranks had taken after they had so kindly offered to let the rebels "submit to their mercy," the British had staged a horrid massacre in retaliation. Sixty Groton men and twelve New Londoners, three-fourths killed after the Americans finally had surrendered, had been bayoneted to death.

Things had not been quite so bloody on this side of the placid River Thames. On the New London side, the dead numbered six British and six Americans. Morgan surmised the lack of organization here, which he had tried unsuccessfully all summer to strengthen, really was a blessing in disguise. For, looking at the Fort Griswold catastrophe, who knew what the slaughter would have been if New Londoners had defied the British and the Hessians. Besides the half a dozen lives including Moses Lockwood and his old butler Joshua, the toll was sixty-five houses, thirty-one stores, twenty barns, nine public buildings, and twelve ships burned. And hundreds homeless and newly destitute.

The morning of September eighth, when the British finally withdrew, gawkers from neighboring towns and counties began to arrive on the streets of New London. Weary of being pointed out—not as the man who had helped fight back, but as the man who had once fought with General Arnold— Morgan stood in the Lockwoods' gardens to let his horse crop grass. Here, in happier, foolish times, he had kissed poor Rina Lockwood when her father and the neighbors could not see them. Today, he watched those neighbors carry out the charred, blanketed remains of Moses Lockwood. Morgan stood, as if at parade attention, but he could not stop himself from glancing down at Governor Trumbull's orders in his hands that one of the governor's aides had just delivered to him.

"I am sending the Lebanon militia to help clean up the town and bury the dead in New London. But I need you back posthaste to report to me, then on to General Washington who will also want to know first hand what happened. He had never given up hope of capturing or killing that Judas, and this will make it worse when he hears . . ."

Morgan clenched his teeth together to keep from crying. He had had that Judas at the end of his musket barrel twice and lost his chance to shoot. The last time, he had hesitated to save Thea when he should have sacrificed her safety, just as he was willing to sacrifice his own. He hated to leave New London now, as if he was running, as if he had something to hide. He could not bear to leave Thea alone with Rina. Rina was so on edge, she blamed Thea for not coming on time and resented the fact that the British had spared Thea's apothecary shop. Rina even refused to stay at the shop. He heaved a huge sigh and walked up behind Thea and Rina to tell them he must go.

The next morning, a merchant donated a wooden box that had once held imported china. It was used as a coffin for Father Lockwood, and they took him in his own carriage to the Ye Olde Ancientest Burying Ground and interred him next to his Samantha. During the final prayer over the open grave, Thea kept staring at the distant site where her family's stones had been, then her eyes drifted to the spot where Benedict Arnold had paused to oversee the ravaging and burning of the town. She put her arms around both Rina and Cassie as they left the new grave behind. Cassie did not hum for once; Rina still shook. She had lost the Lockwood warehouses and most of the furniture factory, as well as the house. Rina, once an heiress, owned the clothes on her back, some land, three carriages, four horses, and whatever Father Lockwood had invested that would come out in his will. Like her fiancé Cullen Varner's home, Thea thought, Rina's rich heritage has gone up in the flames of war.

At the carriage, Jemmy Smith, who had been one of Thea's shop boys, stopped her, hat in hands. "Thought you oughta know, Mistress Arnold, a crowd's gonna burn your shop, 'cause the general left it just for you, they said."

Thea's insides cartwheeled. Her first impulse was to charge down the hill and try to save all she'd worked for and inherited and loved. But the shop was not a living thing any more than the tombstones had been. Even if she lost the shop, it could not compare to Rina's loss of Father Lockwood. No, she thought calmly through her panic and pain, even if they burned her mother's book and notes to her, which were still hidden in the root cellar, it did not mean they were burning her past. She would always have her parents' love inside her, always have the shop, perfect and intact in her mind. She would always have the beautiful memories of her days with Morgan, though he had departed when Governor Trumbull had called him back to fight the war elsewhere. And if she never saw him again, nor got to tell him how much she really loved him, she would have him yet pressed perfectly in the pages of the woman's heart he had awakened in her.

And, maybe, just maybe, if the crowd burned her shop, Thea thought dazedly, she could be one of them, as if that burning could purge her assumed guilt and their bitter hate. None of this was fair, but then nothing had seemed fair for such a long time.

She stood stock-still, while everyone held their breath for

her reaction, staring up at her, lost in thought. "Good-bye, my dearest friend and ally Morgan," she had said to him just yesterday in the Lockwood gardens before he had ridden back to Lebanon. "I hope you will come back when things are over. I—things will never be over for us. I hope you know what I mean."

He had kissed both her hands and then, briefly, sadly, her lips. That touch, a quick caress, was over so soon. "I do know what you mean," he had whispered. "I will not forget, either—"

In those words she remembered now, it was as if she was saying farewell to her dear shop down the hill, to all the people she had helped in New London before the war, before Cousin Benedict had ruined everything. It was as if she bid farewell to Father Lockwood, who had been so dear, who had trusted and helped her to become the person she was. And if Rina never forgave her for not coming sooner the other day, if Rina kept repeating that Thea's parents could have saved her mother years ago, perhaps it was a sort of farewell to Rina's friendship, too.

Tears tracked down Thea's face. At last she moved to help Rina up into the carriage.

"Mistress, din't you hear me?" the boy repeated. "The crowd's down there aburning your shop!"

"I heard you, Jemmy. Go on down and tell them I hope it also burns away their hate against me."

She helped Cassie up into the carriage, and then climbed in herself. And when Rina's arms circled her shoulders and she whispered brokenly, "I'm sorry, dear Thea. We'll get through this together, somehow!" sobs finally swamped Thea, too. If losing the shop assured her of Rina's friendship, it almost made suffering through these firelands worthwhile.

Chapter Nine

"The dandelion has many valuable uses, tho' 'tis hardly so pretty as other herbal flowers. Dug in its youth, when its leaves are a red-gold tangle, the whole plant is medicinal. In summer, the root must be peeled to show its inner wonders. If it completely matures, it construes a much stronger drink for those in need. 'Tis then we realize that through its strength comes its real beauty."

MORGAN GLENN OFTEN thought of Thea Arnold. Even here in Governor Trumbull's office in Lebanon, Connecticut, where he and several other men had been summoned for a meeting, he thought of Thea Arnold. During the long march south and the battle for Yorktown in Virginia, he worried about her and wrote her when he could. During the twenty-two months back on Washington's staff, those nights sleeping in a small officer's tent up and down the colonies he had fought to free, his dreams had been haunted by Thea, red-gold haired, beautiful and strong. Brought together first by Gen. Arnold in their youth, then by common pain and persecution, they had somehow grown, even when apart, like some of her sturdy herbs, mentally and emotionally tangled. Besides those inner wonders, all they needed now was the fruition of physical union he longed for. Was that enough for forever? Soon, very soon, he intended to find out by staking his future on it.

He had tried to convey all that to her, reasonably and calmly, in his letters. But he could tell in the six epistles he received from her that some of their correspondence on both sides had not gotten through in the unreliable military postal system that had to chase a man all over with enemy lines between. He knew she was safe and living with Rina in some woman's New London house since the wretches of that town had burned her shop. He'd asked every eastern Connecticut soldier who'd been home on leave about her. Dang, here he sat in an old storefront that served as Governor Trumbull's war office for an important, if mysterious, meeting, and he was still struggling to pay attention. He snapped out of his longings for Thea Arnold and forced himself to listen.

"I shall get started in just a moment, gentlemen," Governor Trumbull informed the four of them. "One more man is yet to arrive to hear this momentous news."

"Not sure what could be more momentous than when I heard Parliament finally voted these colonies are now free and independent states," Capt. Paul Asbury of Norwalk, Connecticut, said. "Now, if they'll only get around to signing a treaty and recalling their blasted Brit army away from their final toehold in New York City, maybe we'll believe them!"

"It's finally going to happen," Stephen Muncey from Fairfield, Connecticut, put in with shining eyes. "And now our task is to somehow rebuild this 'free and independent state' the bastards burned!"

"Exactly," Governor Trumbull agreed as he leaned on gnarled fists over his big, worn desk. "And that's why we're here today, key Connecticuters from the major devastated cities—and Colonel Glenn."

All eyes turned to him, the Pennsylvanian. The man who had served Benedict Arnold assiduously. The man who had been in New London when the British torched it. The man, it was whispered, who had courted the traitor's cousin, the tall, red-haired apothecary they had all heard tell of. And, just at that moment when Morgan, too, wondered what he was doing here, the last man they were awaiting came in the door.

"Ah, gentlemen," the governor said hastily to break the awkward silence, "I believe you all know Cullen Varner of Danbury, whose fine home and rich heritage was one of the first burned out—and, may I add with profound sadness, whose future father-in-law, the esteemed Moses Lockwood, was burned to death by the fireland fiends under the traitor in New London."

Everyone stood to greet Cullen. Two men saluted. Morgan thought Cullen accepted their greetings as if he were a con-

quering hero instead of an officer who had cast his lot with
a general who had also gone bad, if not in the dramatic way
Arnold had. Cullen's eyes met Morgan's at last. Cullen
looked most annoyed to see him.

"Cullen. It's been a long time," Morgan said and thrust
out his hand.

"Lieutenant Colonel Glenn," Cullen clipped out as if to
say, "not long enough." Cullen sat stiffly without deigning
to shake hands. Morgan frowned, cleared his throat, and sat,
too. Cullen's noble face looked fallen and slightly unbalanced
by the missing earlobe; yet something fierce burned deep and
dark in those narrowed, blue eyes.

At least Morgan was relieved to note that he felt no more
resentment toward Cullen for stealing away Rina or for his
lofty snubbing of him. He was quits with the man and that
was that, he assured himself. If he wooed and won Thea, he'd
never have to see this pompous prig again, even if Thea had
to say farewell to Rina and move to Pennsylvania. Still, there
was something in him that grieved for Thea and Rina's separation and made him want to reach out to Cullen Varner,
for the old, bold days with General Arnold they'd once
shared.

"Now, let me get right down to it about why you particular
men are here," the governor announced in sonorous tones.
"I know most of you are still under orders, but if you accept
my revolutionary—I use that word with pride—challenge,
you will be out of uniform this spring and off to a new and
great task to save this state's people once again. But let me
explain . . ."

Explain he did while they sat, stunned. Thousands of Connecticuters who had been burned out of their homes and live-
lihoods were clamoring for reparations from their state
government. But the state treasury was greatly depleted from
fighting the war. So the governor proposed recompense to
the "fireland sufferers" in free land—land held by the state
in the distant Connecticut Western Reserve.

"But, sir," Clayton Cranston from New Haven said, "in
1780, this state and all the others gave up such wilderness

lands to the Continental congress for the entire nation's future uses."

"Connecticut released all but a huge plot of one-half million acres lying south of Lake Erie near the Ohio country," the governor noted. "And that is why you've been judiciously selected from the areas most severely burned."

"You mean," Cullen said, "you intend to set up a sort of committee where we return to our areas and decide who deserves what parcels of land and encourage them to head west *pro patria*?"

"No, gentlemen," Governor Trumbull said and rose to his feet behind his big desk. "You know the good book says the Lord God had Moses send some brave souls to 'spy out the promised land.' So, through me, the Lord God sends you to travel to this parcel we are calling The Firelands in remembrance of the sufferers here. With a helpmate at your side—"

Morgan's astounded brain seized on that—a helpmate, a wife—as he listened to the rest of the daring plan. With three-hundred dollars seed money each, five married couples would set out from Lebanon in three months, on May 1, 1783. Claiming they were only moving west into New York State, in case they did not return for some reason, they would head west up the Mohawk Valley to a place called Buffalo Creek on the eastern end of Lake Erie. There, the governor would have flatboats called bateaux waiting to take them westward on Lake Erie to the sites of the homesteads, where they would stay for seventeen months—to get in one entire planting and harvest season—and then return to Lebanon by January 1, 1785 for a reward. Those who returned by that date would divide ten thousand dollars and receive large land grants in the Firelands when it was finally surveyed and parceled out. And on their success hung the entire plan to encourage folks whose lives had been devastated in the war to make a new life in the west.

"But what about Indians, Governor?" Stephen Muncey demanded. "Your offer is a great monetary and patriotic challenge, but I'll not take my Hannah into hostile Indian lands!"

"The Mohawk Valley has been peaceful since the British

were beaten there, and the Western Reserve's never had any flare-ups to speak of. And now, with the exodus of the British, who used to rile the savages, all's quiet."

"But will it still be quiet when five white families move into the Indians' untouched lands to plant and not just trade?" Morgan asked.

"For now, you can make it known you're not there to stay." the governor answered. "Besides, we have word from a few reliable trappers in the area that they've built a cabin or two with no fuss from the savages."

Morgan almost interrupted again to argue that most Indians he had known in his youth were far less savage than the whites who took their land or, lately, the British who paid for scalps and gave them firewater to urge them on. But he respected Jonathan Trumbull's judgment and held his tongue. Besides, the Indians he'd known were Iroquois, and that fierce tribe had never gone that far west.

"No, gentlemen," the governor went on, "the danger will be simple survival in the wilds, but the rewards for you and for our people will be abundant. And, once you've been there and looked things over, you may choose to rebuild here with your prize money and the sale of your land grant to others. On the other hand, if you wish to return to the western Firelands, you will have generous grants making you master of all you survey. I regret only, sirs," he concluded as he came around his desk to shake hands with each of them, "that this will have to be kept a secret from the masses until they can be told that at least some of you have succeeded and can recommend the area. And, the Lord God knows, I'm sorry I'm too old to go myself."

"But, may I ask," Cullen said, "why Morgan Glenn is here? We are all proud Connecticuters, but—"

"Because he's paid the price of New London lost, just as dearly as those who owned a home there!" the governor's voice rang out like the Old Testament prophets he often quoted. "Because he's been ever loyal to our cause, and yet there are those who gaze at Morgan Glenn askance and whisper about that Judas Iscariot general who burned his reputation for him. And because, sir, his background in the fields and forests of Pennsylvania gave him the skills he needs to tame the wilderness—more perhaps than some of our own townfolk, however bold, disciplined military men they be."

Cullen's jaw set hard. Morgan blinked back tears of gratitude. He must be tired and battle-burned to almost cry, he thought.

"Now, I'm giving all of you a bit of time to decide if you accept. If not, you'll be replaced by others from your areas," Governor Trumbull announced. "And I realize two of you are not wed—yet."

But Morgan Glenn was already thinking about Thea Arnold again.

"Morgan," Governor Trumbull said, taking his arm as the others filed out, "a private word with you." He steered him from his office into a vast, empty storeroom out back.

"I can't thank you enough for your words of support, sir."

"Well deserved. I knew you were a man to trust from that first time I met you—the week of the traitor's parade in New London. And you served me well during the war, no matter what fate befell New London. It's only that you were too loyal, too trusting with that traitor, but I take it you've learned that lesson now."

"Yes, sir," Morgan said, recalling Rina Lockwood as well as Benedict Arnold.

"Now, about Thea Arnold in New London. Ah, I see by your face I took you by surprise there. I've been keeping a watch on her safety, just as you asked, Morgan. And I've found out that someone has been stopping some of her correspondence with you. Well, don't explode, man. You know she's living in a seething hotbed of folks who still don't trust her, maybe never will—unless of course, she opens up the Firelands with you."

"My thoughts exactly."

"You're going to see her, then?"

"I was, but now I'll have to head home first to Pennsylvania to get a sound Conestoga wagon for the westward journey. I know a man who can make one in a month or so, and then I'll be back here by early April to—to ask her. I was going to ask her, anyway."

"I thought so. Still, a few weeks in April's not much woo-ing time. Sure you're not going after a sturdy Pennsylvania girl as well as a sturdy wagon?"

"No, sir. If Thea turns me down, then—" His voice trailed off. He was determined to help open up the Firelands. It was an opportunity to aid the folks who had been burned out, a chance to show them he was always on their side. He'd prove he despised what Benedict Arnold and his British sol-diers had done before Arnold had turned tail and fled to Eng-land, where he lived now. Besides, Morgan had not wanted to take a wife back to the small family farm his brother was working, and he hardly had enough Continental dollars saved to buy one of his own. The Firelands challenge an-swered all his prayers.

"Thea Arnold is the perfect wife for me," he told the gov-ernor, whose head barely came to his shoulder. "I'll just have to convince her. Besides," he added with a grim smile, "by now, as stubborn as she is, she might be ready to change her last name. But if our letters have been tampered with, could I ask a favor? Is there someone you know and trust going to New London, because I've got to send a letter sure to reach her."

"Cullen Varner's riding there, I hear, to see his fiancée. But," the governor paused and frowned, "perhaps it is best we don't bother a man of his burdens with your note. Yes, I'll see it's delivered into Thea Arnold's hands and that she's kept safe in that volatile town until you return, too, that I will!"

Gratitude and relief flowed through Morgan. Here was a good friend and mentor who had proved he was trustworthy. And yet, the thought gnawed at him, he'd learned to guard his feelings with everyone he thought he could trust, includ-ing, he supposed, his dear, dear Thea.

Even in the hubbub of Mercy Bigler's small, crowded house, Thea Arnold kept a quiet place in her soul as she sat reading from her mother's thick herbal book. Amidst Cas-sie's singing, and Rina's telling a visitor how Cullen wanted her to go west to New York State for a while, and Mercy

Bigler's playing with her noisy son while Susan bargained at
the door with an old, bearded Yankee peddler, Thea recited
again in her heart parts of Morgan's letter that a government
courier had delivered to her four days ago:

> *Our times apart and all the years of war have made
> me realize how much our friendship sustained me, dear
> Thea. "More than friendship," I believe you called it
> once. I must take a trip to my home state to bid my family
> farewell for a while and bring back something really spe-
> cial for you. I shall call on you as soon as I return, and
> I hope you are still considering the lifelong commitment
> we have shared our thoughts on. How cold are written
> words compared to what I feel! Forgive me for not coming
> now, but I will explain, I pray, to your satisfaction. Early
> April, I judge, we shall be reunited as friends and, dare
> I say, more, if you are willing and have missed me, too . . .*

"Oh, yes, I'm willing," she said aloud as if he stood tall
and strong before her right now. "And I have missed you,
too—desperately!"

"Wha'd you say, Mistress Arnold?" Mercy's five-year-old
Joseph asked and came to lean against her knee.

Thea smiled down at the flaxen-haired lad. How long ago
that night seemed when she had helped a midwife bring this
child into the world, and then visited Father Lockwood to
tell him. That night, she thought as her gaze lifted to the animated Rina across the room, he told me all about the tragedy
of Rina's cruel mother. But as soon as Rina wed Cullen and
was a mother herself, perhaps all that grief could be turned
to good. "I said, my boy, you're not to believe everything
Mistress Cassie tells you about the forest folk," she reiterated
her earlier warning to him.

"The *'afeared* forest folk'," he parroted Cassie's words,
wide-eyed. "Never can tell what's gonna get you in the forest!" he cried and darted off.

"Drat," Thea whispered as she closed the pharmacopoeia

and stood to step over his tumble of wooden blocks. "Cassie, I need a word with you."

But even as Thea explained to Cassie again not to scare the boy about the forest, Thea longed for it. In a few weeks, when this February weather passed, she would be able to move out to her little bark-covered hut where she had lived most of last summer, tending her herb beds. With Avery Payne sent to Lebanon and Philadelphia as the town's spokesman to plead for compensation for the fire sufferers, she had felt so free and safe out there. And when Morgan returned in April, she intended to have a well-tended spot in which to greet him privately. Their reunion would be spoiled in this noisy, busy, crowded parlor or on the many-eyed streets of this town, where people still frowned and gawked and pointed!

"So, do you understand, Cassie?" Thea prompted. "You're not to frighten Joseph about the forest folk again."

"But they've never forgiven a one of us who love Mistress Rina," Cassie leaned close to whisper conspiratorially. "Not after Father Lockwood cut so many trees to get himself that big house her and Mr. Varner's going to rebuild after their trip to New York State. 'Tis true if you weren't a forest healer, the fairies wouldn't trust you one bit, either, Thea. They'd send someone to get you out there, they would!"

"That's enough!" Thea added her voice to the hubbub. "No one wants to hear any more of that, I said!"

But later, many times, Thea wished that she had listened.

On April 6, 1783, Morgan Glenn rumbled into New London driving a bright red and blue Pennsylvania Conestoga wagon with white linsey-woolsey stretched overhead like sails. The day was warm and sunny, the sky so blue. He breathed in and exhaled, then pulled on the reins to turn his team of six horses and a yoke of oxen down Blinman Street where he heard Mercy Bigler lived. The big, strong oxen were dun-hued, the horses matched bays. In these hard times, he had paid too much for them, but the effect was worth it. He owed other folks his best, but sometimes, he thought, he owed himself something, too. He'd put most of his saved salary and half of the governor's seed money in this rig and team. With some left for supplies and some for Thea, he'd have to tame the Firelands and be back here on time to share that prize money and get some land, or he'd be poor as a danged church mouse!

But he had made it to Pennsylvania and back in record time, he thought proudly. Everything was in place in his plans—and Governor Trumbull's—except the helpmate, the wife. Sitting in the high seat of the kind of wagon he used to dream of as a lad, he surveyed the town excitedly, hoping to see Thea on the street as he had once before.

He noted that few of the burned areas had been rebuilt; folks just didn't have the money. Governor Trumbull had said that even the Lockwood mansion could not be resurrected from its sepulcher until some of Moses Lockwood's investments were freed up, or Cullen Varner earned his share of the Firelands prize.

Cullen Varner. That name slapped down Morgan's high-flying, happy thoughts. The other three men heading west had drawn homestead sites on Cold Creek, Fire Creek, or old Woman's Creek. But, as providence would have it, he and Cullen had both drawn the same waterway, a longer river so it could take two families and yet have them keep their distance. Cullen had complained that a civilized gentleman could not even pronounce the name of the place: Pequotting River. Morgan had kept his mouth shut when he saw how Cullen, the man who tossed fancy Latin phrases here and there, brooded. But Morgan even knew what *pequotting* meant from his early days picking up bits of Indian dialects that sometimes overlapped one another. *Pequotting* meant "pay nothing."

"Pay nothing!" Morgan said aloud and even slapped his knee at the thought, despite the reins wrapped around his hands. "Pay nothing, when we might be paying with everything we've ever had for this little Firelands adventure!"

That sobered him again, and his stomach twisted in knots at the thought of seeing Thea after all this time. What if she had changed or suddenly promised herself to someone else? He'd yearned for her long before the governor dumped this scheme on all of them, and he meant to tell her—and show her—just how much! But he'd learned before that people you thought you knew just could not be fully trusted.

"Hey, boy!" he called to a flaxen-haired lad who gawked at his grand rig from a yard. "Which house is Bigler's? I'm looking for Mistress Thea Arnold."

"Thea? She's a friend a mine," the lad boasted, thumbs hooked in the waistband of his breeches. His blue eyes were round as saucers at the brightly painted wagon and the matched teams. Morgan knew that look. As a boy he'd stood along the Lehigh Hill roads and gawked at Conestogas. "But she's out at her medicine beds. That's what my mother call 'em," the lad went on. "Out by the forest. There's 'nother man, Mr. Payne, who's real 'portant here 'bouts and been away a lot asking for money for everyone, my mother says. He just now come by with two other men asking where Thea was, too. He went out there hisself—"

But at that, the boy could only stare and jump back as Morgan shouted at him. He swung his teams and wagon around in the street and yard and urged them to a faster clip that left only his dust.

Thea swept out her little hut with the broom she'd sewn herself and replaced the straw tick mattress inside and the single chair in the doorway in the sun. Stuck in old bottles of Daffy's Elixir, bouquets of early white violets and fragrant lilies of the valley scented the little house. And her front door's view of the dandelion-speckled fields and ravines and forest all with hints of coming yellow-green leaves was splendid—more splendid since the land was hers. At least they could not take that away from her.

She kept her big calico apron on as she sat in the sun and ate the bread and cheese she'd brought for dinner. Each day she finished her work of clearing brush and raking early in the morning. After that, she changed her garb and took care to keep her clothes and hands as clean as possible. For any day now, late morning on, she judged, Morgan Glenn might arrive! Her insides fluttered when she saw a distant rider—

no, three of them. But two fanned out along the forest and only one continued on.

Her heart beat louder as his horse's hoofbeats did. She almost wished she'd taken Cassie's offer of the four-leafed clover for good luck today. Putting aside her food, she squinted into the sun. She hastily untied her apron and fluffed out the skirts of her only good gown, a faded, pale blue dress dotted with flower sprigs. Was the rider Morgan? But she saw that the man looked stocky and not that tall. And then she knew.

"Drat! Avery Payne!" she cracked out and ducked inside for her digging spade. She'd feel better with something to swing in her hands, she thought, as she stood waiting for him outside her door. Avery Payne had been away for months, forced, she had assumed, to play the noble benefactor to save face in a town he might have helped to destroy. And someday, somehow, she was going to confront him with everything she suspected to prove he was the depraved demon no one else recognized. But not if she had to face him out here alone.

"You, sir, are not welcome on my land," she greeted him and lifted her spade, blade up, when he dismounted, anyway.

"It won't be yours much longer, unless you learn who runs this town," he said and stepped warily closer. "Thea, I can do so much for you—rebuild your shop, buy you more land than this—if you but give the word. With so much water over the dam, et cetera, can't we be friends at last?" he wheedled.

"No, and it's because of that water over the dam. The way you treated your poor wife, your covert partnership with Benedict Arnold, the way you conveniently disappeared after all your threats to me the night the town burned—" she gave in to her bottled-up fury before she could halt her muted accusations.

"My threats?" he challenged. "They've never been threats, my Thea. Only promises of what I am so weary of waiting for from you. I've admired your independence and wanted you to come to me on your own. That's a compliment, you know. But since you have remained so stubborn, I am totally out of patience. So, I'm here to take advantage of this lovely, romantic, private place—well, private but for my two friends keeping watch—a place you've obviously prepared for us."

How dare he taunt her with all the things she had planned for her and Morgan! And now this vile seducer and murderer reached for her, and she swung the spade.

"No!" she cried. He ducked, then yanked the spade from her hands. She scrambled inside for another weapon, but he was too fast.

"Scream, then!" he threatened as he kicked her rake and broom to the floor and backed her into a corner in the little hut. "Scream so the men guarding this place know what a good time we're having—"

He came at her low and encircled her hips with his arms. His head butted her belly. She beat on his shoulder and head, but his weight took her to the ground, half on, half off her straw mattress. Bottles of flowers flew and dumped their water to make tiny mud puddles on the floor. She kicked, she thrashed, but did not scream. She needed all her strength, all her breath, to fight him.

Thea's thoughts ran wild. Had it been like this for Charity that last night in her bed? He turned her facedown and pressed her into the mattress tick while his hands yanked at her skirts. Her hair, which she had carefully combed and knotted for Morgan, tore free and tumbled over her in a blinding mass.

"You'll not unman me as you did once before," he grunted as he pinned her down. He pulled one arm up behind her back to still her. "Lie quiet now. I swear you'll like this! Then, I'm going to take you away after we seal this little bargain, set you up like a princess outside of town. You'll see how—"

They both froze at the sound of a distant gunshot. And another. Thea grasped for air, her face pressed into the prickly linen ticking. "Damn it to perdition," Avery spat out and, still holding her arm to control her, added, "get up. Get up!"

She tried to stand, but he yanked her to her feet and walked her to the door. He held her wrist behind her back and, with his other hand, roughly fondled her breasts. "Just someone hunting, no doubt," he said and bent to nuzzle her throat with a low growl.

Then, out the door, across the field, she saw Morgan. Riding like the wind on a bay horse with no saddle, he sent clods of her fresh-dug herb beds flying. But that didn't matter. Nothing mattered anymore if Morgan was here!

Avery saw him, too. He clipped out a curse and shoved her to her knees in the hut. He ran to his horse, but it shied away and he had to scramble after it. Thea grabbed the rake and chased him, though her arm had gone numb from his force.

"You bastard!" she cried and smacked the handle hard across his ribs as he mounted. Outrage and Morgan's hellbent charge made her bold. "You smothered Charity, I know you did! I'll tell them all! You were involved with the traitor, I just know it, and I'll prove it if it's the last thing I do!"

"Then it will be!" he grunted as he mounted. "It will be!"

She didn't care what Avery Payne did or said now, as long as he got off her land and out of her life! But he managed to mount just as Morgan reined in. Morgan took one look at Thea's torn, wild appearance and exploded right off his horse onto Avery's, pulling him to the ground.

Though Avery swung and thrashed, Morgan punched the man until he looked more like a ragged, bloodied scarecrow. "Morgan, Morgan, you'll kill him!?" she cried. "Stop, or they'll get you for this your first day back, and then what will we do?" She tried to pull him off, her arms hard around him. He didn't budge at first, but then stood and turned to her. Suddenly, they were in each other's arms, panting, shaking, holding tight.

They both had wondered how it was going to be—their mutual greeting after so long. Whether to hug, to shake hands. To speak first, what to say. But they had not fathomed this desperate greeting, this clinging to each other through her tears and his furious mutterings at Avery even as he clasped her so hard he nearly lifted her from her feet to swing her back and forth like a rag doll. At last, he set her back to look her over even as Payne reared his bleeding face to glare up at them with gleaming, feral eyes they did not see.

Morgan brushed Thea's wild red tresses back from her bruised, dirtied face. His gaze took in her torn gown, pulled askew at the bodice, the tear tracks on her face. And then, before she realized what was happening, he was pummeling Avery Payne again.

"I'll kill you, Payne, if you get near her again! You're even too damned low to challenge to a duel!" Morgan hefted the bleeding man and heaved him, belly-down, over his saddle. "Now get the hell off the lady's land!" He slapped the horse's rump, and the beast took off running madly toward the forest with Avery bouncing along, trying to stay on. Morgan turned and pulled Thea into his arms again.

"He didn't get very far with what he intended, I take it," Morgan muttered. She nodded, her head tucked in the hollow of his throat. "Some old bearded codger at the forest edge told me to watch out for a man guarding the path just down a ways, and another man across the field. He took a pot shot at the one for me, and I winged the other. Don't know who the old man was, but I'd like to thank him."

Thea shook her head. She could think of no one of that description at the forest edge or anywhere else. But Morgan's very presence shoved all such thoughts away.

"You're certain you are all right, Thea?" he tried again when she didn't speak. "That—Avery Payne, he didn't really hurt you?"

"I am certain I am all right, now that you're here," she told him, cuddling closer. She didn't even care that Morgan had found her dirty and ragged once again. She had forgotten how tall he stood, how straight, how he moved with such lanky grace, anyway. She had not quite remembered how low his voice was or how that deep-woods drawl lilted through his speech compared to the clipped east coast English—or was it American now? "I am so very glad to see you!" she said, and blinked back tears of joy as she leaned into his embrace and gazed slightly up at him.

"Me, too," he said and, stiff-armed, held her by her shoulders to look her over despite her blush. He stared openly, as if he'd never seen her before—her proud stance, that tilt of chin, the grass green of her eyes. Yes, he'd remembered the eyes, though he'd never caught that wild cascade of red-gold hair in sunlight quite right in his memory. Tipped back like this, her full breasts strained against her soiled, ripped bodice, which tapered to her slender waist. Without all the stuffings, her skirts fondled the shape of her legs the way he longed to.

"You're so—strong and beautiful," he said as though he'd lost the gift of speech but to babble childish thoughts.

"For you, I want to be."

He almost blurted it out then, all his plans for them. His proposal, his deepest feelings and needs. But he had so much to explain first. And he had to retrieve and show her the wagon he'd left back in the forest fringe when he'd feared the oxen would slow the horses. Maybe, when she saw the wagon, she would understand all his dreams for them.

"I think I've said this once before," he muttered, "that we'd best wash up." His big finger shook as he traced the soil marks on her chin and down her throat to where the slant of her shoulder disappeared into her pale blue, flower-sprigged gown.

"I've a little water inside, and there's a stream—"

"Shhh!"

He kissed each smear of soil on her cheeks, then her nose. Her lips looked puffed where that bastard had abused her. He laved them lovingly with the tip of his tongue, tracing their pouted curves the way he yearned to trace every inch of her. She startled at first, then smiled, though her limbs still felt tense. Her tongue touched his as if they would wash each other's pain away. He slid his tongue deeply into her sweetness, and she moaned. They matched each other in tiny parries and quickening thrusts. She pressed against him. Her full breasts felt so ripe with longing.

He turned his head to deepen the kiss; he dropped his splayed hands to pin her to his hard length, first to her taut rib cage, then her waist, and then lower, to cup her soft bottom right through her skirts. She held hard to him; she did not protest even when, he knew, she could feel the press of him yearning for her. And when she kissed him on her own, the sun blazed hot inside them both. And the whole cup of blue heavens and dandelion meadows tilted and whirled.

Thea seemed as excited as he when they rode together on his horse to retrieve the Conestoga. They had shared so much as they washed by the stream. And through all their conversation, she had not protested that he could not keep his hands and mouth off her. "To match my thoughts that have been on you for months—years!" he admitted. He explained carefully, honestly, about the opportunity he had to go to the Firelands. But he stressed that he had wanted to marry her *before* that opportunity came up; it was not just that he suddenly needed a wife for a new venture.

"And now you—we have a chance to make good things happen here by going there," she concluded for him.

"Yes, sweetheart, together, we do!" he declared and clamped his arms around her even harder as she rode in front of him on his horse. But the gentle jog, jog of her bottom against his lap kept him from thinking as clearly as he liked.

"You know," she said shakily, "New London is a firelands not only for what that traitor and his British soldiers did, but because people are consumed with hatred and mistrust here. I just hope things won't be the same out there. I pray it will actually be a safer, fairer place where folks know and trust each other for what they really are."

At that, he almost blurted out his confession about Rina. But at that moment, Thea caught a glimpse of the Conestoga where he'd left it in the woods, and she nearly vaulted off the horse in her excitement before he lifted her down.

"Oh, it's so big and bright, Morgan!" she said, awed at the red wheels, the back ones bigger than the front, and the deep blue body. He boosted her to step on the sturdy hickory spokes of a wooden wheel. He joined her on the wide seat he'd had specially built. He explained how the wagon could be driven from here or with the driver riding the front, left horse. "Oh, Morgan. Lots of room and with its own mattress and pillows! And it's curved inside like a boat!"

"To keep loads from shifting too suddenly."

"And an iron pot and kettle hanging back there on—"

"On the ridgepole," he put in proudly. "I'm sure they're good for mixing herbal brews as much as fresh meat stew. And I've got bells for the harness, but I didn't want to put them on today. I'm saving them for wedding bells, if you'll just marry me and come along. We'll show this town and the whole state that we're the best patriots around, and that we can forge a future for ourselves and them in this new nation."

But she had stopped listening when he said "marry me." He could tell by the rapt, faraway look on her face. It scared him that he hadn't worked his way up to this. He had meant to tell her about him and Rina first. Thea Arnold was a bold, independent woman who had been making her own decisions for years, in her own way. And he figured he'd hurt her once with Rina, and knew he had to explain all about that, then let the chips fall where they may.

"You can't know," she said, luminous-faced, halting the confession on his lips, "how good it is to really trust someone else besides just Rina, after the deceit and treachery I've seen. If it weren't for my friendship and trust in her, I don't know how I would have lasted in one piece waiting for this dratted war to end and you to come back for me, Morgan. Now I've got both you and Rina to thank for restoring my faith in people!"

He just gaped at her for a breathless minute. Danged if he could tell her right now and ruin all that for her. "And I'm so thrilled," she bubbled on, "that Rina and Cullen will be going to the Firelands, too, and not just to New York State as Cullen evidently told her to say. I can certainly understand that little lie the governor is using to make sure things work out. I know you said Cullen doesn't trust you, but Rina and I will win him over! And I do want,"—she took a big breath and smiled at him through tears shimmering greener than the sea—"to marry you and go with you. The Barbary Coast would do, the farthest desert, the nearest star, anywhere. But yes, a honeymoon to the western Firelands would do just fine. How far is it, anyway?" she hurried on, so inebriated with joy, she could hardly stop her flow of words.

"Six hundred miles," he said. His voice shook. "Six hundred miles there and six hundred back with a lot of hardships in between. But we'd be together, you and I. Cullen and Rina—they'd be off a ways. So you will be my wife? I don't deserve you, but I'll do everything I can to make you happy. And if you want an apothecary shop here or on the Barbary Coast or wherever you want to live after we come back, it's yours. And I am, too!"

They held hard to each other, perched on the high seat of the brightly painted wagon until a horse still in harness snorted and shied at her mate, which was cropping the grass she could not reach. And that was how, in the forest, Benedict Arnold's cousin and his former protégé settled on the promises and trust between them.

Chapter Ten

THE ALTHEA PLANT. "My dear little daughter, we named
you for this herb with my favorite, large pink-purple blooms.
The very root is sweet when chewed and eases pain. Applied
externally, althea balm diminishes skin irritation. It is soothing for domestic poultices and for the eyes. To be sweet and
useful, soothing and domestic—I could wish no more blessings
for you in the years you grow to womanhood and in a marriage of your own. (Another name for this herb is marshmal-
low. We sell the roots to housewives all over town as a
confectionery sweetener.)"

THEA AND MORGAN spent the rest of that happy day on
her land, where they cooked an evening meal from supplies
he had stowed in the Conestoga. They kissed and cuddled
and almost bedded together on the hemp-covered straw mattress in the wagon. But when he laid her down in its softness
under the hooped white roof over their heads, Thea murmured gently in his ear, "This will be our bed the first weeks
we are wed, and then even after while we build a cabin."

"Yes. Yes!" he muttered and nuzzled her throat.

"Our marriage bed," her words pursued him as he slid his
lips down to the sweet cleft between her breasts and gently
lifted her skirts to clasp a bare, shapely knee with his left
hand. He stopped and leaned away on one elbow to study
her in the semidarkness of the wagon. He sighed inwardly.
He didn't mean to rush her after they'd been apart so long
and after what Avery Payne had tried today. And not when
she thought everything was above board between them, as
he hadn't told her about Rina yet. But she made his blood
pound in his veins and he wanted her desperately. He
smoothed her skirt down and once more, lightly, kissed the
satin skin above her breasts.

"Just wanted to make sure you liked the view here, Thea.
On your back, looking up, I mean," he tried a bit of levity.

"Oh, I do. And I will, clear out to our new home and then
back again."

And so instead of having an early wedding night, they drove their big, rumbling land-boat into town to ask the rector in the Episcopal church the British hadn't burned to marry them as soon as the banns could be read. They set their wedding for April 20, only fourteen days away. The rector kindly offered to let Morgan keep his wagon out behind the rectory, near a field where his animals could graze. After dark, Morgan walked her home to Mercy Bigler's house. Thea wanted Morgan to help her tell Rina their news and ask her to stand up for them in the small ceremony, but Morgan suggested she talk to Rina alone.

Again, he meant to tell Thea about him and Rina, but she was so happy that words failed him. Besides, what if Thea refused him when he confessed? What if she felt as betrayed by him as she had by her cousin? No, there would be time to tell her later, after he showed her how much he loved her. Besides, if Rina hadn't told Thea about him by now, she obviously didn't intend to. If he told, Thea might turn on Rina, too. Cullen Varner might find out, and both their coming marriages would be devastated. No, better to let something from the distant past remain the past for just a little while longer, until both marriages were solid. Dang, he hoped neither Rina nor Cullen were at Mercy Bigler's tonight when they arrived!

Morgan got his wish. After he met the others who were there and promised the Bigler boy a ride in his wagon, he kissed Thea good night and beat a quick retreat.

When Morgan had gone and the others went to bed, Thea realized she was still shaken by Avery Payne's attack and threats earlier that day. She carefully checked the small house and locked both the front and back doors. She sat up late in the tiny parlor, enjoying the fresh April air through a window set ajar, waiting drowsily for Cullen to bring Rina back from Cullen's friends' house, where he was staying. They were no doubt planning the large, elaborate wedding Rina had already asked her to participate in, no matter what the other New London guests said! When the lantern guttered out, Thea did not relight it. Dreaming her own dreams, she cherished the stillness of the house as she watched a big block of moonlight slant in the window and slowly move across the floor toward her chair.

She heard footsteps and voices. She peered out to be certain it was Rina and Cullen. How she longed to burst right out the door to share her good news, but they had melded to one shadow out there now. She decided to unlock the door for Rina, then tiptoe upstairs to wait for her. Thea understood a lover's need for privacy all too well. Quietly, she unbolted the front door and went into the parlor to close and latch the open window. But then, Cullen's voice floated to her on the breeze.

"I don't doubt that he'll propose to her, Varina. The man needs a wife to head west. Besides, he's always felt sorry for her, *sub rosa,* with all the Arnold-hatred she's faced here. He knows how that goes, and rightly so, believe me!"

"You don't think Morgan Glenn is guilty of complicity with the traitor, do you? Cullen, he's no more guilty than she is!"

" 'Avoid all appearances of evil,' the Bible says. How I'd like to throw that at our Bible-babbling governor for coddling Morgan Glenn, just as General Arnold used to. I tell you, my darling, I don't want you mixing with Thea Arnold here or out there in the Firelands *ad perpetuam.* "

Thea's hand froze as it reached to close the casement. She sank back into the chair. Her first impulse was to bounce right up again and march outside to rebuke Cullen Varner. How dare he imply that Morgan had known Benedict Arnold intended to defect! Or that Morgan wanted to marry her for such selfish, pitiable reasons! She'd not believe that, however much the words hurt. But it would make everything worse for Rina if she berated Cullen. She wanted to defend herself, but her friend Rina did it for her.

"Well, I think you're being rather narrow-minded, Cullen. Thea's been dear to me for—for as long as I can remember. And you said you and Morgan drew lots for living on the same river what's-its-name out there, so we'd best all be friends."

"We're to be on our own as early settlers would be. Governor Trumbull's made that very clear," he insisted.

"Bosh! Early settlers have to rely on each other, too. If Morgan takes Thea along as his wife, she and I will be thicker friends than ever! I do want to be a good and obedient wife, Cullen, but the reason I fell in love with you after all the time I'd known you was that you let me make up my own mind. I learned from Thea how to be independent, just like our new nation. I made some mistakes, but I know that now. And I just could not possibly get married and go west to some savage land without knowing Thea and I are still friends, however much I love you!"

Tears coursed down Thea's face. Bless Rina. Bless Rina and Morgan! She stood and began to push the window closed, but Cullen's words still assailed her: "I do love and adore you, my darling Varina. Yes, all right. But you must remember that we are in competition with anyone else who goes along on this journey, Thea and Morgan included. I want to do a fine job for our state, and be the first to return. I want to be known as the man who opened up the Firelands. And I want to be a perfect husband to you always—"

Thea closed the window and fled upstairs without lighting a candle. She scrubbed at her wet cheeks with her flannel face rag and hurried to get out of her clothes in the moonlight. She yanked on her night rail and got into her side of the bed. She heard the door below close and Rina in the hall. Rina came in with a wavering candle and began to disrobe. Drat, Thea thought, as she lay there stiff and still as a stone. She wasn't going to start pretending with Rina, not when they had so few days left together after all these years.

"Rina, I'm awake," she said and sat up in bed. "I might as well tell the truth. When I unlocked the door and closed the window, I heard some of what Cullen said. And what you said back. I've never been so proud to have a friend like you! And I have been waiting up to tell you my and Morgan's good news!"

"Oh, Thea!" Rina whispered and bounced down on the bed as if her legs had turned to water. "Then, you mean he proposed?"

Thea nodded, tears in her eyes again. "You're happy for me, aren't you?" she asked. "Even if Cullen and Morgan don't see eye to eye, we can patch that up."

The strangest looks flitted across Rina's pretty face in the wavering candle glow, looks that even Thea could not read. *She's just worried this will come between her and Cullen,* Thea thought.

"I'm so happy for you," Rina choked out, obviously moved. "I know you've loved him from that first—almost always!"

They hugged each other hard. Rina's shoulders shook, and tears flew from Thea's lashes when she blinked. "And, Rina, I'm sorry, but Morgan and I are being wed four days before you. We'll be heading up toward Lebanon to prepare for the trip west, so I won't be able to be here for your wedding. Now, don't fuss. It will soothe things between you and Cullen and not rile your other guests. You can tell me everything when we meet the day the wagons head out. But, if you can, I would still like you to be with me on my wedding day. Both Morgan and I would!"

Thea saw Rina bite her lip hard, the way she often did when she was agonizing over some decision. "So everything—all the bad things in the past are settled between you and Morgan?" Rina asked.

"There's nothing for us to settle. You don't mean that Avery's bothered me or that Morgan was too close to the traitor, do you?"

"No, no," she said, then plunged on to turn the topic. "Oh, Thea, I'm so fussed-up about this journey, but it's the best thing for all of us to build new lives. Cullen's so determined to do this perfectly, partly to make up, I think, for throwing in with General Gates who was only good at hiding in his tent or retreating."

"Gates turned out to be an angel, next to Arnold," Thea said and heaved a sigh. "And Cullen, next to Morgan in everyone's eyes, so—"

"Well!" Rina said and bounced off the bed to continue disrobing for bed. "Let's not ever compare our men—our future husbands. We both love our own and that's that. Good-bye

Connecticut firelands! And Western Reserve Firelands, here we come!"

" 'Rina and Thea, two peas in a pod, have been best friends every step they have trod,' " Thea recited their old childhood rhyme.

"And will be best friends!" Rina said, but she didn't meet Thea's eyes. "Just wait until Cassie hears about you and Morgan! I told Cullen we have to take her with us, Thea, or who knows what would happen to her here," Rina's words were muffled as she pulled her gown up over her head.

"But who knows what will happen to her there. If she's too much for Cullen, maybe we can share her on the trip out, just as we have here."

"Mm. She much prefers Morgan, I must admit. I just wonder what she'll think when we all end up living in the biggest forest she's ever seen, with her fears of curses and abductions and all."

"Yes," Thea said and snuggled back down into the linen bedclothes, suddenly exhausted at the thought of traveling so far into the unknown. Rina crept into her side of the bed and blew out the candle. They both lay there, suddenly silent. Thoughts sifted like sand through Thea's tired, excited mind. All the love she and Morgan had shared today had invigorated her, but sapped her strength, too. He was so eager to possess her, and she was eager, too, but yet shy. She, like Rina, had never had anyone really tell her what it was like, man and woman love in the depths of night and the depths of a bed. They had once vowed that whoever found out first would tell, but she would marry Morgan Glenn and then be gone before Rina became Cullen's bride.

Thea studied Morgan's face in the pages of her mind. Then Cassie's, Rina's, Cullen's, all heading west. All heading toward the forests of the distant, dreamy Firelands.

Althea Arnold married Morgan Glenn on a sunny day at the Episcopal church on a hill overlooking what was left of New London. It was the happiest day of her life. Cassie and Rina wore flower wreaths in their hair, and Thea carried a big bouquet of forest wildflowers from her herb gardens. Two pearl hairpins, her wedding gift from Rina, held back the bounty of Thea's red-gold hair. She wore a blue calico gown made from a bolt of cloth Morgan had brought from Pennsylvania, but he had brought her something more wondrous than that. When the minister asked by what token he pledged his troth, Morgan drew from his dark blue waistcoat pocket a thin gold band to slip on her finger. It fit her finger perfectly, delicately, making her feel she glowed golden all over.

"My grandmother's ring—from Scotland," he told her later. "We always said she was a laird's daughter from the proud way she carried herself through whatever hard times she faced."

"A laird?" she asked.

"A lord of the clan, the father of the tribe, so to speak. I'm sorry I never knew your father, Thea, but I think your parents did a beautiful job to make you so bold and strong and proud. When I told my mother about you, she insisted her mother's wedding ring should go to you."

"Oh, Morgan, thank you!" she said for the first time of many today and could not stem her tears of joy.

During the service, Thea tried to keep her eyes on the minister reciting his sonorous words. But she also darted glances at her Morgan, trying to reconcile him with the idea of *husband*. He looked so solemn, but he shot her a quick grin when he caught her looking. When Rina held her bouquet and Thea's eyes met hers, Rina looked more than solemn, almost grim. Worries for her own wedding without me here to prop her up, Thea thought. So the minute she and Morgan strode to the back of the church and out the door, Thea turned back to hug Rina and whisper, "Everything will be this beautiful for you and Cullen, too. You've always loved only him, my dear friend, just as I have Morgan."

After cakes and ale in the rector's house, Thea kissed Rina and Cassie farewell—Cullen was busy with preparations for their trip west—and the newlyweds climbed into their Conestoga and departed to the jingle of the harness bells. The little band of wedding guests waved and waved: Rina, Mercy and little Joseph Bigler, Susan, Widow Middleton, the rector's wife, and Cassie. "Those bells are to let the forest folk out west know we're all coming, we are!" was the last thing Thea heard as they headed out of town.

But on the way, Morgan stopped by the cemetery, where last week he had erected two carved wooden tombstones to replace the ruined ones over her parents' and grandparents' graves. "Not many people visit a cemetery on their wedding day, but I thought we should say good-bye to your folks together, since we won't be back for a while," he told her, his arm strong around her waist. "And when we get our share of that Firelands prize money, we'll replace these markers with fine ones, ones people around here will point out someday and say, 'That's the family of the woman who helped open up the western Firelands for us, you know.'"

Unshed tears matting her thick, copper lashes, she turned to stare at this wonder of a man who was her husband now. "How can I ever thank you for everything?" she asked. "How can I ever show you what your trust and honesty and love have meant to me?" She held tightly to him, her arms around his strong neck, her body pressed to his. Here was love and security and her future! Everything bad was over now! She blinked, and tears flew from her lashes to speckle his shoulders and lapels. "Oh, dear, crying again, and I'm so happy, really!" she choked out.

He smiled and picked her up to carry her back to the wagon. At that moment, his own joy mingled with pain at not clearing the air with her about Rina, but he could not trust himself to speak. Finally, on the seat beside her as he cracked the long bullwhip high over the heads of his team, he managed, "Say good-bye to New London for a while, my love. As Governor Trumbull says, we're off for the New Jerusalem!"

"But not before ten days of honeymoon!" she declared and held to his arm. They jolted back against the seat and headed out of town. And she did not look back.

The inn where they stayed the first night, twelve miles out of town, had long been known as The King's Arms, but since the war had been renamed The Eagle's Wings. Morgan paid for their second-floor room overlooking a broad back lawn with a bowling green. He unpacked things they would need from the wagon and staked out the horses and the oxen. Thea bathed while he fed the animals and washed in a stream out back.

"I'm famished," she told him when he came upstairs to escort her down to dinner.

"Me, too," he whispered, and his dark brown eyes swept her. "For you. But supper first, or I'll never have the strength for all that I have planned."

"Braggart!" she teased and laughed.

"I'll let you decide tomorrow, and all of our tomorrows together." he countered with another thorough, teasing perusal of her and an almost devilish grin.

They took their supper in the fairly crowded common room, chatting excitedly about the day and making toasts to their future with mugs of Madeira. "Look, Morgan," she whispered. "These people don't know us. Privacy and anonymity at last! No frowns and narrowed eyes as if to say, 'There are those two who—' "

He seized her hand to halt her words. "It will be this way out in the west, too! Freedom! The past forgotten!"

"Except for the others we might see on the way, especially Cullen and Rina," she added, as if regretfully.

At that, they both quieted. Besides, Thea was only too aware of the big, soft bed awaiting them upstairs and how Morgan's thigh pressed so hard to hers on the bench. She was both eager and anxious to go upstairs with him. And yet, each moment he looked at her or touched her, she knew everything would be wonderful.

He would have liked to have undressed her the moment they had first seen their room. But he did not want her to think he did not value her and cherish her—only her—in every way. And, dang it, having her want him in bed as badly as he did her was so important to him! He was starting to feel like a schoolboy who had never even seen a woman naked, though he'd had a few before the war to let him know what was what and how to pleasure a woman. Those tawny-skinned Iroquois gals, and the two farm girls who had been so willing, and then, almost, Rina—

He cleared his throat and stood, furious with himself. Tonight, why did he have to think of that big mistake he'd made? Hell, there was no way on their honeymoon, let alone on their wedding night, that he could spring on Thea the fact he'd proposed to her best friend first!

"You won't believe what I was just thinking," she told him to jolt him from his agonizings.

"What?"

"How when Rina and I were girls, we used to always talk about how we'd have dancing on our wedding days. She was always so graceful at the minuet, and I was the gawkiest, gangliest thing with the most artless feet you've ever seen!"

He just nodded when she thought he would laugh. She was surprised when he steered her out the side door of the tavern into the graying dusk of a delightful evening. "They don't look so big now," he said and lifted up her skirt hems to display her feet. He put his big boots next to her buckled shoes. "See? And as for the minuet, that's enough to make any tall person feel the fool, trying to twirl under someone's arm and going down that arch of all the little folks' hands."

He grinned, and she laughed delightedly. How special to have someone taller and bigger than she was! Someone who understood and cherished her so completely just the way she was! "Come on, then," he said, "we'll have a little frisk—before the one upstairs."

"Where are we going?" she demanded as he pulled her around to the back of the tavern. He escorted her onto the deserted bowling green. The grass here seemed a lush, green carpet under the grand ceiling of open sky. "Whatever are you doing, Morgan Glenn?"

He turned her to him and took her hands. "You said you wanted dancing for your wedding day, Mrs. Glenn. Come on, now, follow me."

"Not the minuet!" she protested, laughing so hard she shook.

"Naw, none of that namby-pamby shuffling! We're pioneers now. I'm gonna teach you the Country Scamperdown and the Pennsylvania Reel! First the gallopade step, and then the hipsy-shay, come on now!"

They whirled and cavorted and galloped and skipped until they were hooting with the exuberance of shared frenzy. All the times Thea had wanted to scream at New Londoners, to march down the main street to give them a sound tongue-lashing, to curse them all fell from her in that wild dance. Morgan's hands were hard and sure on her waist and back as he swung her. She felt very much the maid Cassie's forest fairies had abducted and danced with until her toes wore away. She was bewitched by this man, beautifully so. A building desire for him, along with all this riotous romping in his arms, made her knees go weak. Then, their eyes met and held. The world receded and stopped. As if he had read her thoughts, he swept her up in his embrace and raced for the tavern.

"Morgan!" she protested dizzily. "What will they all say? What—"

"They will say the bridegroom has waited six years through war and hell for the woman he loves, and he's not waiting any longer!" he boomed out in a voice much too loud as he sprinted past the common room of the tavern to clamber up the stairs.

The locals and travelers in the taproom who saw them laughed and even clapped and cheered. Thea's skin flushed hotter than ever at that, but the noise muted with Morgan's decisive closing and bolting of their door. He put her down on the oval rag rug before the unlit hearth and kissed her. Her head still spun from the day, from the dancing, from her desire.

His hands were already on her, unhooking her gown. She helped him. Then, throwing her hesitancy to the winds, she shoved off his frock coat and unbuttoned his waistcoat. They kicked off their shoes in unison. She unwound his cravat, but their hands tangled as he unhooked her stays to loose her breasts. They laughed nervously, but when their eyes met this time they both stood frozen, breathless, solemn. He reached up to take the lace cap from her hair and tumbled her glorious tresses loose from its pearl pins.

"My Althea, you're so stunning. I have wanted so long to make you mine!"

Cool air licked at their damp bodies. Wearing only his breeches, which did nothing to hide his powerful desire for her, he lifted her hand and led her to the bed. His eyes were on her; he looked awestruck, she thought. It felt so natural to be naked like this with him. He lay her carefully back on the soft mattress and bent instantly over her to kiss her lips. He propped his hands on either side of her shoulders. And then his lips drifted lower.

Down her arched throat, over her fluted collarbone, to the valley between her breasts. She kept her eyes wide open. She wanted to see everything, learn and remember everything. The tip of his tongue traced little circles around her dusky-hued nipples, closer, closer. Even that made her dizzy, as if she still spun in his arms. His big hand lifted to cup a knee, then slid higher while his mouth marauded closer, closer, then settled over a perky peak to tease and suckle it. A shower of sparks radiated through her from every place he licked or touched. She struggled with the overwhelming urge to bring him closer, to pin him to her, but she held back, letting him set the pace. Suddenly, next to her, he looked so big everywhere.

He hastily fumbled to unbutton his breeches and peel them off. He sat naked beside her on the bed, and it sagged, rolling her toward him. She scooted back to give him room, her green eyes wide on him. She looked tense and so very serious. He felt himself swell even more when he thought he was at a white hot peak already. He did not know how he could possibly control himself from just taking his wife. Mustering all his self-discipline, he steeled himself to woo her body.

His calloused hands tingled her silken skin. His mouth—meandering places she had never imagined—moved to evoke passions she had never fathomed. Nothing existed but their need for each other and their touch, now fiercer each moment. He rolled her atop him and clasped her bottom. "Yes, like that, fine," he told her when her legs separated naturally to straddle his hips. He drowned in her curtain of copper hair and reveled in the press of her soft curves caressing his angles and planes. But when she thrust her tongue into his mouth as he had taught her, he passed beyond control.

He tumbled her over until he was atop. He kept his weight off her, but he had no fear this strong woman would break as he had felt once about—another. He pressed her down, his fingers working skillfully between her soft, spread thighs until she tensed and tossed her tresses back and forth to make him feel his power over her. He ravaged her damp skin with kisses. He took her mouth again and again until she mewed like a kitten against him and moved her hips in little, yearning circles. At that, he lifted and pressed himself at last against the soft, warm entry to her luscious body.

Thea gazed up at him, awed, anxious. His rugged face looked transported, so tense. She held to his sinewy neck as he lowered himself over her, spreading his legs wider between hers to press the tip of himself against her woman's core. She felt him carefully edge in. She sucked in a breath of fervid expectation.

"Oh, it's lovely," she whispered.

"Just a beginning."

"Really? I sense you know a great deal about all this."

He frowned. "I am only beginning," he rasped out, "to learn everything about you, and I like everything I see and feel."

"And I do, too, and—" was all she managed before he covered her lips with his and settled even closer inside her.

She could feel herself flower for him. But then he stopped. "I adore you, love you, want you," he said hotly in her ear and covered her mouth once more as he thrust his hips forward for total entry.

There was a tiny tear of pain, but it passed. He held still in her; they were perfectly joined. It felt marvelous, so right! But then, when she thought perhaps the ecstasy was over until another time, he began to move within her. Pushing, pulling, he took her with him. Everything spun even farther out of her control—her thinking, her feelings, her breathing. She could only gasp.

"I'm hurting you?" he said and lifted slightly away.

She tugged him back down with her arms around his neck and her long legs wrapped around his muscled thighs. "No, you're not! I was just surprised. I—it's wonderful, everything!"

He was so touched, he almost cried. But he pushed them to a steady pace, and then a faster one, faster. Her supple hips began to move with him; her hands wildly wandered his back and waist and hips to drive him onward toward the crest of victory. He sucked in ragged breaths; she panted in his ear. But she went stunned and still as something dark and delicious she had never discovered exploded deep within her. She felt on fire everywhere, caught in waves of shimmering, convulsing heat.

"Yes, oh yes, my Thea!" he cried, evidently as surprised and soul-struck as she. Then he moaned and thrust and filled her with proof of his passion and love before they quieted, clinging dazedly together on their wedding night.

That night of the Glenn–Arnold wedding, Avery Payne sat facing Jed Clapper and Levi Dobson across the desk in his study. He had no choice, he thought, but to trust these two. He was certainly not going out to the Firelands for his revenge, any more than he'd gone out on the Atlantic to make his privateering fortune! So, to open this important meeting in the language both men understood, he slid a pile of British pounds across the polished desk to both of them. Jed's eyes popped at the size of the stack, and Levi grabbed for his, despite the wound in his arm that had festered, causing him all kinds of pain in the two weeks since Morgan Glenn had shot him.

"Just the beginning, men," Avery assured them. "A great risk, but even greater rewards, et cetera."

"But why do we have to trail them clear out to these so-called Firelands? They couldn't've gotten too far out of town in that Conestoga, Mr. Payne," Levi told him. "Why not just let us put a bullet in Glenn right away and hold her somewhere until you get there?"

"Because I refuse to be linked to any sort of unlawful violence, at least here in civilization! Governor Trumbull has evidently taken a liking to Glenn, and I don't need Trumbull's long arm reaching out to investigate me! When Glenn meets some sad fate in the distant Firelands, the governor won't think a thing of it—and the woman will come back broken or not at all. Now we'll do this my way, or you can both go back to hauling rigging on an outbound ship, and I'll get someone who is interested in enough money to set them up for life when they return!"

"Sure, sure. Didn't mean to throw my own ideas in here, boss. Besides, I got a score to settle with Morgan Glenn for putting a bullet in my arm that day you went visiting the Arnold woman."

"All right, then it's settled. And, if worse comes to worst, I've kept their precious letters, the ones we managed to detour. With a little fixing up," Avery said and tapped his locked desk drawer, "I think these letters could reveal how the two of them were in collusion with General Arnold. But I'd much rather just have that bastard Glenn disappear and the Arnold bitch broken and begging. I've waited much too long for her, but I'll have to wait some more, since they're both in with Trumbull now," he insisted, and leaned back in his big leather wingchair. "I suggest you two just count your money and blessings, and take orders with your mouths shut."

Thea's frenzied accusations still haunted him and made him even a bit afraid of her, Avery admitted to himself as he watched the men rifle through their money, counting it. But that only added to the allure of humbling and ruining her. And since she evidently hadn't come forward with those accusations while Morgan Glenn was here in town, she must not have anything but suspicions. Still, he told himself, if there was no way to have her even with this last desperate ploy, he'd have no choice but to dispatch her once and for all, the way he'd eliminated Charity when she had meddled in his life. He'd have her first, if it was the last thing he did!

Avery stood and paced to the windows to peer out between his curtains at the barren street that once had been lined with fine mansions. Now only three stood beside the empty hulks or shacks where destitute people still clung to their ruined lots.

Damn, but he was always walking on eggshells here in

town lately! The fact that he, a privateer, had not had his house burned had caused more talk than he'd expected. It had forced him to be a strident spokesman for the rights of these damned fire sufferers when all he wanted was to make more money off this war before it was over and have his revenge on Thea Arnold and Morgan Glenn. But at least his petitioning the governor on behalf of New Londoners had made him some state government contacts. He'd managed to bribe them in return for word of the Firelands challenge and copies of the same map the five pioneer couples were given. Now, if only he could discover who the governor had assigned to watch over Thea Arnold and to look into the disappearances of her letters, he could dispense with that problem, too.

"Mr. Payne, this money's real generous of you. But being in British pounds and all," Jed Clapper said, "I mean, the other half of this you promised us when we come back with our job done, it won't be British, too, will it? After a year or so it might take us, wouldn't people wonder?"

"That part of the fortune I offer you will be in American exchange, whatever that is when this rampant war inflation ends," he told them. "Then, you'll both be set for life, and I'll expect you to go back to your own homes and never see me again."

"Suits me fine," bull-necked Levi put in before he realized what he'd said and cleared his throat.

"Then, we definitely have a deal?" Avery demanded and leaned over his desk to stare down each man in turn.

"A deal!" they chorused. "Though I, for one, would like a little something in writing," Jed Clapper dared, and Payne reluctantly agreed. They shook hands heartily, though Avery suddenly had no desire to touch either of them. He gave each a glass of port and let them out the back door. Then he hurried upstairs, his thoughts and passions still seething with Thea Arnold—now Thea Glenn, damn her. And tonight Morgan Glenn was reveling between those sweet, defiant thighs that should—and would—be his.

He felt himself swell and strain against his breeches as he strode the upstairs hall to his bedroom. He banged the door in so hard, the parrot squawked from its corner cage, though it was draped.

"Oh, Mr. Payne, are your guests gone?" Sarah, the new, fetching young housemaid he'd brought back from his stay in Philadelphia asked. She jumped to her feet from where she'd sat, buffing her fingernails in a black silk satin wrapper before the low-burning hearth. She waited, wide-eyed as he closed the door without answering. He really liked the way she was still afraid of him. When she ceased to do his bidding, he'd be rid of her for another, though Sarah's height, her voluptuous body, and reddish hair had prompted him to keep her this long. And now with this added henna he'd had another maid put on her hair to redden it even more . . .

"Do you like it—the new color you wanted?" she asked as he came over to stare closer at her.

"I do, but you're much too covered to please me," he said and yanked her wrapper back and down to expose her alabaster nudeness to her waist. She startled, but did not protest. Shaking, she untied her satin belt and let the rest of the wrapper puddle at her feet. He narrowed his eyes. Yes, he could imagine Thea Arnold better now, and in the dark, the ruse would be perfect. He could almost feel how it would be to have Thea at last after he dispensed with Morgan Glenn and took her somewhere else to live with the fortune he had made from the war.

"Shall—shall I get in bed now?" Sarah's voice quavered.

"Yes," he said, but seized her soft upper arms to stay her a moment. "But I want you to fight me tonight, more than usual. Fight and struggle, and then just take whatever it gets you, The—my darling Sarah."

His eyes clawed her body, not really seeing her. She was trembling already and he liked that. Trembling just as she would after he had her husband murdered and she came back here broken and ready, just like this.

He lifted one hand to her throat and walked her backwards across the room to shove her down on the bed. She dared to protest and struggle! He slapped her once to spill her red hair loose across the waiting sheets. He fondled her full breasts roughly while she thrashed and moaned. And then, not waiting longer to break Thea Arnold, he threw himself upon her.

Late in the velvet darkness of their marriage bed, Thea jerked in Morgan's arms to wake him.

"What is it? Are you all right, my love?" he asked.

"Mm. Just a bad dream, I guess, but I can't remember what."

"No more bad dreams, only good ones of our future."

She nodded, her head tucked under his chin, her bottom back in the curve of his lap as if they were two spoons cuddled on their sides. She felt him grow against her there and marveled how he could start everything over again after each delicious bout. And now, just awakened from a groggy sleep!

"We've a lot of years apart to make up for, Thea." He lowered his head to whisper hot in her ear. He trailed kisses through her hair-swept temples. "I should have gotten down on my knees, weak though I was, that first day in your shop and said, 'Will you wed with me tomorrow, Mistress Arnold?' "

"You tease."

"I'm not teasing. You yourself were the herb that finally cured me of—of many things."

"There *is* an herb named Althea," she murmured through her haze of languorous exhaustion and growing passion. "I was named for it."

But it was obvious to her from the way his lips nibbled her bare shoulder and his big hand lowered to work wicked finger magic between her thighs that all discussions were at an end for now. Her heart soared with love for this man. She felt almost giddy in her joy that they were now one forever. Boldly, she reached back to take the length of him in her hand.

"I know how to cure this fever now, too," she told him.

"Oh, yes, oh, Thea!" was all he managed before he turned her to him and mounted her. She held tightly to his big, rocking body and smiled up in the dark as they loved.

Chapter Eleven

"A sore eye remedy for a sleepless night or too much grief: gather purple loosestrife from the streambank. Its flowers make a fine eye lotion."

NEW LONDONERS PACKED the early Georgian style Congregational church for Cullen Varner and Varina Lockwood's wedding. Friends and relatives of Cullen's had come in from Danbury, too, though they had to be housed on the fringes of the town. In a beige ruffled and ribboned gown which Cullen had borrowed from an aunt, Rina said her vows with hundreds of eyes on her. She received many kisses and shook many hands in the presence of nearly a hundred guests at the reception. Yet in the whirl of the day, she longed for the presence of her dear friend Thea. Perhaps it was partly Cassie's fault that, even during the sacred vows, Thea and Morgan had haunted her mind.

That morning, Cassie's comforting hands had shaped her coif with curls and woven ribbons, but her words had been most disturbing. " 'Tis a good thing Cullen Varner has not riled the forest folk like you and Morgan did that time," Cassie said as she patted the last upswept, silver-blond tress in place.

Rina's hands clasped her looking glass. She tilted it up to catch Cassie's face. "What time? What do you mean?" she asked shakily as memories she had tried to bury flew back to taunt her.

"You know! You and Morgan going right by those fairy rings, maybe walking direct on them, too! I'll bet you kissed him in there, too, and the forest folk don't take to all of that without permission!"

Rina stood to flounce out her skirts. "I saw no fairy rings, Cassie." For one moment, she had feared what the girl meant by "kissing, too" or "all of that," as if she'd known what else they'd almost done out there. But it was only her guilty imagination. Cassie had stayed across the stream. But why, why, did these thoughts have to torment her today, just before she went in Father's old carriage to the church to wed Cullen? And why last night had she dreamed that old nightmare about Mother screaming at her and Thea's voice joining in? She'd hardly slept a wink, and her eyes were burning. If only Thea were here, she'd have something to soothe their pink color and soreness!

"You're not to cry, mistress, not on your wedding day," Cassie chided as she draped the satin shawl around Rina's shoulders. Rina turned to study Cassie's eyes as if she somehow had the answers to her own future hidden in that forest-thick brain.

"Come on, Cassie. It's time for our new life to start. No looking back at fairy rings or anything else," Rina said and went out with a taut smile on her lovely face, sweetly framed by ribbon-captured cascades of curly hair.

"I'd be glad to comb that glorious golden hair out for you," Cullen volunteered. Rina sat dawdling at the dressing table that night in the big, back, upstairs bedroom of his friends' house on Williams Street. Cassie had helped her undress, but had gone back to Mercy Bigler's since the newly married couple did not want her hovering outside their door. Tomorrow they were taking Cassie along and heading for Danbury, and then on to Lebanon in a wagon Cullen had purchased. Rina hoped he thought her on edge only because they faced that long jaunt and not because she could not stem her guilt over how she had once secretly pledged herself to Morgan in a passion she had never yet recaptured. Strange, how tonight that one whirlwind week long ago with another man seemed so real and recent.

But Rina smiled up at her nightshirted husband as he took

her carved bone comb from her hand and pulled it gently through her shoulder-blade length hair. "I never knew your hair was really straight," he told her. "It always looked so curly. What other secrets shall I discover about my darling?"

She jumped as if he'd yanked a snarl. He was just teasing, but it seemed he'd read her thoughts. He put the comb down and feathered his fingers through her tresses. "It's Thea who always had the curly hair," she admitted, tipping her head back against his firm belly to gaze up so he appeared upside down. "I've just curled mine, and that afternoon shower quite straightened it. As for other secrets—that's a lady's prerogative!"

He grinned down and hiked both arched eyebrows. "We'll just see," he said, but his voice was light. She began to relax, despite the tightening knot in her stomach. She gave in to the good feel of his hands in her hair, then kneading her shoulders as she leaned lightly back against him. He bent to caress her temples, her cheeks, her throat, first with fingers, and then kisses. She reached up to cover his hands with hers as he edged her rose silk wrapper down to bare her shoulders. He became emboldened when he discovered she wore nothing underneath. Awestruck at the sight of her, he pulled her to her feet to face him.

"My dearest Varina, you're so lovely, always were, so perfect. And as for the future, we've a real task ahead, but we will win, together, and go on to greater heights from there."

"I'm only wondering," she said, "if the real task you refer to lies out there,"—she swept her arm westward—"or over there!" She nodded toward the big feather bed, turned down for them. She was grateful to him for a lovely day and trying so to show him.

"My darling, I want to be the perfect man and mate for you always!"

Passionately, at least for Cullen, she thought, he led her to the bed and slowly removed her wrapper as if he were uncovering a precious package. She saw how deliberate he intended to be, despite his verbal outbursts. She felt just the opposite, outwardly nervous but inwardly unmoved, and that scared her. She realized that the faster, the wilder this happened, perhaps the better for her—just this time.

She let the silk slither from her arms and kicked it away. She hugged him to her and nibbled at his throat the way he liked. Careful to put her head on his left side to avoid the disfigured ear he always tried to hide with his own hair or wigs, she pressed her naked body against his nightshirt. And just as she had hoped, his need for her exploded like powder in the pan.

"Varina—Rina!" he cried as he took her down onto the soft linen sheets. He had never called her Rina. She didn't want him to. It wasn't like him, it was like others she did not want to think of now—Father and Mother, Thea and . . .

She kissed him back to match his verve. Her body responded, but her mind remained a thing apart. Thoughts jumped into her head, things people had said today, Thea's last words to her on that other wedding day: "My dearest friend Rina, married or not, western Firelands or not, we will still trust each other, still share things!"

Cullen had not pulled his nightshirt off, though she supposed as florid as his face looked and as hard as he breathed, he might have just forgotten it. His hands glided up and down her torso, stopping every time to fondle her petite, pointed breasts. "Am I—am I going too fast, my darling?" he rasped in her ear.

"No! Fast is fine! I want you, only you so—"

He tumbled her on her back, her bottom on a pillow as if to put that part of her on a pedestal. She clung to him; he was panting as if he had run miles, while deep inside, she felt still so deadly calm. And yet she loved him, wanted him and their new life together, didn't she, even if it had to begin way out there in the unknown?

"I realize this is all new, my love. I'll be careful, always careful *inter nos,*" he promised and hiked his nightshirt up to his waist.

She pinned him closer with her nails in his lower bare back to urge him on. He moaned and pressed against her. His weight surprised her. They were one! Everything was fine now. He moved heavily within her. Not much pain, she thought, but not much else, either. She stared straight up at the white ceiling while she clung to him. She wanted to love and desire Cullen! It was just such a busy day that she was not swept away as she had been once when this had almost happened to her before, that was all.

And yet, she adored how he cradled her, how he was beside himself with passion for her, the formal, disciplined Cullen Varner! Should she pretend it hurt, that she felt more than she did? But no, she wanted no more lies to build on. Other than in one thing to protect them all, she would tell the truth. Besides, Mercy Bigler had tried to mother her the other day by telling her that sometimes it took awhile to get used to liking the marriage act men so doted on. But then why had Morgan's arousing touch seemed so wild and wonderful before, even though it had never gone this far?

Cullen Varner thundered his passion into his new wife while she held hard to him, her hands caressing his neck and head. Cullen's hot breathing quieted in her ear; he pulled slightly away.

"Wonderful! You were—are wonderful!" he told her and dropped a kiss on her mouth before rolling off. The past was behind her now, and there was only her dedication and duty to this man. Surely, she really loved him. She adored how he adored her. Over the years in the west and then back here in New London where he had promised her a big new mansion on the site of the old one, she would grow to love him even more than she did now.

"I shall always treasure you, husband," she told him, then added boldly, "and what we just did together."

"You'll be sore in the morning," he warned, but looked most pleased. "And here I meant to be so careful so there would be no Varner heir before we're safely and triumphantly returned here. I wouldn't be surprised," he boasted as he pulled her into his warm embrace, "if they don't give us our own parade here someday for opening the Firelands for them all."

She cursed the fact that got her mind spinning back again to other parade days she'd best not remember. Not now that she was Mrs. Cullen Varner and heading out into the future.

"Oh," was all she managed as he began to nibble up and down her flesh. Her wedding night, the night she tried to bury all the bad things from her past, went on and on.

A spanking breeze cooled the bright sun on the day the Firelands pioneers met to set out from the warehouse behind the governor's war office in Lebanon. Each couple positioned their wagons—the Glenns had the only Conestoga—in the empty building and pointed their teams' noses—the Glenns had the only oxen amidst all the horses—toward the big doors. Though the journey was being kept secret from the masses, old Governor Jonathan Trumbull had arranged a send-off ceremony, and he had not yet appeared. But a little speaker's platform was draped with red, white, and blue bunting, and five boxes of departure gifts were lined up on a makeshift table there. Meanwhile, everyone exchanged nervous greetings. Some of the men restudied their maps of the Hudson-Mohawk Valley and squinted down at markings indicating where they would meet the flatboats called bateaux at Buffalo Creek to take them along Lake Erie. Thea and Rina huddled behind the Varner wagon, while Cassie, whom the Varners had special permission to take with them, hovered nearby.

"Now we've got to talk them into at least camping near each other at night," Thea insisted.

"Cullen says we're stopping at good inns until we're past Albany," Rina countered. "Cullen says he heard the Dutch marketplace there never lacks for goods."

"Rina, dearest friend, we are hardly going to shop our way out west. Besides, once we're past those Falls of Cohoe, it's much wilder."

"Falls of what? You mean you've been studying Morgan's map?"

"Cullen and Morgan are going to need all the help we can give them on this journey. I don't mean to scold the minute we're back together with so much to share, but—"

"Well, really, Thea, it's a relief you haven't changed. I'd be distraught if you didn't scold. You—you haven't changed in just ten days, have you?"

Thea's eyes grew misty. "Yes, of course I have. Surely you have, too. But it only means things will be better for us as more mature, married friends than before, don't you think?"

"I suppose," Rina said and sighed. "If we can get our men to patch things up. But really, it's important each family go west on its own," she added. It made her uncomfortable to be around Morgan and Thea, too, even though she'd put the past behind her. "Cullen says it's the rule that we all settle out there independently, and I'm hardly going to argue with my new husband!"

"But you've argued with him on that very thing before, if I recall. Has Cullen got you convinced he's always right already and marriage makes everything perfect?"

Rina's graceful hands shot to her waist. "I thought you were blissfully happy!"

"Yes. Never happier, except maybe in the old, old days when I was just a child with my parents and didn't even know such a thing as grief or lonely nights or tear-burned eyes existed."

"Yes!" Rina said and nodded fiercely, but Thea wasn't sure at what and didn't have time to ask. Cullen came around the end of the wagon and beckoned Rina to him. She started away, and then turned back to Thea.

"It's just that I'm fussed-up about this big, long trip, Thea, and haven't slept much lately, if you know what I mean. We'll see each other every chance we get, I promise!" she concluded and came back to hug her friend.

"Just remember," Thea told her, "that you used to long for freedom and independence, and now you've really got a chance to build a new life. To really help Cullen, just as I'm going to help Morgan."

Rina nodded again and stepped back. She looked as if she would speak again, but turned and joined Cullen as Governor Trumbull entered across the way.

Thea strode to Morgan's side, standing near the platform as the other couples gathered. She had briefly met them all, and the way they had looked at her and whispered reminded her again of how it felt to be the traitor's cousin. But Governor Trumbull shook her hand warmly and smiled up at her.

"My dear, an honor to meet Morgan Glenn's new bride." She was nearly as tall as Morgan, the governor thought, a fine match for his former aide in every way. And she looked such a colorful person with that flaming hair and green eyes. Perhaps her character was such, too, a glowing, biblical rose of Sharon in the desert among paler blooms. Ah, yes, he was more relieved than ever he had decided to send his best scout to watch over her before she wed Morgan. And when Morgan returned to New London, his man had still helped save her from three men who had surrounded her just outside the town. But it was time now to return that scout to the Firelands he knew as few white men did. Besides, he needed him to watch over the pioneers to assure him the rules had been followed. Ah, yes, and now he'd best get to that.

Governor Trumbull mounted the low platform and held up his hands for order while his aide put a box from the governor in each of the wagons. "I believe you all know the rules and the rewards," he told them. His deep stentorian voice echoed in the warehouse emptied now of war goods. "I send you out, wishing you bounteous success. I pray I will see all of you returned by January 1, 1785 after your sojourn in our promised land. Until that grand and glorious day, I give to you these charges from the Good Book:

> *Until the spirit be poured upon us from on high, and the wilderness be a fruitful field and the fruitful field be counted for a forest, then judgment shall dwell in the wilderness . . . And my people shall dwell in a peaceable habitation, and in sure dwellings, and in quiet resting places; when it shall hail, coming down on the forest, blessed are ye that sow beside all waters that send forth thither.*

"I send you forth thither now to the great forests and the wilderness. God bless you as you sow there beside the waters of the Firelands," the governor concluded and lifted his hand as if in benediction.

"What does he mean about the forests?" Cassie cried and

plucked at the sleeve of Thea's sturdy brown dress just before Morgan lifted his new wife up on the wagon seat.

"He means, even in the forests, we can find peace and blessings, Cassie," Thea said down to her. "Now remember what I said about coming to visit our wagon anytime you see us. Best go with Rina now."

"And give us all a good farewell with 'Danny Boy'!" Morgan called after the girl as she scurried to clamber up in the back of the heavily loaded Varner wagon with its flat, braced canvas top. "Hee-ya!" Morgan shouted to his team of horses and the two stolid oxen and cracked his whip high in the air. The warehouse doors swung open to the narrow back street and the wide country beyond. The team jerked the wagon forward. It fell into line just behind Cullen's, where Cassie was waving out the back and singing, "Then come ye back when summer's in the meadow." Morgan grinned and turned to drop a quick, hard kiss on Thea's cheek. Under them, the weight of the bright Conestoga swayed and creaked. And, from the harnesses, their wedding bells kept counterpoint to Cassie's clear, beckoning song.

The five wagons rolling west stayed close together for that first festive day, then separated to different camping spots at night to fan them out farther apart day by day. Still on well-worn roads and turnpikes, the Glenns reached the Hudson River near West Point, where they would head north along the east bank toward Albany.

"This area brings back bad memories," Morgan told Thea as he held her in the wagon along the forested bank of the Hudson the fourth night out. "Only a few miles from here, Arnold defected and left all of us holding the bag for him when Washington rode in for what he thought was to be just a quick breakfast with a friend."

"You know, I pitied Cousin Benedict's young wife when I first heard. But then, to think she encouraged him to be a traitor and even drove him to it!"

"I shouldn't have brought it all up," he said quickly. "Let's just concentrate on what you can drive your husband to, my sweetheart." He turned her toward him in the little nook they had hollowed out among the packed-in goods. It made them sleep quite close together for two tall, big people, but they reveled in it. And in each other. Now. Again. And always so astounded by the sweeping needs they shared.

They took the ferry across the Hudson to Albany, and it was the first time Morgan had spent any of their precious coins. The governor's gift had been bottles of port and a firkin of Madeira. Added to their own barrel of ale, which Thea intended to use for a laundry tub and bathing when it was empty, they had not even needed to buy drinks from the inns where the Varners stopped every night. When it became clear to the Glenns that Cullen was going to be cold to them, they had not sought them out in Albany, although it saddened them. Still, Thea thought, perhaps Rina was busy shopping as she had said, to add more weight to the lumbering wagon Cullen's six brown horses pulled. But if they saw them on the Mohawk Trail, Thea vowed, she was going to talk to Rina, no matter what Cullen Varner said.

Although the other wagons, no doubt, set out with no extra day's rest in Albany, the Glenns stayed behind another day when their right lead horse threw a shoe. On May 11, they headed to Schenectady over a flat, sandy road and followed the south bank of the Mohawk west.

"That's our last town until we see Schenectady again in over a year," Thea said, but she looked straight ahead. "I don't mind. After New London, I welcome the change."

"There will be villages along the way, though," he told her. "Those cabins and campfires on the map indicate German farmers' settlements or Indian camps. And I've got a surprise for you about forty miles up the river."

"What?" she demanded and reached to tickle his ribs. She had accidentally learned something else about her husband just the other night: he was uproariously ticklish. "Tell me!"

"Thea, dang it, not while I'm driving! I'll tell, woman, I'll tell! I've got a friend from the war who also served under Washington. He has a large estate, where we'll stop for the night. He's really well-known around these parts, I take it.

He's got a French wife who gives theatricals with their two daughters, and he told me to stop if I ever passed through."

"Oh, Morgan! And she's French? And theatricals, out in the middle of all this?"

"His name's Ethan Trent, and he's had the place called Eden's Gate, since before the old Indians wars. I just hope he's home. Someday, my sweetheart, we'll have a place like that," he promised her with a distant look in his eye, which she was coming to think of as "the Firelands look." "Well-established, filled with children, a place built somewhere we both choose," he went on. "I hear the Trents have a trading post for Indians and settlers attached to their house, but we'll have an apothecary shop attached to our big home."

"And we'll help anyone who wants some of Thea's cures," she said. "I like that name—Eden's Gate. It sounds like our own entrance to the west, Morgan. Maybe we'll find our own paradise beyond."

She smiled and linked her hands around his arms. Despite the bouncing motion of the wagon, she rested her head on his shoulder as they jolted along, heading deeper into the thickly treed forests of New York State.

The next day they saw their first Mohawk Indian with the distinctive bald head and standing roach of hair bisecting his scalp. But he paid them no heed and disappeared into the thicket just ahead as they passed. The very thought of scalps, the memory of that story of poor murdered and scalped Jane McCrea that wretch Avery Payne had told in her shop one day made Thea jumpy. But the Indians were at peace here now and, in the Connecticut Reserve, they had never been much riled, as Morgan put it.

They hallooed at flatboats and canoes, which were always moving up and down the river. They passed occasional settlers' cabins, most on the other bank along the trail once called the Kingsroad. They rolled the big wagon across rocky fords, and once the animals had to swim to pull them across. In spots where the dim forest had been hacked away, sun-lit fields with early planted rye, bluegrass, and clover lay off to the side like multihued carpets. They saw occasional folks

to talk to—always, by agreement with the governor—telling
them they were heading west to the far edge of the uncharted
wilderness and not plunging into it. And every time they saw
a neat patch of planted garden, or domestic animals grazing,
or a crude sod cabin, they planned together their own temporary homestead in the Firelands. Then, the third afternoon
out along the Mohawk, they came to Eden's Gate.

"Oh, it's amazing, especially to find it here!" Thea said and
stood in the wagon to gaze up the hill at the impressive house
and outbuildings. "Why, it's far grander than the old Lockwood house!" They both fell silent after seeing sod and chink-
logged cabins these last days. They paused before a tall,
wrought-iron gate, which stood open to a well-worn boat
landing, studded with both canoes and bateaux with their
owners bustling here and there, some with piles of furs on
their backs.

The team dragged the wagon up the slanted lane from the
river. The main house was three stories of white-painted
wood with black shutters and a leaden roof. Glass windows
glinted gaily in the slant of sun. In and out the door to the
trading post to the right of the house bustled braves and
squaws, trappers, and traders of all descriptions. And there,
pulled up near the barracks building on the left, sat Cullen
and Rina's wagon already unhitched.

A beautiful, middle-aged woman, with blond hair etched
with silver came out to greet them. "Welcome to Eden's
Gate," she called as she descended the steps like a queen.
"I'm Mrs. Ethan Trent. It's a day for visitors, it seems, and
we're so happy to have you!"

She was unutterably graceful. Her elegant hands seemed
to float, just like Rina's, Thea thought as Morgan jumped
down and helped her after him. Mrs. Trent—she said to call
her Claire—had such an animated face and lively personality!
And then, Thea spotted Cassie and Rina waving at her from
the front window, framed by green draperies. She waved
back, hardly lifting her calloused, soiled hand. Strange, how
when she felt most free and loved, that old feeling of unease,
of gawkiness, could come back to haunt her. But she did not
have long to worry about that. Claire escorted Thea up into

her beautiful home while Cassie came charging down the hall
with open arms to hug her.

While Thea washed up and sipped tea from a gilt-edged
saucer, Morgan unhitched the team with help from the
Trents' nephew, Dirck Vandervort, a lawyer visiting from
Albany. Then Dirck took Morgan to join the men out back
by the small brewery near the stream. Though he chatted
with Dirck, Morgan's eyes took in the fine array of outbuildings: a cooper's house and shop, bake house, mill, sheep
house, barn, and stable all set in well-tended gardens and
fields. "It's so idyllic here on the edge of the frontier," Morgan marveled.

"It all came under attack in the French and Indian Wars
and the Revolution," Dirck told him. "I could show you the
bullet holes in the buildings. But they fought for it, the
women, too, when Mr. Trent and his two sons were away
serving with Trent's old friend Washington in the east. But
the rewards of peace and prosperity along the Mohawk are
worth it all."

Silently, Morgan prayed that the women he knew—Thea,
Rina, Cassie, and the other Firelands settlers' wives—would
never have to fight Indians along the Pequotting or any Firelands river. But he had no doubt that Thea could fight if she
must, and he intended to teach her how to shoot his Brown
Bess musket first chance he got.

"There are the men, Morgan," Dirck told him and
pointed. "Down by the stream, you might know, fishing out
some bottles of cold spruce beer for dinner tonight to toast
the peace treaty that's to be signed soon. I'll see you back
at the house later then."

Morgan strode toward Ethan Trent and Cullen, who were
talking earnestly with their backs to him. Ethan was gestur-
ing out toward the hills and forests, but he spun when Morgan stepped on a dry twig. The man, every bit as tall as he,
squinted into the sun to see him, then hurried up from the
stream with his hand outstretched.

"Morgan Glenn! A fellow timber beast, if from that hellfire
state of Pennsylvania! Mrs. Varner said you were heading

west, too! I hoped you recalled my invitation at Valley Forge to stop by if you were ever this far out!"

They shook hands heartily. Cullen walked slowly up, dripping bottles in his hands, so he could not offer Morgan a shake. "You two should travel on together," Ethan Trent, buckskin-clad and dark-haired with silver at the temples, insisted buoyantly. "Safety in numbers even with no current Indian threats, since you still never know what's out here around the next bend," his voice trailed off as he noted the strained current between the two men. "I thought you two knew each other pretty well," he added.

"Probably not as well as you and Morgan know each other from serving on Washington's staff," Cullen clipped out, sounding colder than he'd intended. Damn Morgan Glenn! Why did men whom Cullen admired always seem to take to the Pennsylvanian more than to him? In the middle of this big Mohawk country, you might know Morgan, a good friend of Ethan's, would turn up. And just when he was starting to get to know Ethan Trent, the legendary white trader who used to live among the feared Mohawks. It was the General Arnold and Governor Trumbull story all over again, Cullen fumed, but he managed an answer. "Morgan and I knew each other early in the war when we served Benedict Arnold long before his defection. And our wives have always been good friends. Anyway, I went on to serve General Gates while Lieutenant Colonel Glenn was with Arnold right up until the traitor showed his true colors."

"Really?" Ethan Trent said as he grasped the root of the ill will this Connecticut gentleman felt for his fellow frontiersman, Morgan. "Hellfire, Cullen, you've gotta admit General Gates went bad, too, in his own way. I don't think much of a man who lets a splinter group in congress try to replace Washington with him, or one who turns tail in a fight, either, like Gates did more than once. But, though you served Gates closely, I'll just bet you weren't a bit guilty in that so-called Conway Cabal scandal everyone tried to cover up, or in any of Gates's lily-livered retreats, either!"

Morgan saw Cullen's jaw set hard. How badly Morgan was torn between thanking Ethan Trent for teaching Cullen a lesson and yet wanting to shake hands with Cullen. But Cullen still clenched the necks of the bottles he held as if he would shatter them in his grip.

"True," Cullen muttered. "Besides, my wife and I were hoping perhaps the Glenns would go on with us if we saw them again, at least as far as Buffalo Creek."

"One hell of an idea!" Ethan Trent cracked out before Morgan could agree. The older man slapped both Cullen and Morgan on the backs as they headed toward the big house.

"Your home is so lovely, and I thank you for the tour," Thea told Claire as they all settled back in one of two cherry-paneled drawing rooms. Thea's eyes drank it all in: the tiled hearth and thick Turkish carpet underfoot. Fine walnut and rosewood upholstered furniture. Green and gold wall hangings and a portrait of the handsome Trent family of two sons and two daughters over the carved mantel. Perhaps someday, just perhaps . . .

"I was wondering how you got along with the savages at first," Rina was asking Claire.

"When I really got to know them and to love them as individuals, they weren't savages to me, only different, fascinating people. Over the years here, some of my dearest friends have been Mohawk Indians, though I must say I was a bit shocked by some of their 'overly friendly' customs involving white folk," she said and smiled at some private thought.

"Even friendly if they lived deep in the forest?" Cassie put in.

"Yes, my dear. Let me share a little secret with you two new brides, and Cassie, too, so you will be aware of something," Claire told them and leaned forward in her chair to pour Cassie another saucer of tea. "Many Iroquois Indian tribes have a custom of sharing their maidens, 'on the blanket' as they call it, with white men visiting their tribe. A rather too broad interpretation of hospitality, if you ask me," she concluded with a shake of her elegant head tempered by a winsome smile.

Rina gasped, and Thea bit her lip, while Cassie sipped her tea. Drat, Thea thought, Morgan used to trade and visit

among some kind of Iroquois tribes back in Pennsylvania all
the time. She'd just have to ask him about that rather primi-
tive custom!

"Well," Rina declared, "I'd never be jealous of a one-night
Indian maid, because I'd never allow it in the first place!"

"Spoken like a true pioneer wife!" Claire said with a tap
of fist to her knee. "But I tell you, overcoming jealousy was
one of the first hard lessons I learned as a bride, and not because I ever had one instance to doubt Ethan's faithfulness
to me after we wed. But, you see, he had a love affair from
across the river in that little town of German Flats before
me, and I had to work through getting over that."

"At least," Thea put in, "with Rina and me settling somewhat near each other, we'll have each other to talk through
any problems, past or present."

"Yes, of course," Rina piped up and slopped some of her
tea on the new blue gown she'd bought already made from
a Dutch seamstress in Albany. Embarrassed for Rina, who
was usually so adept in social situations while she blundered,
Thea quickly returned the subject to how Claire could improve her medicinal herb garden out back.

That day and night at Eden's Gate refreshed the travelers'
tired bodies and anxious minds. The meal was delicious, the
conversation and the beer heady and exhilarating. After supper, Ethan got Cullen and Morgan to talk over pipe-smoking
and port in the other drawing room. They listened avidly to
Ethan's comments about natural signposts and dangers along
the route they were taking; he knew this territory like the
back of his hand. He would have gone along with them at
least to Fort Trent, he said, if he hadn't been away at war
so long. But recalling Governor Trumbull's rules, both men
assured him they would find their own way.

That evening, Claire and her two lovely daughters,
Merinda and Suzanne, entertained them with amateur theatricals Claire herself had written. The guests slept in thick
featherbeds and set out with full stomachs—and fuller
hearts—after a hearty breakfast the next morning. Thea and
Rina were thrilled that they would, temporarily at least, be

traveling together. Morgan and Cullen seemed resigned to strength in numbers in the wild. The Glenn Conestoga rumbled off down the rutted river road away from Eden's Gate just a bit ahead of the Varner wagon.

Late the next day, they came to the Mohawk Indian village called Canajoharie. To everyone's, including Thea's, amazement and delight, Morgan conversed with the people in broken Iroquois dialect. He came back to their little wagon camp with a big clay jar of honey and an entire basket of fresh, hot cornbread to make a feast for the five of them. But that night in the shelter of their wagon, Thea found she was as disturbed by the closeness of the Indians as Cassie had been, and she couldn't sleep. Just as Morgan reached for her in the darkness, she asked, "I heard about the Iroquois custom of sharing maidens 'on the blanket' for visiting white traders."

He tugged her closer to his big, hard body, silent for a moment. "All that was long before I knew you, Thea."

"Then you—once or twice, I mean—"

"Yes. You think a red-blooded young man could turn down such a thing? Besides, it would have insulted them."

"So—really, was it—different from us?"

"Of course, it was different from us! I never loved them, nor wanted to build a life with them!"

" 'Them'? It sounds like lots. Or was it the same maiden more than once? Drat, I don't want to sound jealous or shrewish or anything, but—"

He cuddled and coddled her that night, regaling her with stories of his early days among the Pennsylvania tribes. He assured her that no Indian maid had ever meant a thing to him beyond a youthful, mutually accepted adventure. And all the while he cursed himself for not telling her he had once planned a future with Rina. But how could he now, with the Varners sleeping in the next wagon? How could he when he feared it might ruin everything he wanted to build with Thea? But he must tell her when they were alone in the Firelands. If such a distant thing as the Indian women he'd known once bothered her so, he had to. That one thing stood between them like an evil spirit he had to exorcise. She would have to understand how Rina had misled him about Thea's being promised to another, even if it drove a wedge between her and Rina. But now, going west, Thea needed to trust him and cherish her friendship with Rina. Now, just as he withheld the truth about their true destination from fine folk like the Trents and even these Indians, he had to hold his tongue.

On May 18, they passed Fort Trent, that log blockhouse that had helped hold back the Canadian Indian hordes in two wars. They delivered messages to some of Ethan Trent's friends there. How good it was to see friendly faces the farther west they went! The men told them that they had seen two other wagons recently, heading the same direction, and the travelers assumed that meant two other Firelands families must be ahead.

Just beyond Fort Trent, they left the mighty Mohawk behind and took the narrow road across what the local tribes called "De-O-Wain-Sta" or "The Great Carrying Place," where canoes and bateaux had to be portaged. Down the Wood Creek Indian trail and along the south shore of beautiful Lake Oneida, even Cullen began to loosen up a bit as he came to realize how Morgan's years in the fields and forests benefited them all.

Cassie rode with the Glenns at times, as her chatter seemed to disturb Cullen and Rina more the deeper they ventured into trackless forest depths. They all marveled at the beauty around them. Deer feeding on water plants and beaver near their humpbacked houses stared liquid-eyed at their passing. Flocks of flapping birds sometimes blotted out the sun. Wild mountain dogwood laced the hills, and stretches of streambeds ran rampant with herbs like wild watercress, yellow dock, and purple loosestrife, which Thea harvested. She also supplemented their wild game and fire cake diet with dandelion greens, wild asparagus, and wild onions. And Rina and Cassie picked what wild strawberries they could reach without stepping one foot beyond the forest fringe. For once, they agreed on that.

" 'Tis true I'd rather be with you than Rina out here," Cassie whispered conspiratorially to Thea as she helped her slice green cattail stems for a salad. "The forest folk have blessed you with the gift of healing, but they might still blame her for Father Lockwood's deeds, even if he did get all burned up."

"The only forest folk out here are Indians, and we're going to make friends with them, Cassie. You just remember that. Besides, now that Cullen and Morgan are getting on so well, that puts a blessing on the forest, don't you think?"

"I 'spose," she drawled. "But there's things about loving in the forest I could tell you of, I could, like—"

"No more stories of the forest folk for now!" Thea insisted. "Let's just get this food ready for everyone."

Thea wiped her hands on the big canvas apron Morgan had bought for her in Lebanon. It reminded her so much of her days in the shop, just to wipe her hands on it, soil and grass-stained as they were. She kept the wagon as neatly as she had the apothecary shop, everything in its place. She climbed up into the wagon to fetch the pewter plates. Yes, she could find things here in the dark if she had to. The pungent smell of newly-gathered herbs hung upside down to dry inside the wagon jabbed her with longing for the shop she had left behind in the ashes of New London.

She sniffed hard to stop the first assault of yearning for home. With Morgan's love, she had longed for nothing, even out here. And yet, in her mind's eye, the shop, the Lockwood house, even poor Charity Payne's bedroom rose up complete and intact, as if she could step out of this little world inside the wagon and stride through the past again. Drat, she was going mushy-minded! She'd have another shop someday with Morgan at her side and Rina as her friend. For now, she could yearn for nothing else!

Heading south of Lake Onondaga, drenching rains bogged them down. On May 20—Rina kept their calendar—the sky cleared and they pushed on through mud and slick prairie grass that appeared to have been matted down by passing wagons, possibly from the other Connecticut couples. Along the Seneca River, named for one of the five once-fierce Iroquois tribes, the skies wept silver tears again. Morgan had

taken the wedding bells from the harness to keep them from
rusting, and forlorn silence reigned. The trail went upward
here, along the north shore of the churning river for a ways,
following another old Indian trail now widened by trappers'
packtrains and the occasional wagon. But it was narrow.
Two wagons could never go abreast past these steep slate
walls, glinting ebony in the wash of gentle rain.

Cullen drove his wagon in the lead today. No singing from
Cassie, Thea thought. The girl huddled inside the Varner
wagon to escape the drizzle. Thea rode outside on the high
seat with Morgan, wrapped in his old blue and buff army
cape, his second-best bicorn on her head. She felt better out
here where she could see. The drop-off on their left side was
steep, and through thick trees, the river foamed like cream
below. She was glad to sit on the right side along the higher
cliff face.

"It can't be like this much farther," she encouraged Morgan. His big hands were fists holding the reins; his jaw
clenched in concentration. Rain ran in rivulets off his wedding bicorn. Twice, in trying to get the Conestoga closer to
the safe cliff wall, he scraped the wagon's side near Thea.

"Just hope the animals' footing holds," he gritted out.
"Danged slick leaves from last autumn on this wet trail—"

They heard a rumble like thunder that shook the wagon.
Thea, her eyes still on Cullen and Rina's wagon just ahead,
screamed. Morgan yanked the reins back as the Conestoga
twisted and shifted under them.

"Out! Get out!" Morgan yelled and elbowed her toward
the safety of the cliff face. She scrambled, thinking he would
follow. But the wagon lurched toward him as some of the
trail gave way in a rumbling avalanche of stone and soil.
Horses neighed and shied as the wagon dragged them back.
The big oxen planted their sturdy feet and bent their bull
necks forward. Before she could climb down, Thea slammed
into Morgan as the wagon tilted more. Under the back left
wheel, the hillside slipped away, and the Conestoga settled
lower in a flurry of snapping saplings.

Thea grabbed for the sloping seat, then Morgan. She heard
Cullen yell and Rina scream something to answer her own

shriek. A big, dead tree ripped through the Conestoga's linsey-woolsey top before it cracked away. On a shuddering tilt, the wagon settled precariously on the edge of the steep, tree-studded slope of the riverbank. Either the reins ripped free from Morgan's grip, or he threw them away. Clinging desperately together, Thea and Morgan tumbled out as barrels and boxes slammed out and spilled after them.

Chapter Twelve

"To combat wracking, staggering pain, the best cures are Dover's Powders or Godfrey Elixir with their opium mixes. For pains that go deeper than that, what indeed can help?"

MORGAN ROLLED THROUGH pine boughs and slammed into a tree trunk before he realized he still held Thea. Despite the pain in his ribs, he grabbed her one-handed by her apron when her cloak tore away. "Thea! Thea!" he gasped. She clawed at the slick pine needle and leaf-littered hill to save herself. Clinging to a tree trunk, he dragged her up where she could hold on to him. He propped them against the tree. Her skin was bruised and scratched; she was panting, terrified, but she held on to him.

He looked up the slope to the big wagon still balanced at a dangerous angle over them. It, too, could come crashing down like the goods it had spilled. It held for now, impaled by a dead tree trunk that had ripped open the roof, and held up by the tautness of the teams' harness. It looked like they had skidded down a damn long way. Cullen, holding to a sapling above, peered carefully over and waved wildly. They could hear Rina's and Cassie's cries from above.

"You got a rope, Cullen?" Morgan bellowed, though the pain around his ribs told him he had broken several. "Fish us up before the whole thing goes. And keep that harness taut!"

"Hold on! I've got an extra harness for plowing! Hold on!"

"Are you all right?" he asked Thea, who looked dazed, her mouth open, her eyes as big as saucers.

"Y—yes. Morgan, my mother's apothecary book. It's in

that box," she said and stared at the wooden case wedged in the brush along the slant of hill. The undergrowth had snagged a few other things, but most had bounced down to the river below.

He almost cursed her mother's book and everything else at the sight of his beautiful Conestoga sitting battered up above, but he didn't. Her book was all she really had from the shop that meant so much to her, like the wagon did to him. "We'll get it up somehow," he told her grimly as Cullen, after what seemed an eternity, tossed the leather straps of a new harness down to them. It didn't quite reach, but if Morgan just planted his feet against this tree trunk and boosted Thea, they might make it.

"We've got it harnessed to one of our horses!" Cullen yelled down. "He'll drag you up. Cassie, damn it! Get away from me and stay there!" floated down to them as, with his hand against her bottom, Morgan shoved Thea higher to seize the reins.

"Close your eyes, and go up on your back!" he ordered her. "Hang on!"

She bumped and slid up the steep, rough hill. Then, Cullen's hands were on her wrists, and she sent a shudder of rolling soil and stones down toward Morgan when they hauled her over the edge. Rina threw a cloak around her, and they all peered over as Cullen dropped the harness again for Morgan. He had to lunge for it. Cullen and the horse dragged him up. For the first time, Thea burst into tears when she saw him safe, but there was much to do.

"We've got to unload what we can from the wagon and then drag it upright and hope the whole thing doesn't topple over in the process," Morgan told them.

"You're not climbing in there to unload," Thea insisted. "Your weight could take it over. I can do it, and—"

"No!" Morgan cut her off. "Rina and Cassie will take what I hand down. I'll put Cullen's harness around my waist while he steadies our team. I'll jump free if it goes over. Thea, I want you to get an axe from Cullen. If the wagon topples, cut the team free. At least then, we'd have our animals to get us there. Let's go before more of this hillside does!"

Sweating despite the cool breeze and drizzle that began again, the five of them worked like demons. Only the oxen were calm throughout. The horses snorted, wide-eyed, Rina cried, and Cassie muttered about the curses of the forest. Thea trembled as she held the axe ready to free the team while Morgan handed down things that Rina and Cassie piled back along the cliff face. Morgan had to cut away more of the fine white linsey-woolsey cover where the tree had ripped it. With the wagon nearly empty, the team tugged and strained and dragged the damaged Conestoga on its side off the edge and down the trail to more solid ground.

"Splintered spokes and a broken axle," Morgan muttered, surveying the damage at close range.

But that wasn't all, Thea thought miserably. About a fourth of their goods had spilled out, a lot of their food, their barrels of ale and flour, some boxes with utensils, dried herbs and her pharmacopoeia. She unknotted the harness from Morgan's waist. He looked white as bleached linen. "It's a good thing I didn't have to dangle by this," he told them. "At least two ribs broken, maybe more."

"Drat. And all my bandages have gone down the cliff."

He pulled Thea to him and took the harness from her trembling hands. He tied it back around him and handed the end of it to Cullen. "Almost forgot that there's one more thing we have to rescue back there. Come on and wrap that around a tree for me, will you, Cullen?"

"No, Morgan!" Thea cried and clung to his wrists when she realized what he intended. "Not with your ribs hurt!" She ran after him as he walked back along the trail where the accident had occurred. "We can just leave the book. I'll understand!" she vowed, but her voice broke. "Or let me go down for it!"

But Morgan was already shuffling carefully to the cliff edge while Cullen wrapped the harness for him. Holding tree to tree, Morgan went down after the box with the big apothecary book. Staring over the edge, hands clenched in prayer, Thea watched him tear off the lid, lift out the precious book, and clasp it to him. "All right, pull!" he shouted, and Cullen

and Thea hauled him up, bit by bit, while he clung one-
handed to slippery trees.

"Oh, Morgan!" she cried when he handed her the book.
"How can I ever thank you?"

"Just—wrap—my ribs with something," he told her and
swayed on his feet toward her before he sank to sit right on
the muddy path that had caused all their pain.

It was nearly dark by the time they managed to drag the
disabled Conestoga to a spot where it could be repaired. Back
from the river, the cliff road left behind, Thea tore her last
dry petticoat into strips to wrap Morgan's bruised and broken ribs. "If we hadn't lost those herbs, I'd have something
for that pain," she told him, but then the thought hit her.
What if there were something along here she could use? Even
common sassafras root brewed in rainwater would help.

While Rina cooked them a light supper, Thea took a brand
from the fire and walked the forest edge in the dusk. No sassafras or much else she recognized growing wild along here.
If only she had some of those Canajoharie Indians to ask
about what herbs they used! But then she saw a bush she recognized. Prickly ash, which some called the tooth-ache bush.
Its bark and berries might help his pain! Quickly, avoiding
the spines, she gathered the oval capsules that contained the
reddish berries and ran back to brew some for him to drink.

That night Thea sat on a blanket on the ground, her back
against a tree. Drained and soul-weary for the first time, she
held Morgan's head in her lap while he slept. A near catastrophe, she thought, and yet they would go on. He had said he
could repair the wheel and axle, though it would take a few
days. Already Cullen had scouted for a tree the right size to
cut down tomorrow. Perhaps, she mused drowsily as insect
sounds creaked away in the woods like some fairyland band,
this terrible thing had happened for the best. After all, Cullen
and Morgan were working together now, and she and Rina
were closer than they had ever been. Yes, even out here in
the dark, even after today, life could be full of promise with
Morgan at her side and Rina near. She clung to that thought

as she drifted off into dreams, a lovely refuge for the nightmare was yet to come.

The next morning Thea awakened to the smell of smoked bacon from Rina's big cast-iron skillet. Morgan was not in sight. She scrambled to her feet before she realized she ached all over.

"He's gone out to look at that tree Cullen marked for a new axle," Rina told her. "Cullen's shaving behind our wagon. Thea," she wiped her hands on a flannel towel as she walked over, "I want you to know I'm going to give you my other skillet and the smaller kettle to help replace what you lost. I know you can't wear my clothes, but we've a blanket to spare, too, and—"

"Varina!" Cullen cut her off as he hurried around the wagon, wiping his strop razor on a cambric handkerchief, "I appreciate your generosity, I'm sure Thea does, too, but we're not going to be close enough to the Glenns to share. And we've brought along what we need to get us through this journey."

Rina's mouth dropped. "But, Cullen, with the accident—"

"Governor Trumbull wasn't even expecting we would be along here to help save them at all, Rina," Cullen insisted. "Part of this trial is to see what people can do on their own, each within his own *status quo.*"

"So that's still the way you want to play this, Cullen?" Morgan's voice rang out behind them. Moving gingerly, he walked toward the campfire, and the four of them faced each other across it. "Then my wife and I thank you for your help yesterday and Rina for her intended generosity today, but we can't even accept that. You want to keep your precious *status quo,* you've got it," he went on. "The repair of this wagon might take me a week, and I would never expect you to lag behind that long and possibly miss the bateau."

"Morgan!" Thea tried to protest.

"We'll catch our own food," Morgan plunged on, "and Thea's obviously skilled at gathering. There are Indian camps along the way where we can trade for cornmeal. I think it would be best for all of us,"—his narrowed gaze challenged Rina, as well as Cullen—"if you kept to your schedule and left us to do things our own way. I pray that won't be the spirit of the westward movement in the future, and it's not what we crude barbarians from Pennsylvania are used to, but believe me, it's for the best here."

"Cullen, surely—" Rina tried, while Thea clasped fistfuls of wrinkled apron.

"You heard him, wife!" Cullen said. "Leave them the bacon or some flour then, and let's go!" He spun and marched away.

"Cullen!" Rina cried, "There have been lots of times when they—Thea, I mean—took good care of me!" But he did not turn back.

"It's all right," Thea comforted Rina as Morgan stalked off, too. "Something like this was bound to happen. We were all riding along on a slippery slope together, just like yesterday. Maybe we'll catch up to you before Buffalo Creek, or if not, we'll see you in the Firelands and have a real reunion then! You'd best take Cassie so we don't have another mouth to feed. We'll be fine! Morgan's always been skilled in the forest, you know!"

Rina's gaze held Thea's. "Yes, we've both got to stick by our men," Rina muttered and fled around the wagon after Cullen.

Rina and Cassie both felt silent tears slick their cheeks as the Varner wagon pulled away from the wounded Conestoga that morning. Thea waved at them briskly, then went back to gathering firewood and pulling mushrooms. Well, Rina thought, and swiped at her wet face, they'll probably eat better than we will, anyway. But it hurt her so to have Cullen be this way, except for one thing. Sometimes Morgan looked at her so disappointed that she suspected he somehow knew she had lied to him about Thea in the beginning, that perhaps he'd even like to talk to her about it. But so far he hadn't, and now he wouldn't. She was safer like this, out here alone with Cullen, no matter how losing Thea pained her.

They rumbled on under a bright sky that morning and stopped for dinner with the sun straight overhead. "Less than a week, Rina, about one hundred thirty miles more to where we'll catch the bateau to travel Lake Erie," Cullen told her over their cold duck and flat firecake. They had not spoken a word to each other all morning.

"Out here, it sounds such a long way to go," she mumbled with her mouth half full, something she would never have done at table at home with Father. Was she changing so much already that manners didn't matter and such things as generosity to a longtime friend had to war with loyalty to a new husband? She leaned back on her hands in the grass and stared at Cullen. She had been trying to love him with all her might lately, in bed and out. She was warming to his possessive lovemaking, yet she never reached the crashing release of passion she sensed was possible. And she could never tell him she suspected such existed for a woman, nor settle herself down enough to let it happen.

She excused herself and went on the other side of the wagon to "make water," as Cassie put it. Cassie was just wandering back into camp from picking big red clover down the way. Rina knew she had to hurry to amuse Cassie, for Cullen's tolerance of her babbling and humming was fragile, and he often scolded Cassie to hurt her feelings.

" 'Tis sad that Morgan riled the forest folk that time," Cassie said to Cullen on the other side of the wagon as her quick fingers wove clover stems into a garland.

He downed the rest of his ale in one gulp. "What time?" he asked without looking at her.

"Now the curse seems to be on him in the forest and not Rina, though she was right there, too, that time," Cassie went on as if she hadn't heard him.

Cullen's head jerked up. "What time?" he repeated. He stood and grabbed Cassie's hand to spill the clover. "What time were they together in your damned forest?"

"I saw them because I saw the fairy rings!" Cassie tried to explain, but she could not shake his hand off. "I didn't mean to see all that, so please—"

"Rina!" Cullen bellowed, and Rina ran back around the wagon. "What in heaven's name is this girl babbling about with you and Morgan off in the forest together? When, Rina?" he yelled, but he still glared at Cassie and gave her another shake.

"Not with you wed!" Cassie said. "Long ago, after the parade, not in Mr. Lockwood's forest, but the other one!"

Cullen spun on Rina. From her blanched face, he knew the little lackbrain somehow spoke the truth this time. He shoved Cassie and stalked Rina as she backed away. "That week after the Benedict Arnold parade when Morgan was ill and at your house?" he demanded. "You went out to the forest with him alone?"

"She wasn't alone!" Cassie said and dared to put herself between him and Rina. "Mr. Lockwood said I had to go along, he did, and I didn't mean to see—"

Cullen elbowed Cassie away. "What *did* she see, wife?" he roared. "Kisses, fondling, more?"

"Stop it!" Rina screamed and covered her ears with her hands. She could not believe this was happening out here this way, not after this wrenching morning. "It was a long time ago, and you and I weren't promised!"

"Then it's true?" he roared and shook Rina by her shoulders until her head bobbed. "No wonder you put me off for so long! Nursed him well that week when I trusted you! How much was there to it? Does Thea know? Damnation, does she? I'll just ride back to ask them both if you don't tell me!"

Rina's first impulse was to face him down and lie to save them all. Perhaps plead guilty to a few kisses, a moment's foolishness. But not of reveling in his touch and wanting him to take her. Not of the fact they were secretly betrothed! But she was weary of pretending, of bearing the regret and guilt alone. Cullen was beet red; he shoved her down and strode away. He was unharnessing a horse! She scrambled to her feet and ran to grab his arm, despite the pains in her stomach and her soul.

"Cullen, just leave them out of this! It was my fault, I could have stopped everything. I was just feeling rebellion in the air. It was all a mistake. Don't go back there to them, please. Let's just go on together and make a new life—"

He yanked away and stepped on the wagon wheel to

mount the barebacked horse. Her grip tore his coat cuff before he shook her off. "Please, Cullen. You can't just leave us here like this. We have to go on!"

He glared down his long nose. "Then tell me now what happened."

"Morgan and I . . . had a little agreement once. But as soon as he was gone, I realized it wasn't right, that I would be a better wife for you."

"You two decided on a *sub rosa* betrothal, you mean?" he clipped out coldly. He seemed more in command of himself again. "And did you somehow seal this illicit bargain in the woods? I take it your father never knew, or he would have told me."

"No—not my father, not Thea, either. They never knew. Please don't get Morgan and poor Thea involved, and let's just go on alone. I'll be the best wife to you I know how, and—"

"I repeat *verbatim,* how did you seal this illicit bargain with him? I have never questioned if I was your first on our wedding night, but at least I was second place to Morgan Glenn again in your affections, wasn't I? Wasn't I?"

"I—I love you, first and always. We didn't—didn't finish, because he stopped. We were only really alone like that once, Cullen, so . . . Please, you said you wouldn't leave if I told you!" she shrieked as he yanked the horse around and kicked him hard to send him in the direction they'd just come.

"Cuuuul–len!" Desperate, she ran after him, but he was quickly swallowed by the turn of trees along the trail.

Concerned over his injured ribs, Thea helped Morgan hack down the tree to replace the broken axle, and they dragged it over to their campsite behind an ox. "If it weren't for George and Jonathan," Morgan told her and patted the big ox on the rump, "that wagon might have gone right over with the horses yesterday. Oxen are worth their weight in gold on the frontier."

"And so you named them for your favorite commander-in-chief and your favorite governor," she said with a little smile. Despite the dangers and hardships, she and Morgan always managed to share a smile, though she knew it pained him to laugh now.

"Right," he told her and kissed her smudged nose, grateful he didn't have to stoop to reach her. But now, with his ribs so sore, the next few weeks he'd have to ask her to be on top of him when they coupled. It seemed the deeper they got into the wilds, the wilder their lovemaking became, and that suited him just fine. Everything about Thea did, he realized, as she set off with the hatchet to search for two straight tree limbs the size of the shattered wheel spokes. He smiled as he watched her go with that smooth-hip swish that so heated his loins. Dang! Here he was sore all over with a wagon to mend and a distant boat to catch by the end of May, and he'd just as soon have a little tumble in the grass with Thea!

He froze where he stood. Could that be hoofbeats? Though it sliced pain through him, he knelt to put his ear to the turf of the trail. Yes, a single rider coming fast. He'd best get the musket and call Thea back so she didn't meet some stranger. But when he stood, he realized the sound was not coming from the direction of civilization but from the west.

He put his musket back in the propped-up wagon when he saw it was Cullen. He strode to meet him. "What happened? Is Rina all right?"

"You ought to know, you backwoods bastard!" Cullen cried and reined in, just missing him. "I never did trust you! Worse traitor than your crony Arnold himself! You knew that Rina was mine! Her father, everyone did!"

"What in perdition—" Morgan got out before Cullen vaulted off the saddle and slammed them both to the ground.

Morgan cried out in pain as the man fell half on top of him and fought to hold him down. "Tried to take her in the woods, like animals, didn't you! You were supposed to be sick, damn you! And I don't believe for one second you were the one who wanted to stop, you vile—" Cullen got out as his fist cracked into Morgan's jaw. Despite Cullen's weight crushing his ribs like a vise, Morgan bucked him off and hit him back.

Morgan tried to sit on Cullen to still his thrashing. He had a good nerve to tell Cullen how Rina had lied to him about

Thea's being betrothed or he never would have looked twice at Rina. But it was too late for talk when Cullen elbowed his ribs to force him off. They kicked and traded blows like wildmen. This had been coming for years. Morgan rolled away with a grunt and stumbled to his feet. Fists clenched, he stood weaving, towering over Cullen while he, too, stumbled to stand.

"You son of a bitch seducer!" Cullen shouted. "Traitor through and through!"

"Damn you, Varner, listen to me! She insisted on a secret betrothal! Besides, she let me down for you, so you're the one she wanted all along!"

"But you, she wanted you first! Anything or anyone you want, you get, you—"

They fell on each other again, but Thea's unearthly scream jolted them apart. She stood, not ten feet away, aghast at what she saw. And, obviously, Morgan grieved, at what she must have heard.

"Rina?" she asked Morgan as she strode forward, the hatchet and chopped tree limbs in her arms. She ignored the bloody-faced Cullen as if he weren't there. "You and Rina in the beginning? Betrothed? Bedded?"

"Not bedded, I swear it, but betrothed—yes. Now, look, both of you," Morgan floundered. "She was unpromised, and it was before you, Thea. I wanted to tell you, I swear I wanted to tell you from the first!"

Thea's mind screamed things, but nothing came out of her mouth. Morgan had betrayed her more than Cousin Benedict or Avery Payne. But suddenly, standing there with her big hands dirtied and her skirts wrinkled and her hair all flyaway, she felt as if a thousand unapproving eyes were on her awkward, plain gawkiness again. Rina, the delicate, the beautiful, the graceful, the high-born had had her way again. Rina had taken from her the only man she had ever wanted, and obviously never earned on her own. Indeed, he must have wed her, as Cullen told Rina once, because he needed a stalwart wife to go west, to cook his meals, to cure his ills, and be handy for him to empty his passion out in the wagon or the forest depths. And even if he and Rina hadn't bedded, they had surely been passionate and intimate together.

"Thea, let me explain everything," Morgan pleaded and walked over. When she just stared into space and didn't move, he took her hand. She flinched back as if his touch burned her.

"Get away—away! I'm going back, I'm going home!"

"Thea, I know it's a shock, but you can't just—"

But she dropped her armload of sticks and the hatchet and walked with shaking shoulders the way they had come on the trail yesterday.

"Damn you, Varner," Morgan muttered. "You're no gentleman like you've always preached. I'm just hellfire sorry us frontier fighters won the war for the likes of you and your damned pious *status quo!*" He did not look at the stunned man. Holding his hands to his painful sides, he hurried after Thea.

Thea's legs were trembling so hard they gave out after she'd walked a short distance. She sank down on a fallen log to stare at her big, scratched, dirty hands clasping her smudged skirt across her knees. No tears came. Only taunting thoughts and the emptiest, crushed feeling that was really no feeling at all. She heard footsteps and stared up, glassy-eyed, at Morgan.

"Just leave me alone," she said.

"I can't have you wandering off where I can't find you."

"Of course not." Her voice sounded lifeless, but for its quavering. "You need me to help you get west, to be your extra workhorse or another oxen to help pull things along. Don't worry. I know I can't really go back now. There's no more there for me than here. But," she said, and huge tears plopped on the bib of her apron, "I believed her, you see. I thought—" her voice trailed off. She was so devastated, she almost wanted revenge on him and Rina. She wanted to tell Rina the secret Father Lockwood had entrusted to her, that Rina's own mother hated her as much as Thea did now. But no. Even in all this, somehow, she could not hate Rina. And she could never, never hate Morgan. The black, reverberating pain inside her was too mountainous to summon up hatred and revenge.

Morgan collapsed on the far end of her log. "I know this is no time to say this, but Rina can't hold a candle to you. True, I was swept away at first, but I thought you were off limits. Thea, I swear that she told me—"

She jerked to her feet. The hurt came screaming out. "I don't care what she told you! I just want you to know that I'm no more to you now than something you've hauled along to use! An axe, a plowshare, some bullets! If we find some eager Indian maids, you might as well share their blanket, because I'll never share yours again! You're worse than Avery Payne, just trying to—"

"You needn't worry I'd ever force anyone, even a so-called wife," Morgan gritted out and stood. He knew she was desperate, but so was he. His dreams for them lay broken like his prized Conestoga, like his plans they would tame the Firelands together. "I swear I meant to tell you, but I—" he hesitated at the horrid import of his words, "I couldn't bear to let you down."

She stared at him, aghast, as if she were discovering all the truth again. Her mind taunted her with her own stupidity. She had trusted Rina. She should have seen their passion for each other that day when they came to the shop and went off together, that week when Rina would not let her near him at Lockwoods' and he sent word he wanted to be left alone.

"Just leave me alone!" she screamed and tore back toward the camp with Morgan hard after her. Cullen and his horse were nowhere in sight now.

"Fine. You want to be alone?" Morgan yelled. "It's good and lonely out here!"

She'd show him, she thought. She'd work her share and then demand her half of the prize money! She'd have her own shop back in Connecticut when they returned and do fine without Morgan Glenn in her life! Independence and hard work had always been her salvation from sadness, from knowing Rina was prettier and more accepted, from knowing deep down Rina resented her in the house with the father she had to share. She'd just exhaust herself every day and forget what a fool she had made of herself with this man and her long-ago childhood friend!

But her shoulders shook and tears spilled down her cheeks, wetting the wood she gathered from the ground. She trembled all over as if she had caught the ague as she stumbled off into the forest a ways. When she heard Morgan's furious hatchet blows from the clearing, she collapsed into a little ball behind a tree and sobbed and sobbed.

It took Morgan and Thea three days of hard work to repair the axle and wheel and remount them with the help of a crude fulcrum. They spoke little, and Morgan slept outside the wagon on the ground. Bedtime and meals were the worst with no talking. Once over a solemn, silent supper, he had begun, "Despite everything, I'm glad you know."

"You prefer it like this between us, you mean?"

"Hardly, Thea. You know I don't."

"I'm not sure I know anything anymore."

"I felt like that once."

"After Rina 'let you down' as you put it?"

"You want the truth? That's right. It was the same time I began to be really disillusioned with General Arnold because a Tory woman was making a fool of him, too. The same time that my father died and I helped those massacre folks at home."

She got up and wiped her pewter plate off with a handful of grass. "Poor Morgan, shattered when the one he loved and wanted to keep forever chose another over him. Now, let's see, how would that feel?"

"There's no comparison, Thea."

She spun on him, her expression sharp enough to rip him deep inside. "Just like there's no comparison between Rina and me? Believe me, I know our differences, so—"

"You're right, you don't know anything anymore!" he roared and jumped up to grab her shoulders. "Rina would have been the biggest mistake of my life, and you were the best thing I ever did. Only I didn't trust you enough to tell you. I didn't want to lose you!"

She stared at him. "You—you have lost me. Let me go."

"No one's allowed one mistake, is that it?" he ground out and released her. "Hell, you should have wed that impeccable gentleman Cullen Varner with his educated Latin phrases and his obsession with his own perfection, and we'd all be happy!" He stomped back to tend to his work, shaving the wheel spokes. For Thea, staring up at the stars through the gaping hole in the ruined canopy, that night was even lonelier and longer than the one before.

They started out four days after the Varners had gone on. That first evening, Morgan insisted he teach Thea how to shoot the musket. She did not argue. She had done what she could to help him, and she, too, would feel better if she learned to shoot. But neither of them had reckoned on their closeness while he taught her to handle the nearly four-foot long Brown Bess firearm. He told her the parts and made her repeat them. Then he lifted it and showed her how to hold it.

"I'll let you load it after you take its kick and get the feel of it once," he said.

"Are you sure we have enough powder and bullets for this?"

"It's one thing that, thank Providence, we didn't lose back there in the slide. Here, put the butt plate against your shoulder and quick-sight it. Now," he went on and stepped so close behind her she could feel his body warmth, "we're going to lower the hammer to half cock." His big hands covered hers carefully and she almost stood in his embrace. She fought to keep from pulling away. She felt the hammer click into place. Drat him! She felt his breath on her cheek. She shifted her stance slightly, but her bottom bumped his hip and she jumped.

"Hold still now. All right," he went on. "Pull on the trigger slow and easy to get the feel when it goes off."

It poofed, and smoke flashed from the pan as the buttplate bumped her shoulder. "Oh, that wasn't bad," she said.

"I only put in a light charge, or it would have really kicked," he told her. His chin almost rested on her shoulder as he bent down to see what limb of the tree she had winged.

"You were a bit high. We'll try again. Now watch the loading."

He tore the cartridge paper with his teeth, then whanged a bullet home with the ramrod. She tried to study his movements, but she kept seeing only him. His lean, austere face with the little smudge on his chin; the golden glint to his chestnut hair in the slant of sun; the slight stubble on his square jaw; each separate lash over those deep-set, loam-brown eyes; the stubborn set to his thin mouth. She realized she ached to reach out and touch him. Maybe to shove that errant lock of hair back from his brown forehead. To just feel again the stony strength of his arms that could be so protective and so tender. She almost swayed on her feet. She had to do something to keep her pride and sanity.

"It smelled funny when it smoked," she blurted.

He squinted at her, then looked away. "I can't tell you how bad it can get in battle. It almost blinds you, and heat shimmers from the barrels in waves. And if the enemy's charging at close range, there's not time to reload. You just use the bayonet or swing the musket like a club. Sorry," he concluded, realizing he was getting carried away. He held it out to her to handle herself this time, Did he dare to hope she looked a bit moved? He was trying to keep such control of himself. All he wanted was to haul her into his arms. He would be crushed if she refused to let him touch her again. But he was going to wage his own war with this woman he wanted so. And, in the heat of this very different battle, he'd use every sensual, emotional weapon he could to win her back again.

"You know what I've wanted for a long time, very, very badly?" he asked as she lifted the gun to sight at the tree again.

The musket wavered. "I haven't the vaguest notion," she said and frowned at him before she squinted down the barrel again. She had seen his hungry look for her, and it really ruined her concentration.

"A Pennsylvania rifle. When I get my half of our prize money, it's one thing I'll buy. They have beautiful, smooth maple stocks, and they're easier to load. More accurate and powerful than this, too, and a joy to even touch—"

Bang! The Brown Bess belched, but Thea had completely missed the tree. "We'll try again, until you get it right," he told her and took the musket back quickly because she looked like she might swing it at him lock, stock, and barrel, just the way he'd said.

Rina was more terrified than ever now that Cullen didn't seem to want her. The dreams of her mother screaming at her woke her in a sweat most every night, and she agonized 'til dawn over what Thea must be thinking of her. She had to make it up to Cullen; she had to get him back. They had argued horribly again yesterday when Cassie had wandered off, evidently along the trail the way they had come.

Rina was beside herself with worry and had begged Cullen to ride back looking for the girl. But he returned after a two-hour search to declare that she must simply be hiding from them, since they both knew she'd not wander into these forests. She was probably just going to wait for the Glenns to come along, he comforted. Still, Rina screamed herself hoarse calling for Cassie around their camp. Although Rina could not bear to leave Cassie to the forests she'd always feared, she knew her maid's presence and obstinate chatter was wreaking havoc on her attempts to make things up to Cullen, so she'd finally agreed to go on the next day.

Now, Rina agonized, without Cassie and Thea, she was going to simply wither and die like one of Thea's upside-down-to-dry herbs if she didn't win Cullen back and he didn't forgive her. In just another night on this lonely trail, they would arrive at Buffalo Creek, where a bateau awaited them. Then they'd be four or five days with strangers, without much of a chance to be reconciled before they reached their home away from home. Rina had to do something—now!

In the wagon that last night before Lake Erie, Varina Lockwood Varner loosed her hair and shook it free. Despite how she detested the gnats outside that swarmed around her face, she draped her shawl about her shoulders over her thin, cotton night rail and ventured out to Cullen's single pallet next to the fading fire. Stars arched overhead, gilded by a sickle of moon rising from the treed horizon.

"Another bad dream?" he asked when he saw her floating toward him like a ghost. His arms were crooked back behind his head. His eyes were in shadow.

"Well, for one thing, I'm still heartsick about Cassie hiding from us," she began warily.

"You know," he mused aloud, "I was thinking. Her real name's probably Cassandra, named for the woman in Greek mythology who used to tell the truth all the time, but she acted so bizarre no one believed her."

"I don't want to talk about myths, Cullen. This is real, this is us. And, speaking of the truth, I came out here because I was longing for you. For your touch. I don't care what you think, it's been that way for me for years. All that other seems so long ago, and I won't have it ruin our future!"

"I never, never thought my own wife would prefer Morgan Glenn, just like everyone else," he said, almost to himself. Benedict Arnold's and then Governor Trumbull's and even Ethan Trent's faces floated before his mind's eye, then faded.

"Back then, I really wasn't the same woman, Cullen. Please try to understand. I didn't know what I wanted or why when Thea seemed to be so sure and settled."

"But you do know what you want now?" he asked and sat up to link his arms loosely around his knees. The musket he kept at the ready glinted dully from the grass like a stiff snake.

"Yes. You! To be your wife! To make you happy! I know I can! I want you to forgive me, and I want us to be together, even out here in this godforsaken wildern—"

"Don't say that!" he cut her off. "Don't think of where we are as cursed or you'll be no help to me, and I simply have to win, to beat them all!"

He reached a hand up to her, and she took it. He tugged her down to tumble her into his lap. She wrapped her arms around his neck. His kisses ravaged her lips, her cheeks, nose, throat, and she reveled in it. "I have always, always desired you, Varina!" he gasped out and rolled them over on the ground to pin her lightly under him. "You're part of my destiny!"

His hands were suddenly everywhere again in this fast, fierce act of passion and possession. She understood his desperation; she welcomed it. She had to make it all up to Cullen. He had to want and love her as she did him! He lifted away from her just enough to tug her night rail up under her chin. His lips captured hers again, again, then slid wetly lower to taunt her breasts and belly. She heard him fumbling with his breeches. He spread her legs.

"Now look at me! Look at me!" he demanded and hovered just over her. Her eyes seemed to glow with reflected moonlight. "You are mine! Only mine forever! Say it, my darling. Say it while I make you mine!"

"Yes! Yes, yours forever! Please, just say you forgive me—" she got out before he pierced her.

But he said nothing else, and this communion had to be enough for now. He rocked wildly over and in her. And, for the first time in her marriage, she shattered the universe with him. He cried out in his mutual release, evidently as stunned as she.

They lay there like that long after, holding tight. Only when the night wind cooled their damp flesh and she began to shudder did he lift her and the rifle in his arms. He scuffed the fire out, then whispered hot in her ear, "There will be no more bad dreams, my darling, I swear it! We're done with the past and with the Glenns, too, *ad perpetuam.*"

Before she could protest that she had to win Thea back, too, he kissed her hard and carried her over to lift her into the back of the wagon. Quickly, he boosted himself inside and reached again for her. But in all the fervent things he said to her that night, "I forgive you" was never one of them.

Chapter Thirteen

"Does the blushing maiden or the moping wife claim she must employ facial beauty to keep her man? Tell her such outward show will not last as long as inner things. But also whisper to her the following you can offer—elder flowers to remove freckles, horsetail and sage tonic to rinse her hair for lustre, and this emulsion to smooth wrinkles: one part chamomile, two parts white pond lily leaves, a few strawberry leaves, and a touch of teasel. Tell her this is teasel, the prickly herb, not teasing the man she adores with prickly words! And tell her, smile more at him to ease everyone's pain."

THE NEXT DAY when the Glenns started out, they received a surprise that walked from behind a tree like an apparition along the trail. "Cassie!" they cried in unison. Morgan reined in the team, and they both climbed down to hurry to her.

"What happened? Why are you here?" Thea cried.

"Can I ride with you? I'm hungry! Eating just leaves and mushrooms I picked last night made me sick."

"But where's—where are they?" Thea asked, as if even using Rina's name would pain her.

"Can't stay with them no more, I can't. Cullen hates me since I—told him," she faltered, her gaze shifting to Morgan.

"You told?" he demanded. "You mean, in the forest that day, you saw—" he began but bit off his words and spun away. This was all he needed, he fumed. Cassie, the harbinger of more pain between him and Thea because of one mistake from the past!

"Does Morgan hate me, too?" Cassie asked Thea. Thea fought another battle with herself. Cassie had been there that time? Cassie had seen them together alone, no doubt in each other's arms, and never said so? But then, just the other day, Thea recalled, she had cut the girl off when she was babbling on about something she'd seen once in the woods.

"No, he doesn't hate you, Cassie," Thea comforted, though her voice trembled. She put her arm around Cassie to lead her toward the wagon. "Of course, you can come with us, but I don't want you to say any more about what you saw, or about Rina right now, either. Come on, we have to go. I'll just boost you up in the wagon and get you something better to eat."

The patched and scraped Conestoga rumbled on with Cassie's occasional humming to haunt them. Morgan's spirits plunged to heavy brooding again, and Thea still mourned. But they rode on, side by side, westward.

On the next-to-last day of May, four days after the Varners had passed through, Morgan, Thea, and Cassie boarded the last waiting bateau at the mouth of Buffalo Creek and set out on Lake Erie. A rope corral contained the team on board, and blocks of wood were wedged under the wheels of the Conestoga so it wouldn't roll. They shared the flatboat willingly with an old trapper named Jacob Roscoe, and his horse. He was a short, wiry man, clad in old-fashioned buckskin, but full of useful advice and woodland lore. He and Morgan talked for hours while Thea and Cassie watched the shore. Thea spoke to Morgan just enough to keep the two bargemen and Jacob from thinking something was amiss.

"So this lake was named for the Erie tribe the Iroquois wiped off the face of the earth years ago," Morgan mused at another of Jacob's pearls of frontier wisdom.

"Yep. The tribes here'bouts—the Wyandot and 'Tawas mostly where you're goin'—been blowin' hot and cold for years. Luck'ly, they been good and cold for a time now."

"There's a Wyandot camp now near where we hope to settle, you say?" Morgan pursued, and Thea perked up her ears to listen.

"Yep. They call the village Pequotting, too, same as the river. Frenchies used to call them Hurons, meaning people with boar heads, 'cause they shaved their scalp but for a standing bristles of hair, jest like the Mohawks. But the red man gave up a lot a' the past now. They cook with iron pots, wear pieces of white-man garb, let their hair grow, and bows and arrows are jest boy's toys nowadays. Some of 'em speak middling English, too."

"Do they know much about medicinal herbs?" Thea asked, and both men turned to face her.

"Yep," Jacob told her with a nod that bobbed the three squirrel tails dangling from his fur cap. "Used to be a famous old medicine man, name a Wabuck, at Pequotting where you're goin', but he died a couple o' winters back. Herbs, incantations, trances, spirit dances, you name it."

As the men's voices droned on, Thea's thoughts lapped like lake waves over what she had heard. The Indians had given up much of their past and had gone on to better, easier ways. And how much easier this water travel was than slogging along with the Conestoga on the land. But knowing it was better to forge ahead and leave some of the painful past behind didn't ease her trail back to Morgan, as she'd come to think of it. Sometimes she came so close to touching him, to a soft word of invitation, or a hint of forgiveness.

But something inside her had frozen hard and wouldn't thaw. She tried to warm it with memories of endearing things he had done for her—replacing her parents' wooden grave markers, fetching her pharmocopoeia from the cliff, even giving her the tin pin in payment for her herbs. But she had been burned too often by trusting others she cared for, and she wasn't ready to trust her beloved betrayer Morgan again. Besides, she couldn't help but think she could never really win him back from memories of his days with beautiful Rina, even if she tried. In the beginning, he had obviously seen them both and chosen Rina.

Out here, Thea thought sadly and tossed her head, the comparison between her and Rina was even worse. Thea's hair was bleached to wild copper and had lost its luster in the dust and wind. Her face was freckled despite the bonnets and hats she wore, and the wind dried and chapped her lips and skin. Rina, however, had still looked lovely when they had parted last week. She had evidently brought along some kind of skin cream, and Cassie had fixed her hair. Her new gowns from Albany clung beautifully to her petite, graceful form, while Thea had lost weight, and her two dresses were absolutely worn and torn. She sighed heavily and turned her face to the endless, blue-gray lake.

Morgan came over to interrupt her thoughts when Jacob Roscoe went back with the bargemen to chat. "Does Jacob seem familiar to you?" he asked, squatting down beside her.

"No." She turned only her profile to him. "Why should he? He said he's lived in these fur trapping parts his whole life."

"I keep thinking I've seen him somewhere. But I'm probably just recalling someone who looked like him among those traders and trappers at Eden's Gate. He's a treasure out here. Says he'll stop by with news when he can, once we're settled."

Once we're settled. The words taunted Thea. How she longed for that, in more ways than one. It would be like putting a curse on their new homesite if they arrived as estranged as this. Yet, she said nothing else, and he stood and moved away. She just stared across the blue waters of the lake to the sandy, grassy banks and shores they passed and chatted quietly with Cassie.

Thea's heart was in her throat as they bid farewell to the men on the bateau and watched them pole out from shore and row away from the broad mouth of the Pequotting River to catch the lake breeze. They would not see them again for over a year, when they took the bateau back toward the east. Jacob shared a final meal of river fish with them and waved back over his shoulder as he set out to run some traps even farther west. "I'll be back 'round when I kin manage!" His farewell floated to them.

"There's the Indian trail on the west bank of the river, like on the map," Morgan said and pointed to a path barely a wagon wide. "Looks like the Varners' recent arrival has beat it down for us. Come on, you two. Let's go."

Both Thea and Morgan became jittery as they headed south into the heart of the Firelands that day. Their home for nearly a year and a half lay up ahead—as did the Varners'. If their map was right and Cullen had followed his plan, the Varners would be camped somewhere along the Pequotting where a tributary called Mud Brook poured in from the west.

"The Pequotting's a lovely, clear river," Thea broke the

human silence while birds jangled their songs overhead. "When you hear a name like Mud Brook coming into it, you picture it all brown."

"Rina won't like living with a lot of mud, she won't, not with those pretty new dresses from Albany," Cassie piped up, and they all fell silent again.

Much later Morgan said in a calm, low voice, "Now don't let this rile you, but I can feel Indians in my bones again."

He had said the same thing along the Mohawk before they saw their first Indian in the wild and just before they arrived at Canajoharie. "Should I get the gun?" Thea asked, trying to match his tone.

"No. Everyone says they're peaceful. It's no good looking hostile when we've got to get along."

His eyes linked with Thea's in personal challenge before he squinted back down the trail. The going was tough through here. It took a lot of steering to keep the wagon from sideswiping saplings or underbrush, despite the wheel tracks which proved the Varners had been through recently.

They jolted in a hole, and Morgan's hard thigh bumped hers. She felt that tiny touch clear up into the very core of her being. More fiery than fear, the feeling feathered up to peak her nipples and down between her thighs to make her shift away from him. Why did it seem the denser the forest wilds, the more she had to fight her desires for this man? Just let him feel Indians in his bones—Indian maidens he could sleep with, too—for she would never give in to the wanton way she acted in the dark with him before! Not after he'd shown what sort of woman he really desired by choosing Rina!

Thea and Cassie kept quiet, but they stared at every shift of shade and shaft of light through the trees. Thea's hair prickled along the back of her neck and chills raced along her spine. It was not just from sensing Indians' eyes on them. Boldly, she folded her hands in her lap and sat ramrod straight, but her trembling at Morgan's mere presence continued.

*　　*　　*

That afternoon, twelve miles south of the lake, they still had not spotted an Indian, but they saw the Varner camp up ahead. On a little rise, Morgan reined in their weary team, and they all stared.

The Varners had pitched camp and already begun to build a log cabin on the flat, broad, grassy, V-shaped plain where a shallow brook warbled over rocks into the river. The canvas top of their wagon had made them a temporary tent; an area was cleared for the cabin, and two-high logs outlined its future form. A bucket on a sweep dangled by the river, and the six horses grazed on rich grass in a rope corral. From the distance came the sound of chopping.

"Neither of them home, though at least Rina should be," Morgan said. "Indians might come along and steal them blind. It's just their way. They think things not hidden or tied down are theirs for the taking, so remember that when we make camp."

Thea blinked back tears; there should have been a joyful reunion for them all here and now. "But—we aren't going to stop, are we?" Thea blurted, suddenly panicked at the thought of facing her once best friend or seeing her and Morgan together.

"No. I want to be there and unloaded by nightfall," he replied curtly, as if that were the only reason they weren't going to call for tea and a cozy chat.

"It looks to me like they have the start of a fine place," Thea attempted in a calmer tone as they clattered down to ford the shallow brook, but Morgan's voice was still edgy.

"It looks to me like Cullen Varner's made two big mistakes, which they may pay for later on."

"Such as?" Thea demanded as Cassie leaned over her shoulder to better hear what they were saying.

"He's building in the flood plain, which might well be part of a roaring river come next spring. And there's a copse of beech trees up by where he'll probably put his field. Beeches kill the soil for crops."

"Oh. Will you tell him all that?"

"You think he'd like to hear my ideas on it?" he countered, and the conversation ended with another terse silence.

Just beyond the Varner camp, the trail got worse. Evidently no wagons and few horses had widened the Indian path here. It took careful driving to wend their way along, then up a gentle slope to higher ground when the bank turned stony and narrow. Thea kept her peace, even when they passed a small waterfall tumbling over a slate ledge that she wanted to remark on as a perfect place for laundry and bathing.

Suddenly, she almost panicked. She had come out here to live with this man for over a year. She was afraid she hardly knew him now. They were at odds and both painfully disappointed in each other: he, no doubt, in settling for his second choice in a wife; she by discovering the terrible truth. But out here, they would have to face dangers both within themselves and without!

He gave Thea their precious, worn map from inside his boot where he'd kept it safe and dry, and she unfolded and smoothed it out over her knees as they got closer to the site marked with an X. "High slate and shale banks along the opposite side of the river with a high bluff on this side," she read Morgan's writing on the bottom, things Jacob Roscoe had said. "Good stands of cottonwood, locust trees, and willows down on the water—yes, they're all below us, Morgan!"

Suddenly, she could not keep the rising excitement from her voice. Six hundred miles, and they were almost here! She steeled herself not to throw her arms around him. Sadly, she pictured how their arrival might have been if she had still been ignorant of how he really felt, or if they were somehow reconciled.

He halted the wagon as they came over a rise to a level, grassy upland plain that rolled away to prairie land with occasional stands of trees. They could hear the waterfall behind them, and the river just below, at the bottom of the treed slope.

"There's a good, short path down to the river and the waterfall for hauling water," he said as he wrapped his reins and stood in the wagon. She also rose to her feet to take it all in. He steadied her elbow, and she did not flinch away.

It looked wild but wonderful, a perfect place for camp or homesite.

Puckerbush and a wild plum thicket grew here to embrace the natural clearing with its thick, blowing grass. Late afternoon sun made islands of light through the leaves of encircling black walnut, hackberry, and paw-paw trees edging the bluff. And scattered through the shorter grass where she could picture their cabin, bold yellow marygold flowers lay like a bright carpet to welcome their arrival.

"It's beautiful," she said. "I see knee-high wild pea vines over there, and wild onions to roast in the embers."

"Rock fish and duck down below and that wild pig we saw in the woods means there are others out there we can catch. I'd say, wife, we have arrived!"

He jumped down and reached up for her while Cassie clambered noisily down the back. Morgan held Thea aloft, his hands lingering hard on her waist for a breathless moment. Then he lowered her slowly to her feet. He had longed, just then, to slide her down along his body. She had yearned to have him spin her until she was so dizzy that she kissed him in joyous celebration at their safe arrival. But they both felt suddenly subdued and did neither. They only gazed deeply into each other's eyes. He reached to cup her chin, then his hand dropped away.

"Let's stake out the team before we explore," he said and stepped back. "They deserve this grass for the job they've done."

Thea watched his brown hands on the harnesses. Cassie was already cavorting, picking flowers. Morgan turned back to Thea and reached for her hand. She gave it and they held palm to warm palm. Their fingers interlocked. Then Cassie screamed. They ran to her, only to see a small, lithe, nearly naked Indian boy sprint away.

"Just like the folk!" Cassie cried. "Long hair and naked with an elf bow, just like the *Sidhe!*"

"Only an Indian lad, Cassie," Morgan told her. "Don't scream again, and maybe he'll be back. I don't want them riled or to think we're frightened because we want to visit their town across the river and trade with them." Thea squinted after the boy while Morgan explained to Cassie. Yes, the lad had halted his headlong flight and was peering back at them. His face looked as sad as curious. She waved.

"Oh, can I go to their village with you?" Cassie was asking Morgan. "It isn't deep in the forest, is it? But how will we get there?" she chattered on and followed Morgan back to his work with the harnesses.

"We'll get there on stones over a shallow part of the river," Morgan told her patiently, and his voice floated to Thea on the breeze. "The boy got over somehow, didn't he? And in the winter, we'll just walk across the ice. Thea, we'd better draw these animals some water before it gets dark!"

"I'll never cross over a river, not me!" Cassie cried. "Did it once and been paying for it since, I have!"

But Thea just hurried the girl along with her to water the animals. They hauled buckets to fill the trough that fit on the side of the wagon—one she figured she might have to use for winter laundry and bathing, too, now that her precious barrels were gone. During all this, they saw their little, long-faced, brown-skinned visitor sidling closer and closer.

"Hello," Thea finally dared to the boy while Cassie just gawked. He wore a breechcloth, moccasins, the strap of his quiver, and nothing else. "Do you speak English?"

"My land," the boy said. "My land." He stomped his foot.

"Oh, I didn't know that," Thea said. "Morgan, he says this is his land!" she explained as Morgan came over at a leisurely pace.

He spoke to the lad in that guttural, windy Indian dialect he knew. The boy, who looked to be seven or eight years, nodded while he chattered away to Morgan. The only word Thea recognized was Pequotting. Then the boy said, "Danilo," and pointed across to the other bank.

"I thought they call that village over there Pequotting, not Danilo," Thea said.

"His name is Danilo, and he lives over in the Wyandot village of Pequotting. His mother is Wintasa, daughter to the great medicine man Wabuck, whom Jacob Roscoe mentioned. Wabuck died two winters back. Danilo's father, Quanemo, said he was not old enough to take south hunting with the village men, so he is running away to look for game on his own. And he wasn't saying, 'My land,' Thea. Milan is evidently their word for these high banks up and down the river. I think he just wanted us to know where we are, and I think he's really run away from home, just like the lot of us."

During Morgan's explanation, the boy looked up, awed at the big, painted Conestoga and the animals eating at its trough. His small brown hand even dared to stroke the rough wood once, then pulled back sharply. The boy's awe at the battered wagon touched Morgan's memory and heart. "Let's give him a gift of that old bicorn of mine you're wearing, Thea, and you can wear your bonnet instead. Then, before darkness falls, I'd better take him back across the river to his family so they don't get the wrong idea we're keeping him."

Danilo's dark brown eyes lit when Thea handed him the bicorn. He almost smiled. It was far too big for him, but he tipped it back and peered up at the tall man and woman and their strange-faced girl, the likes of which he had never seen.

"I'll leave the musket for you," Morgan told Thea, "but I don't expect you to have to shoot it. If I'm not back until after dark, don't worry, as the Indians insist on feeding their visitors."

Thea bit her lip to keep from blurting out whether he also expected to be entertained on some maiden's blanket for returning the boy. Morgan spoke low to the lad in his dialect. "Now don't wait up, and don't worry," he comforted and squeezed her arm. "Danilo says there are no warriors around, and everyone is at peace along these milan banks." He looked as if he'd like to kiss her, but he just started away. The boy was the only one who looked back. When he grabbed the big hat to keep it off his small brown face, he seemed to be tipping it to her and Cassie like the finest gentleman. Thea smiled, and the lad's grin flashed like lightning on his dark face before it faded. Then the two of them disappeared down the path to the river.

*   *   *

Thea and Cassie worked hard to rope corral the team, just like they'd seen at Varners' place, and unload the wagon. They built a little fire in a place where Cassie, much to her chagrin and dire mutterings about fairy curses, had to dig up the grass in a circle. They ate the last of their dried meat, some fresh hackberries, and the bulbous, sliced roots of the beargrass from the lake's edge, which Jacob Roscoe told them was a good substitute for bread. Bread, Thea thought as she settled down by the fire while Cassie rolled herself up in a blanket inside the empty Conestoga. She could almost smell fresh bread baking in the Lockwood kitchen back in New London or taste that rich walnut-raisin loaf Charity Payne's cooks used to make for teatime. Here, they would have to trade for Indian cornmeal since they'd lost the flour barrel, Morgan said, for it would be months before they'd have their own crop. Despite her meal, her stomach rumbled and despite her exhaustion, she could not sleep as the sky darkened to flaunt all its stars.

She was still agonizing over Morgan going to that village. Not so much that she feared for his safety. What if he shared an eager Indian maiden's blanket? Drat, what did she care? She had told him to. But there were almost no men over in the village, the boy had said. Wouldn't the women there be grateful to Morgan for returning the boy? And Morgan, of course, would want to make a good impression on them at first and be willing . . .

"Drat!" she said aloud and flopped over on the grass to yank her blanket up around her ears. Here in the drifting smoke of the fire, the buzzing of mosquitoes was not so bad. It was her own pride and passions plaguing her, and there was no herbal cure for that pain. A buzzing mosquito landed on her forehead. She smacked at it and ruffled her thick hair down to cover herself better. Morgan had said these insects were not so bad as the big deerflies that came in August because they bit like bears, but of course she didn't believe that. Didn't believe Morgan—that he still wanted her, only her, and had married her and loved her for herself. Her thoughts floated through her brain like firesmoke in half-sleep.

"Oh!" she sat up and reached for the gun when she heard

a twig crack. Morgan loomed over her. He put his big foot on the musket barrel when she reached for it by instinct. Her pulse pounded; her heart thudded in her chest.

"Just me," he said, his voice low. He sat down next to her, cross-legged. He didn't add that she'd never have saved herself in time if it hadn't been him. "You're on guard at my spot. Cassie inside the wagon?"

"Yes," she said and sat up, shoving her hair back from her face. "I take it the Indians were very friendly."

"Very." His voice wrapped around her, lazy and warm. She said nothing else, so he went on, "It's a good-sized village with four longhouses and quite a few bark wigwams. Two sweathouses, maybe a hundred women and children, and a few old men. The braves, like Danilo said, have all gone south toward the Ohio River on a summer hunting trip. I invited his mother Wintasa, to visit us."

"Just Wintasa?" she spoke at last. "Was she special for some reason?"

He swatted a mosquito. "If we get too many Wyandots over here, they'll all expect gifts, and we don't have much to give," he clipped out, his voice wary again. "Besides, I thought she'd be the best Pequotting friend for you as her section of a bark longhouse had drying herbs hanging all over it. Of course, if you've now renounced making friends as well as having husbands out here—"

"No, I didn't mean that," she choked out as her face flushed hot. "I was just curious."

"And, Thea, I didn't so much as touch anyone over there, if you're curious about that, too."

"Of course I'm not."

"Good. That will make it easier in the future," he said and stood.

She almost rose to that bait, but he might not have meant what she read into it, and she'd make a fool of herself again. All her agonizing made her feel so alone out here, so estranged from him when she didn't want to be!

"Tomorrow I'll tell you about some of the other Indian women I met, Thea." He broke the awkward little silence between them as he stared at her face, lit only by starlight.

"I've brought back a sack of corn so you can make meal and some bread cakes."

"Fine, but I don't know how."

"I've seen it done. I'll show you, or if Wintasa comes across tomorrow, maybe she can."

"I'd like to learn. I do intend to be a help and support to you out here so we both earn that prize money," she said.

Even in the darkness, she could feel his face harden. Somehow, she always managed to say the wrong thing lately.

"Great," he said. "But if I only wanted a cook or a laundress, I could have brought one. I admire your apothecary skills more than I can tell you, but that's not what I'm longing for from you either, and you know it. Thea, don't pretend you don't. I think we're both done with pretending. Now get on inside the wagon with Cassie, or these blood-hungry insects or something even bigger will be all over you."

She gaped at him for a moment. In the warm night, the luring silence between them stretched taut and tense. Crickets creaked. The darkness seemed to snare them in its warmth. He was giving her a choice, a challenge. In answer, she longed to lean against his leg, to open her arms and pull him back down on the ground with her. Here they were alone—almost alone—together. But what stood between them still hurt so much. Then a mosquito saved her, and she broke the forest spell by swatting at her cheek as if to jar herself to her senses.

"Yes, fine," she blurted like a coward and struggled to unwind the blanket from her legs. "I'll just sleep in the wagon with Cassie, like before."

He turned quickly away to toss another green log on the fire to get more smoke to ward off insects. A shower of sparks lit his solemn, stony profile.

"Good night, then, Morgan."

"Good night, Thea. But I have to tell you, I'm only building one bed for us inside the cabin and a pallet for Cassie if she stays. And I'm not going to sleep out here, come cold weather."

Trembling at her own desires, she hurried away, crawled in the back of the Conestoga, and curled up in her blanket, despite the sheen of sweat on her now. She felt flushed and shaky, inside and out. She felt hot between her legs, just as she did when he actually touched her there. She tried to thrust all those sorts of thoughts aside, but they tormented her. She had to forgive Morgan, even if she couldn't forget. After all, Claire Trent at Eden's Gate had said it was hard for her to come to terms with her jealousy over her husband's previous lover, but she managed and was happy now. She had to forgive Morgan at least so they could get along. Otherwise, she'd be like some blushing maid every time he looked her way or said something like that.

She had to find a way to forgive Rina, too, perhaps go to visit her after they got the cabin built, just to talk. Rina had wanted to give her cooking utensils and food after the accident. Rina had defended her against Avery Payne more than once. Rina had wanted to head west with them even when Cullen had not. Thea shuddered. Or had Rina just wanted to be near Morgan still, even when she was wed to Cullen?

What woman could want any other man over Morgan Glenn, no matter what had passed between them? And that included Thea Arnold Glenn. With just one moment's recklessness, she could walk out there right now and share his blanket so he wouldn't be tempted to look elsewhere. But her pride would be gone in the morning. Would the pain be gone then, too? She flopped and turned until the big wagon creaked in protest and she lay still. Finally, an aching eternity later, she slept.

The hot summer days passed for the Glenns in a haze of hurried work. There was much to do before the crisp winds of autumn began to blow. Morgan, bare-backed in the sun, worked to clear the floor space and erect a bark log cabin. His skin turned bronze as an Indian's, and little white crowfeet marked the corners of his deep brown eyes. The already powerful muscles in his upper torso and legs rippled and hardened; his thighs and calves swelled his breeches and the stockings Thea labored so to keep clean. Finally, he traded a tin tole candle holder for a bolt of blue broadcloth in Pequotting, and Thea made leggings for him and a matching skirt for herself. She wore it with a cool, loose shirt she sewed from a hemp sack she'd brought for storing certain herbs. The root cellar she was digging between two big chestnut trees behind the cabin would have to do for all her herb and food storage. She had been picking and storing the bright marygold flowers from around the cabin to make a winter salve to ward off frostbite.

The cabin itself kept them all busy and exhausted the first four weeks. "The Indians I knew in Pennsylvania used layers of shaved bark over framing logs for winter cabins on the hunt," he told Thea. "It won't be as fine as what you saw Cullen Varner starting to build back there, but it will be a dang site better for our uses. Besides, like I said, his is likely to be swept away come spring."

"We should tell them that, whatever they think of us or our advice," Thea admitted.

"I know. But he's the one who insisted on everyone doing everything by themselves. I was hoping Jacob Roscoe might be through these parts soon and would advise them. We can barely spare a day here, but one or the other of us should go. Or we could send Danilo with a note, but I'd never forgive myself if something happened to that boy."

"I agree. Wintasa seems to fear something dire before his father returns. You don't suppose she's had some dream about it, as much as they put stock in those?"

"No," he told her, leaning against the waist-high wall of their cabin, "I don't think it's that. It's something her husband must have said to her, some threat she's terrified he will follow through on when he returns," he added, leaning his forearms on the top poles to rest and stretch his aching back muscles. He almost chanced asking Thea to rub his back, but he decided to play this out the long-suffering, subtly seductive way. When she came to him it was going to be because she was crackling hot as flame and wanted to touch him so badly she could not hold back.

From the shade of her bonnet brim, Thea studied her husband as he spoke. His big brown shoulders gleamed in the sun; curly auburn hair matted his powerful chest. Suddenly, she could recall the feel of him against her: the crisp resiliency of the springy curl of hair, the way she ran her fingers through it when she rested her cheek there after they . . . She startled guiltily and yanked her attention back to what he was saying.

"As for our cabin," he went on, "I don't suppose either of the Varners would think much of these ugly layers of bark. But it's gonna be warmer. And less work, so we can do autumn plowing and build up our winter stores of wood and fodder to get the animals through the cold weather. If we ever do return for good, I'd build us a more permanent cabin. But with the Conestoga tipped against the north wall to insulate us even more, we'll be cozy as bugs in a rug this winter," he said and went back to work humming just the way Cassie always did.

She recalled his earlier promise he would build one bed for them to share. That mere thought made her stomach drop away. She could barely stand not to touch him now. And when he cuddled next to her in a crisp autumn night under the meager blankets they had to share on that single mattress, she could just imagine the results. But, thank God, autumn was weeks off yet, and he hadn't even begun to build a bed. Taking her long forked stick with her—they all carried one against the fat yellow rattlesnakes hereabouts—she turned quickly back to digging her root cellar.

The framing logs Morgan laid for the cabin were about fifteen feet long, with posts driven into the ground at each end to keep them stacked together. Twelve-foot logs made up the other two walls. The frame was seven feet tall, so neither of them would have to stoop. The door opening and single, narrow window were on the south side to take advantage of the winter sun and shut out the coldest winds. He drove big, wooden Y-shaped logs into the ground at the corners, and leaned large logs across in those. Then he laid poles instead of rafters across those and vine-tied extra thick hunks of bark along the roof and sides to shed rain and snow. He made a squat stone hearth and chimney that vented out the top of the back wall. Meanwhile, Thea and Cassie chinked every little crack or hole with moss and river mud.

Thea's hands were filthier than they'd ever been, with brown, half-moon fingernails she took to soaking daily in the river. In the hot weather, she washed her hair each day and rinsed it in sage water to bring back its luster. She kept it carefully piled under her bonnet, which also minimized the freckles on her face. She picked elder flowers from the berry bushes and rubbed juice from them on her skin every day, and even made a crude skin emulsion by pounding together pond lily leaves and some chamomile she joyously discovered on an herbal expedition along the river. With Morgan's trading and hunting here, Cassie's fishing, and her gathering of berries, mushrooms, and roots, they ate better than they had on the journey. That in turn, filled out her body again, and the two dresses she owned fit without gaping now.

She knew Morgan noticed all this, too, and sometimes she felt she was intentionally tempting him. Still, she couldn't help herself. She was glad his eyes followed her that way, that he looked sometimes as if he'd like to seize her and carry her into the forest depths. It made her feel so feminine to walk that fragile edge of both their desires. Only, still, she wasn't certain if she meant to punish him by flaunting what he had passed up for another. Or, by fanning her own longing for him, was she punishing herself for being so stupid to be taken in by both her best friend and the only man she had ever loved? Yes, loved! Even the pain of finding out the truth had not destroyed her love for Morgan Glenn. It grew each hot summer day like a fire feeding on everything in its path.

As for Morgan, he worked like the very devil to exhaust himself and beat down his own body's desire for her. He played mental games at night to keep from just going to her and carting her off into the woods, Cassie and the mosquitoes be damned! More than once he almost stopped his frenzied work and pulled Thea away to try to talk things out again. He almost blurted to her that Rina had lied to him, evidently about both her and Thea's arrangements with other men. But he worried all that might just sound like sour grapes to Thea. Rina was not here to defend herself, and when Thea asked her, she might just deny it. It was as if he and the stunning wife he so hungered for walked on delicate eggs around each other.

But Thea must be growing to trust him, Morgan encouraged himself. She might even want him again. Things had been so hot between them once, it was a constant torment to think of what they might have lost because he was too much of a coward to risk honesty from the first. Maybe, just maybe, he'd start to build their bed before he even did the front door, he mused with a grim expression as he crawled along the rough bark roof, tying everything together.

One of the things that pleased Thea most about the Firelands was the change in Cassie. Her fear of both the forest and crossing the river, even at the shallow Indian fording place, soon disappeared. Perhaps becoming friends with some of the Indians soothed her fears of her "other forest folk." As Wintasa began to visit their Camp Milan with Danilo almost daily, Cassie went back with them more often than even Thea did. Morgan and Thea were amazed to see that the Wyandots were in awe of Cassie, even though most of them could not understand a thing she said unless Wintasa translated—and sometimes not even then. They looked up to Cassie and hung on her strange pronouncements, instead of mocking or shunning her like more "civilized" folk had done.

Thea and Morgan both recalled the story of how Benedict Arnold had once used a dim-witted soul to panic the Indian allies of the British. As Jacob Roscoe had explained it to them on the bateau on the lake, "The Indians think the tetched in the head, like your little Irish girl there, gotta direct line to God Hisself. The red man thinks the tetched know the future and reveal the truth that others is too blind to see, for everybody's sakes." So, Thea thought, if living in the Firelands had freed Cassie from her painful fears, why couldn't the same thing happen to her?

Now, every time Cassie chattered or sang Morgan's favorite song, which she now called "Danilo Boy" for the little Indian lad who had learned to smile at last, Thea thought of Jacob's rustic wisdom and the Indians' beliefs. What Morgan and Rina had tried to hide, Cassie had revealed to Cullen and Thea. Thea realized she had, as Jacob Roscoe said, been too blind to see the truth. So maybe God, through Cassie, had cleared everything up. But had it really been for everybody's sakes, or had it ruined her future with Morgan? If only, *if only,* she could just let it all go and find her way back to trusting him as well as desperately desiring him here in this new eden they were building together!

Chapter Fourteen

"From what we have learned over the years, Indian medicines are far better healers than many European ones. Chewing the inside bark of willow trees lessens all sorts of pain, and the slippery elm bark may allay stomach upsets. For deep cuts, unless near the heart, poultice of boiled spruce is best. You see, the red man has his own cures and pains."

AT MORGAN AND Thea's Camp Milan, there were frequent guests from the Wyandot village across the river. Danilo often tagged after Morgan on his daily chores or went along to hunt. The boy loved to sit in the high seat of the silent Conestoga or jingle the harness bells Morgan kept under the seat.

"I thought," Thea said to Morgan once during a dinner break just before they took the wheels off the wagon and tilted it against the north wall of the cabin, "you said we would hang those bells from a tree here. Danilo would love to hear them in the breeze."

"I would, too," he told her, his mouth full of rabbit and wild onions. "But I think of those as our wedding bells, and I won't be using them again until we're both ready to act wedded. I'd like to get the bells out, but I'm afraid it's all up to you."

Her spoon had dinged against her pewter plate in surprise. She felt knocked in the stomach. They had avoided discussing that dilemma for weeks. Had he been waiting for her to bring it up again or make the first move? Before she could even think of what to say, he had put his empty plate down and was back to work.

Their other visitor, whom Thea came to cherish, was Danilo's young, moon-faced mother, Wintasa, daughter to the departed medicine man, Wabuck, and wife to Quanemo. Her husband was still gone on a long hunting journey to the south, along what the Wyandots called the O-hee-zuh River. Wintasa wore a knee-length calico skirt with a sleeveless, fringed buckskin blouse and many porcelain-bead necklaces. Her raven hair was oiled and tied back with eelskin to make her face look even rounder, though her body was slender and lithe. She usually went barefoot, but kept her legs and arms oiled against insects and snakes. Her jewelry jingled when she walked.

Thea and Wintasa, who spoke halting English, loved to trade herbs and share medicinal lore. In the beginning, even when Thea showed her every herb she'd found in the vicinity, Wintasa had merely nodded, hardly answering. But when Thea showed her the big pharmocopoeia she kept in the root cellar she was digging, the woman's eyes widened to the size of river clams.

"This book your magic?" she had asked.

"Not magic, but wisdom from my father and mother. They were healers back where we came from."

After she had seen the big book, though she could not read a word of it, and heard that Thea's people were revered in medicine like her father Wabuck had been, Wintasa listened to everything Thea said and began to confide in her, too.

"This son to me, Danilo," she began one day in mid-August as she showed Thea how to bruise green acorns to make a drink to stop the dysentery that had plagued Cassie for a week. "To Wintasa, Danilo the sun in the sky, the cloud, too. Before your Mor-gan come to take him to hunt, Danilo very sad."

"He misses his father, Quanemo, you mean?" Thea prodded in the long pause that followed as she took the crude stone mortar and pestle from Wintasa.

Wintasa nodded, and her beads rattled. "Wintasa very sad Quanemo not in the village now. Quanemo follows a long trail of many suns. When his footsteps return, it will be the time of the dance. For that, my heart shakes like the leaves of the trees." Her huge brown eyes shifted to watch her son as he in turn watched Morgan feed the oxen long grass that had been cut and raked from the prairie just beyond. Wintasa gestured to the boy to move farther away. Scowling the way he did at any order from a woman, even Thea whom he liked and the revered Cassie, he walked off into the bright yellow marygolds and tall grass.

"The time of what dance?" Thea asked.

"When the cord of joining can be cut," she said and made a downward chop motion with one hand.

"What cord?"

"Man and woman bound together to make a house and make a child," she explained, her face showing pained emotion Thea had never seen from her. The usually stoic, placid features wrenched to a frown before her face went calm again. Wintasa clamped her hands flat together, palm to palm. "Like you and your man, Mor-gan. One summer night a year, when the moon is round like a woman's belly with a child, the cord can be cut."

"Marriage?" Thea asked, and her hands stilled. "Cut the marriage bonds even if there is a child like Danilo?"

Wintasa hung her head; her heavy porcelain beads settled lower on her rounded breasts. "If the woman or man no longer lights the path of the other," she muttered without looking up. "The man or woman must only dance with another on that night."

Thea stared, her hands tensed, her mind racing. Divorce, just for the asking? And Wintasa feared Quanemo would cut her off and choose another in this sacred dance? Thea covered the woman's clenched hands with hers, but it was not poor Wintasa she saw in her mind's eye. Rina. Herself. Morgan. Would Morgan want such a thing if it were for the taking in their culture? Would she herself have danced off alone under a full moon, away from Morgan, if she had the chance? She knew the answer to that, for her, was no. Never! But Morgan . . . what of him and . . .

Danilo's cry shot Wintasa to her feet. She ran to him, before Thea scrambled after her. When Danilo cried out again, Wintasa shrieked back over her shoulder, "Snake! Yellow snake with big rattles!"

Thea ran back for her heavy pounding rock. Danilo was

hobbling. Wintasa pulled him to the ground and bent close over his leg. Her knife flashed silver in the sun as she cut an X over the bite while Thea threw her rock to crush the snake. Morgan had killed two of these snakes last week and warned them all to watch for them, as their bite was lethal and there was nothing to cure the poison.

"Yellow root!" Wintasa was screaming. "Yellow root by the river stones for yellow snakes!"

"But that will only make him vomit!" Thea protested.

"Yellow root!" Wintasa cried, and Thea tore away for some, just as Morgan came into the clearing from the forest.

Thea half ran, half skidded down the curved river path. She splashed water as she yanked at what Wintasa had told her just last week some of the braves used to purge themselves before using the sweating hut in the village. She yanked up two, three plants and dunked them once in the water. She pulled her dagger from the pouch Morgan had made from a squirrel skin as she started up the path. Wintasa and Morgan, with the boy in Morgan's arms, were sprinting toward her.

Wintasa grabbed the roots from Thea and pulped them on a rock with the handle of her knife. She jammed the yellow mass into the boy's throat while his eyes rolled and he struggled to breathe. She screamed at the boy in their language, and Morgan repeated it, shouting in Danilo's ear. The boy gulped and swallowed. Thea pounded more, and Wintasa stuffed it down. Danilo shuddered as he lay along the bank. Death throes, Thea thought and mourned already for Wintasa and Danilo and the hunter Quanemo who would surely cut the cord to his wife now. Danilo's sleek little brown body heaved and convulsed. Wintasa rolled him facedown as he retched and retched.

"Now, my son will breathe again," Wintasa said and stood over the boy. "Now his father will give thanks to the Great Spirit and Wintasa his son lives."

Eye-to-eye with Morgan, Thea stared dumbfounded over the strange scene as the boy retched again, and then rolled over exhausted on his back to stare dazedly up at them, as if to ask how he got clear down to the riverbank.

*   *   *

That same day in mid-August, Cullen and Rina welcomed
the old white trapper Jacob Roscoe as a guest in their newly
finished cabin. Rina breathed a sigh of relief again when he
assured them Cassie had traveled Lake Erie with Thea and
Morgan, although they had heard about "the special white
woman" at Pequotting from Indian squaws on berry-
gathering expeditions.

"I can't tell you how good it is to see our first white face
in these parts!" Rina told him as she made stew from the
haunch of venison he'd brought them. Why she didn't cook
outside instead of at this inside hearth in this tiny, warm
cabin Jacob couldn't figure, but then maybe she just felt safer
in her new cabin.

"That's a right nice couple, the Glenns, livin' jest south
o' here. I met them along Lake Erie," Jacob went on from
his spot on the small, single split-log bench next to Cullen.
"Dint you see them when they passed on through here?"

"We saw their tracks," Rina said, "but they were in a
hurry, I guess, and couldn't stop."

"Then you'll jest have to get on a couple of your horses
and go visitin' now that you got things so far 'long here,"
Jacob insisted and kept his sharp eyes on the petite blond
woman's pouting profile.

"*Inter nos*—just between us, I mean—I doubt we'll have
the time," Cullen Varner put in. "Besides, we can't take a
chance on some savages stealing the other horses or stripping
the place clean when we're gone. They've stolen things, including cooling bread right out of the window, and run off
with it."

"Say, speaking of seein' white faces, you sure you've not
seen any other trappers or such passin' through?" Jacob inquired and downed another swallow of the fine port Cullen
Varner had offered him.

"No," Cullen replied warily. "Why do you ask?"

"Up the bank a ways, a pair o' boot tracks and horseshoe
prints from his half-lame horse. For sure a white man's. Toes
turn out like a duck's—white man. In like a pigeon—red

man. Now, don't let it rile you none, like I said. Jest another trapper."

"It couldn't be Morgan Glenn, could it?" Cullen blurted before he wished he hadn't. The look Varina shot him could have pinned him to the puncheon wall.

"Naw," Jacob told him. "It weren't no tall, big man like that. Morgan's tracks would be a whole lot deeper. This man's smaller and kinda' leans forward when he walks, rather than lookin' 'round, so he's not a real good woodsman."

Silently, Rina and Cullen marveled at all he could tell from just tracks. But Cullen wished he hadn't mentioned Morgan's name in an accusatory tone when old Jacob had told him he'd shared the Glenns' bateau ride and admired them both. Worse, Varina would think he didn't trust her again, even though their nights in bed almost made up for the doubts that ate at him during their days. Was he really as dear to her as Morgan must have been once? Had he ever swept her away the way Morgan must have in a mere week? Why, *why,* had she ever chosen Morgan Glenn of the Pennsylvania wilds over Cullen Varner of Danbury, Connecticut, when she evidently could have had either? And if she had the choice again, whom would she pick? He worked hard to make life here easier for her, but he was literally a babe in the woods compared to Morgan Glenn. So in her deepest dreams, even in his arms, did she ever long for that other man she had promised herself to first?

Over dinner, Cullen pumped the wily old trapper for news and got more than he'd bargained for. Jacob Roscoe told them he'd heard the Continental congress was really "feeling its oats" since the British had agreed to sign a formal peace treaty in Paris next month. And so, congress had been scolding the Indian tribes for taking England's part in the past conflict.

"American officials been tellin' the tribes they must be punished," Jacob explained, his voice bitter. "But the bullies in Philadelphia been sayin' they'd 'be kind to their red children' to let them keep a small reservation somewheres 'round here. The gov'ment wants to negotiate sep'rate with the tribes—you know, divide and conquer." Jacob's shake of head swayed the shaggy squirrel-skin cap that he never removed, not even in the cabin. "But, mark my words, some splinter groups of tribes, if not the whole bunch of 'em, will get plenty riled over this!"

"You mean we might have Indian trouble around *here*?" Cullen demanded, his spoon halfway to his mouth. "But we were promised things would be peaceful!"

"Have been, 'cept for a massacre of some Christian Indians by some renegade colonial regiment last year over by a place called Gnadenhutten," Jacob said and downed the rest of his port. "But you gotta re'lize that livin' in the frontier's like walking in that river mud down there in the spring. Never quite know when a risin' flood's gonna pull you in or the mud's gonna drag you down. Sorry, ma'am, for that Indian news over your fine dinner," he apologized to Varina Varner as he laid his spoon down next to his pewter bowl on the two-board wide table. "It's jest that, out here, tellin' the truth always works the best so's folks can be prepared to face whatever comes their way."

When he saw the frightened and yet guilty look that passed between the Varners, Jacob wished he hadn't come with such disturbing news. But, bless it, truth telling *was* the best way. Except, of course, he couldn't tell them who he was really working for, any more than they would tell him why they were really here. He regretted, too, that he would have to tell this man he had built his cabin a bit too close along the Pequotting for safety in the spring rains, but perhaps he'd invite Cullen out for a smoke and tell him that much on the sly without upsetting Mrs. Varner more.

"I'm glad you told us about the Indians," she said, but Jacob thought the poor thing looked as if she might cry. She seemed much more delicate out here than she had back in New London when he'd glimpsed her once or twice. Though sometimes the slend'rest gals was made of the sternest stuff, he'd seen from a distance Thea Arnold Glenn fight off an attacker before rescue came in New London, and he wasn't sure this other woman could do the same. He followed Cullen

Varner out into the sun, grateful not to be closed in by those four small walls and all the goods they had piled in there. He gazed around the vast openness outside and pulled in a good, deep breath as he looked southward down the river toward the Glenns' homestead, which he'd be visiting next in a couple of days after he ran some traps 'tween here and there.

Too bad the ladies had a few miles keeping them apart out here, 'cause it surely would have given them both a lift to visit, Jacob mused. That lovely butterfly of a gal in there was starting to look plumb worn through, and winter hadn't even come clomping in on them all yet. Jacob hit flint against steel in his kit to light the precious tobacco mixed with sumac leaves in his clay pipe. He sucked on it once, then passed it to the Connecticut gentleman who had been forced to play pioneer in this raw land Jonathan Trumbull called the Firelands.

After the men went out, Rina covered the rest of the stew in the kettle and took it off the flames. It would at least do for supper tonight, too. She was tired of bone-filled river fish and small mud clams, but she worried when Cullen went off hunting. At least she'd feel better if she had Cassie for company—and to help with these endless chores. And it was funny how that old trapper had looked at her when he spoke about telling the truth, as if he knew what had obsessed her these weeks here, however hard she had tried to be such a perfect helpmate for Cullen.

Rina missed both Thea and Cassie desperately and yearned to make everything up to them, too. But when she'd merely hinted once to Cullen that they should go visiting the Glenns so she could talk to Thea and be sure Cassie was all right, he had exploded.

"Don't you realize all that's over now, Varina!" he had shouted and slammed a fist into the new door of the house to make it bang on the fine brass hinges they'd hauled clear from Danbury. "You're best off *ad perpetuam* rid of Mrs. Morgan Glenn and that superstitious dimwit Irish chatterbox, too! Or was it Morgan Glenn you really wanted to see?

Maybe he's built a finer cabin or plowed a better field? Maybe he's really the one you wished had brought you west after all, is that it?"

She had stared aghast at his tirade, her hands pressed to her cramped belly. This had obviously been bottled up inside Cullen for weeks. "No, I—Thea and Cassie were my friends for years, that's all. You know that when my mother died—" she'd begun, but he had cut her off.

"I know. But your mother's gone and so are Cassie and Thea, so let's just go on together from here," he had said and hugged her hard to him. She pictured that harsh embrace now in her mind as if she stared at two strangers clamped together in terror. Why did he have to hurt her so sometimes? Her mother was dead and Thea was gone, Cullen had said. Yes, that was true, but she didn't want to think of it that way. When her mother died, Thea had come and taken over the empty places in her life and finally soothed away the bad dreams at night. But she had taken over the house and Father, too, hadn't she?

No one really wanted Varina Lockwood Varner anymore, Rina agonized. Even Cullen, for all his fierce possession, didn't forgive her or believe her or trust her to love him. He thought of all her weaknesses out here as rejections of him or as ploys to see Morgan Glenn, when it was only Cassie and Thea she needed to help her through this long, hard, lonely, frightening, time out here! Thea would know what to do. Thea would be bold and independent enough to stand up to Cullen and yet win his affections out of bed, too!

Staggered by the vastness of her need and the jabbing pains that had returned to twist her stomach, she sank to her knees. She hit her fist on the small stone hearth Cullen had struggled to build, but had not made broad enough so that sparks sometimes spit out on the puncheon floor. Tears blinded her. When she blinked, they splattered her cheeks and the green gown across her knees. Only then did she smell the bit of burning cloth and notice her skirt was near a silver-embered log. She smacked the ashes off her gown with her fingertips, however much that hurt, too.

*　　*　　*

The day after his snake bite, Danilo's ankle was too swollen to walk, so Morgan and Thea went over to see him for once. He was the only one Thea had ever known to live through a rattlesnake bite and all because of some river weed called yellow root, which her thick London-printed pharmacopoeia had never mentioned. Cassie had gone to the village, too, and stayed behind with Wintasa and the boy. With all that had passed to link them to these Wyandot Indians, they had no fear now that any of their animals or precious goods would disappear from Camp Milan while they were gone.

After their visit, Thea and Morgan walked home weighted down with gifts from the Indian women for their part in saving Danilo's life. The most precious, which Thea carried in her arms, was a fine, thick black bear rug, which would be a blessing on their bed come cold weather. Despite the heat of the day, Thea shivered in dangerous delight at that thought, for Morgan had the bed nearly done. When they got home in just a few minutes and draped the soft fur over the bed to try it on for size . . .

"Oh, Morgan, just smell the chamomile along here!" she blurted to save herself from her thoughts as they approached the stone-strewn shallows where they always crossed the river. "Doesn't it remind you of apple blossoms at home?"

"I guess it does at that," he admitted and shifted his pack of food and seeds from the villagers.

"You know, that's one gift the Firelands has given me," she said as they stepped from stone to stone. "Back in the shop I never smelled a thing anymore, but out here, I think I got my nose cleansed, and I smell everything again. Strange how I recall that Cousin Benedict told me to enjoy things while I can when he noticed how good the shop smelled that day of the parade."

"Good advice, even from him," Morgan mused aloud. They stopped to face each other on the west bank of the river. "He was a mix of wisdom and stupidity, just like the rest of us," he added and shook his head. "The best advice Benedict Arnold ever gave me was to charge ahead and make things happen, not to sit back and wait." His eyes went over her, warm as sun splotches through the trees. His sharp gaze took in her face in the shadow of her bonnet, then dropped to her full breasts above where she clasped the robe's furry softness to her, much more tightly now. "I haven't been doing that, Thea, and I'm about at the end of my rope for just hanging back like 'Granny' Gates. So I'm going to take Arnold's advice now in this little standoff between you and me."

"What do you mean?" she said warily, but she almost tilted toward him at the raw magnetism he evoked even without touching her.

"I want you too much in every way to play the long-suffering soldier boy serving time for some kind of court-martial. We've just talked about the traitor Arnold, so I'm going to tell you something about the traitor Rina."

"What? Something else besides—"

"Just listen! That day of the parade at the Lockwood house when she took me upstairs because I was sick, I asked her if you were promised to anyone, and she said yes!"

"She couldn't! I mean, I wasn't."

"Evertt Edwards, she said, and gave me the impression you were rather intimately involved with him. She also said she was not promised to Cullen, and I believed her. Like Cassie's forest folk, she threw a spell on me, and after that . . . Dang it, Thea, I should have asked you, but I had no reason not to believe her. And, you know, I'm just hoping she admits it to you someday, but if she doesn't, it's still all true, and like I said . . . Hell," he muttered, "I'm rambling like an idiot. There's something I want to show you downriver. Let's hide this stuff along here in the bushes and go now, all right?"

"What is it?"

"Just don't argue. I want you to believe me, but if you don't, you don't."

She felt dazed by all he'd said. Yes, she believed him, though a part of her still wanted to rush to Rina's defense. But she had no time to agonize or argue now. Morgan clambered up the bank a ways to secrete his sack, then took the bear rug from her to hide it, too.

"Are you all right?" he asked, his eyes narrowing. "If you won't walk with me downriver, I'm going to carry you."

She nodded her agreement, and they were off along the

bank at a good clip, hand-in-hand. Suddenly, all her senses became poignantly aware of everything, not just river or forest smells. The water burbled at their feet; birds lilted from tree to tree. The sun was hot on her neck, and the coziness of her hand tucked into his bigger one was heaven itself. Her legs shook, but she kept up.

"Are you going to show me the cold sulfur medicine spring down this way?" she asked him when he didn't speak. "Wintasa showed me."

"Not that," he said as they walked on. Maybe he'd tell her later how even bathing in that chilly, smelly water had not cured him of wanting his stunning wife spread naked under him on the ground, thrashing, moaning the way she used to. When his loins had been too heated, it had doused his immediate ardor several times, but his longings for Thea always returned tenfold. He fumbled for his flint and steel kit in his boottop to be sure it was still there. He'd only brought two along, compared to the six Cullen had boasted he had packed, so he always kept one where he could find it.

"Here," he said and stopped so fast she bumped into his shoulder. "Danilo showed this to me last week on one of our little hunting expeditions, and all I could think of was us."

Thea's curious eyes scanned the rock face where he stared. "I don't see anything special. What is it?"

"Stand right there, and I'll show you. The boy says it used to be sacred to the Indians."

She smelled a bit of sulfur, perhaps she thought, drifting over from the medicine creek nearby. She watched, mystified, as Morgan scavenged for a piece of punk and lit it with his flint and steel kit. He blew on it to get it going, then said, "Watch now!" He waved the smoldering punk over the top of a waist-high rock. A three-foot orange and blue flame leaped straight up from the rock face.

"Oh, a natural flare!" she cried as they watched it continue to burn, even when Morgan stepped away. "No wonder the Indians used to think it was sacred. Wouldn't it give Governor Trumbull a thrill to know there's another reason to call this area the Firelands? There's nothing there, and then suddenly—"

"But it needs the flame—some help to make it burn again!" he told her and turned her to him with his big hands hard on her shoulders. "Thea, I have felt like that flame since the truth about me and Rina came out. Invisible, burning up inside. Yes, dang it!" he cried and held her harder when she tried to look away. "I thought I loved her once! How she really felt, I don't know! I admit my mistake! We can't bury it, but we can go on. Every time I so much as breathe the same air you do, Thea, I'm like that flare going off. I burn for you, my sweetheart. I want *you*, I need *you*. And don't think I couldn't have married a good Pennsylvania girl and brought her west with me if I didn't want you! I know one or two who would have been happy enough—"

"I'll just bet!" she countered, but she was no longer angry. Tears blurred her eyes. "Morgan, I have longed for you so much, I can't tell you—"

His big hand lifted to gently cover her mouth. "Then don't tell me. Show me!"

She nodded. Their lips drifted closer. But when they touched, they ignited like the flame which still roared from the rock. Morgan's hands tugged her blouse from her blue skirt and reached up under it to cup her full breasts. She seldom wore a corset out here, and it was driving him mad.

Their tongues, their hands, their legs intertwined as they both shed clothing to shiver in the shade, however warm the day. Morgan removed her bonnet and tumbled her crimson hair free. She gasped as she helped him from his breeches and he yanked off his boots. He was so ready for her, so much bigger and bolder than she had recalled—but then, they'd never done this in broad daylight.

He laid her back on the grassy riverbank atop their pile of clothing. He ravished her mouth and throat. His hard, calloused hands were everywhere and yet so gentle. She reached for him and clung to speckle kisses on his shoulders and chest. They gasped in breaths as if they'd both run miles. "So long, you made me wait so long," he rasped out.

"We can make it up. Make everything up!" she managed between mutually devouring kisses.

On his back, he lifted her up over him at her waist and

trailed her soft flesh and her incandescent hair along his face and chest. She tried to tickle him. He settled her across his hips until he pierced her fully. She looked so surprised. Dang, he'd gone too fast, he thought, but then she smiled.

"We were only really wed a few weeks, my sweetheart," he told her, "and there are other things about all this you ought to know."

"Like this?" she challenged and rested her open hands on his hair-flecked chest to lift herself up and rock against him to set her own quick pace. He sucked in a breath at the thrill of that. He lifted his hands to cup her full, bobbing breasts every time she moved. So bold and beautiful, his Thea!

But as the flame between them built and spiraled higher, he had to seize control. It was something he'd felt was out of his grasp for weeks, months, making this woman want him as much as he did her. Ever since he'd come into the Firelands with Thea, he'd felt he was in a crucible being melted and heated and tested. He rolled over and straddled her, plunging into her willing body at a deliberate walking pace, then a running, pounding one.

"Oh. Oh!" was all she managed when he whispered a string of hot challenges in her ear.

"I love you, wife, and always will!" he cried and watched her face, dazzled with desire.

Thea gazed up at him so close, rocking over and into her. Her blood roared through her; the colors of the searing, sacred flame reddened her view of Morgan's passion-taut face and the whirling treetops over his head. All bad thoughts burned away between them. This mutual act linked them loin to loin and soul to soul. "Oh, Morgan, I just can't hold back—"

"Then don't, never from me!" he rasped in her ear. Together, they flared to one mutual fire that consumed them both.

Afterward, she felt both bold and shy. Still nude, they bathed and splashed in the river, then sat on a big flat rock to dry all but their dangling feet. He sat behind her with his legs on either side of her long legs. His kisses smoothed her damp, wild hair back from her temples.

"I don't think we should sit out here buck naked like this," she murmured. "What if someone from Pequotting comes along?"

"Or one of Cassie's forest folk?" he teased and nipped at her shoulder while his hands marauded elsewhere on her cooling flesh.

"Morgan, don't joke. Shouldn't we walk on back?"

"I am eager to try that bearskin on our new bed," he said, his voice devilishly low. "We've never christened the cabin properly, and I'm itching to get those wedding bells out."

She turned sideways in his arms to link her hands around his neck. "Morgan," she said, her voice so still he almost couldn't hear her over the churning of the river. "I do want everything to be wonderful for us. Out here alone, like this, I think we can make it if we keep working at it."

"Alone like this?" he teased, but then his voice became somber. "Of course, we'll make it. In every way. I know things take time, I've tried to give you time—"

"You've given me a great deal more."

"You forgive me?"

She nodded. But she knew, even now, until she was reconciled with Rina and understood why she'd lied to both Morgan and her, she could not really forget. She had to know how her childhood friend could do that to her. She had to understand it to really put it away.

The next two days were like a second honeymoon at Camp Milan. The harness bells dangled from the chestnut tree just outside the cabin door to sprinkle their tinny tinkles to the wind. The new bearskin was tested against Thea's naked back and bottom on the floor of the cabin, and then stretched across the rope ties of the four-post bed to be tested again. Thea surrendered to her longings and passions; Morgan buried his regrets in his wife's beautiful, willing body. They barely got the animals fed or food hunted. In their blur of emotions, nothing of the past existed. The coming of cold weather or the eventual long trip back to all the hatred they had left behind seemed but a fantasy. Bewitched by each other as if caught in a spell of the Firelands forests, they loved and lingered and loved again.

They had no idea their cabin was being watched. Since the observers were not Indians, Morgan's special sense had not alarmed him. Jacob Roscoe was yet miles away, checking his deadfall traps along the marsh and riverbanks. But one of Avery Payne's hired assassins, the bull-necked Levi Dobson had found his way at last to the Glenn camp marked on his stolen Firelands map. Levi had left his companion Jed Clapper weak with fever up by the lake and picked his way slowly down the Pequotting on his half-lame horse. He had seen only Indian women fishing in the river, but they had not seen him. He had spied on the Varner camp a few days before, but kept well out of sight. He did not like the idea of having to trap or shoot that tall Glenn man by himself without Jed for backup, but if Jed died of the shakes back there, he'd claim all the credit and the money for himself when the Arnold woman came back a widow to suit Avery at last.

He didn't dare just shoot Glenn the minute he came out alone from whatever they were doing in there. Payne didn't want the woman to have any way to link the shooting back to him, so he'd wait until Glenn got himself somewhere off alone. He hunkered down behind the clump of puckerbushes with the cabin in view and waited, but his wait was not long. Clapping on his bicorn, the tall man came to the door of the even taller rough bark cabin. The woman followed him to the door, half dressed, holding a brown gown in front of her like a towel as they kissed lingeringly.

Jumping Jehoshaphat, wouldn't you know it! Levi thought and snickered. And wouldn't Avery Payne just piss his fancy breeches if he knew how the woman he coveted was carrying on out here. She clung to Glenn a moment, and he whispered to her so long in that spill of red hair that Levi reached down to ease his tight britches at his crotch. Damned, if Payne wouldn't probably find out, after he laid the man low, he'd like to come back here for a taste of that tall, flame-haired Arnold gal!

Just as he hoped, Glenn went off in the opposite direction,
calling something to the six horses and two big oxen he kept
in a sapling and rope corral. He could use one of those fresh
horses too, Levi thought, but he dare not risk that, either.
Nope, he told himself as he skirted around the clearing to
keep his target in sight, just one good clean shot to the heart
to drop Glenn in his tracks and then he'd have to make tracks
to his horse, tethered down on the far side of a waterfall. He
moved the hammer of the fine, accurate Pennsylvania rifle
Payne had bought him to half cock. He flexed his bad arm,
which still pained him where Morgan Glenn had shot him
back in New London. Then he stalked even closer.

Thea washed and dressed herself, then stretched luxuriously, lazily after Morgan went out to fetch fodder for the
animals. They had both become such slugabeds these last two
days since they had been making up for weeks of celibacy.
Her body had come alive; her heart had soared. Morgan
cared for her, her only. She knew it! Such a man of honor,
he had believed that she was promised to Evertt Edwards.
So it was Rina who had actually betrayed her, though that
was little consolation in the end. It hurt terribly to have lost
Rina, to finally know their long-tended friendship meant so
little to her. Perhaps Rina had really hated her for years. All
those chances when she could have told the truth . . .

A single distant shot seemed to rock the cabin. But—but
Morgan had left his musket here and only gone to rake up
some grass for the team!

She grabbed his loaded musket from its pegs on the wall
and raced in the direction of the sound. Foreboding wracked
her; fear made her feet fly. Now that she and Morgan were
reconciled, surely nothing could take that—or him—away!

She saw nothing where he should be raking up the waist-
high grass. She lifted and cocked the Brown Bess and swung
it in a half circle around her above the waving grass prairie.

"Morgan!" she called.

She quick-sighted the barrel at the first blur. Danilo! He
hadn't been over since the snake bite. The boy pointed down
at something in the grass she could not see and rattled off

something she could not understand except for "Mor-gan blood. Dead!"

She screamed as her long legs churned through the grass. Morgan lay face up, his eyes open, blood blossoming bright red on his right shoulder.

"Morgan!"

He blinked. Alive! He moved his hand up to the wound. "Keep down," he grunted, obviously wracked with pain. "Someone shot me from over there. Oh," he said and his eyes jumped to the Indian boy as if surprised, "Danilo."

"Dead. The man dead," the boy insisted and tugged at Thea's arm. "Dead. You see."

She helped Morgan sit up. "Go see then," Morgan gritted out. "Be careful." Holding her musket up and cocked, her heart thudding, Thea shuffled through the tall grass after the excited boy. And there, facedown with Danilo's arrow square in his back, lay a bull-necked man she had never seen. Beyond him, in the thick grass, where the man had dropped it, lay a shiny rifle. But the man was not dead. He breathed, and she squatted down beside him to see his face turned at a grostesque angle toward her.

"What?" he said and stared at her, wide-eyed to twist her stomach and her heart.

"Why did you shoot my husband? I'll try to help you if you tell."

"Av—Av'ry Payne sent—" he said but then just made a gurgling sound deep in his throat.

Avery Payne! With an arm that reached clear out here? It could not be, and yet he had clearly said so. "But why?" she demanded. "Tell me!"

"Av'ry Payne, damn his soul—to hell—" he said and whooshed out a breath that was his last.

She ran back to Morgan and helped him to his feet. "Yes, he's dead now. But first, he said Avery Payne sent him. I can't believe it. I don't know who the man is, but Danilo killed him. Didn't Jacob Roscoe say Indians have gotten their tribes in terrible trouble for killing whites or something, that massacre in retaliation—"

"Yes. We'll have to bury him. Avery Payne?" Morgan replied shakily and flopped his good arm over her shoulders. Bent under his weight, she helped him up and back toward the cabin. Danilo trailed behind, carrying his bow and their musket. "We can't let anyone know the boy put an arrow in his back, even if it was to save me," Morgan muttered as pain began to wrack him. "His arrow threw the bastard's aim off. Thea, you're gonna have to dig this bullet out. Then we'll bury Payne's henchman, and just hope there's no more like him—from Payne—out there."

He was sorry he said that, but Thea didn't flinch as she bent to her work. Danilo, wide-eyed and obviously proud of the prowess, which he did not realize could bring wrath on his whole tribe, held the candle for her as night fell. She used Indian medicines Wintasa had helped her store in her new root cellar: boiled spruce poultice to cleanse the wound after she dug the bullet out, alder bark to keep down fever, horse chestnut as a narcotic for the pain.

When Morgan fell at last into heavy sleep, Thea and the boy went out to bury the man Avery Payne had sent. And, without Danilo noticing, Thea edged his Pennsylvania rifle back under a bush with her foot.

Chapter Fifteen

*"My husband's father, an apothecary from whom we inherited
this shop, once told me thus: a proper healer's sign over the
door must bear the Grant of Arms for the Apothecary Society
in London, the Greek god Apollo astride a dragon. Does not
that sign imply that the forces of good must tame the forces of
evil to effect a cure?"*

THE WYANDOT VILLAGE of Pequotting tensed with excitement and activity now that their able-bodied men had returned from a successful hunting and exploring expedition
clear down to the what they called the O-hee-zuh River. The
Indian braves had regarded the nearby Glenn homestead
with suspicion until Morgan assured them in their tongue
they would be leaving next year. That is, he had assured most
of the men. He had not appeased the grim Wyandot
Quanemo, Wintasa's man, however much Wintasa tried to
smooth things over.

Now, thudding drums called everyone within hearing to
the Wyandot feast of the first full autumn moon. Their
rhythms rumbled in Morgan's ears as Wintasa led him toward the farthest bark wigwam in the village to show him
her handiwork. With Cassie and Thea helping lay out food,
it was Morgan's chance to see how Wintasa had carried out
the secret task they shared.

"You like good?" she asked immediately as she pulled an
old blanket off the wooden sign the old village carver had
made according to Morgan's scratchings on a piece of slate.

"I like very good," he told her. From his recall of the
painted apothecary sign Thea had been so proud of in New
London, they had made her a new one. He would give it to
her for Christmas, even if it ended up hanging over not much
more than a root cellar or log hut out here. On the sign, the

Greek god Apollo, father of healing, conquered the evil dragon of disease by bridling and riding him. Morgan himself had carved the words ALTHEA MORGAN, APOTHECARY under it. Someday, he knew, when these western Firelands were finally open to more easterners, a healer would be needed. Now that Thea had healed his heart by forgiving him for loving Rina once, he had no doubt his dynamic wife would be the first white woman apothecary when they someday returned here.

Wintasa covered the sign again, and they went out into the busy village as dusk fell. Her hands darting, her words tumbling out, the Indian woman explained to him how she would dye different sections of the wood to achieve the dark and light tones they had discussed. Morgan knew she was very nervous this night, not only to have her beloved husband home despite how stern he was with Danilo. Tonight was the cutting of the cord ceremony when wife or husband could exchange their mates by merely dancing with another. And though she chattered on about other things, Morgan, having suffered through months of estrangement in his own young marriage, sympathized deeply.

"Willow bark dye will make the black for that demon horse's body," Wintasa told him in her dialect. "And hickory and sumac for your holy God riding the demon horse like the wind."

"The one astride the demon horse—the dragon—is not our holy God, Wintasa," he began, wondering how he was ever going to explain making a sign with a dead civilization's Greek god they didn't even believe in. "But long ago, the ones who began the art of medicine—" he floundered.

"So," a man's deep voice interrupted, "here walks my woman with the white blood man Mor-gan." Wintasa's husband Quanemo blocked their path, his muscular arms crossed over his bare, painted chest. "Quanemo sees it is not only Danilo whose eyes look with favor on this Mor-gan while Quanemo is away."

"Your words are not straight, my husband," Wintasa chided and gently put her hand on his arm.

His frown etched deeper. "Then, is there not more work to do in our longhouse for this fine feast, woman?"

Wintasa began to explain, but Quanemo cut her off with a downward slice of movement that threw her hand from his arm. Wintasa said no more, but her expression echoed fear. Gripping her hands tightly together, her head down, she scurried away. In a tribe where the women were important and proud, her humble acquiescence to Quanemo's dismissal surprised Morgan.

He explained to Quanemo where they had been and offered to show him the wooden sign. The man agreed, and they went back to the wigwam. Morgan stood a head taller than this bronze warrior, who looked carved from dark oak with his rigid features and black, deep-set eyes. Like the other villagers, Quanemo was bedecked in fringed buckskins, leggings, and beads; wild turkey feathers stuck from his thick, oiled hair in precise profusion. Garish arm, chest, and face paint turned his skin to an intricate pattern of lines and whorls. That set Morgan's teeth on edge, though he knew it was strictly ceremonial designs and not war paint. The Wyandots had once battled the bloody Iroquois for seventy summers, for the same problem of contested land, which the new American government was making a dangerous issue.

From their long expedition, the Pequotting hunters had brought back news that some of the tribes were in an uproar. For siding with the British in the war, the Indians had been told by congress to clear out of this area and retire to a piece of land along the Miami River farther west. That sort of thing didn't sit well with white men like Morgan and Jacob Roscoe who admired the Indians, let alone with these insulted "red men children of the great Philadelphia father" themselves.

"See," Morgan told Quanemo in the pidgin Iroquois dialect they shared as he revealed the wooden apothecary sign. "Your woman has many good skills and special gifts. She will dye colors on this gift for my wife. Wintasa's wise ways have guided the feet of my woman and me in this Pequotting land we share."

Quanemo only grunted and stepped back outside where Morgan followed. Large bonfires were being lit now, and

Quanemo's well-oiled and painted body gleamed like a dark mirror.

"When you were away," Morgan dared, wondering if this solemn man would truly break poor Wintasa's heart by taking another mate to him this night, "your woman's care for your son Danilo was great to see. She saved him from the snakebite and—"

"With your help, I hear. And did let him go hunt with you when Quanemo said to him no," the Indian cut him off. "Now my woman goes to the white blood house across the river more than to Wyandot houses. More than when Quanemo set his feet on the hunting path, Wintasa's Wyandot blood now turns white as snow! And in these times of troubles out there—" he swept the forest with his outstretched arm, "—as well as in here!" He hit his chest with his fist so hard his beads bounced. "Wintasa believes in her heart as her father Wabuck before her that the new ways— the white blood ways—are best. But I say no! So how can Quanemo, who once wanted no other woman, stay with Wintasa in these times? She frowns on my path to protect our lands and our old ways! And can Quanemo have his son who must fight for all this someday be in her house?"

He did not look at Morgan. The outburst was obviously aimed at himself. With a sharp, dismissive nod, he stalked off toward his people gathering around the fires. Still shaken by the import of his words, Morgan found Thea with Cassie, still laying out the food they'd brought to the feast. Morgan bent to take a quick kiss from Thea as he always did to reassure himself everything was still sound between them. Cassie was garbed much like an Indian, since she lived over here most of the time, but Thea had donned her blue calico wedding gown as if this were a marriage and not a divorce feast.

"I like everything these Indians eat, I do," Cassie was chattering, "except that 'coon boiled in molasses. The Indians say 'coons change to snakes in the summer, but I think that's just their silly forest talk, and I'll not believe a thing of it, I won't!"

"Good idea not to be taken in by superstitions," Morgan told the girl, straight-faced, but Thea had to hide her smile behind her hand. He steered Thea away the first chance he got.

"Wintasa may be in for it, just like we feared," he told her as they headed for the spot Wintasa assigned them near the fires. "Quanemo thinks Wintasa let Danilo spend too much time with us. He thinks we're a bad influence, and says she's soft on the whites. I'm afraid, especially now that he'd heard the orders our new government is dishing out to the Indians, he's not a bit soft on 'white bloods' in general, or us in particular."

"Drat! Do you think he'll stir up the village?"

"According to what Jacob Roscoe said, the Wyandots are not as committed to some sort of protest as the Ottawas are, but it remains to be seen."

"Thank the Lord we have Wyandots and none of those so-called 'Tawas living right across the river!"

"All I know is," Morgan told her as they seated themselves on a blanket Wintasa had spread on the ground for them, "this place is seething with bad feelings tonight. We'd just better pray for Wintasa with that danged Quanemo, let alone for the rest of us."

Morgan's mind kept poking at possibilities to keep them safe if Indian trouble did kick up before they headed back to Connecticut next year. He had made it known to the Pequotting Wyandots that they were only here for "two summers," as they reckoned time, and then would be taking the path back toward the rising sun. But did they believe him? Did they trust his words when time after time other "white bloods" had lied to them in the east and shoved them farther west? It was his own predicament precisely of being betrayed and becoming wary of trusting even those he most wanted and needed and loved. And he had no doubt Thea, who had too often been let down by those she believed in, felt the same way about trusting these Pequotting Wyandots.

He glanced sideways at Thea's animated face as the tribe gathered to sit in a huge circle to be served food before the dancing. He trusted Thea now not to go back on her word that she forgave him for his mistake with Rina. And yet, there was some unseen wall still between them, something he hoped would be settled when he took her later this winter to visit her old friend. And—Cullen Varner be damned—he would encourage the two women to mend their own relationship somehow.

"I just realized who Wintasa's husband reminds me of," he whispered to Thea.

"Who?"

"The pompous, the precise, the perfect Cullen Varner."

Frowning, Thea only nodded as the wooden trencher before them was heaped with food from Indian maids and the excited, smiling Cassie. Using their fingers and then wiping their hands on big leaves, they partook of *anoo,* a venison ragout; fish and turtle meat; and *coinkia,* balls of steamed rabbit wrapped in corn leaves and boiled. The flat corncakes baked with elderberries and walnuts, which Thea had brought, were mingled with the other food. Later, one by one, members of the tribe got up to form separate lines of men and women dancing in two twisting figure eights around the two campfires to the thunder of water drums and turtle-shell rattles. Cassie came to sit behind them. They soon spotted Quanemo among the men. Slowly, reluctantly, Wintasa rose to join the women.

"What are those two words they keep saying?" Thea shouted in Morgan's ear when she realized what they chanted was not really a song at all.

"The word *kweya* is for joy, and that other word—the one Quanemo is chanting—means 'take courage.' "

"That doesn't sound so bad," Thea said, but her heart fell when Morgan shook his head.

"*Estagon* is also their word of warning or trouble, of challenge and even warfare, Thea. I suppose the ones who intend to find a new mate use that one and the ones who are content, the other."

Thea's hand gripped his between them on the blanket. "Poor Wintasa," she said. "The way you and I danced on our wedding night at that inn was so joyous. I don't think I can bear to sit here watching a dance for divorce, not if he deserts Wintasa."

"It's bad manners to leave right now," Morgan told her

and looped an arm around her shoulders. "For a while at least, we 'white bloods' will have to stay. You know, tonight I almost told Quanemo about Danilo's killing that white man to save my life, since Wintasa wanted us to explain it to him. But he cut me off, and then I held my tongue when I learned he even resented that Danilo hunted with me."

Thea nodded, but her eyes were on this living, flashing spectacle. The mingled musky smells of damp forest floors and leaping Indians and burning wood enveloped them. The loops of the double figure eights interwove so the men and women passed each other twice each time around. Already a few participants had gone over into the other line by merely taking hold of another person's garment fringe. And the chants of *"Estagon!"* and *"Kweya!"* drowned out the stomp of feet. Somewhere, a woman wailed. Then, through the writhing lines of people, Thea saw Danilo standing across the way, arms crossed over his painted chest in imitation of his father. His face was so sad, the way it had been before they made him smile. And then the ranks closed and she saw him no more as other mates were chosen.

"I don't mean to judge their ways, but this is wrong," she insisted to the rapt Morgan.

"Doesn't make for much commitment, does it? And yet, if things go very wrong between a pair, and someone's made a bad mistake that might ruin a whole life—" he mused.

Thea tugged her hand back from his. "You don't really believe that, not for civilized folk at least," she began, but halted when she saw Wintasa, fringed skirt, beads, and braids flying, run toward them.

"Quanemo," she said breathlessly. "My man is gone. Did—did you see him choose another?"

"No," Morgan said. "He was just there in the line."

"Perhaps he is just resting for a moment," Thea said and got to her feet. "Or talking somewhere to Danilo. I just saw him, too."

"No!" Wintasa cried and seized Thea's wrists as if for strength. Her face glistened with sweat; her sleek ebony hair reflected the fires. "Quanemo is with no other woman in the lines, but he is gone with Danilo! His feet have not led him to another woman this night, but have taken him away!" she wailed.

With their distraught friend, they scanned the dancers and then walked the village. Much later, when the dancing was nearly done and the full moon had heaved itself above the treetops at last, they heard. The old wood-carver shuffled up to them from his blanket where he had sat watching the dancing for hours and whispered to Wintasa. When she spun to face them, her face had gone still and pale, like the moon itself.

"Quanemo has taken Danilo hunting. So his feet have not departed from the path of our joining." She turned away, and Morgan heard her words in her own language: "Not yet at least. But has Quanemo taken my son away to hunt animals for food, or white bloods for revenge?"

Thea, who did not understand the last as Morgan did, approached Wintasa and put her hand on her shoulder. "Like your departed father, my friend, you are a great healer of your people. If Quanemo has hard thoughts in his heart, your love will heal those, too."

"If his feet come back to me. *If* his feet come back," they heard her say as she went into her family longhouse alone.

Rina was beside herself with worry when the first hard snow fell in late December and Cullen had not yet returned from hunting for their Christmas dinner. Worse, the howling wind blew the gate to the sapling corral open, and the horses wandered out. She had to bundle up to go out after them. Her teeth chattered, and she shook all over by the time she spotted the last of five, for Cullen had taken one with him to carry back the game he shot. The horse, a big gelding they called Charley, was down by the half frozen river's edge as if he could drink through the ice along the shore.

"Damn you, Charley!" she cursed the animal soundly as she wrapped her heavy cape tighter and clambered through the foot-deep snow after him.

Her toes and fingers tingled in the chill. Her nose was so cold, it felt like a separate thing she could lift off her face. When she was a girl in New London, she and Cassie and

Thea had reveled in playing fox and geese in the big Lockwood backyard in the snow, but playing woman and horse out here alone in the wilds did not suit her one whit! If only Cullen would get back! If only she could mount Charley and it were warm spring already and she could gallop upriver to visit Thea as if all were well between them! How bitter the wind was, but how much more bitter her separation from her dear friend. Worse than leaving New London behind, worse even than the loss of Father in the fire that night, worse than . . .

"Charley!" she shouted into the swirling mist of snow as the horse dared to edge out on the ice. "Stop and get back where you belong, you—you Benedict Arnold!"

She felt like she was flailing through a blinding, white nightmare to reach the horse. Drifts shifted and wind whipped and whispered. It was that same blank helplessness of the bad dream where Mother screamed at her. She was never able to understand what she had done wrong to displease the laughing, beautiful woman in the portrait. Or when she tried to run in the dream, just like this, why did something cold have to make her footsteps slip and pull her back?

Barely out past the river's fringe, she reached for the horse's snow-swept mane to pull him back. If the ice along here held Charley, it would certainly hold her. She edged out just a bit and grabbed for the horse's neck. But the fractious gelding shook its head playfully. Rina slipped and the horse backed farther out with an indignant snort. The ice cracked like cannon shot, and they both plunged through.

The frigid, drenching smack took Rina's breath away. She floundered in the water, breaking more ice, wanting to scream in horror, but needing all her strength. The horse snorted, righted itself, and headed for the shore, crunching more ice. At least it was not deep here, but her soaked gown and cape and hair made her so heavy that it took her an endless time to get to her knees and feet. She crawled to the bank and lay there, gasping, sobbing frozen tears until she realized dazedly that her legs must still be in the water. Dragging in breaths of air that sliced her insides like a knife, she clawed her way farther up on the slick, cold bank.

Rina knew what she had to do and fast, but she found it so hard to move. It seemed she must have fallen through the ice yesterday. Cullen! Where was Cullen? Of course, he had gone hunting and the surprise snowfall had slowed him down. He would be here soon, sooner maybe if she could just scream his name.

She tried to stand; her sodden garb weighed her down like stone. Her legs seemed so numb she wondered if they were still there, just like in the dream. She swayed up the bank toward the house, toppling more than once into a soft snowbank to rest. Each time she lay there a moment, wishing it were their bed inside. Was she warmer now? Was she dreaming cold tears, or was that still snow falling on her face? How long had she really been in that river?

It seemed an eternity later when she made it into the house and stumbled to the hearth. She tried to throw on a new log, but her hand wouldn't work any more than her thoughts seemed to. She threw off her cloak with a plop, but the more she tried to undress herself to get warm, the colder she got. Her fingers would not obey her head. Finally, she kicked two logs into the hearth and dragged a quilt off the bed between her pressed together wrists.

Cullen would be here soon. Perhaps he had gone to the apothecary shop to get Thea to cure this fever. She was hot now, too, though her teeth rattled louder than her thoughts. She would just warm up right here by the fire, and Cullen and Thea could undress her when they came in. Cullen was always willing to undress her and hold her tight in bed. But did he really love her and trust her and forgive her for wanting Morgan first? Did Thea and did Father and did Mother forgive her, too?

She sank to the hearth, huddled in the quilt while the new logs caught and blazed. Her head nodded. Yes, she was warmer now. That hot crackling sound made her feel so good, and the heavy smoke from the kitchen down below where the cooks were preparing Father's favorite Christmas goose made her feel so at home.

*   *   *

Cullen Varner cursed his mediocre shooting ability as he trudged through growing snowdrifts back toward the cabin. After all, gentlemen were never trained as musketmen, nor did they serve in the infantry. They were officers meant to inspire and oversee the others. Give him a sword or a fine officer's pistol and he was instantly at home, but he'd never had to put food on his own table before this insane idea Governor Trumbull had somehow talked them all into! At least the deadfall traps the Indians hereabouts used and the snare traps Jacob Roscoe had shown him how to set had supplemented their winter meals so far, and Rina had learned to make jerky by smoking strips of meat over green saplings. But this unforgiving winter in this unforgiving land could not be over soon enough for him. He couldn't wait to get this skinny wild boar he hauled behind him on his plodding horse back to the cabin. No fat goose or side of beef this Christmas, but he'd humor Rina by telling her they'd just sing "The Boar's Head Carol" over it. Not much farther now through this last stand of snow-etched trees.

He smelled the fire before he saw it. Suddenly, there was more on the wind than mere curling smoke from the hearth. Cinders and pieces of charred debris drifted down with big snowflakes to speckle his path. Despite the nearly two-foot depth of snow, he began to run in great clomping, heaving steps.

Indians? Indians? Surely, not Indians, despite what Jacob Roscoe had told them. Then he saw an orange wall of flame where the cabin had been.

"Varina! Var–iiii–na!" he shrieked in a voice so high-pitched he sounded like a woman. He ran faster, pulling the laden horse after him until it tugged back. He loosed the reins and ran on, floundering in the cold white to reach the glowing heat.

Varina, thank God, lay opposite where the door had been, just beyond the circle of snow melted by the flames. He was amazed her garments were sopping wet and icy when he turned her face up. Perhaps that had saved her from severe burns. But was she even alive out here? He was too terrified he had lost her to do anything but croak out her name now. "Varina!"

Her eyes flew open and she blinked in the shower of snow and soot without seeming to see him. Her complexion looked grotesquely painted. Her pretty, heart-shaped face and pouted lips were as pale blue as her eyes, but for the feverish flush of her cheeks.

"My darling, are you all right?" he cried. "Oh, your hands are burned! What happened, what happened?" He gathered her even closer. She seemed suddenly so frail and fragile. It was then he realized how much he loved and valued Varina. No matter what she'd done to him with Morgan Glenn. No matter how wayward and stubborn she'd been at times. No matter if she wasn't perfect as he'd always wanted her to be. No matter how she'd gotten like this or how she'd let the cabin that was their very survival burn!

She tried to talk, but only gasped at first. "They came and set the house on fire," she choked out before a jag of coughing wracked her.

"Indians?" he rasped and spun to scan the trees and river.

"The British. Benedict Arnold. I tried to save Father. Thea didn't come in time—it's Thea's fault, just like when Mother died—Thea . . ." her delirious outburst ended on a wail that chilled his very bones.

Thea! That was it, Cullen thought desperately. No matter what had passed between them months ago, he had to get Varina to Thea so she wouldn't die. Somehow she had gotten all wet and chilled. Then in some feverish accident, she had burned their cabin and all they had in it. Despite this cold and deepening snow, he had to get Varina to the Glenns' place upriver! The cabin, the Firelands prize—none of that was worth anything to him if Varina died!

He staggered under her weight to the horse, until he realized he should bring the horse to her. He cut the dead boar from the saddle and shoved it in the snow. He took off his own cape, then quickly stripped Rina naked while she mumbled about her father still being in the house. He unbuckled the saddle from the horse and yanked the saddle blanket off to wrap her in as an afterthought. Quickly, he rebuckled the saddle on the nervous horse. He threw Rina's sopping garments over the poor horse's rump. He lifted her onto the horse. She was unconscious now, wrapped in the blanket and his cape with his bicorn on her head. Wearing only breeches, shoes, hose, shirt, and waistcoat, he mounted quickly behind her. Holding her to him for what little body warmth he had to spare, he clucked the tired horse upriver through the swirl of snow while their cabin and their dreams settled heavily to silver ashes behind him.

Despite the shrieking storm outside, their first Christmas together in the Firelands suited both Thea and Morgan. They roasted chestnuts on the hearth and stuffed themselves with rich venison stew and dried wild plums and corncake. "I was hoping you wouldn't clean under the bed today!" Morgan told her smugly and patted her bottom while she stoked up the fire. "I believe I have a present hidden there for you, only a little less precious than gold, frankincense, and myrrh."

"And I have something that you've always wanted very, very, much!" she told him with a teasing grin.

From beside their bed where he'd gone to fetch her gift, he eyed her up and down until she blushed, as if an inner fire had polished her cheeks to rosy apples. "Come over here, then, and give it to me," he challenged.

"Not that—not yet, at least!" she insisted with a laugh. "I have something different from what you got just last night!"

"Nothing I like better from my Thea than what I got last night!" he declared as he bent to reach far under their four-post bed with its grapevine-strung grass mattress. "Aha! Here's a little something just arrived from dear old Mother England via the last packet ship up the Pequotting," he announced grandly, and produced a big wooden object wrapped in an old Wyandot blanket he removed with a flourish.

"Oh, Morgan!" she shrieked in delight at the sight of the apothecary sign. She hugged him hard, and tears speckled both her cheeks and his.

"It may have to hang over that little root cellar for now, and your only customers may be Cassie, Jacob Roscoe, and a few Wyandots, but eventually . . ." he told her and let the words hang suspended at her obvious joy.

"It's perfect!" she declared. "Far better than that other one the New London bullies ruined when Cousin Benedict turned traitor! But now, sit down here. Sit down! Wait 'til you see what I have for you!"

Wrapped in cornshucks and vines and hidden under a pile of drying herbs behind the door was the Pennsylvania rifle Avery Payne's assassin had brought west. "Looks like a new stick to keep you in line with," Morgan teased. "Or a new drying rack for all these herbs I love to keep or a pole to mount this new sign," he chattered on, excited as a boy, while his big hands yanked away the coverings. He gaped amazed. "Thea! Where in tarnation did you get a Pennsylvania rifle way out here? Not Jacob Roscoe, as he'd give his eye teeth to have one, too. Thea?"

"That's the strange part about this," she admitted, quieting a bit. "Out here, you get things where you can. I'll wager this expensive gun was purchased by that dratted Avery Payne himself and given to the henchman that Danilo killed. Maybe we can even use it for evidence against Avery when we go back. It's the rifle that shot you, Morgan, but I couldn't see just burying it with the man nor the shot and powder with it I have hidden in the root cellar out back."

They hugged each other wordlessly after the rush of chatter and excitement. In the middle of the wild Firelands, they had each given and been given something dear from the worlds they'd left behind. It was like reaching out to find each other again in the upheaval of their pasts. Thea was convinced, at last, that whenever she did see Rina once again, she could find some way to understand and forgive both her and Morgan for good. He was certain that Thea would never forsake him now, as others had done.

The wooden sign and the rifle leaned against the wall by their bed as they tumbled into it together. The fire warmed the small cabin, though it also blackened the pole-and-bark ceiling with shiny soot. But nothing happening outside, not even cold air creeping through the cracks mattered to them now. His hands were sure and hard under her skirts as he stroked and grasped the warm flesh of her thighs above her knitted, leather-thong gartered stockings. Her supple fingers unbuttoned his woolen breeches to stoke his desire higher, and they both kicked off their shoes to snuggle under their black bearskin rug.

They were joined again before they got more undressed than that, but then they quieted to caress and kiss. It was their habit now at times to be one and then to talk and love and try to hold the ultimate frenzy back until it simply swamped them both.

"I have never been happier or felt closer to you," he told her, his brown eyes so golden in fireglow. He thrust once inside her with a devilish look and tease she could not help but get the point of.

"And I—to you," she managed breathlessly with a wiggle back.

"You are so beautiful, so wild, like these lands we've come to tame and never really will," he went on with a tremulous smile as he hovered over her like a second protective roof against the storms out there. Her flame-hued hair spread in great wings streaming from her temples and forehead. Her wide, green eyes promised unleashed passion. Her full lips, already sweetly plumped from his kisses, trembled into a pert pout.

"And you, my dearest love," she whispered, "are only and always everything I have ever wanted. You know, I've always valued making my own decisions, but I remember that first time you lifted me up on your horse without asking. I like how you sometimes make a few decisions for me. And that first day we rode to Lockwoods' house together, bouncing just like this—" she began and dared to shift her hips up and down.

It was enough to set them off. Together they rocked their creaky little bed, and then the entire world. Afterward, their breathing slowly stilled. They clung yet, barely parted.

"Look," she murmured drowsily. "This close to the wall, I can see our breaths. Brrr!"

"I won't let you get cold," he promised and nuzzled her neck as he gathered her closer in his arms. "But suddenly,

I'm starved. Let's eat again, and then get back into bed, and I'll show you more than a little breath!"

"Braggart!" she said, but she giggled like a little girl. She hoped it snowed for days so they couldn't get out but to feed the horses, or maybe hike over to see sad Wintasa, whom Cassie was living with now. But then Thea heard a sound outside and jerked bolt upright in his arms.

"What, Thea?"

"A noise. One of the horses, I guess."

He was on his feet instantly. "Not a danged hungry wolf, I hope," he gritted out. He had shoved his feet in his boots and grabbed his musket when a rap sounded on the door. Thea scrambled out of bed, smoothing her skirts down and straightening her bodice while Morgan pointed the gun barrel at the door and cocked the hammer. "Who is it?"

Nothing else. "Maybe just the wind, Morgan—"

"Shh!" He shuffled to the door with her following. He pushed her back behind it, then unlatched it to peer out. The wind shoved it inward, and snow swirled across the packed-dirt floor. And from the void outside walked an iceman with a winter white bundle clamped in his arms.

"Cullen!" they chorused and jumped to action. He stumbled in. Morgan took his burden from his shaking arms. Thea slammed the door and raced to uncover Rina's face.

"She's not dead!" Cullen managed, his voice as creaky as the door.

"No," Thea said, but her throat constricted so she could not say the terrifying words that came to her next: Not yet.

For the next three long days and nights, Thea nursed Rina's burns, her frostbite, and the wracking chills which alternated with raging fever. Rina knew none of them. She either babbled delirious nonsense or lay still as a stone through hours of silence. Cullen's stunned recital of the horrors of the burning cabin and his terrible trip through the snow barely permeated Thea's thoughts. Rina, her other beloved betrayer, lay here in her care. No matter what, she had to save Rina so they could mend the other sickness that had grown between them during this painful separation. What if she just died here like this, without explanation, without forgiveness? What if they had to bury her out there in this blizzard? The ground was so hard, the root cellar would be the only place. But those possibilities were too dreadful for Thea to accept.

Cullen and Morgan slept on the floor near the hearth. In their united struggle to save Rina's life, there was no mention of the harsh words or even the reason they had all come west. Wrapped in a blanket, Thea slept on the bed with Rina, so she could care for her when she stirred in the night. She dosed her with boiled birch bark water, and salved her skin with coltsfoot balm and a poultice of winterbloom, the way Wintasa had shown her.

Holding Rina's delicate hand in her big one—when Cullen was not holding it—Thea sometimes stared through her exhaustion at her new apothecary sign leaning by the bed. The god Apollo rode astride the dragon of disease while Thea despaired that Rina would ever recover. Or Thea studied the pale, thin face of her friend and wondered how it had all come to this. Not just that the fine Lockwood mansion of their mutual girlhood was now as burned as the crude Varner cabin. Not that they lived now in the Firelands of the frontier instead of the firelands Benedict Arnold had made of the old Connecticut towns. But that their friendship and love had come to this sharp estrangement, pierced by lies and mistrust and deceit. Again and again, she bathed Rina's face and dosed her, but the fever would not abate.

"Thea, Thea!" Rina muttered through fever-cracked lips on the fourth day when the men were outside checking traps and feeding the livestock. Morgan had practically had to drag Cullen out to keep him from going crackbrained agonizing over Rina. But now, Thea's heart beat against her ribs as she bent close over her patient. Rina's eyes were open, but she did not really seem to see her.

"I'm here, Rina."

"You came at last. You came. Now Father has two daughters. He talks to you more than me. He trusts you."

She was rambling again as she had so much, but her words

seemed at least coherent now. "Just sleep, Rina. I am here, Cullen, too. I'm taking care of you, so—"

The blue eyes widened. "Why should we take care of you!" a harsh voice, so unlike Rina, demanded. "Your parents did not save my mother. They let her die of typhus fever! Why should you come, and now Father has another daughter!"

Thea's tears of helplessness and exhaustion blurred the frail form on the bed to make two Rinas. Father Lockwood's entrusting his terrible secret of Rina's mother roared through Thea's thoughts, but she could not say all that now when Rina was raving that Father Lockwood trusted her more. She chose her words carefully, not knowing if they would be heard or heeded.

"Rina, we can't be accountable for what our parents did. And anyway, you mustn't blame my parents that your mother died. That isn't fair," she pleaded gently.

Suddenly, the blue eyes focused. Thea realized for the first time since Cullen had brought her here that Rina really saw her, perhaps really heard her, too. "Fair? My mother died and I can't even remember her," Rina whispered in a trembling voice. "You and Cassie recall your mothers, have things they gave you, too! All I keep dreaming of, all I can remember is her screaming—screaming at me—" she plunged on louder and louder and tried to sit.

Quickly, Thea plumped up the pillow to support her, but she did not interrupt. Rina's face was too terrible, her voice too strong to stem. "She is screaming at me to get away, Thea!" she shrieked as if she saw the scene before her now. "She hates me! She hates me, and I hate her, too, and I wanted her to die, and then she did!" The words came out in one ragged shriek so loud Cullen and Morgan clomped back inside and hurried to the foot of the bed to gape wide-eyed at the tirade.

Rina ignored the men as if they weren't there. With her wide, shocked gaze on Thea's pain-wracked face, she repeated the words, "I told her I wanted her to die, and then she did!"

"Listen to me, Rina," Thea insisted and seized both her wrists where she had pressed her hands over her mouth.

"Just because a child who's been hurt thinks she wants her mother to die and then she does, doesn't mean it's your fault. You didn't mean it. It's her fault for not loving you! She wasn't a good mother, and you wanted her to be. But Father Lockwood loved you, Cassie and I did—still do! Cullen does! You have to remember that. It wasn't anyone's fault your mother got typhus fever and died! Not my parents' who tried to nurse her, not Father Lockwood's, and certainly not her young daughter's who only wanted to love her and to be loved in return!"

Rina's eyes darted to Cullen, and then back to Thea. "I couldn't help feeling I hated her, however pretty and however much she laughed with other people at the parties," she said shakily.

"That's right. It wasn't your fault she died."

"But," Rina said to shock them all, "it was my fault I killed our friendship, Thea, and almost both our marriages, too. I hurt all of you. It made my stomach pains return and without you to help them," she got out before she wilted back on her pillow and closed her eyes. Thea loosened her grip on Rina's wrists. She seemed to sleep almost instantly. It was only then, after that poison had poured out, Thea realized that Rina's fever was broken at last.

In the next few days as Rina regained her strength, Thea did share with her all that Father Lockwood had said about Rina's mother screaming her hatred at the girl for her own selfish reasons. They cried together and spoke almost always of old times, especially when the men went back downriver to the burned cabin to bring the Varner horses back and see what could be salvaged.

Morgan had insisted he would help Cullen rebuild at least a sturdy lean-to farther up on the bank before the spring rains came. And the Glenns intended to split household goods and foodstores with them, too, despite Cullen's embarrassed protests, and then his shame for accepting. Cullen had argued that Morgan's help in rebuilding would make Morgan's crop-planting late, but the Pennsylvanian could not be deterred. Sobered and humbled, Cullen acquiesced, but if the two men

ever spoke of or apologized for the other problems between
them, the women never heard. Finally, though, Rina sobbed
out all her confessions on Thea's shoulder, and they were
mostly reconciled.

"It was like something came over me to make me lie to
Morgan and you back then," she explained brokenly as if
groping for the words. "That's no excuse, I know, nor is there
one for hurting you and him the way I did. At least you two
are together in love and trust now. And, well, I'm just so re-
gretful it all happened, Thea. I only pray you can find forgiveness in your heart."

"I've been searching there for it, that's sure," Thea told
her truthfully. "You know, at first I told myself you were
just rebelling from the dratted strict way Father Lockwood
treated you compared to me. Then I thought, it's because her
mother didn't teach her a woman's love. After all, I suppose
I could have blamed your mother and then you for the fact
my parents probably caught their typhus nursing her, but I
just never thought that way. I wish you'd shared all this earlier, but you hadn't even figured it out. As I said, Rina, you
can't blame parents for your own failings, any more than I
can blame mine for this wild red hair and my height and
green as grass eyes."

"You'd blame them for that?" she questioned and sat up
straighter in bed with a Wyandot blanket around her shoulders. "But that's what always made you special in New London, that and your freedom and pride and kindness even to
those—like me—who didn't deserve it. It's part of what I admired so much in you, I guess I resented it."

"But I always envied your petite size and grace and blond
English good looks, Varina Lockwood Varner!"

Rina beamed, though tears filled her eyes, and the saucer
of sassafras tea trembled in her hands. "But I always envied
you so, Thea, even that you were bigger! I felt safe with you.
It was sort of like you were both my friend and mother, always scolding me, taking care of me—and see how things
haven't changed a bit!"

They slopped the remnants of the tea on the bear rug as
they hugged. Surely, Thea thought, they could go on from

here. All mistrust and doubt was now cured as surely as Rina's fever. "As soon as the men come back," Thea said as she blotted the spilled tea up with her apron, "we'll send them to the Wyandot village to fetch Cassie over for a visit. You won't believe how she's changed. She realizes at last the Wyandots aren't the forest folk because they are so good to her. Now, she thinks the *Sidhes* would want to punish us all for cutting down their trees and invading their territory. She tells me she thinks they'll run from the woods someday and spirit us all away!"

Rina just shook her head. "I'd love for all three of us to be back together," Rina told her, "despite Cassie's infernal humming and the way she riles poor Cullen. And the first thing she'll probably say is 'Rina and Thea, two peas in a pod, have been best friends every step they have trod.'"

"No doubt!" Thea said and smiled through tears that threatened again. At peace with Morgan, and now with Rina, she had never been happier. Finally, everything was settled, wasn't it? "No doubt," she repeated as Rina closed her eyes. Thea bustled back to her herbs. The rest of their stay in the Firelands would be spent in perfect harmony, just like this, she thought. No doubt!

Chapter Sixteen

" 'Tis said the herb called nightshade or thorn apple is the oddest curative the red men have. In gentle, medicinal doses, it cloaks pain and serves as an ointment for burns and scalds. Yet in larger amounts, it is a narcotic causing strange hallucinations. And in larger doses yet, it is a poison where the victims suffer dreadful agonies. Likewise, it seems to me, depending on its dose and its intent, any human emotion or experience can be beneficial, or alarming, or most deadly."

WHEN THE SAP began to run in mid-March, Thea became certain she was pregnant. She had missed her second monthly flux, though she was usually so regular, and she felt quite queasy in the mornings. Over the years she had dispensed enough mint and treacle water with both sympathy and good wishes to know what those signs meant. And she knew that the same phenomenon of harboring a new life affected different women in far different ways.

She told no one at first, but savored and treasured the idea, rolling it through her mind and heart the way she did the sweet taste of the sap in her mouth. Besides, there was only Wintasa, Rina, and Cassie to tell right now, and she wanted Morgan to know first. The men were downriver at Mud Brook for a week, building a log lean-to to get the Varners through until next autumn.

But every third day, Morgan rode back to Camp Milan to have noon dinner with them. He checked the banks for strange tracks between their homesteads, and made certain the animals he'd turned out to forage had not strayed far. Tomorrow, when he came again, if she could get him alone, she would tell him of the baby.

It had been difficult for them to find privacy after they'd taken the Varners in, and then had Cassie and Wintasa often visiting, too. Since Rina had recovered, Thea noted, Morgan and Rina pointedly avoided each other in look, word, and deed, even though they lived in such close quarters. Perhaps it was just as well. Next time both men returned, Rina would be going back with Cullen.

With the rumors of unrest among the Ottawas, at the first February thaw the villagers of Pequotting had moved to join with another Wyandot village called Anioton on Cold Creek to the west. Only Wintasa had stayed behind, convinced, she said, that Quanemo and Danilo would soon return for her there. The once bustling Indian village on the opposite bank was now a sad, desolate sight. It seemed more forlorn, Thea thought, with its empty standing buildings than the whole burned town of New London. And so, while Rina regained the strength and flesh she'd lost and Wintasa mourned the village of haunted memories across the river, Thea taught them both to shoot the Brown Bess musket that was hers now. And in return, Wintasa showed them how to cut the V's to drain sap from the sugar maples, and how to insert a trough of rounded bark to drip the sweetness out into a gathering pot beneath.

They flavored much of their food—even snow from the last melting patches—with the sweetness of sap sugar now. Sap in sassafras tea calmed Thea's stomach in the mornings, but it didn't calm her heart. The idea of carrying Morgan's child, of starting their family, pleased her immensely, but for one thing. As best she could figure it, the baby would arrive just before they would be making the long, late-autumn trip back to Connecticut in time to partake in the Firelands prize they needed so desperately to make a future life somewhere. And to take a newborn all that way—and what if it were late, making them late getting started back . . .

"Looks like you're gathering daydreams again instead of sap, Thea," Rina's voice interrupted her worried musings.

Thea realized she'd just been leaning against a tree, staring off into the forest. "I'm just a bit tired this afternoon. But I think I will take these early jack-in-the-pulpits I found and dry them in the root cellar. I see purple stems of nightshade poking up here, too. I'll have to remember they're here. They're an excellent narcotic for pain, but you have to be careful not to overdo the dose or it's a poison."

"Narcotic and poison? No curative doses of that for me, if you please," Rina teased as she poured the sap from yet another pot into her big wooden bucket. "I don't think I can ever abide one more healing dose of one more of your tonics, Thea."

"Don't complain. You're back to normal, aren't you?"

"Yes, Thea," Rina said, sounding like a chastised child. "Much better since all four of us are getting on at last."

Thea almost remarked that of the four of them, Rina and Morgan seemed to have no relationship at all, but she'd best leave that unsaid. They walked back companionably to camp, Thea carrying her armful of infant herbs and the musket, always loaded and half-cocked these days. Rina toted a bucket of sap to add to the kettle, which Cassie had been ordered to stir continually with her wooden paddle while Wintasa checked the maples on the riverbank.

When Thea and Rina returned to the cabin, the others were testing the thickness of the bubbling sap to judge when to pour it out to cool for sugar. Thea went around in back to put her herbs in the five-foot deep root cellar where she also kept her apothecary sign until the spring rains passed. From here, she could hear her friends on the far side of the cabin talking, even laughing, and it made her feel so safe and good.

She unlatched and lifted the heavy wooden door Morgan had made for the cellar, half hidden by two chestnut trees. Leaning the gun inside, she eased herself down the three wooden steps and spread the tender jack-in-the-pulpits out to dry on the piece of Conestoga linsey-woolsey which covered her pharmacopoeia. It was then she heard Wintasa scream, " 'Tawas! 'Tawas! Run!"

Thea grabbed her gun and peeked her head above the ground. Unhuman shrieks shredded the air. On the other side of the cabin, Indian braves with bayoneted muskets streaked from the trees to chase the three fleeing women. Ten, maybe twelve, they kept spilling from the forest, shouting *"Chok! Chok!"*

Thea knew she could drop one of them from here. But by the time she reloaded, they would be on her. Her three

friends had sprinted off into the woods already with the howling Ottawas at their heels. Should she run, too? Could she
outrun them, especially as tired and dizzy as she felt lately?
Or should she just hide and . . .

She decided the moment she saw Wintasa, one of the Ottawas' own race, led back into the village by a brave's hand
hard around her single fat braid of loosened hair. Quickly,
Thea bent down inside the cellar and pulled the door closed
after her, but for an inch to peek out. Her heart thundered
in her chest. She would hide for the baby's sake. Perhaps she
could sneak away to fetch Cullen and Morgan.

Biting her lip so hard she tasted blood, Thea watched in
silent dread as the Ottawas tied Wintasa by a neck leash to
a big tree in the corner of the clearing. Rina was carted back
slung over one man's shoulder, her gold hair spilling down
his buckskinned back. At least she looked unharmed! They
made her stand beside Wintasa, and also tied her to the tree
by a thong around her neck like some sort of animal. Squinting out of the darkness into the light, Thea saw that the Ottawas wore their hair pulled back in knots high off their
foreheads. Their faces gleamed with bright red paint and,
where she could see their skin, they looked tattooed.

She almost vomited in fear as she recalled the story of poor
Jane McCrea's scalping and death during the war. But these
braves seemed more interested in scooping up the boiling sap
by the wooden ladle and cooling it on pewter plates that they
carted from inside the cabin. One brave appeared carrying
their precious bearskin, while they evidently waited for their
other companions to return. And then, Thea saw them bring
back Cassie.

Only, she was neither pulled nor hauled back like the other
two had been. She walked from the forest with a bronze, pow-
erfully built Indian brave as if she were a queen. The brave
not only did not touch her, but seemed to escort her, almost
to guard her from the others. Thea heard Wintasa speak to
their captors in her language, her voice strong and unafraid,
but she could not catch the words. Only Rina looked quite
terrified now.

One Indian cut Wintasa and Rina's neck cords. The others

made a little circle around Cassie, staring, as if they were afraid to touch her. Did these Indians revere those "tetched in the head," too? Thea didn't have long to wonder about that. Cassie suddenly glanced her way, and Rina squinted in the same direction. At that, Thea closed the root cellar door. In the dark, she hid the musket and began desperately to burrow under the piles of drying herbs and the heavy wooden sign. She had no more settled herself in, her back wedged against the big herbal book when someone yanked the wooden door up and light flooded her hiding place.

She squeezed her eyes shut, praying she was hidden. She did not breathe; even her terrified thoughts halted. She waited for a hand to yank her out, even for the poke of a bayonet or worse. The urge to sneeze among these drying leaves bit far back in her head. Cassie's melodious voice drifted to her, so much closer than it had been before. "I want to fly to the forest with you now," she demanded petulantly. A guttural man's voice spoke just above Thea in words she did not know. Another answered. The door banged back down, and the voices moved away just before her sneeze exploded. How much later she did not know, she thought she heard Cassie's sweet voice singing "Danny Boy."

Thea feared that tomorrow afternoon when Morgan should be back would never come. What if this same marauding band of Ottawas had found and fought the men downriver when they'd put their guns aside to build the lean-to? And what were they doing outside now?

With her eyes tightly closed, she lay in double darkness. But a memory came to comfort her: that sunny afternoon she and Morgan had spent in the small limestone cave down the riverbank. Her lips trembled in a half smile. Perhaps it was the day she conceived this child she carried.

Being in such close proximity to Cullen and Rina had worn on them because they never had a moment alone anymore, and they yearned for each other. Stolen kisses, quick caresses outside during chores, and long, lingering looks only stoked their smothered desires. So they had left the cabin to the Varners that sunny February day, telling them they were going to walk to the sulfur spring for a bucket of good tonic.

The cave had been on a little ledge above the river, a place Danilo had showed Morgan months before. It was dark inside, but Morgan had brought a candle. And, lo and behold, she thought as the warm memory steadied her a bit now, Morgan had been there earlier to prepare their stay with a blanket and even some food.

"You see, my sweetheart," his deep voice echoed in her heart even now, "I must admit I've calculated this little retreat of ours for days. It's touching you've been nursing Rina, but I need a bit of touching and nursing myself."

"Really?" she'd replied and laughed throatily. "Just where does there seem to be a problem?"

"I think you know the answer to that," he'd told her and sat so close their long legs touched hip to knee to ankle. He guided her hand to touch him right through the swelling tautness of his breeches. "Looking at you with Rina always there in the way," he told her in broken thoughts as she caressed him, "hearing you two laugh—dang it, woman, I want you, only you!"

Want you, only you, the words revolved in her mind. But he had said looking at Rina made him want his own wife, hadn't he? Suddenly, the painful way he and Rina tiptoed around each other didn't matter. The way Rina still frowned sometimes when Thea saw her watching Morgan didn't matter. All that mattered was that everything was fine now, and they had managed to get alone together here in this lovely, dusky, hidden cave above the murmuring river.

"I know it's chilly and a bit damp in here," he apologized as his eyes devoured her, "but it's been so long since I've really seen and touched and kissed all of you. I promise, you won't get cold," he'd vowed, and she'd gladly helped him remove every stitch of clothing from both of them.

They had been ravenous for each other, like the pent-up wintertime yearning for something fresh and green or sunny warmth on naked skin. Strange how their desire for each other came in different doses with far different results at times. Soon it seemed the cave was not damp or chilly; it reflected their passion and fierce mutual possession. His hands and mouth and love enveloped her. She responded mindlessly to whatever he asked. No, not mindlessly, for she could recall each delicious movement of their joining that afternoon. Finally, darkness began to descend outside and, reluctantly, they had started back. She felt a delicious tingle all over in the soft places he had held and kneaded with his hands and mouth. She felt absolutely wonderful, even when they came in the door and knew Rina and Cullen had probably spent the afternoon much as they had. The two men's eyes met, then looked away with a curt, understanding nod. For some reason, though Thea was proud and glowing, Rina would not meet her steady gaze. But now the blur of those thoughts faded, and the cold, damp root cellar replaced that lovely hidden cave of memory.

Thea huddled there just a bit longer, praying for everyone's safety, hearing nothing else outside. How much time had passed? Had they gone, or was it all a trick to flush her out like a plump partridge for the picking? She had seen Wyandots set their traps with care and wait with stony patience for them to be filled, and the Ottawas had a more dreadful reputation. But, if these Indians had departed, they had surely taken her three friends. Had they ransacked or burned the cabin? At least the animals were loose in the woods.

Thea's limbs ached from the rigidity of her muscles and her trembling. She sat up, half dizzy, and cupped her palms over her flat belly as if to protect the new life growing there. She crouched and groped for the musket under the leaves in the dark. Slowly, she cracked the heavy door open above her and peered out. Darkness had fallen!

She breathed in crisp night air. She lifted the door another inch slowly, then another. The musket went to full cock, incredibly loud. She froze, but nothing happened. Without letting the door thud open, she squeezed out and crawled to the next big tree closest to the cabin.

It still stood. No sounds but moaning, crackling tree limbs in the chill March wind and an owl somewhere nearby asking "Who? Who?" had taken her friends. She almost felt as if she'd dreamed or hallucinated it all. How many hours ago had the Indians gone with their prisoners, if Cassie could be called that considering the way she had looked, bold yet awed, as if she'd found her precious forest folk at last.

When the small band of Ottawa braves finally let their captives rest as dusk fell, they had reached Old Woman's Creek. The Indians kept a respectful distance from Cassie, all but the brave Tochingo who had found her and touched her before he realized she was sacred, even before the Wyandot woman Wintasa explained that the snow-skinned girl with golden eyes and golden sun drops sprinkled on her face was blessed of the Great Spirit. That alone made them treat all three women with special care, when otherwise they would have been tied and run at a dog trot all the way to the Ottawa gathering by the Cuyahoga River.

There, on the banks of that big river, Tochingo and his band had hoped to earn praise from the great Ottawa chief Garihoua for bringing captives. They were young braves, unproved in the age-old battle to keep the white bloods from Indian lands. Such captives would be sold as squaws or slaves to tribes in Canada or traded for guns. But now, with this sacred woman given to them as a gift from the Great Spirit, Tochingo knew he could never release her from his sight and care, not even if it meant making war with her people.

All this tumbled through his mind like loud water over the stones of Old Woman's Creek where he sat. Now, his braves would just sell the other two, including the Wyandot woman. Tochingo knew her man Quanemo from a recent gathering to the south. Though the woman had proudly named her man when she demanded to be released, Tochingo knew pain had pierced Quanemo's heart for his woman's walking in the white man's ways. Now Tochingo would help Quanemo by sending her away forever for the guns she would bring. At Cuyahoga the third captive, the golden-haired, white-blood woman whose eyes made tears, would have to be closely guarded. If fire water or the narcotic nightshade were used there, some drunken or drugged brave would think to make her yellow hair a fine long scalp for his belt.

With wide, awed eyes, Tochingo watched Cassie as she cupped cold water in her hands and brought it to him to

drink. Tochingo did as she indicated, but he was certain he
was not worthy of her touch. At first he had been afraid to
speak to her in her words, which he had learned from his
white mother in an Ottawa village south on the Scioto. But
she smiled at him, so he spoke now.

"You must not serve Tochingo like a slave," he told her.
"Tochingo care for you."

" 'Tis my way to help out others, it is. But look. I've made
you a clover crown, and clover's not easy to find right now,
especially four-leafed ones." She extended an intricately
woven wreath to him and, shyly, he let her drape it on his
head. It snagged in the topknot of his thick, ebony hair, and
she giggled.

Tochingo wore winter leggings, muskrat fur-lined moccasins, and a wide belt where he hung his shot pouch, powder
horn, and hunting knife. Only a leather vest covered his
broad chest on this chilly night, for he had already given this
woman his winter shirt with rabbit fur to keep her warm.
In the pierced places in his ears where he usually wore his
polished copper ear disks, he had only swansdown now to
avoid frostbite from the metal. The sacred woman Cassie had
laughed at his ears and blown the swansdown to tickle him
there.

He would have struck a white-blood woman for that just
yesterday, but no more—not this woman. He was enthralled.
How brave she was. She had turned and waited for him in
the forest when he chased her. She had asked him not to hurt
her friends' cabin and promised to go with him willingly to
meet his forest people. And how strange her voice echoed
from the Great Spirit when she sang or hummed her sacred
chants as now. No, this Cassie woman might be white-blood
like his own mother, but she was nothing like her, cowering,
crying, and afraid of being taken by an Ottawa brave. This
woman was a drug like a ritual herb in Tochingo's blood,
making him dream new dreams that had nothing to do with
the path to bloody war.

"I am glad you forest folk have a human appearance so
I can see you," she told him, her golden eyes still glowing
as dusk deepened. "And I know that women you folk fancy

are kidnapped for concubines, and I'm willing if you are, even if we dance my toes clean away."

Tochingo frowned. Sometimes she spoke a language that was not even that of the white bloods. What had she just said?

"You do live in the forest, don't you?" she pursued. "And you hate the white men for coming in to cut down your trees and sometimes you go naked and fly about on feet like wings?"

"Yes, *aiyee,*" he told her and relaxed a bit. "Feet like wings we take to the meeting of the Ottawas on the great waters of the Cuyahoga by the English Lake. You will like it there."

"I will like it the rest of my life, now that I've found you! I told Thea and Rina time and again I'd find the forest folk, didn't I, Mistress Rina?" she called to the yellow-haired woman so victoriously that Tochingo was once more awed to silence. He sat proudly by the sacred, humming woman while another brave named Ogochin brought her more venison jerky to eat, and even bowed when he walked away from her. Later, the sacred woman went over to talk to the other two. The Wyandot squaw looked sad, and the yellow-haired one afraid, but the sacred woman always smiled, and mostly straight at him.

By the feeble glow of her best tole lamp and the light of a half moon, Thea and the first horse she called from the forest picked their way up the river to fetch Morgan and Cullen. Yellow dawn already smeared the sky when she saw the Varner camp. She breathed a sigh of relief to see both men were still sleeping bundles on the ground, Cullen by the newly completed lean-to way up beyond the bank; Morgan by the ashes of the fire.

Her throat constricted as she opened her mouth to call to them. How different she had wanted things when she saw Morgan. But now the news of the baby she carried in her exhausted, aching body would have to wait for better times. Now, nothing mattered but rescuing the others.

"Morgan! Cullen! An Ottawa raiding party has taken Rina, Cassie, and Wintasa, too!"

The men ran to her. Morgan lifted her down. She crumpled against him; his strong arms felt so good. And then she saw that another man had slept in the fringe of trees—and a boy. They leaped to their feet and ran toward her.

"Oh, I didn't know," she cried. "Quanemo and Danilo! But now you all can help. I had the gun, but I hid in the root cellar and didn't shoot. Oh, Morgan, I wish you had been there!"

The men barraged her with questions while they saddled horses and packed food. Quanemo was the only one who spoke not a word, but he nodded when Cullen offered him a horse.

"Danilo goes, too," the boy boasted. "I can hunt Ottawas as well as deer!" But Quanemo only shook his head.

"I was hoping the boy could stay with Thea," Morgan told Quanemo. "He has protected our camp well once before."

"It is so," Quanemo said, his voice not so gruff as usual. "Quanemo came back to Wintasa and to you, Mor-gan, because Danilo speak to me on our trip. Tell me how you bury the white-blood man Danilo killed. How you tell no one. Most white bloods want kill an Indian boy for that. They shoot the white-blood guns at the whole tribe—massacre."

"Never that! Danilo saved my life. Some white men might, but it is not my way," Morgan insisted as he lifted Thea on a fresh horse of Cullen's and mounted another. "I tell you, Quanemo, white skin doesn't mean a man is bad inside. Some are good. Only some are pure poison. Besides, I'll bet I bleed as red as you."

Quanemo only nodded solemnly again, but Thea knew it was a great victory for Morgan—and hopefully for Wintasa, too, if only they could find her. "The boy Danilo stays at your Camp Milan to protect your woman, Mor-gan," were Quanemo's last words as they set out.

They rode south quickly on the river path so the men could pick up the trail. Cullen looked white as bleached linen at the thought of Rina's being captive. "At the idea of any other savage bastard barbarian's damned hands on her!" he had blurted before his eyes met Morgan's and he turned away.

"Unlike the 'civilized, gentlemanly' whites, Cullen," Morgan exploded, " 'savage bastard barbarians' like the Indians don't rape women they take to the forest!"

Thea breathed a sigh of relief for Rina, but her heart wrenched for Morgan and Cullen. She had thought they were reconciled now, as she and Rina were. Yet how well were she and Rina really getting on when she yet feared unspoken feelings between her friend and her husband? But Morgan Glenn was hers! This wedding ring on her hand, this secret baby she carried said so! Now, he was going after Rina without knowing Thea carried his child. Should she just tell him about it as he left her? What if something happened to him on the trail and he never knew? What if . . .

"Thea, I know you're exhausted, sweetheart, but are you dozing? We're here," Morgan repeated and helped her down. He pulled her hard into his arms for a farewell embrace, and, suddenly panicked, she clung desperately. From here, the men were going on foot into the woodlands. Danilo was already shooing their horses into the corral. "They've got a good start on us, Thea, but we'll find them," Morgan said, but in her inner turmoil she hardly heard his assurances. "I've done some tracking in my day, and Quanemo will be a blessing."

"Yes, a blessing."

Stiff-armed, he set her back and studied her face. She could not stem the tears, though she longed to send him off like a bold, brave pioneer wife.

"You'll be all right here with Danilo?" he asked.

"Of course. And I'll have dinner ready for you when you bring them all back!"

"That's my Thea. Your Rina," he said and shouldered his pack as he moved away, "is one hell of a lot of trouble."

"Not my Rina! Not anyone but Cullen's!" was the last thing she called after him as the three men went quickly single file along the riverbank with their heads down, looking for a trail.

"Here! Over here, feet go, many!" Quanemo's voice carried back to Thea and Danilo. The boy had come to stand beside her as if to buck her up. "And here—my woman's moccasins in the wet mud!"

"Before, Quanemo say he leave Wintasa," the boy told her quietly. "Now, his feet take him back to her. Quanemo say a man must stay with his first woman. Quanemo put aside his other path and return only to her."

"I hope so, Danilo," Thea managed, but his innocent words unsettled her so that she shivered. She fought down the urge to run after Morgan and turned forlornly back toward the cabin.

Cassie asked two other 'Tawa braves for their warm shirts and gave them to Rina and Wintasa. "Cassie, don't you see?" Rina whispered and grabbed her wrist. "These Indians will do anything you say! Tell them they have to take us back!"

"The forest folk do things their own way," she declared solemnly. "Finally, you must admit I found them, I did."

"No!" Rina whispered and gave her an angry shake. "They are hostile Ottawa Indians, and they hate the whites. Governor Trumbull should never have sent us here. Cassie, even if you're staying with them, help Wintasa and me to escape!"

" 'Tis a good girl I've been to you, Mistress Rina, that I have. I've loved you and especially Thea, too, but I'll not insult the *Sidhe,* not me! So don't you, either!" she added and returned to where Tochingo sat watching her with his back against the big tree. He lay down again, obviously surprised when Cassie cuddled up against him on the ground the way she'd seen Rina do with Cullen and Thea with Morgan. She'd longed for a man of her own, too, though she'd never said one word on it. But perhaps, Cassie thought, Rina was right about these men because this one was rock-hard bone and warm, real flesh. Surely, the *Sidhe* would be something lighter, like sunbeams or forest breezes.

She put her head on his arm for a pillow and bumped her hips back closer into his lap. He grunted and stiffened his arm—and another part of him, too, which she could feel. She did believe in the Irish *Sidhe,* she really did, but like Thea had tried to tell her more than once, this wasn't Ireland. Indian land would have to do. She felt the funniest stirring in her belly and between her legs at being held this way. And she was not a bit afraid anymore of the forest or crossing streams or leaving Connecticut or anything. No, perhaps Tochingo wasn't a *Sidhe,* but she'd never admit it aloud.

She smiled and settled back farther against Tochingo's hard thighs. His arm crept tighter around her waist. His knees lifted to the backs of hers as if she sat in his lap, sideways, on the ground.

It was a long, tense time before the sacred woman Cassie and the forest folk Tochingo fell asleep.

The three men tracking the Ottawas followed the trail until darkness fell and were up again at first light. Morgan was adept at following tracks and spotted broken branches, but Quanemo's ability to read signs amazed him. Moss crunched down or kicked awry, broken twigs or bent grass, or a piece of cloth caught on a thornbush caught his eye. At midmorning they had reached Old Woman's Creek and found where the braves and their captives had spent the night.

"Nine, ten braves sleep here," Quanemo grunted. "Two women here, one my woman. Another woman over here close to a man."

"Sons-of-bitches, I'll kill them!" Cullen cracked out.

"Don't assume anything, Cullen," Morgan told him. "You should have learned that by now!"

They plunged on eastward, fording two more creeks. The day was brisk, though they all kept up a sheen of sweat. But only Cullen's breathing labored. And only Cullen cried aloud when they disturbed an unseen flock of ducks that shot into the sky in a dark cloud. Through mucky marshes, down and then up ravines, they hurried on. It reminded Morgan of the relentless charge on the British that day at Freeman's Farm when Benedict Arnold had won the day and then been shot at the very crest of his heroics. But it was Cullen who got hurt at Vermilion Creek.

While they searched for traces of the Ottawas along the banks, Cullen accidentally triggered a deadfall Indian trap meant for beaver or muskrat. The big, suspended, secreted log whacked down on his foot with a force that would have stunned or killed the animal.

"Damn! Oh!" Cullen cried and crumpled to the ground.

Morgan got to him first. Even in his boot, Cullen's foot looked flattened. "Here, let's soak it quick in the creek to keep the swelling down!"

"Ugh. Maybe just broken toes. No, no! You can't stop for me, I—damn I can't even put weight on it. I'll do what I can and come on when I rig a crutch. Go on, keep up, please, Morgan. Bring her back safely to me! Despite—despite our troubles—Rina's and mine—yours, too, I know I need her. Go on!"

Morgan nodded. He understood. And it was the closest Cullen Varner had ever come to reaching out to him. "We'll be back for you, Cullen—with Rina." He shouldered his musket again and plunged on behind the silent Quanemo. It was almost an hour later when Quanemo thrust out his arm to halt him.

"Look, Mor-gan. Tracks go two paths here. My woman goes with most braves toward the rising sun. Two white women go that path with only one brave."

"We'll have to split up."

Quanemo nodded. "Some 'Tawas tell of a great powwow. That way," he said and pointed westward, "to the Cuyahoga. There, they hear their Chief Garihoua. I go there now with many 'Tawas. They think I walk their path, they give my woman back. They think my words not straight, they kill me."

Morgan's brown eyes locked with Quanemo's black ones. "Then you no longer plan to follow the war path if the Ottawas go that way?"

The solemn Indian shook his head. "I think my woman speak wise words of white bloods like you, Mor-gan. I find her, our feet return to our Danilo. I go now. You find the white-blood women. My feet not return again, Quanemo's heart smiles you take Danilo hunting."

Before Morgan could respond, the Indian strode into the brush; fir branches swept closed behind him. Morgan started out the other way, his rifle up, his eyes down. The single Ottawa's tracks with Rina and Cassie walking just behind him were easy enough to follow. Their captor must have assumed no one could pick up their trail so fast, and especially not just a white blood. But if both women were trusted enough to walk behind the Ottawa brave, could they perhaps bolt or hit him with a stone? No, probably the brave had even leashed or at least bound them, but there never seemed to be a stumbled step here, at least from the larger woman's tracks. Rina's smaller shoeprints seemed to drag a bit. And then at a shallow, rock-strewn spot with stones and hard clay along the banks, the tracks simply disappeared as if they'd all flown away into the forest depths beyond.

Morgan retraced his steps, then crossed over to the other side to search. It was growing dark and cold for mid-March as he tramped up and down the banks looking for where they could have emerged from walking the river stones. The birds quieted and the night breeze sprang up. Frustration and desolation crushed his spirit.

"Damn, damn!" he cursed and collapsed wearily on a rock. Then a limb cracked behind him, and he spun with uplifted rifle barrel.

"Don't shoot! Oh, Morgan, thank God. It is you! Where's Cullen?"

"Rina?" Mouth agape, he squinted into the forest gloom as Rina emerged alone from behind a tree. "Cullen—he's miles back. He hurt his foot. Where are the others?"

She ran to him now, but stopped a few feet away. Her voice snagged on a sob. "They think Cassie's sacred! And she thinks she's found the forest folk. When I admitted to her she was always right about them, she talked them into leaving me behind. Her brave Tochingo brought me this far and said to follow this river to the lake. They're going someplace called the Cuyahoga for a powwow or something, but I think Cassie's just going off alone to live with that savage!"

And then, despite all the painful things in their past, she just couldn't help it. She was so relieved she would not have to find her own way back, so grateful to see a white face in this terrifying, wild maze of trees and creeks, she exploded into Morgan's arms and sobbed and sobbed.

"Are you sure we ought to have a fire?" Rina asked Morgan later. "What if other hostile Indians are passing through here for that war council?"

Morgan could tell her teeth chattered, and she shook with cold—and nerves. He'd already given her his heavy hunting shirt to replace the rabbit shirt she'd said a brave had let her wear last night. Dang, he was cold, too, and could see his breath when he talked.

"The Indians aren't likely to travel at night, Rina. We've got to do something to keep warm until dawn breaks and we go back to help Cullen."

"All I could think of each step of the way with those savages was how much I love Cullen," she admitted, and then a sneeze shook her. "Well, I'm glad you know right where he is," she said, wiping her nose with the back of her hand. "I wish we could go now."

"So do I, Rina. So do I, but we'd probably lose our way in the dark. And it's not going to help Thea and Cullen when we tell them we were together alone in the forest all night, is it?"

"No, but Cullen trusts me now."

"Good, because this time, we're going to explain everything, the truth, flat out, the minute we see both of them, and trust them to deal with it."

That silenced her for a while, but for another ragged sneeze. Finally, while they shared his venison jerky, chewing slowly to make the little last, she began, "I never told you how sorry I was for everything, Morgan."

"For everything. That covers a lot."

"I was so foolish and rebellious then, so set on defying my father and Cullen, too. And you were so—different."

"That's a good reason to pledge eternal love and marriage." His voice came cold as the night breeze.

"You're very angry yet. Well, I don't blame you. I guess I was—sort of a Benedict Arnold to both you and Thea, and neither of you needed another traitor. But I didn't mean to mislead and—and use you. I thought I loved you very much when it all happened."

He sighed. A burden he had been carrying around with him for years lightened. "And I you, Rina."

"But what's important now," she hurried on, "and always should have been, is that I admire Thea, Morgan. I always have, you see, but I guess I was a bit jealous of her, too. I told her so and apologized to set things straight with her, you know."

"I know, and so we'll bury this between us for good. We've been edging around each other for months because we were both so ashamed of the mess we made of things. You're good with Cullen, I'm good with Thea, so it all worked out for the best. I just hope Cassie's safe and happy—and that you and I end up that way after we explain things to our respective mates."

They made two beds of dried leaves and huddled under them. But he could hear Rina's teeth chattering again and her frequent sneezes made him almost hear Thea's voice telling him to take better care of the patient she'd saved this winter. He was cold, too. But he could also hear Thea's voice wavering out the words, "You chose Rina first? You and Rina?" Damn! Thea trusted him now, and he knew she'd never desert him, didn't he?

"Rina, it's danged cold. We're going to have to get closer for body heat. I won't take you back to Cullen sick again when he's going to need your help at planting time with that broken foot of his."

Not a dried leaf stirred.

"Rina."

"Yes, I'm so cold. But it might be better if I was sick again and just died rather than the two of us hurting them."

"I'll tell them both you said so," he muttered and moved both himself and his gun over behind her. He almost couldn't touch her. That other time in the woods he had been wrong to touch her passionately and then propose marriage. But this was dire necessity, and he'd just have to fight Cullen again and take Thea's scorn if they didn't both at least trust him by now. "Hold still and just go to sleep!" he ordered much too gruffly as he moved close and threw one arm over her. They both lay still and stiff a moment, hardly breathing. But the shared body warmth was better.

What had once seemed so precious to both of them was

only past poisoned regret now. If only it were Thea in his arms, he mourned. She grieved for Cullen, too, and foolish mistakes she'd made. Unmoving as two statues, they lay there, warmer, and yet so cold. Finally, exhaustion and slumber drugged them lying so close together, but so very far apart.

Chapter Seventeen

"Do not become careless or waste precious herbal ingredients. Weigh or measure each medicine for its worth: keep the scales, the proper funnels, and the flasks ever ready to judge true proportions for the cure."

THE NEXT MORNING Rina and Morgan returned to where he'd left Cullen the day before. He was not there! Soon Morgan found tracks which told them he had set out with a crude crutch. They tracked him farther up Vermilion Creek toward the lake. An hour later, they saw him, the musket slung across his back glinting in the chill sun. Rina let out a squeal and raced toward him as he turned and cheered. She almost knocked his Y-shaped tree limb crutch away, but they clung hard together as Morgan strode slowly toward them.

"I can never repay you for this, Morgan, never!" Cullen told him and, for the first time in years, extended his hand for Morgan to shake.

"Seeing you two back together's good enough," Morgan said.

"I was going to walk clear to the Cuyahoga to find her if I had to!"

"They didn't hurt her, Cullen. Thanks to Cassie."

"Cassie?" he said. "Then they did believe she's some sort of holy goddess?"

"Yes," Rina put in. "But after Cassie made them let me go, it was Morgan who found me. Cullen, I have to tell you we spent last night together in the woods, close together because it was cold. But nothing happened," she blurted in a rush as if to obey Morgan's stern command they would be promptly truthful this time.

Cullen's blue eyes darkened; his aristocratic jaw set hard. "I think something did happen," he declared to freeze Rina in his embrace. "I think my wife grew up, and stubborn fool that I am, I realize I have a good friend in Morgan Glenn."

Rina heaved a sigh and clung close again. "It's been a long, hard process, *ad perpetuam*," she said and squeezed Cullen even harder.

They decided that the only way to get Cullen back in a reasonable time was for Morgan to hike the rest of the way up this river, west along the lake to the mouth of the Pequotting, and then down to bring back three horses from Cullen's place. It would mean a longer time away from Thea, but it had to be done. He helped the two of them hollow out a hiding place in the woods and left them most of the meager food he had to supplement Cullen's. At least the weather seemed to be warming now, but he had no fear they'd be cold as they'd been last night. With Cullen's musket for protection and their flint kit, they would survive in mutual bliss until he could get back, he thought looking at them. He warned them about staying mostly hidden should more Ottawas come through heading for the big gathering on the Cuyahoga. By noon, he had set out northward at a good clip.

Along the lake, it was he who had to hide occasionally as parties of single-file Indians and several flotillas of canoes went by toward the east. He agonized over the five Connecticut couples having to remain through the coming planting and harvest months if the Ottawas flared up further. Morgan thought that congress's orders handed down from distant Philadelphia to the Indians were too painfully reminiscent of the king's ministers' decrees proclaimed from London to the colonists. And that had led to war. But he and Thea had staked all their worldly goods on this Firelands venture. Their share of the prize money to get them going either here or back east was an absolute necessity. Somewhere, somehow, he intended to buy or build her an apothecary shop, and he'd never do that or get them a decent house without some seed money. But their safety was most important, and they might have to flee if everything exploded around them here.

Two days later on his return trip, Morgan saw no Indians along the lake; perhaps the great Cuyahoga powwow had begun. As he thundered along sandy or stony shores of the great lake, pulling two others horses behind, he pictured large sailing vessels docked here someday, bringing those who wanted to settle. He imagined villages and fine farms springing from the rich, rolling prairie loam. He saw it as clearly in his mind's eye as Cassie must have envisioned her precious forest folk—and believed it all could happen, too.

He found Cullen and Rina safe and happy. He prayed, as they all headed back, that he would find Thea the same.

To keep busy, Thea planted some of her herb garden early. Next time it frosted, she would just cover the tender shoots with last year's dry leaves. But there seemed to be a warming trend from the chilly weather of the last few days. She had carefully measured in her mind how much of which Indian and which traditional herbs she would need to replenish her stores and get them through the next seven months before they departed for Connecticut—if an Ottawa uprising did not send them fleeing before then. She would share what she had with Wintasa—if the men got Wintasa back, she thought, and stood to wipe her soiled hands on her apron.

She walked over and leaned against the corner of the cabin. The morning nausea was not so bad now—either that or else her constantly knotted stomach over the Indian raid and Morgan's absence just cloaked it. She'd judiciously dosed herself with teas and tonics, but she could never quite escape the tense feeling that Morgan would surely walk from those forest depths or come striding back down the river any moment now. Though he worked hard to keep them in meat and feed the team, Danilo often gazed up wistfully in the direction the three men had gone after the captured women.

The thought that she should have done more when the raid occurred tormented her. She should have shot one Indian, run into the forest to reload. Perhaps she could have scattered them, frightened them to think a band of white men were surrounding them. And that glimpse of poor, terrified Rina glancing over toward the root cellar burned in her brain. Had Rina been wondering again why her friend was not there to help, like the night Father Lockwood was lost? Did Rina still blame her for things that she couldn't help or that Rina had brought on herself?

She jumped when Danilo's voice sliced through her reverie. "Man come on a horse, old man!"

Thea grabbed her gun, though Danilo sprinted for the trees with his bow and arrows. She cocked and lifted her trusty Brown Bess musket as Jacob Roscoe rode up the trail. "It's all right, Danilo!" Thea cried. "He's a good friend."

"Right glad to hear you say that!" the grizzled, bearded man told her with a grin.

"I almost didn't recognize you with that beard," she admitted as he dismounted and handed down a haunch of venison to the boy.

"Winter warmth for this ugly face and jest hain't shaved it yet," he told them. "Varners here? See they hain't up on their own place."

She told him everything she knew. He nodded, looking so worried it terrified her more. "Heard tell of 'Tawas having a big gatherin' on the Cuyahoga." He shook his head. "It don't look good. Never expected this," he admitted. Nor, Jacob Roscoe thought, could Governor Trumbull have foreseen this when he sent these folks out here and paid him to come along to report on them and take care of them best he could. Times like this, though, his job made him feel like a traitor as well as a spy when jest coming clean could probably buck this woman up.

"You know, Miz Glenn, the 'Tawas are a real int'restin' tribe," he explained as they walked to the corral to put his horse in. "Pontiac was their great, legendary chief from their big rebellion some twenty years back. Got together a huge alliance of tribes 'gainst them Brits and fought them fierce as fire. But Pontiac got hisself assassinated over in Illini lands. Now here's the important thing. The 'Tawas claim they can never go to war 'gain 'less Pontiac hisself comes back to lead them. Aye, really. Lots of 'em think he's gonna rise from the dead like some frontier Jesus Christ or somethin'. This new chief they got, Garihoua, some's claimin' he's the one. My guess is, 'less Garihoua can convince them he's Pontiac, maybe jest nothin' will come o' all this."

"What folly, everything hanging on superstitions!" Thea said.

"Sure, that's it. Superstitions. Folks just hopin' so hard things turn out the way they want will grab on to anything," Jacob said.

She nodded, thinking of her own plight. How badly she wanted Rina, Morgan, Cullen, Wintasa, and Quanemo to be safe. And how desperately she needed Morgan back here to love her, and this baby she carried, too.

"Say, you don't mind if I set up camp and trap 'long these banks 'til Morgan comes on back with the others, do you?"

"Oh, of course not! Danilo and I would love to have you in our little makeshift family," she said and placed her hands protectively on her belly before she realized Jacob Roscoe was staring. Quickly, she wiped her hands on her apron there. "And somewhere out here, I'll even find us some early greens to have with this venison tonight. I'm grateful you brought so much, as I'm sure they'll all be back soon."

It was just as she was starting to cook those greens that she heard Danilo give a whoop. She jolted at the memory of the Ottawa attack, but he was shouting Morgan's name! She ran to the door, wiping her hands. Yes, Morgan, alone, but he had come on a horse from the direction of Varners, not the way she had been watching for so long!

She ran toward him, arms outstretched. He dismounted and threw the reins to Danilo. She was in Morgan's arms, really in Morgan's arms, and he had come back to her!

"The others?" she got out after a crushing kiss.

"Rina and Cullen back home, Cullen with some danged broken toe bones from a deadfall trap, but the 'Tawas didn't harm the women, at least as far as I know. Quanemo has gone on after Wintasa to the Cuyahoga, Danilo," he said and explained all he knew to the boy.

"And Cassie?" Thea asked.

"Gone off willingly with a brave who seems to love her as a woman as well as adore her as a goddess."

"Yes, I know which brave he was," Thea said, picturing the raid again. "Imagine that—Cassie. But what happens to her if they find out she's not a gift from the Great Spirit at all but just—" her voice faltered.

"But Cassie's always been a strange and special gift to us, Thea, and we've spent a lot of time protecting her. Perhaps the Ottawa brave will do the same. Come inside, as I have much to tell."

Just then he saw Jacob Roscoe hurrying up from the river-bank. Thea was surprised to see Morgan frown. "Just Jacob with his winter beard," Thea said.

The men shook hands. "Welcome back, jest in time for a real good supper," the old man told him.

"Oh, yes!" Thea said. "Come in! Morgan, I promised you there'd be a nice meal waiting when you came back! And I have so much to tell you!" she cried and ran back inside to save her greens from turning to mush.

"I recognize you now," Morgan told the man quietly while Danilo led his winded horse away.

"Jest a winter beard."

"No, I mean, you're the man who warned me that there were men in the woods that day outside New London when Avery Payne attacked Thea. I wounded one, and, I believe, you shot at the other."

"Avery Payne?" old Jacob said. "Was it that blowhard his-self botherin' her? Sure, I was jest passing through that day and glad to be of help."

"Just passing through—a frontier trader like you in New London? And you were just passing through Eden's Gate on the Mohawk River that very day we visited there," Morgan challenged.

Jacob's sharp eyes bored into the tall man's questioning gaze. "An old trapper like me gets 'round. 'Nough said for now," Jacob retorted and followed Thea inside the bark-covered cabin.

At last, Morgan thought, he'd discovered who good old

Governor Trumbull must have assigned to watch over Thea after Benedict Arnold defected. But was he watching over all of them now—perhaps sworn to secrecy? Dang, he'd keep Jacob Roscoe's secret if that was it, but he wasn't going to keep his own. The first moment he got Thea alone he was going to tell her about him and Rina's night in the woods. Cullen had accepted it, and Thea surely would, too. He was staking their whole future on it!

But there were two more for supper by the time a strangely balmy night fell. The warmth was so pleasant after the chill snap, they even ate outside. All their chatter stopped when Danilo jumped to his feet. His twice-emptied plate flew. "Quanemo's owl cry," he shouted. "Quanemo, he is here!"

They all stood and looked the way the boy ran as one, then two figures emerged from the forest fringe on the bank above the river. "Wintasa?" Thea cried. "Wintasa, too? Blessed day!"

Morgan only hoped it would be so as he, too, rushed to greet their Wyandot friends. But as for sharing his new confession privately with Thea or hearing what news was keeping her so shy and smug over supper, he would obviously have to wait a bit longer.

"On high wood bank, setting sun side of great Cuyahoga, Quanemo find Wintasa," Quanemo solemnly began his story. Everyone sat around a small campfire outside the cabin, enjoying the early spring warmth. Thea saw unspoken emotion flow between the Indian couple when Wintasa's eyes met her husband's. They all listened intently to the measured, careful words of Quanemo.

He explained that he had argued with the Ottawas, who wanted to trade Wintasa north for guns. After all, hadn't he said just last summer he was renouncing her for her feet on the white man's path? He had actually feared they might not return Wintasa to him for his own broken words. But Cassie was there, too, with the Indian brave Tochingo. Tochingo was proud to protect her. Cassie, the sacred woman, said she came to see all the forest folk gathered in their secret place before Cassie and her man Tochingo went west to live.

"Cassie's going farther west to live with Tochingo?" Thea blurted, but Morgan's hand on hers in her lap stilled her.

"The sacred woman saved for me Wintasa," Quanemo pronounced with a slow nod. "The sacred woman turned the feet of all that tribe from the path of war."

Now it was Jacob Roscoe's turn to interrupt. "You mean that little gal told them not to fight her white friends and so they won't? Damned unbelievable!"

"Cassie's never been believable," Thea said. "Yet somehow, everything she says comes true."

At another nod from Quanemo, it was Wintasa who picked up the story. "On the trail, Cassie tell the 'Tawas free Rina and they did. On the Cuyahoga, Cassie tell them free Wintasa to her man Quanemo. Most of all, she tell them their Chief Garihoua not the great chief Pontiac, come back from the dead," she explained.

"I can't believe she managed to reason all that out," Morgan marveled.

"Not that," Wintasa answered. "The sacred woman Cassie just say Chief Garihoua is king of forest folk and cannot be their Pontiac. And she sing the song of Danilo boy. Then 'Tawas turn their eyes away from the words of Garihoua."

"Yes, my song, Danilo Boy!" Danilo put in proudly.

"So the 'Tawas did give to me my woman back and say no war now," Quanemo concluded their tale.

Thea just shook her head. Wait until Rina heard all that, she thought. Jacob Roscoe swore under his breath in amazement, then added, "Out o' the mouths of babes like Cassie, sometimes the truth comes the long way 'round."

Morgan stood and pulled Thea to her feet beside him. "The last thing in the world I want is to be rude to our best friends," he announced to them all. "But that good news has about done me in. I've been on foot or saddle for over a week now, and I'm going to take my wife inside for a little welcome home."

"Morgan!" she gasped, embarrassed.

"A little welcome home talk," he amended, and though

the others grinned and Quanemo nodded, Morgan bid them all good night and led her firmly into the cabin.

"Sorry if I upset you out there," he said.

"I'm sure they didn't mind. You just surprised me. It's been so long since we've really been alone, and I've been hankering, as Jacob says, to talk to you."

He sailed his worn bicorn to the bed and took her hands in his. "Me, too. But first—"

He tugged her close, and she came willingly. They melted in an embrace that plunged to passion in a searing kiss. They tilted their eager mouths to deepen their closeness. His tongue explored the sweet shape of her mouth as if he had all the time in the world with her. But he feared he might not, once he told her what he had to say.

She answered the slick, hot probe of his thrusting tongue with dazzling forays and teases of her own. She clamped them both together, hard-muscled stomach to soft belly, thigh to thigh. He had come home to her with no more thoughts of Rina, she exulted. She had just sensed the tension between Rina and Morgan during all these months of close proximity. He had helped rescue Rina only for Cullen and not for anything they had ever shared because he asked Rina to wed him first! And when she told him of the babe, all would be well. Peace between them always, just as with the Indian tribes of the Firelands!

She felt dizzy when he suddenly set her back, leaned her against the wall, and loosed her. He crossed his arms over his chest defensively, as if to hold her off. "I have something to tell you that happened on the trip," he said, his voice shaky at first, but then it rolled on crisper, even hard.

"Not more harsh words between you and Cullen?"

"No, no need for that anymore. Thea, when Cullen was hurt and couldn't go on after Rina, I did. I found her first."

"You found her first—"

"Just listen. Night fell, and so we had to spend the night together in the forest. It was cold, and she was getting the shakes and sneezes again like when you were nursing her. And so," he took a breath before he plunged on, "I insisted we sleep close together for both our sakes—for warmth. She said she thought it was better if she got sick and died, but I insisted. As Rina put it to Cullen, 'nothing happened,' but I had to tell you, and that's that."

She gaped at him a moment, grateful for the wall behind her. She had intended to just blurt out about the baby, but now . . . "And that's what?" she managed.

"The whole truth right out, so you can deal with it any way you want to. Cullen was so glad to get Rina back untouched and in one piece, it hasn't hit him yet—or else he's finally realized Rina loves him and I love only you. Look, sweetheart, I can see you're upset, and I'm dog tired. I wouldn't think of even asking to get in bed with you with a week of trail dust and sweat on me, so I'm going out to wash. And when I come in, if you don't want me sharing that—" he pointed to their bed, "with you, just say so, and that's that, too."

He made a strange beseeching motion with his hand, then slapped it down on his thigh. Before she could ask another question or say a thing, he yanked open the cabin door and plunged out into the night.

She stared after him with her mouth hanging open before she clamped it shut. To have all that spilled on her when she was dog tired, too! And after how she'd been fretting how a man who had loved Rina so passionately to become betrothed to her in one week could never let her go! She had worried for weeks how Rina and Morgan scooted around each other in close quarters here. And then he'd told her they spent a night in each other's arms out there and just for warmth! Suddenly, her knees wobbled and she slid down the rough wall to sit right on the packed-earth floor.

"But those nights were cold, before this warming spell," she said aloud to the terribly empty cabin. "And he told me right out, told me the truth."

This is Morgan Glenn, the honorable, the dedicated, the fiercely loyal, she thought. The man whose sense of duty made him follow Benedict Arnold to the end. The man who kept his pride, even when people spat at him in the streets. She knew with all her being that Morgan was not a traitor to his country, nor had he knowingly been a traitor to her.

It was only that he had been trapped once in his promise to another. He himself had been misled and betrayed and suffered for it, even as she had. She could not bear for him to suffer again. She and Morgan were bound together by so much—their pasts, their love, this child.

"This child!" cried aloud and scrambled to her feet. She had not told him about the child! She had not told him she believed him and trusted him and loved him and always would!

She pulled open the cabin door, but it was so dark outside she went back for the tole lantern. He had said he had gone to wash? Where? Down on the river or at the waterfall? She'd try that first. She could just wait in bed for him, but what if he took too long or decided not to come back in? She had to tell him everything *now!*

She saw no one else around. Jacob must have returned to his camp, and perhaps the Wyandots had even gone back across the river to empty Pequotting.

Her feet knew the way to the waterfall in the dark, but she held aloft the wavering lantern. Camp Milan was as dear and familiar to her now as her shop had been once where she could locate anything she needed in the night. She would surely hate to leave here come next autumn. Next autumn, if the baby just came in time for them to make their deadline. Drat, if it didn't she would just have to bear it in the wagon on the way!

Down closer to the river, wisps of white mist drifted upward from the mingling of warm air on cooler ground. She stood silently at the entrance to the little sheltered grotto where the small falls threaded over a slate ledge. She'd done much laundry here and washed her herbs and herself. Yes, she heard him splashing here. She walked through a patch of fog like through a dream. She put the lamp down to just stare at him as her eyes grew accustomed to the dark. The scene seemed enchanted with silvered spray and silvered sounds.

He neither heard nor saw her light, as he stood ghostly naked under the tumble of water. Though from the waist up his brown skin had faded somewhat in the winter, his lower

torso gleamed gilded alabaster. Like a child, he splashed and
snorted in the roll of water. He turned, and she could see his
broad chest and the darker hair there that narrowed to a V
down his trim belly, as if pointing to his loins. His thighs and
calves, like his arms and shoulders, bulged with muscles
molded by his frontier endeavors. She felt desire for him
surge through her, stronger than the force of the white water
over the cliff. The spring air still had a nip in it, and the water
was no doubt still crisp, but she felt warm all over.

She envied the water touching him. She kicked off her
shoes. It was then she spun around so fast, he flicked droplets
on her from his loosed, wild hair.

"Thea? Thea! It's still danged cold!"

"Not like it has been. Besides, I bet I'll never notice!"

He strode over to her as if he were fully garbed and stared
slack-jawed while she scooted her gown down and peeled off
one stocking. He stood ankle-deep in the wading pool of
water caught by rocks before it tumbled down to the river.
"Have you decided you trust me then?" he demanded, hands
on his lean hips.

She hopped on one foot, trying to get her last stocking off.
And she could not keep her eyes off him. "There was nothing
to decide about loving you, so there's nothing to decide about
trusting you," she got out while she peeled the other stocking
off. "Watching you and Rina together these last few months
riled me, but—"

"It riled me, too! She made me so jumpy, always getting
in the way when I wanted you. It just kept reminding me
what a fool I'd been once not to tell you what had happened.
Dang, but you've always had the most stubborn, independent
mind!"

"Me? You told me you liked that, frontiersman!" she
threw at him with her last scrap of clothing. He caught the
petticoat and tossed it back on the bank. Through the swirl
of river mist and night wind in the wavering glow of her
lamp, his eyes heated her cooling flesh as if he touched her
everywhere.

"You know," he said and swished two steps closer, "I
thought I was tired and cold tonight, and now I'm neither.

Suddenly, I'm burning up in here, and it's too early for real warm water."

Before she could wade in, he strode up on the ledge and caught her in his arms. He sat on the pile of their garments, bringing her down with him. "Our bed may be waiting, but I can't wait that long," he murmured as his mouth covered hers.

His skin was tingly cool against her warm flesh. That was the only thing that told her where he ended and her body began. But his lips were warm everywhere on her, along her eyelids and the slant of her cheeks. Down her throat and over her shoulders to her fluted collarbone. His mouth plundered the sweet valley between her breasts, and then nipped and licked both nipples, pouted from the gentle breeze and stronger passion. He marauded lower across her belly, where the baby grew.

She jolted from her drugged reverie. She should tell him, right now. But his mouth slid lower and she soon cried out other things.

He was on her and over her and in her. Their separation, all the danger past and yet to come, were nothing now. He rocked gently, then fiercely.

"Morgan. Morgan!"

"What, my darling? I'm so hot for you, no time for a love chat now. And I told you, you could never change your mind!"

"No, never. But I have to tell you one thing! I'm—we're going to have a family. Only it might be as late as November, I don't know, so—"

He propped himself barely off her on stiff elbows and knees, panting hard. The lantern she had abandoned in her haste etched half of their faces in a gentle golden glow. "That's wonderful! But I could have hurt you, I—"

"No," she told him and placed three fingertips over his trembling lips. "We'll never hurt each other again. And please don't stop. Don't ever stop loving me!"

He grinned and let out a half-muffled shout she was afraid might bring the old trapper from the river. Drat, she thought, let Jacob Roscoe and the whole world come to stare! She loved Morgan Glenn and he loved only her, and that was all that mattered. That—and the baby—was all!

He began to move so gently inside her again. Smooth, feathery soft, the union shook her again and made goose bumps tremble her flesh through the sheen of her body and heart heat for this man. When his love pulsed into her, it was as powerful as the promises he whispered in her ear. A bit later, it took the waterfall dusting them with spray to cool their shared bodies and their precious dreams.

Thea's pregnancy grew apace with their first real crop of summer corn and squash. How fertile and rich the land was here. Wintasa showed them how to weave the squash vines amongst the corn for a double crop in the same plowed space. The corn held up the squash, which let the squash lace itself around to support the cornstalks. Like in a good marriage, Wintasa told Thea with a taut smile, the two held each other up even when rains beat down and winds blew.

Thea's vegetable and herb gardens also popped and flourished as she did. By late summer, she had taken to wearing Morgan's big extra shirt over a loose-fitting skirt or a doeskin sack garment Wintasa gave her. Some of the Pequotting villagers had straggled back, now that the threat of an Ottawa uprising was evidently past. But the returned Wyandots had brought back a lung cough they called "Croaking Like Frogs," which Thea recognized as Whooping Cough. Among Indians, especially male adults, it seemed quite deadly.

Thea helped Wintasa care for the stricken Wyandots, but Morgan and Wintasa would not let her directly nurse those ill, lest she catch the malady with the baby coming. She had almost argued, but she remembered Rina's mother and her own parents' fate, and agreed to dose the Wyandots from afar. So, even in her heaviest autumn months, she visited the village to help Wintasa, but did not go in the huts or near the sweathouses the sick visited to help themselves breathe.

In a big central cooking pot, Thea made black spruce tea and mixed the boiled onions with honey, the traditional Indian internal cure for this disease. With a mortar and pestle made of river rocks, she carefully ground and mixed salve of marygolds and lard for a chest rub that eased muscles wracked from the spasmodic fits of coughing.

She wished she had comfrey and thyme, which she had tended in her New London herb beds for such an illness, but those precious plants and seeds had gone over the edge of the cliff on the way west. She studied her pharmacopoeia for possible hints from her mother about Whooping Cough cures, but found nothing special, until she saw a little note wedged in between two lines that "maidenhair is also good for any wracking chest cough that ails one."

It was not a day too soon! Quanemo, strong as he was, had fallen ill, too, and was hacking up the streaks of blood that often portended death. Thea hurried along the muddy banks of the river to the spot where she'd seen abundant maidenhair ferns in the summer. If only a few were left this late! How she wished she'd found this use for the tall, delicate, and graceful ferns earlier! She'd seen the Wyandots use them only for fans to whisk off mosquitoes and no-see-ums on the hottest days of summer.

Yes, there was a patch of bedraggled ferns left, but the bank was steep and muddy here. Her bulk and lack of balance these last weeks had robbed her of her surefootedness. Perhaps she should go back and fetch Danilo or even Morgan to help. But by then she could have them pulled and boiling!

"We're just going along here a little way," she talked to the unborn baby as she often did now. She held on to saplings, concentrating on each step. "Got to get some herbs to help our Wyandot friends," she said and reached out to pluck a handful.

She gave a little squeal as she felt her foot nearest the water slip and give way. Her body twisted around the sapling she held, and sat down hard. When the slender tree bent under her weight, she grabbed for ferns and weeds to stop her skidding plunge toward the rocks at the river's edge. She couldn't let herself pitch over or roll! She seized another sapling. That perilous plunge down the cliffside with Morgan and the Conestoga flashed through her brain.

But then, she held. Still sitting on the bank with her skirts shoved up, still holding to the ferns and weeds with her left hand, she sat very quiet. Trusting the sapling she held in her right hand, she sidled her hips backwards, inching up, away from the edge. She sat leaning heavily against a bigger tree, trying to calm her heartbeat and slow her galloping breaths.

She had misjudged the danger, she scolded herself. In one reckless move, she could have hurt the baby, ruined everything. Would she never learn? Would she always plunge ahead when she wanted something, even if it was for someone else? Suddenly, that shortcoming made her feel closer than ever to willful Rina. Yes, they were so different, but at their very cores, perhaps greatly the same. Independent, willing to help others, but fiercely proud and needful when it came to love. A stab of longing for her friend jabbed her so hard, it took her a moment to realize that pain was in her mind and not her body.

She glanced down and saw she still held a torn fistful of maidenhair fern. It would make enough lung tonic to help Quanemo and some of the others. Then she could send Danilo down for more before the early frosts that portended a hard winter reached into this little valley where the Pequotting still flowed warm and free.

Carefully, she got to her knees and steadied herself on the tree trunk to rise. She stood there concentrating on how she felt, for after all, as Morgan said, she was her own patient now, too. Yes, a sturdy, hardy child grew within. No kicking or thrashing for that bump and panic back there. Maybe, just like his or her parents, this new life would be stubborn, too.

"We still don't know what we're going to name you," she told the child as she started slowly back up the trail to Pequotting, "but it will be a name that means something strong and good!"

Quanemo was one of the few adult males struck with Whooping Cough who regained his health. On the far side of the village, many Wyandots had been wrapped and buried, with food left on their graves for their supposedly restless spirits. Thea thanked God that Wintasa had not lost her beloved man a second time. She knew she could not bear it if she lost Morgan.

As October neared its end with a fine harvest and spectacular blaze of forest color, the Indian father and son went up and down the river hunting again. They brought word that the coats of the animals they shot or trapped were unusually thick already, a warning of an early, hard winter. And after each trip, they brought news from the Varners. By Quanemo and Danilo's hands, Thea and Rina wrote letters back and forth. Before it was time to head for home, Rina promised, they were coming for a visit to Camp Milan. Despite facing childbirth and the long trip back, Thea had never felt happier or more hopeful than now that all would go well.

When Cullen and Rina came for two days, the good times among the four of them were just as they always should have been, Thea thought. Too bad their days in the Firelands were dwindling. But, she mused, when they got back to that other life, could it remain like this for the four of them? When Cullen and Rina rebuilt the Lockwood mansion and rejoined the social circles of a new New London, could they all stay friends? And could they somehow prove the evil deeds of that "pillar of the community," Avery Payne, or would he outfox them again? Would they still be Arnold-tainted, the couple who wanted to return here or start some little apothecary shop somewhere back east? Lately, Thea and Morgan had been focusing so hard on what was happening here and now that they had not yet decided their future, as it all hinged on the Firelands prize.

"Well, time is going, that's all I know!" Rina's voice interrupted Thea's agonizings. "What's that phrase you always say for that, my love?" she asked Cullen.

"Tempus fugit," he said and coughed. "Or maybe *carpe diem,* meaning 'seize today and enjoy it right now,' so—" Cullen went on before Rina cut him off. They often finished each other's thoughts lately, Thea noted.

"Yes, that's it," Rina declared. "You have simply got to birth this child before we all head back east, Thea, posthaste! You just tell it—him or her—when you talk to the baby next time. Honestly, and we used to think Cassie was half-cracked, chattering away to forest folk she couldn't see."

At the mention of Cassie, they all observed a moment's silence as if someone dear had died. They had heard no more of her and her Ottawa brave Tochingo, and could only hope for her safety and happiness out in her once-feared forest depths.

"Enough of that," Rina piped up again. "This is a celebration of almost surviving the Firelands here, not to mention back home. But I think we'd better plan ahead a bit. Now, Cullen says by Governor Trumbull's orders, the last lake bateau at the mouth of this river will depart on November tenth, whether we're there or not. We can't take the same bateau with our two wagons, but I think—"

"I think we will somehow meet on the trail past Buffalo Creek and return the rest of the way together!" Cullen put in, his arm around Rina, his eyes on Morgan. "Safety in numbers. Governor Trumbull surely would understand the code to help others out here. After all, in the Firelands, who's a gentleman and who is not should be judged by how a pioneer keeps himself and helps his neighbors, and not by anyone's past. Out here, it's who's a man that matters."

Thea and Rina strolled out along the riverbank, arm-in-arm, while the men sat outside the cabin door to share harvest talk and ideas of taking some Firelands corn back east to Governor Trumbull.

"I'd love to have a baby, too," Rina admitted to Thea, "but not facing that long trip home. I envy how you've always been so brave and strong, Thea."

"Sometimes, lately, I don't feel either. Oh, I've never been happier with Morgan, but I'm afraid this won't be over in time for him to get a good start back when we need our share of the prize money. I will blame myself if we literally miss that boat. We'll never make it back in time if we do. And I've heard about a lot of first babies carried high in the mother like this that came ever so late to be born!"

"But don't you know some good herb to hurry the baby if it goes overlong?"

"No. I've looked through Mother's book and her hand-written messages. We can gather more feverfew down in the valley today to help with my labor once it starts, but that won't bring the child. Besides, something like that is in God's hands, not an apothecary's. He gave us herbs to help, but things like birth and death—those are His doings."

"Ugh, this pregnancy has made you even more serious and fretful! Now that I've faced the past, I'm just looking to the future. Finally, Cullen really trusts and loves me, and I'm not letting go of that!"

Thea hugged her, then stepped back. "Never let go of that, Rina, never!"

"And, promise you will send Danilo for me when your time comes. It will be any day now, I just know it. I will be a big help!"

"If you don't faint at the first sight of blood. I'm just teasing. If it happens before you have to go with Cullen, I will send for you."

"But I could stay behind and catch up with Cullen later. You'll not have this child in the wilds alone, Thea!"

"My dearest friend, I won't be alone. I'll have Morgan and Wintasa, and I've seen a few babies birthed in my time. And to me, this place will never be the wilds. I only hope and pray we'll get back here someday—"

"Oh, don't cry, Thea, just because I don't ever intend to come back and don't want you to, either! You can't cry, please don't!" Rina pleaded and hugged her, despite her height and bulk.

"Drat!" Thea said and sniffed hard. "It's just my ragged emotions with this baby. But if you can't be here with me, I'll know your good thoughts are with me, and that will keep my spirits up! Come on now. Are you going to help me pick some feverfew for helping birth this little laggard, and some yellow marygolds in the meadow to help the Wyandots get through the lung disease this winter or not?"

Their last day in the Firelands together, Thea and Rina gathered armloads of the precious, dying golden blooms and hearts full of their newly blooming friendship.

Chapter Eighteen

"Marygold is a bright yellow, aromatic annual flower to cheer the heart. But it earns its way in the herbal kingdom with its precious petals and leaves, which make a fine healing salve. It is a hardy wildflower unto itself, not be be confused with the tamely-tended pot marigold."

WHEN THE FIRST week of November dragged by with no baby yet, Thea felt stirrings of frustration and anger. Why could it not be born now, for it must be fully grown! She told the child so in no uncertain terms, but still it clung to its warm world inside her and would not budge. Morgan remained tender and outwardly calm, but she knew waiting for the child's arrival so they could depart for Connecticut weighed as heavily on him as her. Their financial future, their hope to return here or start a business there hung on getting to that last Lake Erie bateau at the mouth of the Pequotting by November tenth. She knew first births were often difficult, and feared Morgan might not be willing to leave for a time after. Worse, winter had come wickedly early with light, sporadic snow squalls sweeping down from the lake and a biting wind, which could make the going hard even when the child did come.

This afternoon of November eighth, Morgan was out in back with Quanemo and Danilo drying meat to make pemmican, the grain-and-suet food Indians often used for journeys. The brisk northwest wind that too often portended storms rattled the door to the cabin and made the hearth fire dance. Thea sat fully dressed on the edge of their bed, brooding, staring at the flames. She loved this small room with its log and bark walls standing guard against the wilderness, but it seemed to be pressing in on her today. Surely, Cullen and

Rina had left their cabin at Mud Brook to head home already. Besides, she would be spending enough time within these walls and in this bed after this stubborn child was born, for Morgan would not hear of setting out before to birth the baby on the trail.

"We're going for a walk, and you're going to realize your time is up in there!" she told the baby and rose heavily to her feet to shuffle over for her woolen cloak on a wall peg. "Come on now, Jonathan or Marygold, it's your welcome to the world day!"

They had decided if the child were a boy they would name it Jonathan for Governor Trumbull. After all, he had given them this chance for retribution and a fine future that hung so precariously now. And it was Morgan's opinion that the governor had sent Jacob Roscoe to watch over her for a while in New London, and as an advisor for all of them here in the western Firelands.

If this obstinate little mule of a child were a girl, Thea had asked to name her Marygold for the bright, hardy flowers which dotted Camp Milan's meadow and were a precious healing herb. Why should her daughter not be named for an herb, even as she had been? She could picture the sunny yellow marygolds the frost killed after she and Rina picked them their last day together. But she realized it was the hard times more than the good ones that had bound her and Rina as friends.

As Thea pulled up her hood and opened the door, the sight outside jolted her. That green, sunny meadow of memory was brown and windswept. She could hear the men's voices from around in back, but she'd not bother them or go far. Besides, Morgan would make her head right back to bed if he saw her.

She paced the clearing as quickly as she could, but her ungainly middle weighed her down. She wondered how the men were keeping their smoke fire going when the wind whipped the tree limbs so. Tiny ice pellets hard as shot peppered her, and she realized she should go back. But with her mind meandering through both the past and future, she plodded on.

She thought of Rina sailing eastward on the bateau. How these winds would fill those sails and make it unnecessary for the men to row. She imagined Rina sailing, flying through the wind toward Connecticut. Rina was free of this burden of a child. Rina, the graceful and ever-elegant, was even more so now that Thea could barely walk this forest edge in a straight path.

"You *will* be born today!" she told the child again. "You must be born in this place *now* because we have to leave it!"

The retort of cold tree limbs from the woods sounded like gunfire or crackling flames. How far away the War of Independence and the fires of New London seemed to her now. These Firelands would be the herb that healed the wounds of the Connecticut fireland sufferers when they got their homes here in this bounteous land. It had to be, had to be . . .

"Oh!" her cry was lost in the sharp cut of wind. A pain from deep inside knifed her, then retreated. Biting her lip, she began to walk again. She inhaled deeply. It smelled good and clean out here: woodsmoke and crisp forest and that distinctive river valley smell even though ice covered puddles and the shallows of the Pequotting already. The pain leaped at her again, this time at the back of her waist, like a fist that smacked right through her. When it passed, she heard the far-off howl of what Quanemo called "the winter wolf." The wild animals kept to themselves when the weather was good; but when winter came, they ventured closer. This year their close proximity suggested a stark, severe season.

A shadow emerged from the trees ahead, and Thea screamed. Not a wolf, but a man with a wolf skin over his back. An Indian! Cassie's Indian! He loomed from the forest the way he had that day of the raid! Then the paler, thinner form stepped from behind the man, as if they had been one.

" 'Tis true, then?" a familiar, lilting voice asked. "Over in the Wyandot village, we heard you going to have a child, we did, Mistress Thea," Cassie started in as if they'd never been apart. "Is Mistress Rina here to help you? I can boil water real good, I can!"

"Cassie!" was all Thea managed as she spread her arms to welcome the girl. But before Cassie could run to her, another pain sliced Thea in two. Tochingo jumped forward to catch her before she pitched to her knees.

"Please," Thea muttered as Tochingo held her upright and

Cassie grasped her other arm. "Fetch Morgan, Cassie. And Wintasa, too."

Except for everyone insisting she leave Thea behind with her baby yet unborn, Rina rejoiced the day they left their Firelands camp. She gave just one glance back at the banks of Mud Brook, then turned away and dreamed of the big house she and Cullen would build in postwar New London. She thought of parties again, of laughter in the new house, just like the old days when her mother was a happy hostess. But Mother, she thought with open grief she accepted at last, had never really been happy at all. A woman who hates her own child—any child—is a sick woman. Rina vowed she would never be like that when she had one of her own or even helped tend Thea's.

As their wagon creaked along the lakeward trail, Rina wished Father would be in Connecticut to greet them, instead of just Governor Trumbull. All those years Father had been ill, he had lived life well, helping others, loving her, even though he was so strict. And, perhaps, she thought with a new comforting insight, he was that way just because he'd lost Mother young, and feared to lose his only child, too. Then Cullen coughed in his gloved fist again to yank her from her revelations.

"I hate to think you're starting out with a chest cold," she commiserated. "I wish we had a few of Thea's cures along, besides sassafras roots to shave for tea."

"It's nothing," he rasped out. "Agues and chills just have to work their course. I'll rest the days we're on the bateau, and be fine by the time we get to Buffalo Creek."

They made their last quick stop before the lake in a natural glade, and Cullen walked off the trail to relieve himself. "There's been a campfire hidden back in here!" he called to her, "and not an Indian one like Quanemo makes." Cullen was proud he'd learned a thing or two about reading signs and following woodland tracks. She joined him off the trail behind a hazelnut thicket. "I'd say, Rina, it was a white man who left these prints in the mud, but surely not Jacob Roscoe, as the feet are so large."

"Cullen, look!" she cried and grabbed his arm. Beneath the thicket, a pair of boots barely protruded.

"Get the gun!" he ordered, but then he saw there was no need and seized her wrist to hold her there. The man was not only dead, but had been for months. He was mere bone and clinging cloth. Perhaps only the cold weather had preserved what was left of him. "Poor bastard!" Cullen muttered. "Don't look!"

She gladly turned away while Cullen went through the leather satchel he found beside the corpse. "You won't believe this, Rina. A lot of British pounds in here." His voice rose in disbelief as he went on. "And a promissory note for more money, evidently to this man 'when the deed is executed.' It looks like his name was Jedediah Clapper. And the note—it's signed Avery Payne!"

"Avery Payne!" she cried and swung to glance at the paper. "Out here? Avery Payne!"

She squinted at the moldy note. "But who was this man? And what does 'when the deed is executed' mean?" she asked, and Cullen shrugged.

"Here," he told her and thrust the satchel into her hands. "Whatever this man did or didn't do, it's only right we bury the rest of him." He coughed hard, and it took him a few moments to wheeze in his breath. "It won't take long."

Rina nodded, despite her concern for Cullen's ague. She marveled at how these Firelands had changed her husband. Back in New London, he would never get his hands soiled for a dead stranger if he were expected somewhere on time or had a chest cold to tend. She admitted to herself she loved the western man more than she ever had the eastern gentleman. "I'll fetch the axe to dig in this cold ground," she told him, "and we'll say a prayer for his soul. But if he was working for Avery Payne, I have my doubts he had much of one."

The labor Thea had struggled to start stretched on into that night and the next day. She tried to keep calm, but when she realized she had no control over what her body was doing to her, she began to panic. She pushed and pushed, but it seemed the baby was yet unwilling to be born. Sounds, voices drifted in and out of her head.

" 'Tis a wolf howling out there," she heard Cassie say once. "That means someone's going to die."

"Quiet, or I'll toss you out in the snow!" Morgan hissed and all was quiet again but her own frenzied grunting and panting.

But she hadn't cried aloud yet. The Wyandot women never did, and often gave birth in the corner of a longhouse or bark wigwam behind a hanging bearskin, squatting without a word while family life went on. But she was not alone. She had Morgan to hold her hand between attacks of pain, and Wintasa's help, and Cassie darting back and forth—that really was Cassie, wasn't it?—so she had to be brave, even if she was burning up with her exertions. Then, later, Father Lockwood smiled at her from the hearth fire, and Charity Payne lay in the bed beside her. She had to nurse Charity and stop her agonies, her gasping for breath! Thea screamed and screamed at Avery to get away when he tried to come in the cabin door with Cousin Benedict at his side to smother her and Charity.

Thea tossed her head and bore down when they told her to. She knew this had to be over soon so she and Morgan could go on into their future, chasing Cullen and Rina back to Connecticut for their share of the prize. Yes, there was Rina, dear Rina. Had she come to help as she had wanted? The thought that she and Rina were still friends reached up far inside Thea and turned things all around from the sad way they used to be.

It was the most pain she had ever experienced, at least, almost as bad as when she learned Morgan had chosen Rina first and had loved her inwardly. Inwardly, that was how this pain attacked.

"Wintasa," she gritted out between pushing so hard, "nothing yet?"

"Soon," her friend said. "Soon."

It seemed that promise would never come true. Thea's mind looked for places to hide from the pain. If she were in her shop right now, she'd know where to look, even in this darkness, for cures for the agony, for salves for aching muscles. She tried hard to push away the longing for an apothecary shop of her own with shiny glass windows and sparkling, pear-shaped carboys filled with elixirs just waiting to be poured. She clung to thoughts of the mingled smells and hanging bunches of her herb garden bounty. She tried to grasp the memory of mint water and rose petals. She flowed into blackness. She settled down in longings for her deep, dark drawers of stored sassafras and sage and basil and marygold.

"Here's Marygold, my sweetheart," Morgan's voice gathered her drifting thoughts. "Open your eyes and meet our daughter, Marygold Charity Glenn!"

The pain had fled, and a bone-melting weariness took its place. She felt lighter, light-headed, too. She slitted her eyes into the light of a glowing hearth and a bright new day muted through their single grease-paper window. Wintasa sat on a blanket across the room, calmly lacing leather thongs through a Wyandot baby board. But Morgan stood here, bigger than ever, leaning over her with a tiny, yellow-headed, reddish-faced mite that fit perfectly in his big hands.

"It took a long time, and you've lost a lot of blood, but she's surely worth it," Morgan told her. "Thank God you didn't leave me!" His deep voice quavered, and tears touched his brown eyes. Thea managed a smile before she looked back down again at the wonder he held.

"Oh! Marygold. She's beautiful!"

"Almost as beautiful and beloved as her mother!" Morgan whispered and laid the baby in her arms.

"She's so small, Morgan. Maybe she will be elegant and graceful when she grows up."

"Of course she will, however tall she grows. You've always been elegant and graceful to me, Thea."

She fought back tears of gratitude for a man like this. Even at this moment of disarray and exhaustion, he made her feel every bit those wondrous things she had always longed to be—things which suddenly didn't matter half as much, now that they had made this child together.

"Her hair's all gold, without a touch of red. We've given her a perfect name, Morgan. And now we can go!" Thea told him. "If this is next day, we've only one left to catch the bateau!"

"Just rest, my love. This is the third day. And even if Cullen somehow talked one of the crews into remaining an extra day or two, we'll never make the bateau now. It's been sleeting. And I'm not taking either you or the child out until I'm sure you're really ready, even if we never make—make it back in time at all."

"But—" she began before she saw the child's eyes had opened at their raised voices. Despite her joy for this baby, her heart fell. All their dreams of earning their way back and starting over, dashed! "Morgan, there has to be a way," she told him low as she opened her gown to nurse the child. "There has to be some way!"

Rina was distraught their second day out on the cold, windy lake. Thank heavens this sleet came *after* they set out on the water, for more of it along the Pequotting trail would have bogged down their wheels or made the trail unbearably slippery. They had grieved when the bateau men told them that they could not wait extra days for the Glenn Conestoga to arrive. "Likely with a new child, they'll decide to sit out the winter, anyway," the head oarsman told them. "This here's a freak season, earliest snap of cold I ever seen. Bad luck for them, but Morgan Glenn, he's a woodsman, and he'll survive."

"Cullen, we can't leave them!" Rina protested.

"I promised him if the boat would not wait, we'd go on and explain to Governor Trumbull," Cullen insisted. "And come hell or high water, pardon the phrase, my darling, I'm keeping my word to my friend Morgan!"

Sadly, Rina and Cullen huddled together in blankets to cut the wind creeping into the body of their wagon. "And to think I once wanted to beat Morgan in this Firelands endeavor more than anything on earth," Cullen admitted, his voice raspy from coughing. "You know, maybe there's another way to help Morgan and Thea get a start, even if they lose out on the Firelands prize. If Morgan weren't so proud and independent, we could share ours with them. But, at least, if Avery Payne doesn't claim this British money we found, that could be theirs!"

"Oh, yes! But—Avery Payne," Rina repeated with a shudder that had nothing to do with the wind. "I would hate to have any of us tangle with that vile wretch again!" She snuggled closer to Cullen. "Maybe I could sell some of the land Father left me and convince Thea to take the money—perhaps for the sake of their child. If Thea knew she had enough seed money in New London, she could open a shop on her old spot! Oh, Cullen, that would be wonderful with all of us together! New London's a fine place to rear a child!"

"I'm planning for us to do just that," Cullen promised, but he had to sit up as another spasm of hacking shook him. Quickly, he hid from Rina the red flecks he'd coughed up in his handkerchief.

Two days later when Thea could sit up in bed without dizziness, Wintasa finally told her how the baby had wanted to come into the world feet first—the sign, she said, of a strong child who would always choose her own paths in life. Wintasa, her arm covered with marygold salve, had reached inside Thea's womb to turn the child so it could finally be born. Thea recalled none of that, any more than she remembered Cassie's departure when she had learned Rina had already set out for home. But it was not for that Thea felt sick at heart.

Morgan came in only for meals and to sleep lately. Though he often cuddled Marygold, "his golden Mary" as he called her, he spent most of his time outside, despite the heavy snow that had fallen while the child was being born. He seemed distracted, brusque, and driven. More than once she had asked him and Wintasa what he, Quanemo, and Danilo were doing outside. But his answers were noncommittal, and she feared he was out in the woods running traps to get them through the winter here. Despite the occasional flare in his eyes, she prayed he had not given up their dream of a Firelands prize. But every time she dared to broach the subject, he put her off. Once, he said, "Thea, there's new snow out there, and it's crazy cold for this danged early. I'm doing the only thing I can."

The Pequotting villagers brought gifts for the baby. Almost all were dried winter foodstuffs or fur robes, but there was a doeskin baby pouch with a shoulder strap for the mother, and two pairs of ash-wood snowshoes. Thea tried hard to settle in her heart that their dream of returning triumphant and forgiven to New London was over.

More than once she heard distant chopping, and she realized Morgan must be cutting firewood to get them through the winter here on land that could never even be legally theirs now. Then the pounding came closer, and she got up to see what was going on, but he must be way around in back. Perhaps, she reasoned when she heard him take the body of the Conestoga away from the north wall of the cabin, he was going to build a second room on the back to keep himself busy and lift her spirits. That was it: he simply wanted to surprise her. She tried to be patient. But then a nightmarish notion punctured her patience. Had he decided to leave her and Marygold safely here with the Wyandots and head back on his own?

"These Wyandot gifts are to get us through the winter here, Morgan, aren't they?" she demanded over dinner. "The tribe, at least, seems to have been told we're staying. Then, I'll just use these snowshoes out there to get over on the other bank to help Wintasa nurse sick Wyandots again this winter."

"No!" Morgan declared so vehemently she jumped. "You'll be too busy nursing golden Mary 'out there' where we're going. You said there had to be a way, and maybe I've found it. I have a surprise for you, something I didn't want to share before in case it didn't work. Let the baby sleep, and bundle yourself up. We're going out."

Thea's heart fluttered when she saw the set of his jaw. Despite the fact she could walk just fine, he wrapped her woolen cloak around her, pressed a warm fur against her for a lap rug, and picked her up in his arms. He carried her outside and behind the cabin to look.

"Oh, Morgan! We can do it now! I knew you'd find a way!"

Before her, back by her root cellar, stood the faded blue Conestoga wagon body, resurrected from the wall of the cabin. Somehow, he had shortened it. Two extra wheels and a pair of wide, sturdy wooden runners to make a huge sleigh, if need be, were attached to the side. The wagon bed had the remainder of the linsey-woolsey stretched over it for a flat, instead of arched, roof, only half as high with the broken hoops and torn top gone. He carried her to the front seat and lifted her up, then climbed after her. The inside had been narrowed and rebuilt. Half of it was lined with warm furs, and the other was filled with bark troughs of dried prairie grass and grain, enough to feed the team during the trip back.

"I'm leaving the slow oxen and two of the horses behind for Danilo to feed," he said. "We're lighter, and we've got to be fast. And I'm looking forward to hearing our wedding bells on the harnesses again." He grasped her closer in his arms. "There's some risk, Thea. You'll have to ride mostly inside to keep Marygold warm. I believe we can do it, maybe even make it back in time this way. But if you don't want to try, we won't. We can trust Cullen to petition Governor Trumbull for us. Or Rina said they'd buy your piece of herb garden land in New London to give us money to get started here or somewhere else."

Tears blurred her view of her big, bold man. She placed three trembling fingers over his lips to halt his doubts. "I don't want us to really put down roots anywhere else but here, if you have your heart set on it, Morgan. Since I lost the shop, *I* can petition for land here over the next few years—if they'll give some to Arnold kin. We haven't dared to doom our future by talking about our share of the prize, have we? Drat, we're as superstitious as Cassie! But I'm not afraid to talk about it now! We can make it back safely, I know we can! Then we'll have money and land so that we can come back here to homestead, and maybe I'll just keep that eastern land where my herb beds grow, so we'll own some of both firelands!"

"Thea, I can't tell you what you mean to me!"

"And you to me. I think we should start out tomorrow!" This time she pulled back her fingertips and covered his mouth with her lips.

Early the second morning on the lake, as Rina and Cullen's bateau passed the broad mouth of the Cuyahoga, one of the oarsmen called in to wake them, "Ma'am! There's a couple o' Indians on the shore, and we'd swear one's 'acalling your name!"

Rina wrapped herself and climbed down, with Cullen peering out behind her. She squinted into the sharp slap of wind and slant of tiny ice pellets. She cupped her hands around her eyes. "Cullen, do you see?" she called. "It couldn't be, could it?"

The voice sounded shrill on the breeze. "Mis-tress Riii-na! Good-bye! Gooooood-bye!"

"Cassie and Tochingo!" Rina gasped. She spun to the oarsman. "Can we put in? We can't leave her in this desolate land!"

"No, ma'am, we can't put in. Them shallows and currents are dangerous there, and the lake's gonna kick up with this wind."

"But she's a white woman. She's my maid, and—"

Cullen climbed down to put his arms around her. "My darling, she's obviously been safe with that Ottawa brave of hers. And she's saying 'good-bye,' not 'take me with you.' "

"But to leave her here!" Rina cried. "To leave her and Thea, too, I can't, Cullen, I just can't!"

"You know," he mused more to himself than to her, "a few months back I would have tried to put a bullet in that Indian brave for abducting you, but I can't summon up the strength or the hatred anymore. I hope he takes good care of her *ad perpetuam.*"

But Rina heard not a word he said. She tore from his arms and stared back again through the gray wall of gathering November lake storm. The two figures looked barely as high as fingers now, but Cassie was still waving, waving. Rina waved wildly, too. "Good-bye, my dear friend! Be happy, like me!"

She cried out things to Cassie long after she knew they could not hear and had slipped into the gray jaws of the devouring horizon.

Thea had never imagined good-byes could be so hard. Wintasa and Quanemo waited, each with a hand on Danilo's shoulder, as Morgan boosted her and Marygold up into the Conestoga the next day. Wintasa stood stoically, her eyes as dark and wet as river pebbles. Danilo's lower lip trembled. Only Quanemo's carved expression did not change, but it was so sad.

"Return to us. Live on these milan banks. Find the path

back to us!" Quanemo called as Morgan clucked to the horses and snapped the reins. With waves and cries of farewell, they jerked away down the slant to the riverbank, the bells on the horses' harnesses jangling in their ears.

Holding the baby close in her doeskin pouch half under her fur robe, Thea twisted to look back. She could not believe they were leaving and might never return. The lovely clearing, her gardens, her root cellar, the dear bark cabin that had served them so well. The friends they had made among the Indians, far better than some of those from civilized New London.

And yet, the Firelands dream was yet unfulfilled. They had to plunge out into this vast world of wilderness. They had to endure to triumph, so this child and many others could share and cherish this land. As if she knew she were going on a long, long trip, Marygold shifted against her mother, searching for another meal. They rumbled down past the little waterfall where they had made love one night and been finally, permanently reconciled. Glazed by frozen spray, the cliff face around it made a cold, carved monument to mark the spot where so much warmth had been shared.

"It's hurting you to leave, too, isn't it?" Morgan asked with a quick glance away from the trail at her.

"Yes, but nothing *really* hurts me anymore if we can be together."

"For me," he said, his voice rough, "wherever we both are is home, even if it's out here on the trail."

She put one hand on the lap robe over his knees. In this leafless, tree-studded world etched with white, nothing looked the same as when they'd first come this way, both hurt and mistrusting the other. But they would find their way. She would not be afraid. She patted his knee and went inside the wagon's warmth to nurse their daughter.

Rina had never been more afraid. Coughing jags drained Cullen's strength as they left the lake behind and headed east past Buffalo Creek. She had finally seen he was hacking blood; he couldn't sleep at night for the attacks that took his breath. After each spasm of coughing, he sucked in air in a long gasp that sounded like a whoop. Rina didn't need Thea to diagnose the disease after things Thea and Quanemo had told her about the Indian malady the Wyandots called "Croaking-Like-Frogs." Thea had said many of the adult male Indians died from this cough, but then Cullen wasn't an Indian!

Rina drove the team often now, since he insisted they plunge on. It was the only way he would agree to stay inside the wagon or snatch bits of sleep. Though she wore his big leather gloves, blisters soon pained her palms and the pads of her fingers. But she, Varina Lockwood Varner of New London, whose hands had never known more pain than the prick of an embroidery needle before she came out here, drove on. What would Connecticuters think of life in the western Firelands when she and Cullen told them how hard things were out here? she wondered. Would any white man or woman ever want to venture farther west than the Mohawk Valley when they learned how it really was?

She spent a lot of time praying as they pushed on. Praying for Cullen, for Thea back there bearing a child. If only there weren't this cold wind and the sky the color of pewter that portended early snow. If only Thea and Morgan were just behind, instead of back there on the Pequotting! She wove frenzied fantasies in which Thea arrived in time to cure Cullen's cough, the way she had helped to save Quanemo. But Thea had been too late when Father died. Rina shuddered when Cullen's jarring, gasping cough shook her even out here. She reined in and scrambled back into the wagon. His face was blue!

"Cullen, my dearest, please don't leave me!" she blurted before she realized how terrible that sounded.

Weakly, he seized her trembling hand. "Whatever happens, I will never, never leave you!" he vowed before coughing convulsed his frame again. When he worsened that night and was almost too weak to open his eyes the next morning, she pulled the wagon off the trail and made camp in a new dusting of snow. She was not driving one more lonely mile until she found some way to save him!

The journey along Lake Erie went better than Thea and Morgan could have hoped. They either followed the shore-

line Indian trail, or if it was too narrow or twisting, they kept
to the grassy banks above the water. The horses tired easily
in the cold and ate grain faster than Morgan had planned,
but he wanted to keep up their strength. If the feed only
lasted until Eden's Gate or even Fort Trent, he hoped to
spend money for more fodder there.

Their only real problem came at the broad mouth of the
Cuyahoga. The waters were so icy, the horses balked at going
in. They had to track several miles inland until they found
a narrower, safe fording place, and then slowly come up the
other side of the river to return to the lake. The cold and the
threat of hovering snow to the north sapped all their strength.
Morgan tried not to count the days, but they had lost precious time not only with the baby, but also with the slower
land travel around the lake.

As Thea regained her strength, she insisted on driving
sometimes, and Morgan sat holding the child. They came
upon Seneca Indians fishing at Conneaut Creek and traded
with them for a supply of fresh fish. The red men were in
awe of the Conestoga, and showed them their travois, the
two-poled platforms they dragged behind their horses to
carry goods. But, as if most Indians had gone into warm winter quarters out here, those were the only humans they saw
the whole length of the lake, and the only time during daylight they did not push ahead.

For the baby's diapers, Thea used cattail down from the
large sack that Wintasa had given her. When it was wet or
soiled, she simply threw it away, an improvement over wash-
ing out linen. Perhaps even "civilized" mothers would admire this innovation. Sometimes she kept Marygold in the
warm cradle board Wintasa had made for her. Already she
missed the quiet, capable Wyandot woman and her family.
And, though she had experienced no cravings for food during
her pregnancy, she longed for an apple now or some fresh
greens. The first thing she would do in the spring after they
got back to New London was go out to her herb gardens,
however wild they'd grown, and pull some good greens!

Of necessity, they both learned to use their snowshoes.
Thea laughed, claiming that the awkwardness of getting
about on them was much the way she felt when she was preg-

nant. But it was so cold, they did little laughing or else their lips would crack. They cuddled together at night in the wagon for body heat, with the child nested between them. They only built a fire to boil water for Thea's herbal teas and to wash the baby, as it took too much time and energy to gather a big supply of wood and feed a roaring fire all night long. Winter did not slacken, even in these early days of December when they finally arrived at Buffalo Creek where the bateau would have put them in. But it lightened their hearts to be at least this far safely. Finally, they headed eastward through New York State.

Tears froze on Rina's face as she desperately searched the ice-skinned shallow streambed near their wagon. She had started out chasing two of their six horses that had strayed, but had given up in exhaustion—and with a new, desperate thought. Maidenhair ferns, Quanemo had told her. Thea had boiled maidenhair ferns to make tea to help him when he was spitting blood! And though the remaining vegetation here was glazed solid or lay crushed under last night's new snow, if she could find some ferns, even dried or dead, she could boil them to save Cullen!

He hardly had the strength to hold her hand this morning. She was terrified he was going to die, and she would be out here alone! She was going to lose him when she had finally found him. They had made a good and loving marriage, and they were on the brink of a happy future at home in Connecticut!

Panicked, she scrambled along the bank, clawing at anything that looked like a plant. Her hands felt numb; soil made her hands look like a gardener's with rims of brown under her fingernails. Maybe she could dig up just the roots of ferns! Thea made tonics from so many things that looked alike to her. Why hadn't she paid better attention? Why had she refused to dirty her hands helping Thea gather herbs?

Finally, defeated, afraid, and bereft, she crawled up the bank with only spruce boughs in her arms. As far as she knew, they were only good for making spruce beer like they'd all drunk that night at Eden's Gate hundreds of snowy, lonely miles from here along the distant Mohawk. She dropped the green boughs outside the wagon and climbed up inside. Cullen was so quiet and peaceful, it terrified her even more.

"Cullen?"

His eyelids fluttered open. "Where have . . . you been?"

"Searching for something besides the sassafras Thea sent with us to make you tea."

"To cure . . . this?" he said and began to cough.

She propped him up and gritted her teeth to hear him gasp for breath. She wanted him to live! She wanted him to live as much as she had once wanted Mother to die, but she somehow knew she would not get her wish this time, and grieved anew.

"Cullen, are you done now?" she asked. "Here, I'll just help you lie back. See, you're not even wheezing now!"

His head flopped back when she laid him down. "Cullen? Cuuuu-llen!"

He did not move. He did not breathe. "Cullen, no!" she cried and threw herself beside him to hug his body and get him warm. "We didn't have enough time!" she heard a woman's shrill voice. "We have so much to say, to do! I used to be so angry when you preached to me about being perfect, Cullen. Cullen," she went on desperately, cradling him against her like a child, "no one is perfect, but we were perfect together. Perfect these last months in the Firelands, and now we have to go home. Home, Cullen, please don't go without me!" her plea ended on a wracking sob.

At last, she sat up and folded his hands on his chest. She touched his bluish cheek, and the scar where he'd lost his earlobe in the war and worried so their children would ask how. Her chin on her chest, she howled more bitterly than the wind outside.

Chapter Nineteen

"The most severe and wracking pain we mortals must bear may be relieved somewhat by laudanums, paregorics, or bleeding—and love of those most dear."

ABOUT FORTY MILES beyond Buffalo Creek, lay flat, open prairie land, which they nearly flew over, even without Morgan fastening on the runners to make the wagon into a sleigh. Now, this new winter snowfall be danged, Morgan thought triumphantly, they were making better speed than usual. It was as if the six inches of snow greased the turning of the wheels. Occasional blowing drifts slowed the horses, but did not impede their progress. The bells even sounded merry today!

But then the trails narrowed, and tree trunks crept close again. He reined in some. He heard his daughter wailing inside, as if she were sympathetic their speed was slackening, too.

"Thea," Morgan called back into the Conestoga, "why is she crying?"

"Her cattail down just needed changing, proud papa," she called to him, and put Marygold back into the body pouch she often slung over her shoulder to keep her against her chest. Balancing the baby and sheltering her from the wind with the fur lap rug, she climbed out and sat by Morgan. His face looked ruddy and sun-browned. Amazing, she thought, how he even got that color amid the snow when her skin just turned pink with windburn. She squinted up ahead on the trail and almost leaped from the wagon.

"Morgan, there! Cullen and Rina's wagon! You don't

think hostile Indians—" she began, but her voice strangled in her throat.

"Cullen! Rina!" he bellowed as they pulled up. Then they both saw her, only her. She was slumped on her knees by a hump of soil and snow covered with green fir boughs. She got slowly to her feet and turned to face them.

"What in blazes?" Morgan cracked out, but Thea had already handed him the baby and was scrambling down from the seat to wheel to ground.

"Am I d—dreaming?" Rina stuttered. She was so cold, still so stunned. "We didn't think you'd get away—"

"Rina. Not Cullen? Not there?" Thea asked, her hands outstretched, one finger pointing to the fresh grave.

Rina didn't move. Her mouth, her entire face, was so stiff when she formed the words. "That c—cough. We thought it was the ague or chest chills. I looked for ferns, Thea!" she cried, and her voice broke. Still, she took not one step forward. Thea heard Morgan climb down behind her, and Marygold began to fuss.

Thea waited for the accusations Rina would hurl at her for not coming in time. Now she would be blamed, even if indirectly, for Cullen's death, as well as Father Lockwood's and her mother's. The friendship she and Rina had resurrected these last months would be ruined again. But Rina only stared blankly, then said, "I wish you would have been here to help, Thea, but it just wasn't to be. It wasn't your fault. You got birth, and I got death out here. The Firelands, I hate them!" she declared, her voice sounding lifelike for the first time as it rose in fury. "The Firelands killed Cullen! I'm going to tell them how horrible it is out here, all of them!" she screamed and threw herself in Thea's open arms.

It was much later Rina asked to see the baby. Her stiff face even softened briefly when Marygold cooed at her. "It's your Auntie Rina," Thea said. "She's come to help your mama take care of you on the way back." Thea put her arm around Rina's shoulders as they huddled in the Conestoga. Outside, Morgan unloaded all the goods from the Varner wagon that they were able to carry, and tied the four remaining horses on the back of the Conestoga. Both women had been crying together for hours, and talking, just talking. Rina was still completely dazed, Thea thought. When Morgan called out that it was time to go, Rina shrugged Thea's arm off and climbed out the back into the snow.

"I can't leave him here! I can't, I can't, I can't!" she screamed as she ran back around to the fresh grave graced by fir boughs. She threw herself on her hands and knees in the snow beside the grave.

"He's not really here, Rina," Morgan spoke directly to her for the first time since he'd extended his condolences. He bent to help her up, but she shook him off.

"All that's left of him on this earth is here! It isn't fair! Just when we were going back home! Cullen wanted to prove he could do this, and the Indians with their Whooping Cough and that godforsaken land killed him!"

"But the Indians and that land gave you back to Cullen once," Morgan said, his voice low as Thea came to stand beside him. "He was never happier than that day you were reunited after being abducted, Rina. And as for the Firelands, it's a hard life there, but a rewarding one. And that's one of the most beautiful graves I've ever seen. When—if—Thea and I come back through here someday, we'll find a good stone for it and etch in his name. And, no, it isn't fair. But I admired Cullen Varner, too, and count it a blessing we were friends in the end."

"Yes," she echoed as tears dripped from her chin, and her thin shoulders shook. "He thought of you as his friend, even at the last. He and I—in the end—we were perfect for each other." She slumped as if she would melt into the snow.

"Let me help you, Rina," Thea coaxed and took her arm to help her up. She brushed her off a bit when she stood, talking soothingly all the time. "Cullen would want you to go with us. Cullen would want you to go back to claim his share of the prize and tell them about some of the good things in the Firelands, just like he would have."

They led Rina away, and Morgan boosted both of them up in the wagon. Rina lay all day as they whisked along, her eyes open, staring up at the blank, flat linsey-woolsey ceiling close over her head. She did not react nor budge until finally that first night when Thea despaired for the darkness of her soul and spoke to her.

"Rina, do you want to talk?" Thea whispered.

"I've lost everyone. You have Morgan and a child. I've lost everyone. My life is over."

"But you're young and beautiful and clever. Besides," Thea dared, "your father went on after your mother died."

"But I needed him. No one needs me."

"I do. And, see, Marygold does, too," Thea declared and bounced the baby before her.

Rina's eyes focused at last, and she stroked the downy head once. "I'd like one just like this, but I can't have it. Cullen's gone forever," she said and rolled over on her side with her knees drawn up and her face to the wagon wall.

"But you're strong, Rina. You've always been strong, even when you didn't know it. And loving, too, even in the hardest times. But you've always been too hard on yourself. You even make yourself sick. Sleep now, and I'll be right here if you need anything."

"Just like that baby needs you?"

Thea startled as if her words and tone had stabbed her. "No, not not like that. She was born my daughter, but time and again, I *chose* you for my friend."

Rina said no more, but Thea worried. She worried over the way Rina gazed endlessly at Marygold without really responding to her. She wondered what Rina was thinking and feeling, or had she gone numb inside? She feared that Rina would slip back into her moods and morals of the past, an attitude that Thea could not understand or accept. But Thea had her hands full with things that meant their very survival out here. She only wished the sorrow and love she felt for Rina could help heal her bitter heart.

They intentionally traveled a bit north to avoid the Seneca River Valley where the Conestoga had almost gone off the cliff heading west. They made good progress south of Lake Ontario, and forded the half-frozen Genessee River safely. But Rina's progress seemed neither good nor safe to Thea. Sometimes she just stared out the back of the wagon in the direction they had come. Thea wondered if her friend still saw Cullen's grave back there—even Cullen himself beckoning them back. Weird expressions often flitted across Rina's face as she stared out over Cullen's four horses following the Conestoga. The rest of the time, Rina seemed passionately attached to little Marygold. Rina either stared at her as she slept, or held her solemnly. Rina hardly talked; she had retreated to some strange, secret place inside herself. Thea even hesitated leaving Marygold in her care in the wagon, and cramped her neck muscles continually glancing back inside when she was on the front seat with Morgan.

"Rina," Thea ventured when they were both in the wagon the fifth day together, "you know, it takes a long time to overcome the pain, even anger, when you lose someone you love. But it's harmful to brood about the past. Believe me, I know."

"I'm not brooding over the past when I remark that I'll never have Cullen's child," Rina clipped out, her eyes still on the sleeping Marygold. "It's a fact of my present and my future. Cullen said he wanted us to rear our child in New London, but all that's as dead as he is now. He's dead! See? I can say it. I've accepted it!" She stroked Marygold's head gently with the edges of her knuckles, but her hand made a hard fist. A chill that had nothing to do with the weather iced Thea's spine and made her shudder.

She had to stop pitying Rina and give her more jobs to do, she reasoned. Then Marygold would not be Rina's only concern—her obsession. There had always been some deep, dark place in Rina's mind because of her mother's death and hatred of her as a child. Thea had thought their times in the Firelands had dragged all that out and cured it. But now Thea agonized in jangling thoughts that matched the harness bells: with Cullen's tragic death, Rina had no child; Thea had a child, Morgan's child; Rina once loved Morgan. Thea wasn't certain what was solved and what wasn't in the recesses of Rina's mind.

"Thea, the Oswego River up ahead!" Morgan called back into the wagon. "And the fording place looks frozen! I'm going to have to get out to test the ice. Can you hold the reins?"

"Be right there!" she called. Her voice low, she said to

Rina, "We'll need your help to get us a bit to eat after we cross. Some pemmican and that corn bread we've thawed will do while I melt some snow for water. All right?"

Rina's eyes met hers for the first time all day. "All right. I just wish my dear little Marygold were weaned, so I could feed her, too."

Thea climbed up to hold the reins for Morgan. She wished she had a moment now to talk to him privately about getting Rina back to her old self, but he would want to be across this river by nightfall. Tonight, she'd get him alone. Over her shoulder, she glanced back inside at Rina. She was getting out the food as Thea had asked, but her eyes were still on Marygold strapped in her Indian cradle, innocently sleeping.

Since this was the first frozen river they had encountered, Morgan decided he would drive the wagon over alone while the others waited on the bank. Then he would walk back over to escort everyone safely across. Thea made sure she held the baby, over Rina's protest, as Morgan first herded their extra horses across the slick white floor of ice. This was the same place they had forded on their way west. Thea recalled the animals had been forced to swim part way then, though it was not that deep near the banks. But with the autumn rains and this cold snap and winter snow, it was hard to tell how deep it was under that ice now.

She held Marygold tightly to her as if to calm the child, though it was she herself who needed comforting at a time like this. After testing the ice as best he could, Morgan led six of the eight horses over and tethered them together with Cullen's harness. He walked back over and, with only two horses to keep the weight lighter, slowly drove the wagon out to the center of the river. Now, the chill wind was welcome, and Thea prayed it had frozen the ice solid enough to take the wagon's weight. She held her breath as Morgan passed the halfway mark of the crossing. Surely, the ice would be the thinnest there.

"Look," she whispered to Rina, "he's almost over."

At first the sound that reached their ears was like cannon or crackling thunder. "No!" Thea shrieked, and Marygold wailed.

Thea ran, slipping along the snowy bank a little way. Oh, no. No! The wagon dipped forward, then settled like a bulky boat into the big, choppy water hole where both horses swam or flailed. More ice cracked away. Thea moved instinctively. No time for thought or fear.

"Rina, take the child! Stay here and keep her warm! I am trusting you to take care of my child!" she said and thrust the baby wrapped in a doeskin bag into Rina's arms.

Thea did not look back. She could not. She only prayed that Rina would do what she said. If they lost the wagon, all their food and supplies would be gone. And if she lost Morgan—

She half ran, half slipped her way across the ice, making a slight circle around where they had gone in. Even from here she could see that the struggling horses and the wagon were cracking an ever larger hole in the ice. Morgan was still in the seat, struggling with the reins, hoping the big animals would right themselves in the icy water before the tilted Conestoga filled with water.

"Morgan!" she screamed. "Morgan, I can help!"

"I'm gonna have to cut the traces, or they'll drown!" he shouted. She knew what that meant. No more reins! Even if they did save the Conestoga, they wouldn't have reins to control the team or pull the wagon. She saw his knife flash silver in the sun as he cut the thrashing beasts loose. But now he was adrift in a widening pool, and the Conestoga was sinking lower and lower. "Here!" he shouted. "I'm going to toss you some things!"

"Just get out!" she screamed at him, cupping her mouth against the stiff wind. "Save yourself!"

He heaved the flint kit from his boot, and it skidded neatly to her on the ice. She stuffed it in her buckskin boot. But why had he given her this unless he thought he was going under?

Thea dared a quick glance back across the ice at Rina. Her stomach careened to her feet. She was nowhere to be seen on the entire bank! Her friend Rina—had she trusted her and lost again?

But then Thea saw her carefully making her way across the slick ice downriver, holding the child carefully to her. Thea's spirit swelled with hope. She knew Rina was terrified of falling through the ice after she'd almost died that way, and yet she was daring it now!

Things Morgan could throw, the Indian baby board, a sack of pemmican, even ears of corn he had wanted to take back to Governor Trumbull came winging at her over the ice. He hurled clothes and the baby's sack of cattail down. He threw out both guns and shot, and fur rugs, one of which Thea had to pluck from the very edge of the jagged ice. The two horses, she saw, had made their way exhausted way up on the bank, but four others had panicked at the retort of breaking ice and pulled free of their tether.

"Get back! Back!" he yelled when he saw how close she'd come.

"No! I'm coming in after you if you don't get out. It's sinking, Morgan! Now! I need you!"

"I needed Cullen, too!" the shrill voice behind her said.

Thea whirled. "Where's Marygold?" she cried when she saw Rina's arms were empty.

Rina pointed. "Asleep all bundled up under that first pine tree. If I go through like I did once before," she said and bent to gather their things off the ice, "I won't have that precious little sweetheart getting wet with me."

Tears flowed down Thea's face. Rina! This catastrophe had brought Rina back! But she still might lose Morgan!

Morgan appeared in the back of the sinking, shifting wagon now. "It worked once before!" he bellowed to them. "Try to get a piece of harness off those horses and toss it to me. I'll have to jump or swim!"

Thea tore up on the bank. The two dry horses were still tethered, but they were snorting, stomping, skittish. She edged her way close to one and grabbed a harness by his mouth bit. "Steady! Steady!" she comforted as she moved back along him and slid the traces from the harness rings of Cullen's horses. Cullen's harness would save Morgan and her future, as it had once before! She yanked the trace from the next horse, then ran down to the bank to heave it to Morgan. But she feared even then it would not work. Please, dear God, she prayed, we can't lose both Cullen and Morgan!

With a loud gurgle the wagon tilted and settled low enough to slip sideways; the back end of it slid under the ice. "Morgan!" she screamed as she strode the jagged edge of the ice, staring into the choppy blue water. She didn't see him anywhere! "Mor–gan!"

Rina ran along the bank behind her. "There he is!" she shrieked. "In the water on the other side!"

He had popped up, head and shoulders on the far side of the jammed, half-sunken wagon, the hatchet in his hands. Thea ran around the big hole and threw the piece of harness to him, but it missed. She hauled it in to throw again.

Suddenly, she realized Rina was right beside her. "Get back!" Thea cried. "Get back!"

Rina grabbed her arm. "If you go in, too, Marygold won't have a mother or a father! Let me do it!"

"She'll have you! I'm going to save him!"

Thea crawled now, clawing her way, belly down across the fragile ice. At the edge of the hole, she heaved the leather strip again at Morgan. But, even when he grabbed it, she and Rina, just behind her, had no leverage to haul him out, and it would never stretch to one of the horses on the bank.

"The hatchet!" Thea cried. "Throw us the hatchet!"

He went under when he heaved it up, but came up again. She grabbed the hatchet and risked sinking it in the ice a ways, just enough to have a handhold. She grabbed the hatchet in one hand and wrapped the strip of leather around her other wrist. Rina held on to her, too. Morgan heaved, then hauled himself half up. The ice cracked away from under him to spill him back in. Again the women held tight; again he tried to clamber up. Thea grabbed his coat; Rina grabbed her and held to the hatchet, too. When the blade tore loose, enough of Morgan's weight was on the ice to save him. Bit by bit, with his help, they hauled him up together.

"Get back now. Get back!" he ordered and inched his way toward them.

An eternity later, all three of them lay panting on the bank. Rina ran to get the baby, and brought her back to the pile of their things strewn there. "Thea," she ordered, her voice more determined than Thea ever recalled, "you've got to get him warm and dry. Believe me, I know what can happen when one's in icy water, even for a while like that!"

Thea jolted to action. Rina scrambled to gather pinecones

from under trees, and lit a fire with the flint and steel kit Morgan had saved from a dousing. Thea hung his sopping clothes on a tree limb near the blaze, and he huddled in their salvaged fur rugs while she boiled him a cup of hot water in the only pewter mug that had survived. They had lost so much: four horses had run off; the icy river had claimed the wagon, the harness, the animal feed, much of their supplies, and all but a little food. They had survived, but Thea feared they would never make it back in time now, if at all.

She held the baby close and rocked her slightly as she nursed her. They had been wrong to think they could defy the forces of the frontier to rush from one firelands to the other in this increasingly hostile weather. It was the same strangling feeling as when the town turned on her for something she did not deserve. For one earth-trembling moment, she despaired when she looked all around at the jagged hole in the ice and at the barren sweep of snow. The wind whistled through the high, tossing pines as if to mock them as mere stupid mortals. But Morgan was safe, and Rina was really a stronger, better Rina again.

"Look, Thea," Rina said and walked toward Thea as if her thoughts had summoned her. "I just spotted this on the bank. Morgan must have thrown it out at the end, and I just missed it at first. Your mother's treasury of herbs. If it's survived this long, I guess we all can, too."

"Yes. Yes, of course," Thea said and smiled even through her tears. She hugged Rina when she sat beside her, placing the book in her lap beside the baby. It was Rina who had been strong for her now, Rina who comforted and healed. "Yes, together, I'm sure we can!"

That first night without the Conestoga, they all huddled together between the two remaining fur rugs. Morgan slept on one end, Thea next with Marygold between them, then Rina on Thea's other side. There was no other protection from the biting wind but fir boughs Rina had cut with the hatchet. Both Rina and Morgan insisted Thea eat the larger, rationed portion of the pemmican to keep her milk up for the child. Rina rotated Morgan's stiff clothes near the fire so they would dry and unfreeze. At Thea's direction, Rina brewed all three of them a mug of spruce tea, and banked and fed the fire before they slept. Tomorrow night, even if they'd been on foot all day, Thea thought as she swam in utter exhaustion, she was going to build them a snow house.

Morgan's whispers woke her the next morning as they lay there, dreading getting up. "There must have been a warm current flowing into that river and pooling in that spot," he was saying. "The ice was fine until we hit that one soft spot."

"It's over," she tried to comfort him. "Don't blame yourself. Now, we've got to go on."

"It's all I've thought about all night—going on," he admitted and moved just enough to let in a blast of chill air between them that jolted them both to get up.

"But," he went on as she helped him scramble into his garments before Rina rose or they roused the baby, "I actually thought of the solution at the last minute yesterday, just when I realized the weight of things and the wet cloth top were going to swamp the wagon," he explained. "That's why I went back for the hatchet and almost got caught underwater."

"What solution?" Thea asked.

"Remember those travois—the two-poled platforms the Indians we met on Lake Erie pulled behind their horses? If I can salvage some of those danged nails out of the wagon wheel sticking up through the ice out there, I'm going to chop wood to make two travois with runners on them for you and Rina to ride behind the two strongest horses. We can salvage short pieces of harness for that. It will be better than your trying to ride with the baby. I'll ride the third horse, and we'll rest the fourth one. Unless we get deeper snow, we may make it yet—even in time for Governor Trumbull's deadline!"

That bold speech warmed them, but to travel nearly half the distance yet sounded impossible. As if they believed it could be done, they set to work with a will to make and rig their separate sleighs while Rina tended the baby and scraped snow away from the bankside to give the four remaining horses something to crop to keep up their strength.

Two days later, they were all glad to leave the scene of the accident behind. Yet, as she had when they departed Camp Milan, Thea looked fondly back, at least, at the single, now

ravaged wheel of their Conestoga showing above the river.
A clean bandage of new-formed ice covered the gaping
wound of the accident. With Marygold cuddled in her arms
and her mother's pharmacopoeia strapped at her feet, the
horse hauled Thea backwards on the next leg of their trip,
sixty miles south of Lake Oneida to Fort Trent.

The next three days were a nightmare. The horses nibbled
bark off trees to supplement their meager diets. Morgan fed
the beasts all but one ear of corn he had intended for Governor Trumbull to show how fine a Firelands harvest could be.
They and the horses ate snow. They gnawed shavings from
the single sassafras root Thea had left to supplement their
daily handful of pemmican ration. Only little Marygold had
her belly filled from Thea, and she feared her milk would stop
out here on this cold ride where they dare not take the time
to forage for food. Besides, even when Morgan saw deer or
rabbit tracks in the shallow snow, he hesitated to leave the
women alone to go off on a stalking expedition. They had
no kettles or pans to cook whatever Morgan could hunt, and
no time to chase or butcher the occasional darting game. No
time, no time. Soon, there would be no time left to reach Connecticut, if they made it at all.

Their bellies cramped, their heads pounding from the glare
of sun off the snow, they pushed on. They were brave for each
other; they had no choice. At night, despite their pine bough
or wet wood fires, they huddled together between their two
bearskins in a makeshift hut of travois tipped on their sides
and padded with mounded snow. But it bonded the three of
them closer together than the weeks in the little cabin at
Camp Milan when Rina was ill. Past deceits and problems
were now silently forgiven and forgotten. Now, the survival
of all four of them depended on their being strong and going
on together. They rejoiced to see the headwaters of the
mighty Mohawk, even edged with ice and snow.

The fourth afternoon, plodding along on snowshoes, dragging the lead horse down the Mohawk River trail, Morgan
halted. The other exhausted animals gladly stopped.

"What is it?" Rina and Thea asked almost together.

"Woodsmoke on the breeze. Maybe we're nearer Fort

Trent than I thought. These dang forests don't look the same with all this snow. Thank God, I think it must be just through here."

When the three of them shouted from the forest outside the log walls of Fort Trent, the skeleton crew inside was amazed. A good night's warmth before a roaring fire, a hot meal, hot wash water, extra food, and they were off again with fresh horses they traded for their own. But both women could tell the dwindling days were wearing on Morgan as much as the physical struggle he'd been through. He looked hollow-faced under his high cheekbones, and his mouth too often twisted to a thin, nervous line.

"I'll just find some sort of work in Lebanon if we don't quite make it," he told Thea the day after they passed the Mohawk Indian village at Canajoharie without stopping this time. "Governor Trumbull will give me a recommendation to someone, even if we let him down here."

"If we do," said Thea, equally exhausted and on edge, "it's his own fault for setting deadlines with no leeway for freaks of nature like childbirth and sudden early cold and snowstorms!" To be heard, she had to call to Morgan as he rode ahead of her to lead the horse that pulled her travois sleigh down the more traveled, runner-rutted trail. "And after the things we've been through, the state government of Connecticut ought to at least pass out dratted consolation prizes for those who tried and lost, Morgan Glenn, and I'm likely to tell them so!"

"Consolation prizes for those who tried and lost," Rina echoed from behind them, where her horse was attached to Thea's. "That would be perfect for me. But I say we'll make it back in time yet!"

"You've ever been the optimist since the accident, Rina," Thea called to her, "and I don't know what we would have done without you!"

"You'd be in dire straits! That's why I want you to stay in New London. I've got some of Father's land yet and a little money, too. I'll help you build a new apothecary shop so my lovely little niece doesn't grow up away from her doting Auntie Rina! And, speaking of money, Morgan," she shouted, "when the sleigh went through the ice, you didn't see a moldy old leather satchel you'd taken out of our wagon, did you?"

It was the first time Rina had thought of that satchel Cullen had found near the dead man back on the Pequotting. Cullen's illness and death and their battle to survive had driven it from her mind.

"No, but I think we had it. Are you sure I didn't throw it out of the sinking wagon?"

"If so, I never saw it," Rina said. "Oh, dear. I forgot to tell you both. It had a stack of British pounds in it I suppose you could have used. And a note to the dead man from Avery Payne!"

She explained everything she remembered about the note, and was amazed to hear Thea and Morgan's story about the man Avery had sent to kill Morgan with a Pennsylvania rifle. "At least we still have the gun if we can find its maker and somehow trace it back to that bastard Payne," Morgan muttered.

"If that rifle's not enough to convict that foul wretch," Rina declared, "I'll testify to what we found in that satchel in court!"

"Drat, it's not enough," Thea said. "As close as you've been to us, Rina, they might not even believe you, not if that bastard still has everyone in New London in his waistcoat pocket!"

"We'll find a way," Morgan declared to echo Thea's earlier vow. "We'll find a way."

An overnight stay at Eden's Gate worked wonders on their bodies and spirits, and they set off for Schenectady and Albany in a fancy sleigh the Trents owned, pulled by four eager, sturdy chestnut horses. Little Marygold was as finely outfitted with Claire Trent's grown daughters' old baby clothes as if they'd taken her shopping up and down the streets of Philadelphia. Now they might really make it, Thea crowed inwardly, but they were all afraid to ruin their apparent good luck by speaking those words aloud anymore. If Cassie were here, Thea wouldn't fuss a bit if she wove them all wreaths of four-leafed clovers, even if she had to look under all this snow to find them! It was December twenty-third already.

They had but eight days to be back at Governor Trumbull's war office to claim their victory over the western Firelands. And then, she wondered, how would they be accepted in New London when the word got out?

But in Albany, their luck turned bad again. A second snowstorm shut down Mohawk River traffic for two days. And they learned that Jonathan Trumbull was no longer Connecticut's governor.

"Surely, that won't mean the Firelands quest is off!" Thea said to Morgan. "It just can't be! Not after all this!"

"He believed in it, and I'd trust him to see it through somehow," Morgan assured her, but the creases perched on his brow and at the corners of his mouth deepened even more.

In Albany, they stayed with Ethan Trent's sister Merinda Vandervort and her son's family in their big home, where Ethan had sent them, thinking it would be for just one night. Merinda entertained them bounteously that Christmas; Thea was almost ashamed at how much they all ate after their hungry days in the wilds. Rina, who usually supped like a graceful bird, put the rich Dutch food away more like a fieldhand at harvesttime. Her petite form blossomed. Perhaps eating like that was just another reaction to their ordeal and losing Cullen, Thea thought.

As soon as the skies cleared, they were off again. Rina and Thea sat close together in the sleigh as they approached the Connecticut state boundary marker on December twenty-eighth. "Hurray! Home!" Rina, who held Marygold right now, shouted, but then Thea saw tears in her blue eyes and put her arm around her.

"I'm all right, really, Thea. And you know what did it?"

"Just your being you, full of love, despite the hurts and hardships of life," Thea offered.

"No. It was standing there with the baby in my arms when you had to run to help Morgan because he went through the ice. You were willing to trust me yet, after all—all we've been through together. I knew you didn't want to leave Marygold, but that even if something happened to you, you'd still be with her because you loved her that much."

"Yes," caught in Thea's throat.

"And I remembered when Cullen was very, very ill, he

vowed he'd never leave me—even, I think, when he knew he was going to die. So he just meant his love would never leave me. I feel it inside me, Thea, I really do!"

Thea cried now, too, silent, grateful tears. She nodded in the only response she could manage as the sleigh raced on into Connecticut toward Lebanon.

Chapter Twenty

"Fireweed is a strange herb—a paradox. It can grow short or tall. It can smell aromatic or fetid. Sometimes its roots, sometimes its leaves work best. Its taste can be invigorating, pungent, or downright bitter. But whatever its varied characteristics, it flourishes anyplace the land has been severely burned."

THEY SLEDDED TOWARD former Governor Trumbull's old war office in Lebanon on the very day of the deadline. Morgan jumped out in the front street instead of the back alley and pounded on the door. Nothing at first, but it swung open as he knocked again.

"Where can we find Governor Trumbull—the former governor?" he demanded of the man who opened the door.

"Well, state government's moved back to New Haven now that danger's past from British raids, but he's in his house just uptown here. You one of the men he's been expecting? Two others come in already, and two are still out. Say, you're the one who worked for him a spell during the war, aren't you, the one who was an aide-de-camp to—"

"Yes. I'm Morgan Glenn. Please let him know we're here."

They went inside his one-time war office to wait while the man went to fetch Trumbull. Morgan paced. Rina sat in the corner, suddenly weak-kneed, holding a fretful Marygold on her lap. Thea stood, looking out the big bowed window. No one spoke.

The door banged open. "Morgan! Morgan Glenn!" the old man's familiar voice boomed out as he rushed in. "Of all the ones who set out, you were most dear to me. I had despaired when it seemed Satan might prevail against us with the threatened rising of the heathen savages, and then this unsea-

sonal weather!" He shook Morgan's hand heartily and
beamed at Thea, standing by his side. "But it is we, *we* who
have prevailed!" he went on. " 'And I shall say to the forest,
hear the word of the Lord! Thus saith the Lord God: Behold
I will kindle a fire in thee.' And in the Firelands and—oh,"
he stopped mid-word when Marygold squealed, and he
turned to see Rina holding the baby.

"A great deal has happened, sir," Morgan said in the awkward silence. "We have much to tell."

Homeless as they were, they accepted Jonathan Trumbull's offer to stay at his house until the winter weather
ended. When they had told their story over dinner and
throughout the next few days, the stern old patriarch finally
yielded up his own tragic tale. During the war years he had
lost wife, son, and daughter; the big Trumbull house seemed
lonely and cavernous to him. "But now I have new purpose
in life!" he declared to them. "The war for America's freedom is won, but the war for our burned-out Connecticuters
to have the freedom of the western Firelands is just begun!"

And so, while Marygold who had been a perfect baby all
the way turned fussy and colicky as if she resented living in
a real house now, they stayed on. Governor Trumbull
awarded prize money to the four families who had returned.
Rina got Cullen's full share, and they all hoped the missing
Stephen Muncey of Fairfield had not been caught in the snow
on the way back. Word went out far and wide that four families had lived in the western Firelands and harvested a crop
and returned to tell about it. Names and claims were gathered anew of those wanting future Firelands grants. Morgan
proudly showed the single ear of corn they had salvaged
every time he spoke with the former governor at his side that
winter. And one day, at first thaw, Jacob Roscoe came to
Jonathan Trumbull's home for dinner with the missing Stephen Muncey and his wife Hannah, whom Roscoe had
helped bring back.

"Our guardian angel!" Morgan greeted the wiry trapper
and scout.

"Don't look much an angel!" Jacob told him gruffly, but
the smile under his full beard showed that he was glad to see

them. "You got two o' your own angels, Morgan. Now," he told them after a large dinner, where Rina to everyone's surprise had outeaten even the men, "we gotta lay plans to trap Avery Payne for all he done to Miz Glenn that day I helped you out in New London. I hain't forgot that, I tell you!"

"Nor have I, my friend," Morgan agreed.

"But we've got a lot more to settle with that dratted Avery Payne than that!" Thea declared. She explained Avery's ties to the two intruders in the Firelands and admitted she was certain Avery had even been in league with Benedict Arnold on the New London raid.

"Then maybe the epistle for you that came into my hands today through the congress in Philadelphia will help establish Avery Payne's guilt," Jonathan Trumbull announced and sent his butler for the letter.

"A letter for me?" Thea asked as all eyes turned to her.

The old man nodded. "From England. From your cousin, no other than that arch Judas Iscariot, Benedict Arnold!"

Thea's startled gaze snagged Morgan's. "I'm afraid," Jonathan Trumbull apologized as he lifted the letter from the butler's silver tray and extended it to her, "considering the source of the letter and the way you were under suspicion once, it's been thoroughly perused by some new safety and secrecy committee in congress before coming on to me for you."

She reached for it slowly. Her fingers closed on it almost as if she thought it could burn her. "It indirectly clears you of all complicity, dear Mrs. Glenn," Jonathan Trumbull assured her when he saw she hesitated to read it. Morgan heaved a sigh of relief. "And it suggests, as you will see, someone else held high in New London's esteem besides you betrayed the town's secrets to the British that night. So, tomorrow, I'm going to ask the new governor to order Avery Payne arrested. The cur is residing right now in New York City, but we'll have him extradited back here. Connecticut justice will coax a confession of guilt from him to completely clear your name, since New Londoners may not accept Benedict Arnold's word, even in written form."

Thea skimmed the letter, studying the familiar, bold signature at the end. So far they had come, she thought, so much had happened since that day Cousin Benedict had come in his parade to sit in the chair of her dear apothecary shop and bring her Morgan. Everyone's eyes on her, she spoke at last.

"Yes, Benedict Arnold implicates Avery Payne here and exonerates me. But Avery Payne is a powerful man and a skilled liar. I doubt he would confess, even with this letter. He twists facts to suit his own ends. Besides, just as important to me as proving his collusion with the British or his attacks on me and Morgan is proving that he killed his wife. She was a friend of mine, almost as dear as Rina . . ." she paused to turn to Rina on her other side before she looked back at Jonathan Trumbull. "So if you and Morgan will only wait until Avery Payne returns to New London and trust me to try, sir, I think I know a way to trap him."

Morgan stared at the wily Jacob Roscoe before looking back to Thea. A loud, long silence followed.

"Aye," Jacob Roscoe declared with a bang of fist on the table that rattled the silver. "We'll work together to flush him out like a fat partridge when he gets hisself back to New London, eh? And have ourselves more fun skewerin' and roastin' him with his own devil's fire than any fresh game we ever shot and cooked ourselves up in the Firelands, right Morgan!"

Morgan frowned and nodded grimly.

"And without him around," Rina put in as she popped another maple sugar candy in her mouth, "New London will be the perfect place for all of us to settle down and spoil little Marygold over the coming years, won't it, Thea?"

"Morgan and I haven't decided yet," Thea said and rose to push her chair back before the butler could get to it. "But speaking of the little lamb, I'd best look in on her upstairs. Excuse me all, please, and I'll join you a bit later in the drawing room."

Holding her squirming daughter in a rocking chair upstairs, Thea soothed her even as she read the Benedict Arnold letter over and over. "Fondly, after all," he had dared to close the letter! The brazen gall of the man! When Marygold reached for the parchment, Thea dropped it on the floor and ground her foot on it every time she rocked. She was done with Cousin Benedict in the new life she and Morgan would forge together. But she still had an even bigger score to settle with that other master deceiver and traitor, Avery Payne!

Rina returned to New London in March, but the Glenns stayed on at Governor Trumbull's home until the end of April. Morgan continued to speak far and wide about their experiences in the Firelands, though never in New London. They were kept apprised of Avery Payne's whereabouts in New York City, where he was attempting to set up a new coastal shipping business. More than once the former governor and Thea had to talk Morgan out of going after Avery with his bare fists to beat a confession out of him as, together, they laid plans to lure him back to New London and into a trap.

Meanwhile, Jacob Roscoe came and went, conducting Jonathan Trumbull's business. Marygold matured, cut teeth, got over the winter croup, and delighted in wadding up the numerous notes her "Auntie Rina" sent with gifts from New London where they planned to visit her soon—and where they would settle things with Avery Payne for good.

Finally, the formal invitation came for the second of May: "The city and citizens of New London invite Morgan and Mrs. (the former Althea Arnold) Glenn to a welcome in their honor at the City Parade Grounds for the opportunity of addressing a town gathering concerning the Western Firelands. Provisions for the stay are offered at the mayor's home. Our other guest of note, former Governor Trumbull, has accepted an invitation to abide with our town's leading citizen, Avery Payne, for the duration of the welcome-home festivities. Mrs. Cullen Varner is serving as advisor for the above said activities."

" 'The welcome home.' " Thea mused to Morgan as they bent over the vellum invitation together. "So it took Rina to arrange a welcome for us back there after all. I just hope she's keeping to her vow not to eat day and night."

"And not to tell a soul about our intentions for dealing with that bastard Payne when he returns for all this," Morgan muttered through gritted teeth.

"We'll be careful. He's both crafty and daring," she admitted. "But our plan's just got to work!"

"After the things we've survived, it *will* work!" he declared, though his voice sounded shaky. "Cullen's loss was bad enough, and I'm not risking you."

She hugged him from behind, her cheek pressed between his shoulder blades, her arms tight around his waist. "You're not risking me, my love. I'm not afraid to face him. I just want us to be able to decide where to live when this is all over. If the town welcomes us, do you think our future could be there, as Rina wants?"

"She needs you," he said, his voice brusque. "And it would be a danged lot safer than heading west again—for all three of us. More than once you've told me I'm the only one you liked sometimes making decisions for you, my sweetheart, but this one may have to be yours." He reached behind for her and pulled her gently around to face him. "Thea, she's making the offers to you, not me," he went on, his face and voice fervid with emotion. "But, as for our future, I think you know what I really want." He dropped a quick kiss on her mouth and hurried upstairs with her when they heard Marygold crying.

They returned to New London on a lovely spring day. They had arranged to stay with Rina at Mercy Bigler's old house on Blinman Street, instead of at the mayor's. When Thea saw Rina after the month they'd been apart, she gasped in shock and gave a little scream. It was not just that Rina was plump; she was obviously a good five or so months with child!

"Rina! Rina!" Thea cried, and they ran together and hugged before Thea pulled back to pat Rina's rounded belly. "I should have known! But the way you ate, when I felt so sick even at the smell of food—"

"If I never guessed it, how could you?" Rina sobbed in joy. "I've only bloomed there in the last few weeks. Cullen said he'd never leave me, Thea. I felt his love still inside me! And here, it was our Firelands baby! Now, you'll have to settle here and help me raise him without Cullen! Oh, Thea, I've got two pieces of Father's land left. One can be for your house, and we'll rear our children together!" her impassioned plea tumbled on. But over Rina's trembling shoulder, Thea noted well the stiff expression that froze Morgan's rugged features. She knew he was worried about her having to face Avery Payne again, but when that was over, surely all the rest of their future could be happily settled.

That evening, just after dark, Thea left Marygold in Mercy Bigler's care and set out for Avery Payne's. Despite her nervousness, with her apothecary's ever-watchful eye, she noted the pink-flowering herb called fireweed had grown rampant in lots where buildings had been burned. She'd have to gather some to dose Marygold, for it made a good tonic to combat the summer complaints of children. Bank Street was a flurry of building activity these days for the few that still had money to build. Several new houses rose like phoenixes from the ashes of the old, including the one Rina was building on the Lockwood lot. But the Payne mansion where Thea had come to call on Charity so long ago yet stood, the venerable, untouched sentinel of the street, watching over all the upstart activity. Only today, in accordance with their carefully-wrought plan, she had come to call on Avery Payne.

Her heart thudding hard enough to shake her, Thea turned up the walk. This had to work! She had to face Avery and bluff him into a rage. But the other two times she had been alone with him and he had lost his temper, he had been violent. Still, she had convinced Morgan this was the only way. Besides, former Governor Trumbull and Jacob Roscoe, posing as his mute valet, were staying here. They would rush in to help her as soon as they overheard Avery confess. And Morgan was following her at a discreet distance. Jacob would let Morgan in the back door, so surely nothing could go wrong!

She rang the bell and shifted from one foot to the other, wondering what Avery had thought when he'd received her note saying she needed to see him privately. No doubt, those other two times he had lunged at her would never be repeated, now that she was a married woman with a child, and Avery knew Morgan's temper.

Lately, she mused, she had felt almost graceful and elegant with new gowns like this handsome deep blue one, made for her to accompany Morgan on some of his speaking engagements. She had her form back to normal, since she was no longer nursing Marygold. But the memories of this town staring at her, blaming her, hating her, not to mention the attacks Avery had perpetrated on her, made her feel momentarily unsteady and awkward again. But then, in her heart and soul, she buried those thoughts forever. She steeled herself not to glance back up the street to see if she could spot Morgan, nor to note if any citizens were staring now. She lifted her head, pulled her shoulders back, and exhaled a deep breath.

Just as she rang again, a shockingly red-haired maid, a girl nearly as tall as she, opened the door to give her a start, like peering in a looking glass. "The master received your note, ma'am, and been expecting you," the girl told her and indicated she should follow her in. With a quick sideways glance into the hall, Thea entered.

The girl escorted her into the parlor just off the hall where Avery had trapped her years ago. What tricks memory played: the room looked much the same. That poor green-and-yellow parrot still sat in his cage in the corner. Thea perched, stiff-backed, on the edge of the same royal blue settee where she and Rina had sat after Charity's funeral. She was jolted back to reality when the maid said on her way out, "The master will be right down, ma'am."

"Not my master, and he shouldn't be yours, either!" Thea whispered to the parrot, rather than the maid. From her knitting bag she withdrew the fragile piece of paper where she had reproduced in Charity's hand, best as she could recall it, the dead woman's death-night accusations of Avery. She prayed it would startle him enough to confess that he had killed his helpless wife. Jonathan Trumbull and his "valet," were primed to follow Avery to the room to eavesdrop on their conversation. Then, as soon as Avery incriminated himself, they would burst in with Morgan.

The door opened. Avery Payne entered and slammed it. He was yet sleekly handsome in an oily, overly polished way, but his jowls had lengthened, and his once glittering gaze had dulled. "Thea, what a surprise, after all these years!" he said and leaned against the door. His eyes slid over her as she stood to avoid feeling at a disadvantage with him. She only hoped Jacob and Jonathan Trumbull would be able to hear enough through that door he'd closed. She strode boldly closer to Avery, so their voices would carry better.

"After all these years, I've no doubt you haven't changed," she went instantly on the offensive. They had all decided she must not appear to be shy, or he might not believe the ploy of Charity's note or the copy of the Benedict Arnold letter she also carried. She studied Avery, hoping she did not look either as shaky or as angry as she felt. She could have gladly slapped his pompous face, yanked off his elaborately curled white wig, and scratched at those smug, glass-gray eyes. At least, he seemed to take the bait as she stopped halfway across the room. He looked most perturbed.

"I see you *have* changed a bit," he observed, and dared to grin. "You always were fiery underneath, but it's more on the surface now. How very nice for both of us."

"I've not come to recall old times, except the ones you'll have to pay dearly for!" she began her long-rehearsed lines. "I've two pieces of written evidence here, one a letter from Benedict Arnold, and one in your own dead—and murdered—wife's hand."

To her stunned chagrin, he dared to laugh. "Always so independent and in charge of things, Thea, that's one reason I wanted you—and wanted to break you, et cetera. But you've ruined it all now. And I'm afraid I'll have to take a bit of that wind out of your sails, my bold little bitch. If you think for one moment my esteemed guest, the former governor I hear you've been residing with, or that strange, wiry valet of his are going to rescue you if you scream for them, I'm afraid they're a bit indisposed right now."

She gasped to give herself away. "I—what do you mean?" she tried to cover her error.

"Just that they've both had such a good dinner this afternoon and a glass of port or two with a little something added—you know, my dear, special herbs—so I'm sure they'll both sleep until our parade in the morning. I'm afraid they've accidentally imbibed a rather heavy dose of the same sleeping potion you used to give poor Charity. Oh, don't worry, the crowds won't be too disappointed on the parade grounds in the morning when you and your husband decide you can't face New Londoners after your betrayal of the town the night of the raid. They'll just have to do with my speeches and a word or two from the former governor and Mrs. Varner. Of course, you two won't show because you'll be on your way out of town permanently."

"You are demented!" she said, trying desperately to go on with the ploy she had practiced. After all, when Jacob did not let Morgan in the back door, he'd be suspicious. He'd surely crash his way in here if he had to. She fought to rein in her rising panic. "My husband and I intend to share both this Benedict Arnold letter indicting you for treason and Charity's note that you were working with the British—the note she scribbled and stuffed in her herbal sleeping pillow just before you smothered her with it!"

At that, he looked as if she'd struck him. "Is that the note?" he demanded and stalked her. "Let me see it!"

"This is just a copy of the original, which is in safe hands!" she insisted. She had to stall. She had to find a way to make him confess in front of someone else who would testify! She had to keep control of this dreadful man until Morgan realized things had gone awry and got in here! But Avery shoved her down onto the settee and sat down heavily close beside her to pin her there. He ripped the paper and her knotting bag from her hands, and blocked her in while he skimmed both notes. His mouth twitched as he glared at her.

"You know," he said, his voice slickly menacing, "I've waited years to have you, or if not, to break you. And tonight, it seems, at last, I shall have both. So I'm telling you now, I've hired a man to waylay your husband from calling on me, too. Ah, I see I have your undivided, passionate attention at last. And you'll never see Morgan Glenn again, unless you comply with my wishes—all the way."

Her flesh crawled. She wasn't sure why, but she believed Avery Payne. Perhaps it was that he had sent two henchmen after them, clear to the Firelands, and only fate—in the form of an Indian boy's arrow and the land itself—had saved them. Fury flamed in her, but she began to tremble. Her thoughts darted about for a way out of this. Morgan—Marygold— their friends would want to save her, but she would have to do this on her own.

"Now, if you ever want to see him alive again," Avery's vile voice went on, "let me tell you how things will be. I have letters, too, you see. Ones passed between you and Morgan Glenn during the war years."

"You stole our missing letters?"

"My, how quickly you catch on. They quite clearly show the two of you were in league with the British for the burning of New London, et cetera."

"They could not. We weren't. It was you! You forged—"

"Hush and listen!" he shouted and bent her back over the arched settee arm. His breath came hot on her throat. His hands imprisoned her. His satin waistcoat and silk stock slid along her breast. His saliva speckled her when he talked. "If you do not want your and Morgan Glenn's traitorous behavior denounced from the platform tomorrow, ruining all your chances to take up any sort of life here, you will take your accusations and be gone by morning. You know New Londoners will be willing to believe the worst of both of you, my dearest. But first, you will let me have anything I want from you, for I saw you before Morgan Glenn, and I wanted you first!"

The words and their import were so terrible, her brain would not encompass them at first. Her thoughts scrambled for a denial, a way out. This defiling murderer had wanted her first; Morgan had wanted Rina first. But that was over now. Avery's threats belonged to the past. She had to save Morgan and help her would-be rescuers. Her panic crashed to anger and defiance.

"Then at least admit you killed Charity!" she demanded and tried to shove him away.

"Killed my dear wife? Hardly. But you are quite tempting me here," he said and seized a satin-tufted pillow from behind him on the settee.

"You smothered her with the embroidered pillow, and Doctor Nelson saw the marks on her face from it, as well as I!" she dared as she tried to hold him off. Her voice rose to a shriek. Perhaps someone, even that frightened-looking maid, would come. "The pillow was one of the few things I saved from the shop when it burned," she lied to fight his dreadful lies. "Charity's doctor is going to testify tomorrow that you smothered her. Doctor Nelson and the mayor are in on this, too, and they'll be here soon. Really, once your wife's murder is publicly proclaimed, whether or not you helped the British will be a moot point and—"

He laughed and yanked her off the settee to pin her to the floor under him. Breath smacked from her. She tried to scratch him. "My dear!" he said as he clawed at her skirts with one hand and pressed the pillow against her face with the other, "Doctor Nelson died last year. You're obviously lying to me. And now I'm going to take just enough of the fight out of you that you're going to lie *with* me! I really had planned to just enjoy you once and let you go, but now I just don't know."

She tried to buck him off. She clawed at him as he pressed the pillow over her face. But then she heard the door smack open.

"Damn it to perdition!" Avery cried. Thea craned her neck to look. For one hovering instant, Morgan stood there with the red-haired maid. His eyes were black slits, but the girl's were wide as saucers. Morgan vaulted into the room to rip Avery away from Thea before he could even get to his feet. Thea scrambled up as fast as Avery.

"Morgan, don't kill him! I'm all right. We want him to stand trial to clear everything up!" she shouted.

After a glance to be certain she was safe, Morgan ignored her. "I never would have let her in here with you at all, despite her pleas, you bastard! You're such a coward, Payne! Won't put your hands on anyone but women!" Morgan taunted and slammed his fist into Avery's jaw so hard he toppled over the back of the settee. Morgan raced around and dragged him to his feet, then smacked him against the marble mantelpiece to hit him once, twice in the belly. "You'd talk, all right, if I had my way!" Morgan vowed. "I didn't bring a gun myself because I would have put a bullet in you, and like the lady says, I'd much rather you go to trial *before* your death!"

"No! No!" Avery cried, gasping for breath. "Just see if I don't mean what I told her that you'll both be publicly ruined tomorrow—again!"

Morgan shook him as if he were a boneless scarecrow.

"Not a coward? You never took one of your ships out during the war! You never enlisted, but bought your way out of serving! You tried to terrorize Thea. You sent two poor hired bastards to the Firelands to do your dirty work for you, and one had a real informative chat with Thea about you before he died."

"And the British money you paid Jedediah Clapper along with the promissory note in your handwriting came into Rina Varner's hands!" Thea added. "But then, it's just what I'd expect from a man who smothers his weak, invalid wife with a pillow and—"

"And beats me every time we bed!" the red-haired maid's voice screeched from the door. "And makes me dye my hair red as this. Now I know why, don't I, master?" she goaded. "I thought he might put the pillow over my face more'n once, too! If he goes to the gaol, I'll tell a thing or two about him!"

"Where the hell are Jacob and the governor?" Morgan demanded of Thea after the girl's outburst. "She's the one who let me in on her way out of here, trying to run away with her satchel.

"Upstairs, I think," Thea said. "Avery drugged them. I'll go see, and then we'll call the mayor and the bailiff in so they can hear and see our evidence."

"Thea, listen, both of you!" Avery demanded, his mouth dribbling blood. "I'll pay you, deed my shipping empire over to you—give you this house, if you want to live here. I'll pay thousands for those notes Mrs. Glenn has—this one from Benedict Arnold, and the one from Charity. Look, from what I've heard around town, I know you can't have much money. My fortune. I'm offering you both a fortune, and all you have to do is wait until morning to say I'm gone!"

"You did murder her," Thea insisted. "You did murder your invalid wife because she found out about your collusion with the British to burn this town. Just admit it, and maybe we'll consider."

"Yes, damn you to perdition. Yes! I was your cousin's silent partner, even helped the British to hook him! Charity— yes, but she was living on borrowed time and—"

"And you, too, you Benedict Arnold to all that's sacred!" Jonathan Trumbull's usually loud voice echoed, strangely weak, in the room. Still stiff-armed, Morgan held Avery nearly off his feet in a stranglehold by his lapels. Thea spun toward the door while the red-haired maid darted farther into the room. There in the doorway wavered the usually immaculate former governor, now wigless and disheveled, as if he'd been out on a binge and just stumbled in. Jacob Roscoe, looking even the worse for wear, leaned against the doorframe as if to prop them both up.

"Aye, you lily-livered son of a bitch," Jacob Roscoe muttered to Avery, then tried to explain to Thea and Morgan. "He jest slipped somethin' in our wine, but I should a knowed to watch a snake like him. I swear, butter-kneed or not, I'm gonna watch the bastard 'til the authorities come, Morgan, that's sure!"

Jacob helped the old man to the couch, and then joined Morgan with his hold on Avery. Thea sank down beside Jonathan Trumbull and felt his pulse. "Steady. It's steady," she said, "but then you've always been that for us," and kissed the still-befuddled man on the cheek.

Thea saw that the maid was still uncertain what to do, so she went to put her hand on her trembling arm. "Don't you worry that any more harm will come to you. You can just wash that dratted red stuff out of your hair now. And," Thea added as a last thought, "take the parrot upstairs with you and let him out of his cage anytime he wants. All right? Just don't leave the house so the authorities can talk to you."

The maid nodded and did as she was told without another backward glance. In fact, Thea thought as she went out to send a servant for the bailiff and the mayor, she had been certain the girl had even smiled on her way out, perhaps for the first time in years. She could sympathize. She herself could barely abide being in the same room with Avery Payne. But, delighted by everyone's deliverance, from the caged parrot to the memory of poor Charity's spirit, Thea hurried back inside to be with Morgan.

In a bold red gown to match her hair and the stripes of the new country's flag, Thea prepared to face New London the next morning. At her side, Morgan stood decked out in his best dark brown breeches and coat with a gold satin waistcoat that made his loam-brown eyes gleam. They were both excited and relieved. Avery Payne would not be standing on the welcoming platform at the parade grounds today; he was firmly ensconced in the newly rebuilt town gaol. And both former governor Trumbull and the mayor had vowed the evidence against him would mean an eventual hanging.

When Jonathan Trumbull arrived at Bigler's, they all left together for the festivities. It was not until then Thea realized there was to be more than only a reception and a speech. A brass band of Connecticut veterans bearing the bold American banner waited outside for them with a bedecked carriage to be pulled by two prancing bays. "A parade," she whispered to Morgan. "A parade of our own!"

"Cullen always dreamed of one," Rina whispered behind them and beamed as she shooed them on. "But you two deserve it! When word spread about what happened at Avery Payne's last night, suddenly it's a parade as well as a reception!"

Settled in two carriages—Jonathan Trumbull was in the second one with the mayor—they rode with Rina, who held little Marygold on her diminishing lap, though a bright blue cape properly covered her condition. Folks along the way seemed subdued at first, as though testing the waters. But when Rina waved, people waved back. Thea and Morgan felt all the eyes on them, as they had during those earlier, difficult days. Morgan sat somewhat stiff and grim, remembering.

But these were better times, Thea told herself. They had been to that other Firelands and back. Perhaps, these citizens, like her and Rina, regretted some things that had gone before. Gently, she poked Morgan's arm and smiled deep into his eyes until Marygold fussed. "Here," Thea told Rina, "I'll take her for a while now," and hoisted the awed child on her lap. Thea lifted Marygold's pudgy little arm to wave at the crowd along the edge of State Street. A woman who had been there the day they ripped her apothecary sign down waved back. Boys along the curb cheered. Someone speckled them with violets. Soon, Morgan, too, lifted a hand and smiled.

A chorus of "Huzzahs!" swelled and grew. "It was that foul braggart Avery Payne, all along," they heard someone

shout, "and not neither of them!" The sprightly state song,
"Yankee Doodle," seemed to sweep them on. The harbor,
now in peacetime with the privateers converted to merchant
ships, glittered with no wharves and building to block it out,
though here and there along the way new frame or stone
buildings sprouted from charred soil where fireweeds now
bobbed their pink heads. And then the once-devastated parade grounds loomed ahead.

"Oh, it looks like half the town's turned out," Thea said.

"I'll bet it's every last person who wasn't along the parade
route," Rina added, sounding very pleased. "The word's been
passed what Avery Payne did—and what you two didn't do!"

Cheers deafened them as they mounted the platform.
When the crowd quieted, the mayor spoke first, then Jonathan Trumbull, who also acknowledged Rina's and Cullen
Varner's bravery. Morgan spoke about the beauties and the
challenge of the Firelands. Loud cheers punctuated almost
every sentence. And then, to Thea's surprise, Rina intro-
duced her to say a few words as a pioneer Firelands wife.

Memories and mingled emotions nearly swamped Thea as
she stood, looking out over the rebuilding of New London
and the sea of upturned faces. "My husband has told you of
the western Fireland's beauty and bold challenge," she
began. Her voice wavered, then strengthened to ring out clear
and strong. "I want to tell you as a woman and a proud Con-
necticuter once again, it's a good place for people. A place
where people need and learn to trust each other. A place for
making new friendships and strengthening old ones. The
Firelands is a place where people learn to love and heal and
forgive. And a beautiful place for a man and wife to rear a
family and start a new life together!"

Cheers like the sea drowned out anything she would have
said next. Waiting for the noise to subside, she glanced over
at Morgan who sat to her right. His face glowed with pride.
Behind him she saw Rina, tears streaming down her face.
Rina, the dear friend of her childhood, offered them so much
here for their future. Morgan, she knew, wanted to go back
west. But for the baby's sake, if the town had forgiven them
and opened their arms this way, wouldn't it be wiser to stay?
Morgan was admired here now. As the mayor had jested in

his speech, Morgan could run for mayor and win. He could be the great town leader Avery Payne had never been. He could help this firelands of her forefathers to rebuild, while Marygold and their other children played with Rina's child and got a fine education with no real dangers or threats lurking in surrounding forests.

And then the mayor spoke again. "In appreciation of the trials of this patriotic man and woman, the town has decided to rebuild the Arnold Apothecary shop on the original site, and to donate one hundred man-hours of work and materials for a new home on the land which Mrs. Varner has donated to the Glenns—"

Thea heard no more. She smiled and cried while she hugged the mayor, hugged Morgan, Rina, Marygold, Jonathan Trumbull. And the sound of the cheering was sweet in her ears.

The next day, despite the reception that had lasted far past midnight at the mayor's home, Thea got out of bed at dawn. She did not disturb Morgan, who had drunk a great deal last night. He was sleeping heavily on his side, a frown crimping his brow. She donned her brown Firelands dress she had come back in and her sturdy walking shoes. She peeked in on Marygold, and knew she would not awaken for an hour or two and that Mercy Bigler would tend her if she fussed.

She left Morgan a note downstairs and took some nut bread from the kitchen to eat on the way. In the small stable Biglers shared with two other houses, she saddled a carriage horse and rode out of town to see her herb gardens. She had to tell Morgan today she favored their taking advantage of the bounty here to start a new life, and she was dreading the look in his eyes. He would probably agree to stay. She would build her practice back up here, just like the boom days of Benedict Arnold's glory.

She rode the periphery of her gardens outside of town and peeked in the dilapidated bark hut. She walked through the tangle of herbs gone back to their wild, untended state. But, strangely, all she could think of was that other bark cabin along the Pequotting at Camp Milan, and her skimpy herb beds there. Drat! She supposed if she went west again, she could take with her more seeds and starts from this chaos of growth here.

She cantered back into town, past the lot near the old Lockwood place where the new Glenn home would rise if they agreed to stay. She and Rina would be neighbors, as well as friends over the years. They had earned that right!

She rode down Bank to Water Street to the site of her old apothecary shop. She had not been able to face the blank, burned lot before, but now that she knew it would rise again with the town's blessing and not their curse, she was ready.

Still, it saddened and shocked her to see the grassy spot with tumbled rubble, decorated only by the tall pink blowing fireweed. She strolled among the ruins, thinking the copper still once stood here, the counter ran right along here. She pulled some boards off where the root cellar had been, and stared into its empty depths. And then she heard Rina's voice.

"I must admit I saw your note on the breakfast table for Morgan!" she called and picked her way around a pile of bricks. "I didn't want you to have to face this mess alone, but just think of all it's going to be! You can even replace that hanging sign you were once so proud of!"

"You know," Thea told her, "I was thinking of that sign Morgan gave me for Christmas, the one Wintasa dyed to look like it was painted. And how New London already has Greenwoods' Apothecary, and the western Firelands have none."

"Thea!" Rina cried. "You aren't really thinking you'd go back! Not with everything perfect for you here!"

Thea sighed. "Morgan's heart is back there, and maybe mine is, too. You see, always, my heart is with him, Rina. I know you understand that."

A flurry of emotions flitted across Rina's plumply pretty face, and Thea read each one. Hurt, fear, anger, willfulness. But Thea saw, too, that Rina mastered herself as once she never would have.

Her friend said, "Yes, I understand that now. Those Indians out there, or new settlers, too, someday—I wouldn't want them to die the way Cullen did."

They clung together for just one moment as the sun rose

higher, and the street and waterfront came alive with activity. But one horse seemed to be riding fast, very fast, and Thea saw it was Morgan. She walked out through where the front door once stood to meet him. He reined in and doffed his hat in his big hands as he dismounted. His hair was a bit rumpled, but it glinted in the morning sun. His rugged, brown face still bore the shadow of morning stubble.

"I didn't mean to sleep so late," he said. "Too many toasts to the future last night." His eyes were wary, and she wanted to soothe all those lines of doubt away from his face. "Making plans for the new shop?" he asked.

"Yes. But I was just telling Rina I want that new shop to be built out west, as near to Camp Milan as we can get."

The smothered fire in his eyes flared anew to thrill her. "You can't mean give up everything they've offered you here?"

"Give it up only for something better that we can build together. Rina not only understands but agrees, don't you?" Thea called over her shoulder as Rina came, almost shyly, up to them.

"I do. I've made Cullen's dream my own, and Thea's only doing the same. I just hope they fix those roads between here and there, because I and my son will have to come visiting you someday, and you will have to bring Marygold back here to see her 'Auntie Rina.' "

Rina's tears started as she turned away. With a jaunty wave back over her shoulder, she strode up the street, leaving them there together. Tears washed her face, but her heart was full, even when she darted a quick look back to see Thea and Morgan in a fierce embrace, joy she would never share again with Cullen.

Over Morgan's shoulder, Thea watched Rina's figure shrink from sight, the way it would when they headed west again. Rina walked almost ungainly now; she no longer floated. But she was wiser and better for all that had gone before, and she had a fine future, too.

Thea and Morgan held each other as if they would never let go. And, at their feet, the healing herbs called fireweed nodded their approval of it all.

Author's Note

IT TOOK YEARS after this story ends for the Firelands to be fully opened to settlement. Because the wheels of government moved slowly even in those days, it took time to gather a complete reckoning of whose eastern losses deserved how much western land. It was not until 1796 that the first official survey party laid out plots. In the summer of 1805, the Indians were induced to formally give up their land, though some lingered for years after. (The Wyandot Indians finally went west in 1842.) By 1817, the full swelling tide of Connecticut immigration crashed into the area to found its fertile farms and New England–style villages.

Today the Firelands is a beautiful region of Ohio. Many charming towns and cities bear Connecticut names: New Haven, Fairfield, Greenwich. The area includes the port towns of Vermilion, Huron, and Sandusky, and the lovely interior towns of Milan (where the Pequotting Indian village stood), Norwalk, and another New London. Milan's current fame comes from being the birthplace of Thomas Alva Edison, born along the banks of the Huron River, once called the Pequotting. The area also contains the famous Castalia Spring, and the popular resort of Cedar Point. And it is the region where my Ohio ancestors from the east first settled.

Benedict Arnold, the man whose name became synonymous with "traitor," became very unpopular in his refuge in England and failed in several business ventures there. He dared to attempt to obtain compensatory funds from the British government for the loss of *his* property in America, after he had devastated so much property of those who had once trusted and even venerated him. But this, too, he was denied. His sons eventually served in the British army with much more honor than their father had in his own.

Although *The Firelands* is a work of fiction, it is based on historical events in the life of Benedict Arnold, the American Revolutionary War, and later pioneer migration to the Connecticut Western Reserve, known yet today in Ohio as the Firelands.

Karen Harper

July 1990